KU-765-285

# SPECIAL MESSAGE TO READERS

## THE ULVERSCROFT FOUNDATION
**(registered UK charity number 264873)**
was established in 1972 to provide funds for
research, diagnosis and treatment of eye diseases.
Examples of major projects funded by
the Ulverscroft Foundation are:-

- The Children's Eye Unit at Moorfields Eye
  Hospital, London
- The Ulverscroft Children's Eye Unit at Great
  Ormond Street Hospital for Sick Children
- Funding research into eye diseases and
  treatment at the Department of Ophthalmology,
  University of Leicester
- The Ulverscroft Vision Research Group,
  Institute of Child Health
- Twin operating theatres at the Western
  Ophthalmic Hospital, London
- The Chair of Ophthalmology at the Royal
  Australian College of Ophthalmologists

You can help further the work of the Foundation
by making a donation or leaving a legacy.
Every contribution is gratefully received. If you
would like to help support the Foundation or
require further information, please contact:

**THE ULVERSCROFT FOUNDATION**
**The Green, Bradgate Road, Anstey**
**Leicester LE7 7FU, England**
**Tel: (0116) 236 4325**

**website: www.foundation.ulverscroft.com**

Quintin Jardine gave up the life of a political spin doctor for the more morally acceptable world of murder and mayhem. Happily married, he hides from critics and creditors in secret locations in Scotland and Spain, but can be tracked down through his website at: www.quintinjardine.com.

# FUNERAL NOTE

After a tip-off, a man's body is exhumed from a shallow grave in Edinburgh. Murder, surely — yet he died from natural causes, so: case closed? Indeed, was there ever a case at all? But Chief Constable Skinner and his people continue digging. Who was the man, why was he buried so reverentially, and by whom? Meanwhile, an investigation into corruption within the force is launched. And, immersed in crises, his marriage heading for the rocks, Skinner's very career is in jeopardy, its fate beyond his control. In this tale of mystery upon mystery, seen through the eyes of each of its leading players, the greatest threat of all facing the Chief is revealed, and a deadly race begins. Can he win out, or will his life implode?

QUINTIN JARDINE

# FUNERAL NOTE

*Complete and Unabridged*

# CHARNWOOD
*Leicester*

2 9 MAR 2013

First published in Great Britain in 2012 by
Headline Publishing Group
London

First Charnwood Edition
published 2013
by arrangement with
Headline Publishing Group
An Hachette UK Company
London

The moral right of the author has been asserted

All characters in this publication are fictitious and
any resemblance to real persons, living or dead,
is purely coincidental.

Copyright © 2012 by Portador Ltd.
All rights reserved

A catalogue record for this book is available
from the British Library.

ISBN 978-1-4448-1591-7

Published by
F. A. Thorpe (Publishing)
Anstey, Leicestershire

Set by Words & Graphics Ltd.
Anstey, Leicestershire
Printed and bound in Great Britain by
T. J. International Ltd., Padstow, Cornwall

This book is printed on acid-free paper

NORFOLK LIBRARY AND
INFORMATION SERVICE

| | |
|---|---|
| SUPPLIER | ULV |
| INVOICE No. | PF 747 |
| ORDER DATE | 2 9 MAR 2013 |
| COPY No. | S10 |

This is for Bett and Bob.

# Foreword

For new readers, and old friends.

I have a birthday today. It's not a big number, unless you're a Satanist with a little imagination, but it's a good day for reflection, to look back on my life and on some of the things that have happened along the way.

When this book appears in its first editions, twenty years will have elapsed since I signed my first contract with Headline, then a thrusting newcomer to UK publishing, now a member of the global Hachette group, and a major industry player. Twenty-two years will have passed since I accepted my late wife's challenge to live up to my assertion that I could do a bloody sight better than the book I'd just finished and tossed away. Twenty-two years of living alongside, and occasionally in the shadow of, Robert Morgan Skinner.

The first decision I ever made about Big Bob, who is not my *alter ego* whatever anyone may say or believe, set the route for what at that time I had no notion would become a twenty-year (so far) journey. Having looked around the crime fiction genre as it existed then, both in printed form and in TV drama, I was struck by the fact that most of the cop protagonists out there, with the possible exception of Fat Andy Dalziel (a name I know how to pronounce, having grown up opposite Dalziel High School in Motherwell), were middle-ranking detectives with one hundred per cent clear-up rates and no prospects of promotion because of character flaws, ranging from alcohol, through arrogance, to sheer unlikeability, or they were toffs who regarded policing as a form of charity work.

Thus Skinner was created as a high flyer who had already flown, a detective chief superintendent on the first page of *Skinner's Rules*, and promoted to assistant chief constable halfway through.

Or was he created? Even now I'm not sure about that. The greatest moments in this writer's life are those in which a character appears on a page without any pre-planning, or warning, as if he's come not from my imagination but from somewhere else. That's how it was with Skinner, and as it was later with the likes of Lennie Plenderleith, Xavi Aislado and Paloma Puig, his abuela, although, with hindsight, she may owe a little to my own paternal grandmother. He imposed himself on me and left me to put shape to his existence. How could that happen? Does the mind work that way? Or is he really a separate entity, a personality in his own right? Could it be that I have a personality disorder? If so, I won't be seeking treatment for it.

Once he was there, and in his place in a police force that is entirely fictional . . .

*Explanation: in the real world, police services are provided in Edinburgh and its surrounding counties by Lothian and Borders Constabulary. That's a phrase you will not encounter in any*

*Skinner novel (I hope!). It's a quirk of mine, to emphasise that his is a fictional world and that he is a clone of no living person.*

. . . the benefits from that first determination about his place in the structure began to bear fruit.

Most significantly, the fact that Bob is where he is in his parallel universe means that he has more subordinates than those other cops and, therefore, that his stories tend to have a greater cast of characters. That has been fundamental to the durability of the series, in that it has allowed me, over the years, to bring people in from the back benches, explore them in more detail, cast them as hero/ines or occasionally villain/esses, then let them step back . . . if they've survived.

Should that make you imagine that the Skinner series possesses some of the elements of a TV soap, I'm fine with that. It's what I've set out to give it, from an early stage in its development, as soon as I realised that I had more stories in me than I could number.

If I've learned one thing in twenty years it's that readers are drawn to series by places, but stay with them because of people.

Today's great British telly institutions such as *Coronation Street* and *EastEnders* won attention initially because they were set in recognisable, identifiable communities, but they haven't held it for all those decades simply because people like Salford or Tower Hamlets. No, they've survived and prospered because of a constantly renewing cast of strong characters and powerful storylines.

New viewers come to these series with every

episode that's broadcast. When they do, they don't need to know that Martha Longhurst sat down and died in the snug of the Rovers in 1964 or that Dirty Den Watts was murdered twice. But the scripts need to give them enough of a reference back for what's happening so that they will understand it as well as anyone who's been watching *Corrie* since December 1960, or been lodging in Walford since the Queen Vic opened twenty-five years later.

It's the same with a long-running crime fiction series. Readers who've been with Bob Skinner since he presented his credentials to them at the dawn of the 1990s will know that the death of his first wife, Myra, wasn't quite the accident he believed it to be, until the truth was revealed in *Skinner's Ghosts*. Those who meet him for the first time on these pages have to be told how her story fits into his, but not necessarily all of it.

Newcomers need to know something of Skinner's past life for certain references in subsequent books to make sense, but not every detail, for inevitably that would get in the way of the current plot, and in addition would cause the premature death of thousands of trees. Similarly, while it's important that readers know George Regan to be a man marked by the loss of a son, so they can understand his situation, they don't need to know how he died. Nor do they need an exact description of Stevie Steele's passing, only the information that it happened on the job, and that he was the second husband of Maggie Rose, after her failed marriage to Mario McGuire. Similarly, Harold Haddock's nickname is

'Sauce', but if I explained in every book that for people in the east of Scotland brown sauce is an essential condiment to a fish supper, it would become wearing.

That's the line of accessibility, the chalk-mark on the floor; to provide the essential information that newcomers need without alienating old friends, or making them think we're patronising them. It's what Martin Fletcher, my editor, and I try to do with every book. We believe we walk that line without leaning too far to either side; I'm pleased to say that so far, feedback indicates that we do. If not, we would like you to tell us, and you can do so through my website, www.quintinjardine.com.

Three years ago, when I finished the twentieth Skinner novel, *Fatal Last Words*, I decided that would be a good moment to take a look back over the series and to appraise where I stood with each character. It didn't take me long to realise that while I had spent quite some time, and turned many doomed trees into paper, developing the characters of cast members including Neil McIlhenney, Andy Martin, Sarah Grace, Jimmy Proud and several others the one of whom I, and as a result my readers, knew least was the main player, Skinner himself.

With that in mind, I embarked on *Grievous Angel*, a story set fifteen years back in Bob's career, and narrated by the man himself as part of a therapeutic process. I set it fifteen years in the past, when my main man was balancing his climb up the CID ladder with the pressures on a single parent with a daughter entering her teenage years. I decided to set the book in the first person, for two reasons. One, I tend to rebel against convention, including that which decrees that cop stories should be told in the third person. Two, I wanted to get deeper into Skinner's head, and to explore the Dark Ages of his life, the period between his first wife's death and the coming of his second marriage.

A year later I felt confident enough to take the experiment a step further, to return to the present and to go further in determining what Chief Constable Bob's colleagues, friends and family actually think about him, and occasionally about each other. That's how *Funeral Note* was born, and that revelation will explain its structure. It has been described as my most ambitious work yet, and I will accept that as a fair assessment.

Like its predecessor, the book is in the first person, but this one is in multiple perspectives. It's a series of inter-related, sequential narrations, each told to an unseen interviewer, and presented almost in the style of a documentary. With each contribution mystery is laid upon mystery and gradually a hidden, shapeless threat becomes terrifyingly apparent.

Along the way readers will find that Bob Skinner's hope of a settled, stable family life was misplaced, they will find that his colleagues admire, fear and dislike him in almost equal measure and they will find that the unshakeable certainty that has made a success of his professional life turns destructive when it is challenged at home.

I've learned a lot about Skinner and his people in writing the last two books, but most of all about the man himself. It hadn't occurred to me before, but now I realise that since the start of our acquaintance, his and mine, Bob has been in denial over the death of Myra, his teenage soulmate and first wife. He has blundered into several injudicious relationships, and a couple of ill-considered marriages, while at work he has become completely ruthless, although it seems that only there is he aware of his own weaknesses, as a conversation with 'Sauce' Haddock reveals in *Funeral Note*.

I know now that Bob Skinner is a very damaged man; I can see that his soul is broken. That's my fault, for I did it to him. Can it be repaired? I can't say for sure, but I'm going to try, even if it leads him to the funeral pyre of a hero.

That's my promise, to him and to you. Now, please, read on, be you newcomer or old hand. When you're finished, we hope that you'll come back for more.

Quintin Jardine
L'Escala, Spain
29 June 2011

Not a drum was heard, not a funeral note,
As his corse to the rampart we hurried;
Not a soldier discharged his farewell shot
O'er the grave where our hero we buried.

'The Burial of Sir John Moore at Corunna',
*Charles Wolfe*

# Detective Chief Superintendent Mario McGuire

'There is no wrong, there is no right; there's only what happens. As a cop you deal with it, and leave the judgments to others . . . to the lawyers, to the jury, and if the verdict goes that way, to the guy on the bench in the wig and the red jacket.'

Paula gave me a long look, from beneath raised eyebrows. 'Be nice if that was true, wouldn't it?' she said, in that long, slow drawl of hers. She slid her long-stemmed goblet across the table. 'Top me up, McGuire.'

I took the sparkling Highland Spring from the ice bucket and obeyed orders; seven months before (or was it eight by then?) it would have been claret, or maybe, if she'd been feeling particularly Italian, a nice Chianti or a Sangiovese. The glass was to preserve the illusion.

'It is,' I insisted as I poured. 'We are objective.'

'Come on,' my beautiful wife laughed. She shook her head, in that deprecating woman's way. A flash of light, reflected from a building across the water, was picked up by her hair, and made it shimmer. I was still getting used to Paula's auburn incarnation. She had been almost jet black when she was younger, as I still am . . . apart from the odd grey flecks that I regard

1

as signs of distinction . . . until some twist in the mother's side of her genes had turned her silver before her thirtieth birthday.

She'd let it stay that colour. Most people who've come to know her only in the last few years thought that she was ash blonde, and she didn't make them any the wiser. But then she'd fallen pregnant: great news for us, and a nice one for Charlie Kettles, her hairdresser. His profits took an instant hike when she decided that it made her look too old to be a first-time mum.

She wasn't done with our discussion. 'Remember that guy,' she persisted, 'the one who slashed Maggie a few years back, when she tried to arrest him? He cut her arm right to the bone, so I heard. Were you objective with him when they had him locked up in the cells at St Leonards?'

'Absolutely,' I insisted . . . perhaps a little too insistently. Was she guessing, I wondered, or had someone been talking out of school?

'Aye, that'll be right,' she scoffed. 'I'll bet you even made sure he was tucked in at night, and had a full Scottish breakfast in the morning.'

I nodded. 'Complete with a slice of fried dumpling.'

'That's if he had teeth left to chew it.'

'He had, I promise you.' That much was true; I hadn't left a mark, for all the pain I'd visited on him.

'Okay, okay, okay.' She held up a hand, as if she was conceding the point. 'So you've always been purer than the driven slush. I assume that explains why you're being so hard on these naughty cops of yours.'

'I'm not,' I protested. 'It's the chief constable who's chucked the book at them.'

'Not quite, Mario,' she argued. 'All that Bob Skinner's done is hand you the book and told you to clobber them with it.'

'No . . . ' I was going to contradict her, but I didn't. I'd have been wasting my time.

I never win arguments with Paula, even when I'm right and she's wrong. She's the most single-minded woman I've ever met in my life; when she sets herself a goal, or takes a position, be it a business decision, a major life issue or in a simple debate, she always scores. Ally that to her determination . . . some might call her obdurate, or obstinate, but there isn't really a word strong enough to define her . . . and you have an exceptional person.

Her pregnancy's a classic example. When I was married to my first wife, we had a phase when we tried to start a family. No, I'll be honest with you: I was always more keen than Maggie was. She went along with the idea for my sake, not from any great desire of her own. We never told anyone about it. That was just as well, for after a year of earnest by-the-book effort, cycle-watching and all that stuff, and Mags never being as much as a day late, we consulted a fertility specialist. He examined us both, gave us the full range of tests. She passed with flying colours. I failed. The cock-doctor, as Neil McIlhenney, who is and always will be my best friend on the planet, christened him when I finally got round to confessing all, pronounced that my baby-juice was entirely unfit for purpose.

I suppose that was the beginning of the end for Maggie Rose Steele and me. In truth, she had sexual hang-ups that went back to her childhood, and I always suspected that marital relations . . . with me, at any rate . . . always did require a certain amount of thinking of Scotland on her part. When I found that I was thinking of Italy at the same time, I knew we were done.

There were no hard feelings on either side when we split, and Paula and I began, those two events being simultaneous. No, any difficulty there was lay within my circle of friends and family, or rather, ours. You see, Paula and I are first cousins.

There's no reason why anyone should think twice about that, but people did. My mother was one of them, for a while, and sure as hell Uncle Beppe, Paula's dad, would have disapproved as loudly as he could, if he'd still been alive to continue his unspoken feud with me.

Fact is, I was in the 'anti' lobby myself for a while. I'm a few years older than Paula, so our paths crossed very little as kids. It was only as young adults that I became properly aware of her, when she started hanging out in the same pubs and clubs as my crew. She claims that she was after me even then; if that was true, and I still doubt it, the guys she pulled made a pretty good smokescreen. And in those days, I was as constrained in my thinking as most people. Sure, she used to flirt with me, but when she came to

4

me for help dealing with a bloke who was showing signs of not taking 'No!' for an answer, I decided that she saw me as Big Brother, and that was it.

Yes, that was it: until there came a morning, after a party we'd both been at and where I'd really tied one on, when I woke up to find the other side of the bed crumpled and heard someone in the *en suite*, brushing teeth. When Paula walked out, wearing a short-sleeved Hibs football outfit, minus the shorts and socks, I stared at her like someone, she said at the time, and still does, who's realising he's been stitched up by the *News of the World*.

'Tell me nothing happened,' I croaked: yes, I had been that drunk. She wouldn't, though; her only reply was a wink and a broad smile. (It took me years to make her confess that she hadn't been able to rouse me, in any way.) When I sobered up, I was shaken up by the incident, confused, and not a little alarmed by the fact that the sight of her in that green and white shirt had made me, instantly, as stiff as a chocolate frog. In the aftermath, I was careful to keep distance between us, even when I was married and she was going through a series of short-term relationships with guys, including Maggie's future second husband, the ill-fated Stevie Steele.

I made myself think of her as just another family member, and even imagined rivalry between us when it came to the future destiny of the Viareggio family businesses, although I'd never had any real interest in running them.

5

Uncle Beppe had taken over after my grandfather's death, and he and I never got on. When I told him that I'd decided to join the police force rather than work with him, he couldn't keep the smile from his face.

He wouldn't have been grinning if he'd been around when, finally, I looked at Paula and saw not a kid cousin, but the woman I'd loved all along, even through the years of my marriage. As it failed, I turned to her for comfort, and discovered that I didn't want to be anywhere else, ever again.

My old inhibitions didn't disappear in a flash, nor in anything like it. For a while the fact that we were sleeping together was a secret to be kept, even from our mothers. When the shackles were finally broken it was by the unlikeliest person: Nana Viareggio, our grandmother, our matriarch. She's a wise old bird and she spotted the difference between us before it had dawned on anyone else. When she asked me about it, I started to apologise to her, to seek her understanding, if not her forgiveness.

She laughed at me. 'You must be a secret Calvinist, boy, for all you were raised in the Holy Catholic Church. That's Scotland for you; where your Papa and I came from, your relationship would have been encouraged. His father and my mother were cousins. Didn't anyone ever tell you that? What's wrong with such marriages? The European royal families have been marrying with each other for hundreds of years.'

She was right; Nana's wisdom encouraged me to do some research on the subject, and I

6

discovered that in many cultures, it's the norm, not an exception. When I showed this to Paula, she laughed, and told me that she knew three women in the Edinburgh merchant community who were in happy marriages with cousins, arranged when they were children.

Nobody's ever told us they disapprove of our relationship . . . or even been foolish enough to try . . . but I know we were the subject of gossip when we moved in together, as we did after a period of maintaining separate homes, for show. The chattering classes were pretty much silenced though, by our friends, first among them Bob Skinner. He made a point of inviting us, as a couple, to every formal dinner with which he was involved, and the chief constable, or deputy as he was then, hosts or organises plenty of those. He and Aileen, his politician wife, and Neil and Louise McIlhenney, were the only non-family guests when Paula and I were married in a private ceremony in Kelso just over a year ago, and they're still among very few people who know that we're man and wife.

It wasn't long after we tied the knot that Paula got broody. Ironically, Maggie, my ex, had a lot to do with it. She remarried and had a baby daughter, born a few months after Stevie, her cop father, was killed, tragically, while on duty, by an explosive device that was meant for someone else. We gave her as much support as we could, saw a lot of her and the wee one, and it was those first few weeks of Stephanie Rose Steele that triggered a full-blown outbreak of the baby blues.

'When you were told you were infertile, what was the diagnosis?'

The question came out of the blue, across the table in a corner of Ondine, a trendy restaurant on King George IV Bridge that Paula had booked for my fortieth birthday dinner. (Just the two of us: I'd warned her that if she organised a surprise party for me, I would tell the world when she hits the same mark.) I was taken aback, but more by the content than the timing, for I'd read the signs by then. However, I'd been expecting her to ask what I thought about adoption. If she had, I'd have said 'Fine', without missing a beat. But I'd misread her. She didn't simply want to be a mother; she wanted to have a child.

I frowned, as I recalled the moment when the cock-doctor had broken the news. 'Diagnosis?' I repeated. 'How many ways are there of telling you your tadpoles don't work?'

'Lots,' she replied. 'What did he actually say?'

I shrugged my shoulders. 'Word for word, I can't recall. He gave me the headline news straight up: 'Mr McGuire, you're the problem.' Then he said I was producing sperm, but that they were no use.'

'You mean the count was too low?' she persisted, like a QC in court.

'I dunno. That was what I assumed.'

She drew me that look, over her glass. 'You did want a baby, though.'

'Yes.'

'Why?'

'Pfffff. Why does any bloke? Because he's

8

married and it's what you do. We did try, you know; we read textbooks on the subject, took her temperature, did it with a cushion under her bum. We even went by the phases of the moon for a while. None of it worked.'

'So you gave up?'

'What else could we do? We weren't left with any choice.'

'My darling boy,' she purred, 'do the words 'second' and 'opinion' have any significance for you?'

'The man who did my tests was an expert, a top consultant,' I protested. 'He cost a load of money.'

'For which you didn't get value,' she suggested, 'if that's all he told you.'

'There was more,' I admitted, 'but I wasn't listening. He gave us a written report, but I never read it.'

'Aw!' she exclaimed, with more than a hint of mockery. 'Poor wee boy. Mario threw a huff. You took it personally, saw yourself as unmanned, so you went away and flexed your muscles in a corner, without even thinking 'underlying cause', and looking into it.'

I felt myself go red. 'If your sperm is useless, love, that's it,' I muttered.

'Not necessarily,' she countered. 'Do you still have the report?'

'Hell no. It hit the bin the next day.'

'Can you get another copy?' she asked.

'I imagine so.'

'Will you?'

I looked her in the eye and I saw something

9

I'd never seen there before, an unspoken thing that was, beyond any doubt, a plea. She wasn't asking me to go back to the cock-doctor; she was begging me.

'Of course I will, love,' I promised. 'With neither hope nor expectation, but I'll do it.' I paused. 'And if it confirms what I believe, then we'll look at other options, like a donor, for example.'

'No.' She reached out and touched my cheek. 'I want your baby, nobody else's.' Then she grinned. 'But I warn you. If the consultant says there's just one viable tadpole in there that'll do the job, and I have to squeeze it out with my own bare hands, then I will.'

Thank God, it didn't come to that. When the copy of the report hit my email inbox and I read it, I found out that it said that the problem required further investigation before the precise cause of my infertility could be established. I went straight back to the consultant and told him to go ahead. My output was collected and observed. It didn't take the specialist long to tell me that I suffer from what he called asthenospermia; what that means is, the little buggers were there, but they were lousy swimmers. That being the case, he proposed that we assist them by trying in-vitro fertilisation. He warned us that the odds were against success, even after several attempts, but he didn't know Paula. The first shot was a bullseye.

When her pregnancy was confirmed, I've never seen her so happy. No, scratch that; I've never seen anyone looking so happy. Me? Looking at her, I couldn't stop myself; I cried

10

like the baby she's expecting.

She picked up the metaphorical bones of our unfinished discussion and gnawed on them some more. 'So how are you going to play it?' she asked.

'Like any other criminal investigation,' I replied.

'Criminal?'

'Yes. Varley and Cowan compromised a CID investigation; worse than that, they leaked information to a suspect. Jack McGurk and Sauce Haddock had a man called Kenny Bass under surveillance in connection with a cigarette smuggling operation; they'd had a tip that he'd imported a cache of dodgy fags, and they were playing him. They had an authorised phone tap in place on Bass's mobile, trying to pull in other people involved in the scam. Late yesterday afternoon, when they were just about to finish for the day, they were told about an exchange of texts setting up a meeting that same evening. They traced the other number to a man called Freddy Welsh. He's a building contractor, and he has no criminal record, but the fact that he initiated the get-together interested my guys. The venue was Lafayette's, Regine Zaliukas's pub out in Slateford.'

Paula looked puzzled. 'Which one's that? I thought I knew everywhere in Edinburgh.'

'It used to be called Caballero's, before Regine made her now departed husband move it upmarket and clear out the pole dancers.'

'Ah, that place.' She smiled. 'I went out with a guy once and he took me there. I did not go out with him twice.'

11

'Did I know him?' I asked.

'No.'

'Just as well for him. Anyway, our two planned to be in there, waiting for Bass and the other man when they turned up, but . . . Jack couldn't make it. He and his partner were going to a wedding rehearsal last night, and he's the best man, so he begged off. Becky Stallings, the DI in overall charge of the operation, called Sammy Pye, down at Leith, and asked him if he could borrow a replacement. Ray Wilding, Pye's DS, was off limits, obviously, not just because he and Becky live together, but also because he was on the verge of leaving on promotion, so big Griff Montell got the call.'

'Montell? As in Alex Skinner's ex?'

'She'd probably deny that, say they were just friends, but yes, him. He and Sauce watched them arrive, Bass first, then Welsh . . . they'd found a picture of him by that time so they knew what he looked like. They let the pair of them get settled into a booth with a table, and then moved in close enough for Sauce to use a very cute wee directional microphone, and eavesdrop on the conversation, while Montell filmed them with a video cam small enough to fit into his hand. They'd only been there for about a minute, talking about nothing much more than the weather, when one of the bar staff asked if there was a Mr Welsh in the place, for there was a phone call for him. He went off to take it. Because he's a good cop, Sauce went with him, still close enough for the mike to pick him up as he took the call at the bar. I've heard the tape.

12

Welsh says, 'Freddy here. Who's this?' There's a pause, and then he says, 'You're fucking joking.' Another pause, and he says, 'Thanks, you're weighed in for this.' Then he hung up, turned around, and walked straight out the door without even looking at Bass.'

Paula was wide-eyed, hooked on the story. 'What did Bass do?'

'He sat there for a while, looking puzzled.' I knew this for sure, because I'd seen the video too. 'Eventually he figured out that Welsh wasn't coming back, finished his drink and left. Sauce sent Montell after him, to make sure they weren't meeting up outside . . . which they weren't . . . while he went and asked the bar staff about the call. The girl who took it could only tell him that it was a man's voice. When he tried to check the number on one four seven one, it came up as unavailable, but BT were able to trace it for him later. And guess what? It was a public phone box, about a hundred yards away from Gayfield Square police station.'

'Which anyone could have used,' she pointed out, 'so how did you link it to your two? Come to that, how did you even think to?'

'Young Sauce is going to be a great cop,' I told her. 'His gut, and some logical thinking told him there had been a leak, and a very recent one at that. So who was new on the team? Montell. He called Stallings on her mobile, and asked her to meet him. He was even bright enough, or brave enough even, to tell her to say nothing to Ray Wilding, because he worked with Montell. He told Becky what had happened. First thing she

13

did was promise him she'd said nothing to Ray. The second thing she did was call me. I went straight to Special Branch, Dorothy Shannon and Tarvil Singh, and I told them to find out as much as there is to know about Freddy Welsh's background. A couple of hours later, Shannon got back to me. Welsh is Inspector Jock Varley's wife's cousin, Jock Varley is DC Alice Cowan's uncle, and Jock Varley's based at Gayfield Square. Tarvil had checked the station CCTV. It shows Varley going out with his coat on a couple of minutes before the call was made, and coming back in ten minutes later. We've even got a usable print off the phone.'

Paula whistled. 'Poor you, having to deal with that. I take it you've known Inspector Varley for a while?'

'All my career. Now I'm going to have to end his, and possibly worse. When Welsh said 'You're weighed in for this', that can be taken to imply reward, and that, my dear, is 'go to jail' territory.'

'So how is Cowan involved?' she asked.

'She works with Montell, and more besides. He's been giving her one for months. He was supposed to see her that evening, and he told her why he had to cancel: in detail, far too much detail. Unfortunately Alice has a track record for helping her uncle; she knew who Welsh was and she called Jock. She's done too. The best I can do for her will be to let her give evidence against him, but she's probably finished in the force. It's a bloody shame for Alice and I hate it, because I like the girl, and because she's put her life on the line for the job in the past, but I can't hold back on either of them.'

'What about Montell?'

I shook my head at that one. 'I'm having nothing to do with that. I told big Bob as much. The guy insists he knew nothing about the family relationship with Welsh, but he'll still face a disciplinary. The boss will pass that on to someone else too, for the personal reasons you mentioned. So I guess our new deputy chief constable will decide his fate.'

She frowned. 'Will Maggie be tough on him? Could she kick him out?'

'Oh yes, she could recommend that. Whether she will or not, we'll have to wait and see. I can't speak to her about it, and neither can the chief, other than to brief her. I'll tell you one thing, though. If her predecessor, Brian Mackie hadn't gone to the top job in Tayside, and he was dealing with it, Detective Constable Montell would be fucked. Brian's a real hardliner.'

'And what about this man Bass, what about the illegal fags?'

'Oh, we picked him up this morning. We knew where the fags were from day one; the lads followed Bass to a lock-up he owns out in West Calder. Actually they were no big deal. They're Spanish, a brand called Ducados; they had tax labels on them, so we found out very quickly they were part of a consignment stolen from a freight depot in Alicante. They're crap. The street value's maybe a few thousand quid, at the very most, and even then only if you could find anyone daft enough to put them on their shelves, or in a cigarette machine, given that a foreign brand would stand out a mile. Bass isn't saying how he found out about them. Indeed he didn't say a dicky bird to Becky and Sauce when they interviewed him and charged him. He is, as his brief's told him to say, maintaining his right to silence; currently maintaining it in the remand wing at Saughton jail.'

'How did he get them to Scotland?'

'Again, we don't know for sure, but given the quantity, he might have paid a trucker to smuggle them in. Either that, or Kenny could have gone for them himself. Maybe Varley'll be able to tell us when we grill him. He was arrested this morning, and he's being held overnight, down at Leith. There's a lot we don't know. Bass has been on our radar in the past, but not for anything like this. Then there's Welsh; he's a substantial businessman, so what was he doing buying dodgy fags from a small-time smuggler?'

Paula lapsed into cop-speak. 'Has Welsh been lifted?'

'For what? We've got no grounds. There was nothing incriminating in the texts they exchanged, and they don't say a single significant word to each other on Sauce's tape. They were inter-rupted by Varley's phone call before they could. I did think about bringing him in for questioning, but Bob vetoed it. He says we need to find out more about him before we do that.'

I must have sighed, for she reached out and stroked the back of my hand. 'You're feeling really isolated just now, aren't you?' she whispered.

16

I knew what she meant, but didn't say so. 'Isolated? Of course not, I've got you . . . you two, even, for wee Eamon's starting to make his presence felt in there.' That was very true; Paula was in her last month and I could see him kicking sometimes.

'Don't dodge the issue,' she said. 'The Glimmer Twins are no more; you don't have Neil alongside you. You've lost your sounding board, and you must miss him a lot.'

I made no further attempt at denial, because I couldn't. She was right. McIlhenney and I have been bosom pals from the day we joined the force. I made CID a few months before he did, but our careers had developed from then on, if not quite in parallel, then pretty close to it. When I made detective chief superintendent, and was appointed head of CID, he was moved in as detective superintendent in charge of all criminal investigation in Edinburgh, and my deputy.

Neil and I are similar physical types, but he's much less volatile than I am, and when he has to be, he's a calming influence on me. I was going to miss him by my side in dealing with the Varley-Cowan affair, and no mistake.

How did his move come about? I suspect that the occasionally subtle hand of Bob Skinner was behind it. He and Neil are pretty close as well, and when the Commissioner of the Met decided to look outside his force to fill a command vacancy in his covert policing department I wasn't surprised when my pal was put in the frame. My suspicion was, and still is, that somehow Bob might have instigated the vacancy, before helping to fill it.

Quite apart from the prestige of the job, and the chief super promotion that came with it, a move to London was timely for Neil. Louise, the lady he married a couple of years after his wonderful wife Olive passed away, and with whom he has a third child, is an actress. She took time off from her career to have wee Louis, but her agent had been pestering her about making a comeback. The chief knew that, and it would be typical of him if he had gone out of his way to help.

But there's another possibility, a suspicion that lingers at the back of my mind and won't go away. He might have realised that it was time for the Glimmer Twins (back in our rock and roll youth, some wag bestowed on us the nickname adopted by Mick Jagger and Keith Richards, and it stuck) to be separated, in the interests of good policing in Edinburgh. You see, neither one of us is the other's strongest critic, and there were times when, probably, one of us should have been.

With Neil's move the old CID city structure is back in place, with Detective Inspectors Sammy Pye, in Leith, Becky Stallings, at Torphichen Place, and, as of the very day of Paula's inquisition, Ray Wilding, on promotion to DI at Gayfield Square, reporting directly to me from their divisions. God help them all, I laugh to myself sometimes, without my mate McIlhenney to hold me down when they screw up.

'What's your next move?' Paula asked, breaking into my musing.

'I'll interview Varley, formally, tomorrow. Because what he's accused of is so bloody serious, the boss and I are agreed that I need to have a senior officer from an outside force alongside me. Bob's persuaded Andy Martin to fill that chair. As head of the Scottish Serious Crimes Agency he outranks me, but what the hell, he lives in Edinburgh now, so it's handy for everybody. Also, he doesn't know Varley, only of him; their paths don't seem to have crossed at all when Andy was one of us. When we've taken his statement . . . that's if he gives us one . . . I'll probably charge him then send a report to the Crown Office. It'll be up to the fiscal to decide whether to go ahead with a prosecution.'

That's the way it works in Scotland; officially, the police investigate crime as agents of the Crown.

'Will he?'

'Too bloody right he will,' I growled, 'or I'll want to know why. But that will only be stage one. As the chief said, we'll have to find out all there is to know about Mrs V's cousin Freddy, the mystery man, and we'll have to go back over Jock's entire career to see if we can find other instances of him having tipped him off about anything. He's putting a separate unit on that. He's going to use David Mackenzie, his executive officer . . . again, he has no history with Varley . . . putting him together with another outside man.'

'Who's that? Do you know yet?'

'He's bringing in a man called Lowell Payne. He's a DCI from Strathclyde; I believe that he and Mackenzie know each other slightly, from our David's days in the west.'

'Strathclyde?' She winced. 'That's a bit like having next door wash your skid-marked underwear, isn't it?'

'This man will be discreet. He's hand-picked. The boss let it slip that he's Alex's uncle: he's married to Bob's sister-in-law, from his first marriage.'

Paula laughed out loud. 'To think that you used to fret about us being cousins! Skinner seems to be filling this whole investigation with his family.'

'Payne never was family, not really,' I pointed out. 'From what the chief told me, Myra Skinner had been dead for about eight years before her sister even met him. The bloke helped him out in an investigation about fifteen years ago, but since then he's seen very little of him, and nothing at all professionally.'

'He's seen plenty of Andy Martin though.'

'Andy's not family.'

'As good as,' she murmured, with a sly grin. 'He was engaged to Alex once, and it's not long since he left his wife for her.'

'Hey,' I cautioned her, 'that's not true. Andy and Karen just came to the end of the road, that's all.'

Her favoured eyebrow rose again. 'Would that have been before or after he got caught shagging Alex?'

'After,' I conceded, 'but the two of them had got over that. It wasn't why they split.'

She smirked. 'You may believe that, but most

of female Edinburgh thinks she's a bitch who crooked her finger and he came running back.'

'Female Edinburgh better not let her father hear them saying it. Me neither, for that matter; Alex Skinner is okay.' I smiled at a memory. 'I don't think I've ever told you about the first job Bob Skinner ever gave me. He had me looking after Alex when he had to bring her along to a crime scene. I was still in uniform at the time, but that night helped me through the door of CID.'

'He did that?' she exclaimed. 'He took that chance?'

'Come on, she was only thirteen at the time, and I was much too careful ever to consider that she might have looked a few years older. No, I repeat; Alex is okay. Besides, she and Andy are both career people now. That's all they have time for.'

'Yes,' she nodded, 'and my school pal Lorna's husband is a taxi driver. Alex has his number and she uses him a lot; from her place to Dean Village is a regular evening trip of his, but he never takes her in the other direction. And who lives in Dean Village? Andy Martin.'

I gasped in sheer admiration. 'Paulie, my love,' I said, 'when the boss put Neil up for that covert policing job, it's as well he had no idea what you're capable of or he might have offered you to the Met instead.'

We were still laughing when the phone rang. I'd thought my life was complicated enough then: but what did I know?

# Chief Constable
# Robert Morgan Skinner

*'I am here to tell you that there ain't nothing in the world I hate worse than that elephant under my ass.'*

The older I get, the more often I'm asked why I chose to be a police officer. My reply has always been simple: unlike too many people, I was lucky enough to find my vocation early in life and to have been able to practise it ever since.

That's absolutely true as far as it goes, but it's a pretty vague response, and I do not invite supplementary questions. If I did, the sharpest would be, 'How did you find it?'

If it was put to me, my honest answer would be, 'Thanks to Big John Wintergreen.'

Beyond doubt, most people would then ask, 'And who the hell is Big John Wintergreen?'

John never existed, not in reality. He's the doomed hero of a movie called *Electra Glide in Blue* that my dad took me to see in an art house cinema in Glasgow when I was fifteen years old, and the line that I've just quoted is the one that sticks most firmly in my mind. There were no big stars in it; the cast were mostly familiar faces of the era in which it was made, and the guy who played John went on to win more notoriety than fame. But somehow my buttons were pushed by

22

the character and by his desperation to get where he wanted to be.

In the film, 'Big' John . . . he was only five feet four . . . is a motorcycle cop in Arizona, whose dream, asleep or awake, is to be a detective, and that elephant under his ass is the Harley Davidson they make him ride and from which the movie's title is drawn. He gets lucky; he's in the right place at the right time and he's promoted to plain clothes, homicide division. But it doesn't work out for him. An unfortunate tendency always to say what he thinks, a dislike for the office politics, and a liking for his boss's girlfriend, combine to see him busted back to traffic and back on board that two-wheeled pachyderm. The story has a very sad, but very beautiful ending, and I was choked up when we left the cinema, so I didn't say anything on the train home, until we were almost at Motherwell. But all the time I was thinking about John and about his determination and about the job he had lived for and ultimately been denied, and as the train pulled into the station I said to my father, 'Dad, I want to be a detective.'

'Now,' he replied. 'That's what you want now. Let's see how you feel in five years or so.'

He didn't say, 'When you're grown up,' because I was almost as tall as he was by that time, but that's what he meant. His ambition for me was never stated, but I knew it was the obvious, that I would follow him into the law practice that he had started after the war. He had a couple of partners who did carry it on eventually, but I have no doubt that he saw me

23

settling into his chair when he was finished with it.

There was a time when circumstances might have made me do that, but the flame that John Wintergreen lit didn't go out overnight as, most probably, he'd hoped it would. It was still burning six years later, when I graduated from university with an arts degree, and when I applied to join the police force in Edinburgh. I ruled out Glasgow because I didn't like the way things were at that time in that city. I'd seen too many cops chasing the wrong people for the wrong reasons, and I wanted no part of that.

I made detective, pretty quickly; once there, I kept Big John's fate in mind. I made a point of being circumspect in what I said and did, and if there was anything about the office politics I didn't like, I made a mental note of it and stored it away, until the day when I was in a position to do something about it. And yes, my DS's girlfriend was strictly off limits.

Myra and I were married by then, we were living in Gullane, my dad having given us the deposit on a nice cottage as a wedding present, and our first child had arrived. Our life was planned out; once Alex was of school age, we'd have another child, Myra would take another two- or three-year sabbatical from her teaching career, and our family would be complete. But Robert Burns was right, even if he did express the truism rather differently; all too often the most sensible of plans wind up being royally fucked up. Ours never came to be either; a very solid tree got in the way of her speeding car

. . . Myra didn't do slow . . . and thank God Alex wasn't in the kiddie seat behind her mother at the time.

I've never said this before, but in a strange way, I reckon that Myra's death helped my career. It brought me to the attention of a couple of people who hadn't taken too much notice of me before, since I was a man of the West, and also, the rebellious kind who wasn't a freemason. One of them was Alf Stein, the Brahma bull of our CID at the time; under his tutelage and, I admit, with the benefit of his patronage, I never looked back. He was kind to me, and exceptionally tolerant on a few occasions when I pushed my luck to a degree that might have been beyond another man's limits. I rode the wave, and instead of being my father's successor, I became Alf's. As a matter of fact, in some ways I might have been closer to old Stein than to my dad. That's something on which I don't dwell, but I'm conscious of it. My father had a bad war, a secret war, and it marked him.

When Alf retired, Jimmy Proud became my mentor. Sir James was the last of the old breed of chief constables, the kind that were appointed for the duration, not for a fixed term, and who had extra power and influence because of it. Once, I heard some clown dismiss him as a career administrator, but he was more than that. Jimmy was a fixer supreme at many levels; he even fixed it for me to have a spell of outside duty that overcame the normal rule that prevents an officer being promoted to chief within his own force. For that's how he saw me from an early stage, as the guy he had measured up for his uniform, and when Jimmy wanted something, he got it. In my case, he encouraged me to overcome my own doubts, not about my ability to do the job, but about the effect it would have on me. I've always been a front-line detective, even as assistant chief, then deputy.

'I didn't join the police to be weighed down by silver braid on my shoulder,' I used to insist, when we spoke about it. I have never liked being in uniform and that's the truth.

That's the elephant under my arse. I will have no truck with the modern habit of making detectives wear the tunic unless they positively have to be in civvies for the purposes of the job. Beat officers have to be visible and recognisable as such, CID do not; end of story.

Jimmy would shrug at my objections, and tell me, 'Then do it your way. Every chief puts his own stamp on his office.'

Eventually he wore me down, with the help of my third wife, Aileen, who was Scotland's Justice Minister, and then briefly First Minister of its government in the devolved Holyrood Parliament, before Labour lost office. She made herself the exception to my inbuilt antipathy towards politicians. She came into my life at a pivotal moment. My second marriage was in a state of chaos and mutual recrimination, on the most jagged rocks you can imagine. Simultaneously something had happened at work, something up close and bloody, that I was having trouble handling on a personal level. Aileen was there for me to lean on; I came through it all. As soon as I had, before I knew it, she'd eased me into the chief constable's office.

Mind you, I did consult my older daughter before I applied for the job. She knows me better than anyone else, and if she'd been against it, she'd have said so. As it was, Alex was neutral. 'There's part of me that would like you to walk away from it all now,' she said, 'and buy the boat that you fantasised about that time we went sailing on the Clyde. But the other part, the realist Alexis, not the romantic, would be afraid of what might happen to you if you did. Your call, Pops.'

Buy that boat or not, I'll always be moored to Alex; I was there when she was born and she'll be there when I die. I can't say that with certainty about anyone else right now, no other adult, that is.

Once the decision to apply was made, and I'd been selected for the post, I took to it better than I thought I would. I kept the promise that I'd made to myself that I'd focus as much as I could on the crime-fighting and crime prevention aspects and delegate as much as I could of the public order side and the admin to my deputy, Brian Mackie, who'd been close to me for fifteen years and more. It wasn't long before he was gone, to the chief constable post in Dundee, but I'd planned for that eventuality and was able to move Maggie Rose Steele, another of the group I think of as my 'trusties', into the vacancy.

It seemed that finally, after years of continuous adjustments and frequent upsets, both my professional and private lives were running smoothly; for sure, that was a first for me in almost twenty-five years. Everything seemed fine. My younger kids were settled and content, Alex seemed to have found balance in her life, and the electorate had freed my wife from the burden of executive politics, as she put it, by sending her party to the opposition benches. My golf handicap went down by a couple of shots, and Aileen even persuaded me to take up a new hobby, one that I had been planning to leave for my retirement. I wrote a memoir, and enjoyed the process so much that it will probably be the first of several.

I should have known that no millpond stays calm for ever.

I'd been happy with the aftermath of my divorce and with the agreement that Sarah, my ex, and I had reached about the children, in the light of her decision to move back to the USA. I told myself that it was a good thing for them to spend school holidays with their mother, that it would give them an understanding of the wider world, and would spare them from the unreality of being shuffled between parents every week-end. Yes, I was happy with it and I thought that Sarah was too.

I still don't know for certain what prompted her to change her mind. She didn't even tell me about it until the decision was made; I found out by accident from Andy Martin, who managed to stay friends with both of us. I have no doubt she'd have kept me in the dark for longer if he hadn't let it slip. For sure, my ex-wife can hold her cards very close to her shapely chest, but I didn't find that out until well into our marriage. Indeed, I'm still learning just how close they can be. Yes . . . and I smile as I say this . . . she is some machine, is Sarah.

Granted, I had not been in the best of humour since her sudden reappearance, but I don't believe that had anything to do with the explosion with Aileen. Also, a major crisis had erupted within the force that very day, and a long-serving ranking officer had been arrested as a result. However I like to think that I'm good at leaving personnel troubles where they belong, in the office, and I'd done that, although it had been difficult. No, our confrontation would have happened regardless of anything.

I had hit the roof earlier, no two ways about that, when Mario told me what had happened with Inspector Varley. A surveillance blown by the deliberate act of a veteran officer, and with more than a hint of corruption as well, in the man Welsh's recorded promise to the caller that he'd be 'weighed in'. I ordered Varley's arrest, and his niece Alice Cowan's instant suspension. I came within a couple of words of suspending DC Montell as well, but I cooled down and decided that if pillow-talk was automatically sackable we were all gone, so I put his file in the hands of the tough but fair Maggie and told her to work out what would be best done with him in the circumstances. I had an idea, but I wanted to see whether she came up with the same solution.

That stuff was all over with; it wasn't done and dusted, but neither was it hanging over the dinner table like a cloud that evening. However, there was one problem that I did bring home in my briefcase, and in my head. My last meeting of the afternoon had been with my fellow Scottish chief officers, a formal gathering of our association, ACPOS, in a committee room in St Andrews House, the big grey government building at the top of Waterloo Place, with Andy Martin in the chair, by rotation.

The only item on the agenda was consideration of a proposal by the Scottish government that all of Scotland's eight police forces should be merged into one. The debate had been forthright, and fierce at times. Not at all to my surprise, the pro lobby had been led by Toni Field, my recently appointed opposite number in Strathclyde. Since her force covers half of the country as it is, it was predictable that she would want to take in the rest.

I sensed also that being new on the block, having parachuted into Scotland from Birmingham, she was out to assert herself as 'Scotland's top cop', as one of her *Daily Mail* acolytes, who thought it was all about geography, had described her. Field believed it, for sure. She'd landed the Strathclyde job on the back of a high-profile hands-on career, that had included a spell in SOCA, the Serious and Organised Crime Agency, the English equivalent of Andy Martin's outfit. While she was there she'd busted a big drugs cartel with links to both Colombia and Mexico and had used it to catapult herself, over the heads of more experienced candidates, into the chief constable's office in the West Midlands force.

I'd met her only once before that afternoon and it had taken me five minutes to realise that she had arrived in Scotland with a very simple plan. Support the unified force, then take the top post and use it as a springboard to the ultimate policing job in Britain: Commissioner of the Metropolitan Police Service. Good luck to her, I thought. If she was happy with reporting to a mop-headed clown elected on a populist ticket, then good for her, but she wasn't going to do it by helping to destroy the force that I knew in Scotland, the one to which I'd dedicated my life. I believe unequivocally in local accountability in policing; maybe that comes from John Wintergreen too.

I wasn't able to hide my antipathy to the woman, but I was careful not to invite any accusation of either sexism or racism. On Maggie Steele's advice, I wore my uniform to the meeting, as I knew Field would, and I addressed her formally, by rank; no first-name terms, lest she accuse me of being patronising.

In the debate, the antis had lined up behind me. At the end of the day it had come down to the casting vote of the chair and Andy was opposed, so I won the day, but I knew quite well that Field would ensure it was raised again at our next meeting, at which the chair would pass to Max Allan, the Strathclyde ACC, and it was assumed that he would side with his boss, not because he's a toady, but

31

because the long-serving Glasgow people are all imperialists at heart.

I wasn't going to talk about the meeting, but Aileen asked me straight out how it had gone, as soon as I settled into my chair in the garden room. I told her what had happened, and what my prediction was for the future.

'The First Minister's trying to railroad ACPOS into backing the proposal,' I said, 'even if it's only by one vote, so he can bang the legislation through before the next election and claim that he has our support. I like Clive Graham, but I'm not letting him get away with this one. I tell you, I'll fight this in the Association, and in public if I have to, right up to the very end.'

'I'd rather you didn't,' my wife murmured.

I stared at her. 'You what?' I gasped. I thought I'd misheard her.

'I said that I'd rather you didn't.'

'Eh?' Yes, I had heard her right, but still I didn't believe her. 'Why the hell not?'

'Because Labour's going to support the government; we're going to back the bill.'

'You're going to WHAT?' I roared. I'd never raised my voice to her before; I'd never been angered by her before, and I'd never imagined that I could be. And yet . . .

I worried that the children might have heard me, until I remembered that the three of them were at their mother's place in Edinburgh. Nevertheless I made an effort to rein myself in.

'How in God's name,' I asked her, as quietly as I'd been loud before, 'can you bring yourself

32

to do that when you know that I'm completely opposed to it? Please tell me you didn't vote for this within your party group; tell me you were overruled.'

'I can't,' she replied, 'because I wasn't; the decision was unanimous. My colleagues and I all believe that it's the best option on cost grounds.'

'Cost?' I hissed. 'You're prepared to jeopardise the efficiency of the police service to save a few quid?'

'It's more than a few quid, Bob,' she shot back at me. 'And how exactly will it affect efficiency?'

'How exactly?' I mimicked. 'The present structure's bad enough; now you're going to ask cops in Lerwick to implement policy decisions that are taken in Glasgow, by someone who most certainly won't have a clue about local conditions.'

'Then he'll have to get up there and find out, won't he? And who says the unified force will be based in Glasgow?'

'I do,' I snorted, 'because that's the way it will play out. But efficiency's not the only issue; the big one is the concept of putting policing power in the hands of one man, the First Minister . . . or one woman, if you and your lot get back in at the next election . . . which you won't if I have anything to do with it.'

Her eyes flared, angrily, like I'd never seen them do before, and she opened her mouth to rip into me, but I cut her off. 'Think back,' I snapped, 'and not that far back either, to when your predecessor, that crooked little bastard Murtagh, tried to do this very thing and you shot him down in flames. The media will go for you if you turn full circle now. They'll throw your own words back at you.'

'And I'll say that it won't be the same proposal at all, that we'll put safeguards in place. As for your political point, the senior appointments won't be made by the First Minister but by a management board that isn't part of government.'

'And who'll appoint that?' I challenged.

'That hasn't been decided yet; Clive and I have to consult about it, and soon too, because you're right about the legislation going through before the next election. There's no need to wait. We don't want to politicise the issue.'

'No, you want a fucking stitch-up, the pair of you,' I growled.

'Damn it, Bob!' It was Aileen's turn to shout. 'Why are you being so difficult?'

'Because I'm dead against it! Dress it up any way you like, it's political policing. If you can do this you can do anything. You'll have us all carrying sidearms next.'

'Who knows?' God, she was sneering at me: I realised that I didn't know this woman, this version of my wife. 'We might, so live with it! We are elected, after all; it's called democracy, a quirky little system, but it works. And by the way, what did you mean, about you having anything to do with it?'

'Work it out, love,' I snapped. 'I've told you. I will oppose this, as loudly and as publicly as I can.'

'Hold on a minute,' she protested, 'you can't.

34

You're a serving chief constable; you can't involve yourself in political debate.'

'Watch me.'

'Bob, I won't allow it, Clive won't allow it. ACPOS won't back you; they'll support us once the bill's published, you know that.'

'Don't you be so sure about that. The Association is split down the middle at the moment, but once my colleagues see that you're getting into bed with Clive Graham and that it's all been carved up, you may find that quite a few move behind me. And what the hell do you mean 'allow'? What's the new political Couple of the Month going to do about it?'

Her eyes narrowed and her mouth tightened. 'You could be suspended,' she snapped. 'Clive could do that if he thought you were trying to interfere with the political process.'

'Define interference,' I countered. 'Usually with your crowd it means not agreeing with you. And what the fuck was that meeting about this afternoon if it wasn't interference with the ACPOS process? We were offered a committee room by the First Minister, so that we could gather to discuss the proposal, specifically. I'll bet you he assumed he could rely on Toni Field and her Strathclyde contingent to carry it through. He was wrong; we voted against . . . democratically. Now you're telling me the whole exercise was a sham.'

'I didn't say that.'

'Of course you did.' I didn't even try to keep my scorn from my voice. 'You and your new Nationalist best friend, you'll join hands and

35

push your bill through the Scottish parliament without giving the people a chance to consider what's at stake, and that is the potential to create a police state.'

'Aww! Listen to yourself,' she mocked. 'A police state.'

'I said, the potential to do it. Look, the more you centralise the police service, the more remote you make it. People don't know who their local cops are any more. When I was born, my home town had its own burgh police force, and its own chief constable. The local people knew him, and they knew their cops. Okay, it wasn't perfect, especially if you'd gone to the wrong school, but it made for good policing. When my wee force was merged with Lanarkshire, something was lost, but it was still socially acceptable. Personally I'd have kept it at that level. In my view Strathclyde's a monster, and even my own force is too big. Create a single police force? I'd create three new ones.'

'What about Andy's agency?' she argued. 'The SCDEA. That's national.'

'You said it: it's an agency, and it co-ordinates investigations against serious crime, working with local forces.'

'Are you sure you've never served in the mounted division?' she laughed, with mockery, not humour. 'For you're really on your high horse now.'

I was having none of it. 'You know what they do in France?' I challenged. 'If they have a major public gathering . . . let's say an anti-war march, or students demonstrating over the issue of the day . . . they will have the riot squad, the CRS, on hand. But those officers won't be local. If the demo's in Paris, they'll have been brought up from Marseille, or vice versa, so they can kick the shit out of the troublemakers without the chance that they might be beating up their nearest and dearest. That's the model you're about to import into Scotland.' No kidding, I was fuming.

'Okay!' she yelled. 'You've said your piece. But it won't change anything. We will put this legislation forward and parliament will vote it through.'

'I am sure you're right,' I told her, 'but it will do so in the face of my determined and public opposition.'

'And then you will look like a complete idiot when you're chosen to head the new force.' She stepped right up to me, this little street fighter I'd never met before, leaning over my chair, right in my face. "This is really about Toni Field, isn't it? You're like all your brother . . . and I use the word deliberately . . . officers. You cannot stand the thought of this force being set up and its first chief constable, or commissioner or whatever the hell we decide to call the commander, being a woman. That's why you're so upset.'

I couldn't believe that. 'Is that what you think of me?' I gasped. 'That I'm your classic Chauvinist pig? I must tell my deputy; it'll come as news to her, and she's known me a fucking sight longer than you have. Aileen, you have known how I feel about a national force since I wrote a paper for you on the subject during my sabbatical. I've studied it, I've looked at models in other countries, and I'm against it.'

'In that case you're going to look ridiculous when the force is set up, because I don't know a single person who expects Toni Field to head it, other than Toni Field herself. Clive and I have already agreed that the First Minister will be taken out of the decision process on the new supervising authority. Why? So that if I'm back in office after the election, I won't be compromised. Everybody assumes that the job will be yours, man. So please don't make it any more difficult for me than it is already. State your objections in ACPOS, then when the legislation is through you can draw a line under it and take the top job without being labelled a hypocrite.'

I stood up and walked across to the window. My back was to her as I looked out over the garden and beyond, out to sea. I'd been having a private debate for some time, away from ACPOS, away from everyone, in my head. I hadn't come to a conclusion, not until then, but my wife had brought me to it, not in anger as she had been, but calmly, as I accepted the inevitable.

I turned and faced her. 'If that is everybody's assumption,' I said, 'it's completely off the mark. Not only would I never seek to command such a force, I couldn't in all conscience even be a member of it. So when your chum introduces his bill, and you stand up to support it, I want you to bear in mind that you are putting my career on the line. So you'd better know this too: if you think for a minute that I won't do everything in my power to defend it, even at the cost to you of yours, then neither of us really knows the person we married.'

I meant every word of it. As I looked at her, and as her angry eyes stared back at me from an uncharacteristically pale face, I knew that I had arrived at a sea-change moment in my life, one as instant and shocking as Myra's death, bigger than my split from Sarah, which had been gradual, and the opposite from the end of my relationship with Alison Higgins, which had been an amicable, mutual decision.

Having said all I had to say, I didn't know what to do. I didn't even know where to go. I might as well have been paralysed.

If I'd planned the exact moment that the phone should ring, I couldn't have done it any better.

# Detective Constable
# Harold 'Sauce' Haddock

'You pick your moments to slope off.'

I couldn't resist having a dig as Jack McGurk unfolded himself from his car. I hadn't seen him since the Lafayette's operation went tits up. But all the big sod did was smile at me, and nod.

'Didn't I just. And am I pleased? You bet your little life I am. If I'd been there, I'd have sent you off after Kenny Bass, and I'd have done the check on that phone call.'

I know when Detective Sergeant McGurk is kidding me, and he wasn't. I felt my eyes narrow. 'Are you saying that you'd have handled it differently?' I asked him.

'No. I'd have done exactly the same as you, and that's why I'm pleased I wasn't there, or it would have been me that called the DI and blew the whistle that's going to call time on the career of two fellow cops, and maybe three. Face it, lad, you will not be the most popular boy in the force when this gets out. The bosses will love you, sure. You might even get the DS vacancy that was earmarked for Montell, with Ray Wilding moving up. But Varley and Alice are liked in the job, especially Alice, so don't be surprised if you ain't, for a while at least.'

I'd worked that out for myself, from the very first moment I'd realised that the caller to the pub almost certainly had been a cop, but Becky Stallings, good gaffer that she is, had promised that she'd keep my name out of it. I told him so.

'Oh yes,' he said. 'And do you think Montell's going to keep your name out of it too?'

'Why shouldn't he?'

Jack stretched to his considerable height and rolled his eyes. 'Figure it out,' he drawled.

I didn't. 'Okay, he works with Alice. But she let him down. So why should he take it out on me?'

He laid a big rugby lock forward's hand on my shoulder. 'Let me lay out a scenario. Suppose a guy has this girlfriend, pillow-talk is exchanged, and she gets him into professional trouble. What's he going to do? Sign up for her firing squad? No, once she's finished crying on his shoulder he's going to give her a big hug and tell her everything's all right. You, of all people, should know that.'

He was getting personal. A few months ago I'd put myself into a very similar situation with a girlfriend. With another chief constable, it might have been career-ending; indeed Bob Skinner can be such a grim, ruthless bastard that at the time I'd expected it would be. Instead, to my astonishment, when I was summoned to his office at Fettes, in the ugly building that's neither old nor modern, he gave me a cup of coffee, so strong that it was probably punishment enough, and told me, with a frankness that astonished me, that I wasn't the first cop who'd let his dick bypass his brain, and that I was sitting beside

41

another. 'The trick, Sauce,' he went on, 'is not to let it do so twice.'

So when Ms Cheeky McCullough turned up on my doorstep a couple of nights later, what did I do? You guessed it. When she'd finished crying on my shoulder, I gave her a big hug and told her everything was all right. I was taking a chance, and I still am, because Cheeky's granddad was . . . and how I hope that past tense is right . . . a villain, big time, but as long as I remember what Mr Skinner told me, it'll be fine.

I'm still naïve at times, though. For example, because they worked together, it hadn't occurred to me for a minute that Montell and Alice Cowan might have been dancing the horizontal mambo out of office hours.

'Oh,' I said to Jack, 'so I'd better steer clear of Leith for a while.'

He laughed. 'And hope you don't get that DS vacancy.' Then his face went straight. 'You want some serious advice? Call Griff. Don't apologise for what you did, because you were right, but for the way it's turned out. He's a sound bloke. He might not thank you, but he'll respect the approach.'

We had been walking as we talked, towards a line of trees; it was late in the evening, but being July, it was still bright enough for us to see well enough. At some point in time, the car park where we'd met up had been created in the centre of a mature wood, and what was left surrounded it. A man was waiting for us, mid-thirties, bad haircut, in uniform: at least we assumed he was waiting for us, since we had

42

walked past three police vehicles and a dark blue van on our way towards him.

'Why are we here?' Jack asked.

'I don't know,' I replied. 'You're the fucking sergeant; you tell me. I had a call from the gaffer telling me to get here sharpish, that's all.'

'Same here.'

'Through there,' the uniform said, standing aside to allow us to pass through a gap between two trees behind him.

McGurk stopped, so abruptly that I almost bumped into him. 'Can I have your name, and your age, Constable?'

'Harkins. What dae you want my age for?'

'Ach, you know. We always like it in the story.'

'Eh?' As he muttered his incredulity, Jack whipped out his warrant card and displayed it; I did the same.

'We could have been *Sun* reporters for all you know, PC Harkins,' the big man told him, not unkindly. 'You want to sharpen up. There's real competition for jobs these days.'

The plod smiled; personally, I'd have preferred to see a little contrition from him. 'Tough for them, eh. Sorry, Sarge.' He chuckled. 'But I've never seen anyone looks more like a polis than you do.' He pointed into the trees, towards an area that had been taped off, and in which we could see people, moving under lights that had been set up. 'It's over there.'

'What is?' I snapped at him, irked by his indifference to everything.

'The body. What did you expect here, son? This is Mortonhall Crematorium ye're at.'

That much I'd known, but that was all the DI had said. She'd sounded flustered, and that was a first for her, in my experience. As she approached us, holding a crime scene tunic in each hand, she looked less than her cool self, too.

'Lads, sorry to haul you out past your bedtimes, but this one isn't the normal run-of-the-mill homicide.'

'A definite homicide, though?' Jack quizzed her as he started to climb into the paper suit that wasn't going to fit him any better than the last one had.

'He didn't bury himself,' she replied.

'How was he found?' I asked, looking across at the sterile area we'd soon be entering. 'This doesn't look like a place where people walk their dogs.' The woods seemed too thick, close though they were to the houses that I could just make out on the other side. I sniffed the air and caught the scent of cat piss: but no putrefaction, I noted.

'He wasn't. We were told where he was.'

'We were told . . . ' Jack repeated.

She nodded. 'You heard me right. There was a phone call, an hour and a half ago, on the public line to the communications centre. The caller said that there was a body buried in the woods, and told us precisely where. He even gave map co-ordinates.'

'And communications called you?' I knew what he was getting at. We were out of our area.

'No, I did.'

The voice came from behind us, but we didn't have to turn to know who owned it, or that he

44

was not best pleased. He joined us, just as I fastened my paper pyjamas. We'd all been advised to walk as if on eggshells around DCS Mario McGuire, our head of CID, ever since his 'soul brother', Neil McIlhenney, had shocked the world by moving to the Met.

In truth walking on eggshells around McGuire is advisable at any time. There are a few people in this world on whose good side you always want to be, and he's one of those for sure. He's just over six feet tall, and built like a brick shit-house, although he's always dressed to disguise the fact. He has thick curly hair, jet-black, but with some grey creeping into it, as you'd expected in someone around the forty mark. He's usually amiable, but as someone once said, 'If Mike Tyson ever gets into bother in Edinburgh, McGuire's the man they'll send to lift him, and Iron Mike will come quietly.' I took a quick look at him, trying to assess his amiability gauge; it seemed to be still above the danger level.

'In a week or so I might have called Ray Wilding,' he said, 'since this is Gayfield territory, but it's his first day there as DI and he's still bedding himself in. Besides . . . ' His voice trailed off, letting us fill in the rest as we saw it. My interpretation was that maybe he wasn't ready to trust Gayfield with anything sensitive for a while.

'I know what you guys are thinking,' he continued. 'People normally bury bodies to hide them from us. They do not call us and ask us to dig them up, and when they don't do that, they most certainly don't use a scrambler to disguise their voice.'

'How long's it been there, sir?' McGurk asked.

'It's fresh,' I chipped in. 'You can't smell it.'

The DCS leaned forward and tapped me on the chest with a thick index finger. 'The sergeant may well call you 'sir' one day, lad, but not for a while yet. Until then, speak when you're fucking spoken to unless I tell you otherwise.' Then he grinned. 'You are spot on though . . . although it was just as possible that it might have been very old. Come on and see for yourself.'

He led the way forward into the taped-off area. The SOCOs were all over the place, some of them working under hand-held lights. I guessed they were looking for traces of the mystery phone caller; people sign their names in the oddest ways these days.

The burial site was located in a small, square clearing, defined by four trees. It was just big enough for the hole to have been dug, grassy but covered in broken twigs and the brown mulch of last year's fallen leaves. The grave itself had been excavated and the answer to Jack's question was indeed apparent. The body was fresh; it had been enshrouded in what looked like a white bedsheet; that had been partly opened, enough to let us see that it was clean, and free of insect activity. The exposed torso was also naked, part of a young adult male with dark hair; the hands folded across it had neat fingernails and its muscular definition looked sharp even in death.

'Okay, Sauce,' McGuire said, 'take a bow. He's fresh all right.'

Emboldened again, I ventured a question. 'How long's he been there, sir?'

'Don't ask me,' he replied, 'ask the pathologist. Can you make an estimate, Sarah?'

I'd been aware of someone else at the edge of the clearing, but I'd been too focused on the body to take in any details. When she stepped forward I, had a sudden, strange illusion; that I'd stepped into a television crime drama. The woman was tall, strikingly attractive, and the hair that had escaped from the hood of her outfit was a rich honey blonde. Mid-thirties, I thought, in the same ball-park as Becky Stallings. The boss looked across at her, one professional to another, having already been introduced, I assumed, waiting for her reply. It was Jack McGurk's reaction that set me on my heels: his mouth fell open and his eyes widened, as if a second hand had come down on his other shoulder in the middle of a prostate examination.

'Hello, Sergeant,' she murmured, smiling. 'If it still is Sergeant, that is.' Another surprise; her accent was American, and a little twangy, like the dead Kennedys. I had a flash of Marilyn Monroe crooning 'Happy Birthday, Mr President', on old grainy black-and-white film.

Jack pulled himself together. 'Yes it is. I'm sorry: I didn't know you were back.'

'No reason why you should,' she replied. 'The university was asked not to make an announcement when I took up my post. I was worried that it might attract the wrong sort of coverage.'

I hadn't a clue what she was talking about, but I was more interested in the poor sod lying at my

47

feet. I took another look; at first glance I had thought he was unmarked, but second time around I saw a dark discoloration, in the centre of his chest.

'I'd rather call it a guess,' she told the DCS in reply. 'Estimate would be too formal; but I'd say he died around midnight last night, give or take a couple of hours. It was warm last night, so I'd expect that rigor mortis would dissipate at the normal rate rather than more slowly, if he'd been colder in the ground. He isn't exactly floppy yet, but it's going. As for cause of death, I won't know for sure till I've seen all of him, but that bruising interests me. It could be post-mortem lividity, but I don't think so.'

'Will you do the examination yourself?' McGuire asked.

'Unless you want to wait for a couple of days for Master Yoda to come back, yes, I'll be doing it, with a postgrad assistant. Is that all right with you?'

He nodded, vigorously. 'Absolutely,' he agreed.

'Who the hell is Master Yoda?' I whispered to Jack. The woman called Sarah heard me.

'It's what the students call Professor Hutchinson, our chief pathologist,' she explained. 'To his secret delight, I should add, even though they only call him that because he's very small and looks a bit like the Muppet in *Star Wars*.'

Beside me, McGurk was still tense. Indeed, I'd have sworn he was quivering, slightly; I make a mental note to threaten to shop him to Lisanne over his reaction to the mystery blonde.

But that was for later. 'Do we know who he

is?' I asked, of nobody in particular.

'No,' someone very particular replied, 'and from the way he's been left, someone's keen that we shouldn't find out too easily.'

I blinked and looked up. The chief constable had arrived quietly, without anyone noticing his approach. He wasn't suited up like the rest of us, but I wasn't going to be the first to point that out, and anyway, the SOCOs had been over the area around the grave.

Bob Skinner's past fifty now, but if it wasn't for the grey hair, which they tell me he's had since he was around thirty, you might not think so. He has a presence about him, and it's common knowledge that he has something of a temper too, although he didn't reveal it to me when I was expecting to see it, and deserving of it.

They say you can tell his mood just by looking at his eyes, but on the rare occasions when I have done, I've sensed an underlying sadness more than anything else, although I've got no doubt that everything they say about his ruthlessness is true. One thing is certain; when he joined us that night, even McGuire seemed to diminish slightly in his presence. Not the blonde pathologist though; she seemed to grow a little taller, and her jawline seemed to firm up.

He looked at her. 'Have you seen all you need to, Doctor?' His tone was formal; but the sparks between them were practically visible.

She nodded. 'Yes; all that I need to here. Can I have him now? The sooner I get him in the fridge the better it'll be tomorrow.'

'Yeah, fine,' the chief agreed. 'I passed the meat wagon on the way in; you might tell them to come and get him when you leave. But I'd like you to take a look at him tonight, if you'd be so good, just in case he's got six toes on each foot, a regimental tattoo, a bar code on his backside, or some other distinguishing feature. Becky and the guys would need to know about that right away.'

As before, his voice was different when he spoke to her; there was a deference in it that I hadn't heard from him.

'I was going to do that anyway,' she replied, calmly. I whistled, mentally; she'd put him in his place. '*I pathologist: you, simple cop.*' The words hung in the air as if she'd actually said them.

She turned to the DI. 'Can I have your mobile number, Ms Stallings?' She took the boss's card as it was handed over, then walked away, taking each step carefully, since it was quite a bit darker than when we had arrived, and illuminating the path with a small torch that she'd taken from her bag.

The five of us who were left stood back from the grave, waiting for the mortuary crew to come in with their black plastic coffin. I tugged Jack's sleeve and drew him a little away from the others. 'Who is she?' I asked, quietly, not wanting to be overheard again, although as I looked away I saw that Skinner, McGuire and Becky had drifted off in the opposite direction.

'Dr Grace,' he murmured, lowering his head as if he was afraid of being lip-read. 'Dr Sarah Grace.'

'So?'

'Sauce,' he hissed, 'were you asleep when you were a plod? She's the chief's ex-wife. She went home to the States after they got divorced, but now it seems she's back, and in her old job. I doubt if she expected him to be turning up at crime scenes any more, though.'

'It didn't seem to faze her much.'

'It wouldn't. She's a cool one, is Sarah.'

'And a looker, as well.'

He frowned. 'I'll forget you said that, and so should you, Sauce. Banish lust from your mind and concentrate on your moll. I tell you, mate, I still worry about you and that one.'

'Then don't. Cheeky and I have an under-standing; she never, ever asks me about the job.'

'That's good to hear,' he drawled. 'And has she given up driving get-away vehicles as well?'

Yes, Jack knows which buttons to push. 'That was a misunderstanding,' I snapped. 'Her mother pleaded guilty, remember. She said she'd spun Cheeky a story, and naturally she believed it.'

'With respect,' he chuckled, 'it was a plea bargain and the fiscal bought it. She might have finished you, Sauce, yet you're still seeing her.'

'Enough, Jack,' I warned him.

He held his hands up, palms out. 'Okay, okay. Your life, your career.'

'Exactly, and I'm not about to risk either.' He was chasing the wrong hare, anyway. My relationship with Cheeky was working in my favour, but he didn't know that.

We drifted back to the senior officers' meeting, which was breaking up with the arrival of the

51

meat porters. We stood together and watched as they lifted the body, shrouded once again, from its temporary resting place, encased it and took it away, the entire exercise completed without a single word being spoken. Just before they folded the sheet over the victim's face I took a last look, and estimated that he must have been close to my own age, maybe a year or two older, but likely under thirty.

That brought it home to me; this was my job, the one I had chosen, but it had its moments of horror. The chief had been doing it for a lot longer than me, and I knew that he'd seen worse than that, much worse. Little wonder then, that it showed in his eyes, and in DCS McGuire's, when I looked more closely. If it didn't, then maybe they'd have a touch of the monster in them. That's something I'll guard against in the future, I promise.

Skinner stepped forward, and crouched down beside the grave, making sure that the bright lights above didn't cast his shadow across it. He peered in, then reached in and touched something. He glanced over his shoulder, at me. 'See that, Sauce?' he murmured. He was frowning; still, it seemed to me, not quite himself. I wondered if something else had unsettled him, as well as the presence of his ex.

I knelt beside him, following his pointing finger, to a piece of living root from the tree alongside. 'It's been cut,' I said.

'Yeah, that and others. But it's clean. It doesn't feel that it was chopped through by a spade. Indeed it's probably too thick for a spade to have got through it in one whack. No, I'd say it's been severed, by a knife.' He picked something up, from the ground where the body had lain. 'See?' He stood and held it up, examining it closely in the light. 'It's the other half, or similar, ripped out and cut off, and not with a bread knife either, but by something very sharp.'

He looked up at Stallings. 'How was it when it was found, Becky, do you know?'

'Yes, sir. I was here when they opened it. The turf had been replaced, after a fashion, and there were branches laid over it, and stones, covered in dirt, as if they'd been in the ground and dug out with the soil, then placed on top.'

'To hide it?'

She frowned, as she thought. 'No. No, the opposite; I'd say they looked more like protection, as a cover, and as a marker, even.'

'Interesting,' the chief said. 'As you can imagine, I've stood over a few informal funerals in my time. Most of you will have too. But I don't recall ever seeing one that was quite like this. The others were all obviously rushed, and most of the victims weren't even properly covered. None of them were unclothed, but none of them was treated with any dignity either. This grave was dug carefully and the body was put in it ... How can I say it? It was buried reverentially, wrapped in a sheet.' He paused. 'I'd say this was dug by hand. I may be proved wrong, but I don't see one person doing it alone, not to a depth of about what, twenty inches or more.'

'Then there was the phone call,' the head of CID added, 'through a voice scrambler. The communications centre usually pins down everything incoming, but not this. It was a mobile number, but untraceable.'

'And they took his clothes,' Skinner added. 'It's as if they were giving him to us, giving this man into our care, and yet they don't seem to want us to know who he is.' His eyes pierced me. 'What do you think of that, Sauce?'

I hesitated; in that group I was so low on the totem pole I was almost holding the thing up. I felt like a student at a practical exam.

'Come on,' he insisted. 'You're the freshest mind here. What are your instincts?'

I took a deep breath then voiced the only thought I had. 'Whoever buried him didn't kill him. They treated him like a friend, not an enemy; like a comrade.' Something from my schooldays offered itself from my memory. 'There's a poem I read once; I don't remember the words, but it was about a soldier being buried on the battlefield.'

The chief constable nodded. 'I know the one. Jesus, I don't like this. Unknown man, a casualty of something. His colleagues can't dispose of his body properly, so they give it to us for safe keeping, more or less. Which probably means they're still here. But why?'

'Surely, sir,' Jack said, 'they must assume that we'll identify him, given our resources. The body's unmarked; we can mock up a lifelike image for the media, and if that fails, there must be a likeness of him on record, somewhere. We

54

can do a national database search, and put a name on him, eventually.'

'On the contrary,' Skinner retorted. 'It's just as well I'm not a betting man, or I'd lay you long odds against any of that working and I'd cover any stake you laid down. I didn't see his hands, but I know his fingertips haven't been sliced off.'

'How do you know for sure?'

'Because they left us his fucking head as well,' he snapped, 'lifelike image and all. The man is not on any database, Jack, not prints, not image, not DNA: not any database that we can access, at any rate.'

'Are you suggesting he's foreign?' Becky Stallings asked.

'I'm suggesting nothing. I'm telling you that as far as we're concerned the guy we've just had carted off to the morgue is a non-person.'

'So where do we start looking?' She sounded impatient. It struck me that her tone might be pushing her luck.

The chief raised his eyebrows, peering down at her. 'Am I wearing a white pointy hat and bejewelled robes?' She stared at him. 'Am I infallible? No, I'm not; I know this because I've met the real Pope. You do all the routine things, photographic databases, fingerprint comparisons, DNA too, when we get a profile. You do them because I might be wrong. But after you find that I'm not, you fall back on the only asset we've got: the body itself. You ever been to the mortuary, Sauce?'

'Yes, sir,' I replied.

'Good, in that case, you won't need directions

there. I want you to attend the post-mortem tomorrow morning.'

'On my own, sir?'

He frowned at me. 'You don't expect me to come with you, do you?'

I gulped, not knowing quite what to read into that, but having enough smarts to keep my mouth shut.

'Sit in with Dr Grace,' he continued, 'and learn from her. Before she begins, I want you to update her on the discussion we've had here and to explain to her that we're looking for any way of identifying her patient, however unlikely it may be. Joe Hutchinson's the best in the business, but he's got nothing left to teach Sarah. If there are any pointers there, she'll find them.'

As he spoke I saw DCS McGuire's forehead gather into a frown. So did the chief. 'Question, Mario?'

'No, boss, not really. I'm just wondering about only one officer attending. Might we not need corroboration for the court at some stage?'

'I don't see why. There'll be two pathologists present. Plus, the way things are, we don't have any evidence that a crime's been committed. We couldn't even do anyone for concealing a death, since they've gone out of their way to make sure that we know about it.'

'What about the media?' Becky asked. 'Do you want me to draft something for the press office?'

'Hell, no!' he exclaimed. 'To tell them what? That someone can't afford the price of a funeral, so they've handed the deceased over to us.'

'Maybe that's all it is.'

I didn't realise that I'd voiced my thought, until four heads turned and eight eyes focused on me.

Then the chief laughed, so loud that a couple of SOCOs looked across, wondering what the joke was. 'Maybe it is, Sauce. Maybe it is. And you know what? If that's so I will never have been so happy to have made a fool of myself.'

# Dr Sarah Grace

Silly me, thinking for one moment that I could operate as a consultant criminal pathologist in Edinburgh without ever crossing the path of the chief constable, especially when he's Bob Skinner. I should have known it had to happen, but I hoped it wouldn't . . . or so I told myself.

I knew there would be talk when I made my decision to move back to Scotland from the US. But hell, I should never have gone in the first place. When Bob offloaded me for that fucking witch of a politician, I should have stayed put and fought my corner.

But I didn't; instead I made nice. When he made his speech about us having fallen out of love, I agreed, and when he said that we should do what was best for our children, well, I could hardly disagree with that one either. Had I known that he was planning to move the witch, Aileen de Marco, into our bed first chance he got, it might have been different.

Okay, our marriage wasn't perfect; we'd both played away games, but in that respect, the score was Bob three, Sarah two, and maybe he'd been involved in other matches that I still don't know about, so he wasn't standing on any high moral ground, not ever.

Looking back, I can see that he sandbagged me when I was at my weakest. I'd lost my parents, and I was still in shock over that, yet he'd left me alone in the USA to take care of the estate and everything, when he could have taken time out at no cost to his precious career. Then someone else died, someone I'd been close with in my younger days and had gotten close with again, someone who'd been filling the void that Bob had left. I might have stayed with him, but it all came to an end.

My husband played Mr Magnanimous then. It was as if my affair had never happened. Sure, he said something about the score between us being even, but the truth was that his great big macho ego made him blank it out. We went back to Scotland, for the new beginning we announced, to establish a stable base for our kids, me full of good intentions, Bob full of . . .

Some would call it bullshit, but I'll be generous and call it the same crusading zeal that had always led him to put his job over me and over our family: apart from Alexis, that is, my former stepdaughter. From the age of around five, he brought her up alone. He had one significant relationship in that time, with another cop, a classy lady called Alison Higgins, but, as he put it when he told me about her, she was as ambitious as him, so it didn't last. It wasn't till I came along, after Alex had left home and gone to university, that he had any meaningful time for anyone else.

I have nothing against Alex, far from it; she never did a thing to undermine me, and we get on perfectly well even now, but she and her long-dead mother are the true loves of his life, even if he doesn't know it. And she is her father's daughter, in every respect. She's as precociously outstanding in her profession, the law, as he was in his, and like him she will go to the top, wherever she decides that might be. But like him also, she sets it above everything else in her life, so anyone with whom she becomes involved, and there have been a few already, had better accept that it leaves her incapable of ever focusing fully on a personal relationship. Of all people, Andy Martin should have known that when they got engaged, given that he's been Bob's protégé from way back, but he didn't, and that thing crashed and burned. Mind you, from what I hear, he's come back for seconds.

When I came back myself, from America that first time, weakened, insecure, and diminished, Alex was perfectly nice to me. She loves her young brother, James Andrew, and being his mother always gave me brownie points with her. There being about twenty years between them in age, Jazz may be the closest thing to a kid of her own that she will ever have: sad but true. But when the witch came along, and Bob decided that our marriage had indeed gone stale and the time had come for a nice amicable separation, that was it for Alex and me. No conflict, but no contest either. We never fell out, but I am damn sure that behind the scenes she was part of the team that advised her father on a split deal that worked out very well for him.

It might seem that as the mother of two young children I was in a strong position, but it wasn't as easy as that. Mark, our other, older, son, was adopted under Scottish law, and that might have been a problem if I had pursued sole custody aggressively. Then there was the property side. Bob's father's estate, combined with the insurance that followed his first wife's early death, left him comfortably off, but my parents left me substantially better fixed than even he was. If that had gone into a common pot, I'd have been a loser. Alex knew that, even if he didn't, so the deal put on the table was that we each took away what we brought, and that we have joint custody of our three children.

Fair enough, but there was one small, but globally enforceable, clause in the deal, put there by Bob's lawyer, a partner in his daughter's firm, that put all the strings in his hands, given the fact that I'd said I was going back to the USA to practise medicine. The children can never be removed permanently from the jurisdiction of the Scottish courts. In theory, I could have gone to the mattresses on that one, but in practice we were negotiating a no-fault divorce . . . Hah! Equal fault was the truth of it . . . so I had little choice but to sign off on it. What it meant in effect was that I was the one to whom my kids went on their school holidays, while they spent the bulk of their time not just with their father, but, as happened very soon after I left, with the witch, Aileen. Ironic, and then some, that Bob always used to talk about 'fucking politicians'!

Deal done, marriage ended, I moved back to the land of my birth, to work in New York; I bought a family home outside of the city, and I went back to practising medicine with the living, among disadvantaged people, since I could afford to do that. I settled in. I made the house welcoming for the kids' first visit, and I arranged my work schedule so that I could spend most of my time with them when they came over. I enjoyed my job too, particularly the novelty of interaction with my patients: by definition, that's not something that pathologists experience. Eventually I found time to begin a new relationship, with a nice single man, a classy New York Latino, who was even smart enough to bond with James Andrew by taking him to baseball matches. When I mentioned that to Bob in one of our occasional conversations, the sound on the other end of the line was that of a lead balloon going down.

So, there I was, a wealthy, professional, attractive, thirty-something woman with all the flexibility she needed in her life, and a guy to take care of all those things she can't do for herself, or would rather not. Ideal, yes? On the face of it, absolutely, but there was one problem that I failed to dissolve: the loneliness that had enveloped me, even as a wife and mother.

Looking back, I believe it started that time when Bob was stabbed, and almost died; it was a ridiculous thing, a random street knife crime incident that could have happened to anyone. He hung on the edge for a while, but he pulled through. He has great physical strength, and his body made a complete recovery, but his mind didn't. It was a different person who emerged from the chemical coma. While the man that I married had been single-minded, the one to whom I found myself married after the stabbing was obsessive, to the exclusion, at times, of everything else.

It was never the same from then on. He shut me out of his life, and for a while I took myself out of his, until I went back, out of stubbornness as much as love. But he never let me close to him again. We had a married life, and we had a second child, but Seonaid's birth gave pleasure, not joy. We had meetings of the body, but never of the mind. I put a face on it, but inside, I was living in a bubble.

When, finally, I left him for good, I believed that I would be a whole person again, an independent spirit able to interrelate completely with another. But it didn't work out that way. Oh, it was fine with my New York guy Armando at first, sex and that was all, but as it can be with these things, we started to drift into something else, and that was okay too, up to a point, until he started wanting more and more from me in commitment terms, and then became more and more frustrated when I found that I couldn't give it, until one night he asked me how it was that he could be in bed with me and still feel alone, and I realised that I felt the same way.

So we split, last January, and that was probably the lowest point of my life, lower even than when the witch stole Bob from me. I'd had suppressed anger to fuel me then and a clear path to a new life that I thought I wanted. But when Armando and I parted, calmly and rationally (that must be the only way I can do it), my tank was drained. All that I had was my isolation. I had a big empty house, I had a job at which I was okay, but at which I knew I did not excel, and I missed my kids so much it hurt. I was back in the bubble, in a country whose passport I carried, but in which I felt alien.

I don't know what I'd have done if Master Yoda hadn't made contact, but he did, on the third Friday in February, out of the blue. His email told me that he'd met Andy Martin at a conference and that Andy had let him have my address, and went on to ask me to please call him on the cellphone number he gave me.

I didn't leap to the phone: Professor Joe Hutchinson was part of the old life I'd left, and even then I'd rarely ever seen him unless we were surrounded by bits and pieces of human beings. I mulled it over for a couple of days, but on the following Sunday I was feeling so low and weepy after a Skype video chat with Mark, Jazz and Seonaid, and more than a little pissed at having seen the witch passing by in the background, that I dialled his number.

'A long time ago,' he began, once we'd got past the 'hello, how are you' stage, 'I found that it was much more fun finding out how the dead died than administering mostly palliative care to the mildly unwell, and pandering to malingerers. Maybe I'm being cynical,' *You could say that, Joe,* I thought, 'but I believe that all doctors should be specialists. You're not a specialist general practitioner, Sarah, and you never will be, but you are a gifted pathologist. There's a vacancy here at Edinburgh University, linked with the health authority at consultant level, and I'm sufficiently eminent for recruitment to be entirely in my hands. The person appointed will be my number two, and will succeed me as Professor of Pathology, by the end of next year, no later. I owe my wife some time, before she becomes my widow. I've put a lot into this department, and I want to leave it in good hands. That's why I'm offering the post to you.'

I was silent for so long that he thought I'd hung up on him, and hung up on me. I waited for five minutes before I called him back.

When I did there were pieces of metaphor all around me on the floor. That bubble was burst. I had purpose; I had self-belief. I was smiling, no, I was beaming.

'What would I have to do?' I asked, as soon as we had reconnected.

'Practise and teach,' he replied, 'as I do. You've been in the academic world before; you know how it works.'

'When do I start?'

'When can you start?'

'Give me three months to extract myself; May.'

'That's ideal, but don't you want to know about salary and conditions?'

'No.'

I resigned my New York job next morning and put my property on the market. The kids were with me for Easter when it sold, but I didn't say anything to them. The only person I told was Andy Martin, out of courtesy because he'd put Joe in touch with me in the first place, but I didn't give him any details other than that I was coming back to Scotland in May. Bob and the witch? They would find out in due course.

And they did, when I moved into a rented apartment in the city centre a few days before I took up my unannounced appointment. By that time, Bob had heard from Andy that I was coming, but he had no idea that I was back for good. I called him, at the office, and invited him to lunch with me in a restaurant of his choice. He wasn't keen on a public meeting; instead he proposed the senior officers' dining room, a small oasis of privilege in the police headquarters building.

We ate there, and I told him about my career move. He congratulated me, without meaning a word of it, I'm sure, but we chatted politely about it, and about his appointment, although he had been in post for nine months by then. We did our real talking afterwards in his office.

'What do you want?' he asked, abruptly, as soon as the door closed on us.

'What do you mean?' I played the innocent, badly; it doesn't come naturally to me.

'You know bloody well what I mean,' he snapped; just like towards the end of our old times.

He'd asked for it, so I laid it out. 'I want what's best for the children,' I told him. 'I've bought a house in the Grange, and I'm moving in in a month. During the school term, I'll have them with me at weekends. Okay?'

'I don't know,' he grunted. 'I'll need to think about that; they have their own weekend routines. The Jazzer plays mini-rugby on Saturday mornings.'

'All year round?'

'Of course not.' He frowned. 'Look, Sarah, you've bounced this new situation at me. The first thing I need to do is explain it to the kids. Then Aileen and I need to discuss it.'

I felt a chill, as if an ice cube had fallen into my cleavage. 'Excuse me.' I suspect that it came out as a hiss. 'This has nothing to do with that woman.'

'Oh, it has,' he murmured. 'And you'd better believe it.'

Two minutes alone and we were at logger-heads: I'd expected it to take at least five. I stood to leave. 'Weekends, Bob,' I repeated. 'And holidays. For a while.'

That's how it's playing out; even if the witch opposed it, although I'm quite certain she didn't, she'd have been overruled by a higher authority. That same evening, after a brief call to check that I was free, I had a visit from Alex. She brought a bottle of wine, and we had a girlie chat. It wasn't until she was leaving that she murmured, 'Sarah, please don't hurt my dad, or embarrass him.'

'I don't want to do either,' I told her truthfully. 'I never did.'

She gave a small smile, and patted me on the shoulder. 'I'll talk to him,' she said.

The arrangement that Alex had brokered was the one I'd proposed, but outside term time, Bob has them at weekends rather than me. Their carer, Trish, is the glue that holds the routine together; she transports them between homes, and has every weekend off.

I had breakfast with them, and said my

farewells, before I left for the morgue, to work on the mystery man from Mortonhall. It was a holiday Friday morning and the boys weren't due back at school for another month at least, but they would be in Gullane by the time I got home again.

Young Sauce Haddock is a keen one; he was waiting for me when I arrived at the horrible brick and grey concrete mortuary on the corner of Cowgate and Infirmary Street. Its appearance is as depressing as its purpose and I never enter it without my spirits being lowered. How bereaved people must feel if they have to go there is beyond my imagination. If I had the power to raze just one building in Edinburgh to the ground and start over again, I would flatten that one.

As Bob had asked, I'd given the victim a quick, preliminary examination the night before. There had been no extra toes, no tattoos, no bar code on his ass, or anywhere else; in fact he didn't have a single distinguishing mark anywhere on his body. Dental records weren't going to be any help either; his teeth were perfect, thirty-two of them, all present and correct. In fact, the only part of him that was missing was his foreskin. But there was saliva foam in his mouth, and that interested me.

'The chief says he wants you to . . . ' Haddock began, but I cut him off.

'I know what he wants,' I said. 'He wants me to make his job, and yours, as easy as possible; but that isn't up to me, that rests with the guy in the next room.'

68

'Sorry, ma'am,' he murmured.

'Don't be. If he wants to spell things out, that's his privilege. I do what I do, regardless. You ready for this?' I asked him, as Roshan, my postgrad assistant, and I stood with him outside the examination room.

'You mean will I faint, Doctor,' he asked, with a Brad Pitt smile, 'or chuck my breakfast? We won't know until we get there, but I hope not. Where do I stand?'

'There's a viewing panel, with a loudspeaker so you can hear us.' I looked at him. 'Or you can come inside, if you want, as long as you suit up like us, and get the hell out at the first sign of queasiness.'

He grinned again. 'Might as well get it over with. Got a suit?'

We waited until he was sterile, then walked into the room, where our subject was waiting for us. He'd been X-rayed earlier, section by section, as a matter of routine, and an image of the torso was displayed on a light board. My technician, Roddy Frame, was fingerprinting the body as we entered. 'All the other exposures are unremarkable, but you might want to take a look at that one, Sarah,' he called across, his voice muffled by his face mask.

'Why are we wearing masks?' Haddock asked. The laugh lines round his eyes were creased. 'Is it in case he catches something off us?'

'The other way around. You can get some nasty molecules in the air in this room.'

I stepped up to the light board and peered at the image, and saw at once what Roddy had meant. 'Indeed,' I murmured. 'Look, Roshan.'

'What?' the DC asked, behind me.

'He had broken ribs,' I told him. I pointed at the X-ray, counting the fractures. 'One, two, three, four.'

'That's from the bruising on his chest?'

'Yes. It must relate.'

'Is that what killed him?'

'No. I'd say it was meant to be the opposite. Injuries such as these are common when CPR is applied, that's . . . '

'Attempted resuscitation?'

'Exactly.'

'So he might have had a heart attack?'

'It's possible, but I won't know until I look inside.' I looked over my shoulder at Roddy. 'Are you finished?'

'Yes, Sarah, he's all yours.'

As I went to work, with Roshan alongside me and Haddock standing stoically a few feet away, but in my eyeline, so that I could spot any signs of weakness, I had a few possibilities in mind. The first was the one that the young cop had raised, the kind of congenital cardiac condition that can strike down the fittest without any prior warning, but when I opened the chest cavity, all the internal organs were in perfect condition. I made a point of checking the lungs and airways for soil or fabric from the sheet in which he'd been wrapped, but they were clear. Given the circumstances, that was important; it meant that he hadn't been buried alive.

Possibility number two was the jackpot winner. As soon as I opened the skull, I knew.

'Massive brain trauma,' I pronounced.

Haddock knew it also, for the blood that had been released made it obvious. He whistled; he was a cool one. 'I can see that,' he exclaimed, drawing a chuckle from Roshan. 'Does that mean he's been shot?'

'I doubt it; I looked for an entry wound, but there was no sign.'

'A blow to the head, then?'

'No, the skull's intact; a blow hard enough to do that would have fractured it and caused obvious external damage. I expect to find that this man, whoever he is, suffered a subarachnoid haemorrhage, that's bleeding between the outer membranes of the brain.'

'So he was hit?'

'I doubt that very much; in fact I'm quite certain that he wasn't. You know the shit that happens to people?' I asked.

He frowned. 'I've got first-hand knowledge.'

'Well, this is an example of it. A person, young and fit like this man, could be walking around with a weakness in the wall of a cerebral artery, usually at the base of the brain, knowing nothing about it until the day it gives out. When it does, there's a fifty per cent chance that it will be fatal, and a good chance that the sufferer won't even make it to hospital. It's subject to completion of my examination, but I'd say right now that there was nothing untoward about the circumstances of this man's death, and that the way in which his body was disposed of played no part in it.'

'So like the chief said,' he ventured 'this might not have been a crime at all?'

I had to laugh at his incredulity. 'He has been known to be right, Constable.' *When it comes to his work*, I added mentally.

'I'd better report this, Dr Grace,' Haddock said, full of eagerness.

'Don't you want to wait till I'm finished?'

'Will you be able to tell me any more than you have already?'

I raised my eyebrows. 'I can't tell you how the book will end till I've read it all.'

His chuckle was muffled by his mask. 'In that case I suppose I'd better not miss a chapter. It'll be colourful, if nothing else.'

# Aileen de Marco Skinner

I know a few people who claim they went into politics for the excitement of the life. Every one of them is a fool. Today in our nation there are two professions whose members are excoriated by the masses, and held in universal scorn. You know who I mean: bankers and politicians.

I'm one of the latter, and while I am shamed and outraged by those of my colleagues who've betrayed the public trust, on balance I'm proud of my job. I'd rather have it than be one of the other lot, and that's for sure. I don't say this in the debating chamber or in my constituency newsletters but I sympathise with most bankers. We've seen the big headlines, but usually, the bonuses for which they take such stick are contractual, and performance-related. They're not the fault of the individual, but of a lousy regulatory system set up by my lot, a fact forgotten by too many of us.

The one advantage that bankers have over me and mine is that, with the exception of the few at the top of the tree who are hauled regularly before self-righteous Commons Select Committees with their caps in their hands, they are anonymous. We legislators, on the other hand, are subjected to relentless public scrutiny and criticism. Some of it is justified, I acknowledge, but much of it is simply the reflex antipathy created by our adversarial system, its fires stoked by the media who line up on either side of the ongoing war.

These days there's no escape in the public domain. Everything we do is scrutinised, and nothing we do is ever one hundred per cent right. We cannot leave our offices without being photographed, often in the least flattering light. This is particularly true for women, fly-away dresses on a windy day being especially popular with the tabloid snappers, and making the wise among us wear trouser suits or tight skirts all the time. The photo libraries have alternative images for us all; the nice ones for a good-news day, the off-guard for the opposite, or all the time, if the newspaper involved is rabidly against the victim's party.

That's the kitchen in which we have to work, and as Harry S. Truman advised, those who can't stand the heat should know what to do about it. Sensitive souls need not apply: nor the paranoid either, for there are physical dangers, make no mistake about it. Those at the very top of the political tree have round-the-clock police protection, but the rest of us are vulnerable, and round the world, many tragedies have happened.

The one place we're entitled to feel safe and relaxed is at home. That's why Bob's explosion was so shocking to me. Yes, I know that I had a history of opposing a unified police force, but I am also a pragmatist, and as such, I'm open to persuasion . . . unlike my husband. Considerations can change, and if I find that cons have become pros on cost grounds, I'm capable of changing with them.

It seems that Bob Skinner isn't like that. I thought I'd married a reasonable man, but I've discovered that his equanimity only applies when he knows he's going to win at the end of the day. When he doesn't, he's blinkered, he's stubborn, he's obdurate, he's implacable, he's unyielding and he's every other adjective meaning that when he takes a position and refuses to listen to even the most reasonable counter-arguments he is quite unshakeable.

When I told him that I'd been persuaded to back the Nationalist administration's bill to unify the police service in Scotland, not by Clive Graham but by the cost arguments in favour of the proposal, I was prepared for him to be disappointed, but I expected him to listen to my rationale and to be persuaded by it. So when he turned on me in fury and the shouting match began, it wasn't just his attitude that set me off, it was the fact that my sanctuary had been invaded. I wasn't in the debating chamber; it was my home.

Well, 'Bugger that for a game of soldiers!' as my constituency agent is fond of saying. I've cared for that man. I've been there for him when he's been down, I've been his confessor, I've become a mother to his ... another woman's ... over-indulged kids even though maternity has never been one of my life goals, I've massaged his prodigious ego and I've fed his sexual appetite, which is not inconsiderable either.

The least I expected was to be treated with respect when I took a position at odds with his own, and for him to make some effort to understand how I had reached it. But no, he turned on me and I saw him at his most intransigent.

Until I met Bob, I had no great history of long-term relationships, nor much time for them, if truth be told, but whenever I was involved with someone I had a rule: never let the sun set on an argument. I didn't have a chance to follow it that night. Our blazing row was interrupted by a phone call. He took it, muttered something about having to go to Edinburgh, and headed for the door. When I went to bed I expected him to join me eventually, but he didn't. I don't know where he slept, but he was in the kitchen when I came down next morning, sweating like a horse in his running gear and guzzling a litre of orange juice straight from the carton.

'Want some breakfast?' I asked.

He crushed the empty carton in his fist, and tossed it into the waste bin. 'That was it,' he replied. 'I'm off for a shower.' He turned and walked out. I looked at his retreating form, and imagined a hand thrust out, keeping me at bay. I'd never felt isolated from him before, and never ever imagined that I could be but . . .

A political commentator, no friend of mine either, once described me as 'an irresistible force'. I was in motion and on a collision course, it seemed, with the immovable object that is my husband. 'Sod him,' I murmured, as I picked up my car keys. 'We'll see who can't be moved.'

Parliament was in recess, but that didn't mean

that the place was deserted when I got to my office. Being a party leader is a year-round job and six days a week at that, although reaction to a Sunday newspaper splash often eats up much of the seventh as well. In opposition, it's worse than being First Minister; the workload isn't much less, but you don't have the civil service support.

I was halfway though a substantial mail-tray . . . yes, some people still communicate on paper . . . when my phone rang. As I picked it up I guessed who it might be, and I was on the mark. 'Ms de Marco,' Russell Moore, the First Minister's principal private secretary, purred in my ear, 'Mr Graham wonders if you could spare him a few minutes. He's in his parliamentary office.'

'Sure,' I sighed. Best get it over with. I finished the letter I'd been reading, a request for a questionnaire contribution to a postgrad's PhD research, and walked the short distance to the room that had been mine until a year earlier, when I'd sacked my coalition partners and left the Nationalists to form a minority administration, in the hope that they'd shoot themselves in both feet.

It was beginning to look as if I'd miscalculated; we were only a point or two ahead in the most recent polls, with an election less than a year away, and I'd been told that there were mutterings on my own back benches. I wasn't worried about the security of my position, as the only people I judge capable of unseating me as leader are too smart to want the job in the circumstances, but on the other hand it didn't please me. It was one reason why I'd done the deal with Clive Graham over support for the unified police force, and the early legislation that he wanted; if I had to fight internal battles I didn't want to be in bitter warfare with the Nationalists at the same time.

The PPS was going to show me into the presence, but I wasn't having that. I told Mr Moore, fairly curtly, that I knew the way and marched in with the briefest of knocks. Clive swung his chair, my old chair, round to face the door as I entered, but he didn't even make a show of standing.

'Don't get up,' I told him, regardless, thinking *My* God, as I saw that he was wearing that fucking tartan waistcoat. I'd assumed that it was the affectation of a professional jock, purely for the cameras, but no, there he was in his private office, in shirtsleeves, and still wearing the thing, in high summer.

He smiled, and nodded. 'Thank you, ma'am,' he laughed. And then I saw that we weren't alone. There was a figure in one of the visitor chairs with her back to me. I could see a tuft of brown hair with just a hint of purple about it, and I knew whose it was. It's impossible to be a member of the Scottish parliament for a Glasgow constituency without bumping into the Chief Constable of Strathclyde Police.

He followed my eyes. 'Toni's dropped in for a chat,' he said, his voice tentative as if he wasn't sure whether I would turn on my heel and walk right back out of there. Neither was I, for a moment. Twenty-four hours earlier I would have, for sure; but that was before everything changed between Bob and me, so I stayed there and eased myself into the other seat, nodding to Chief Constable Field as I did. She was in her uniform too, all black, tunic and skirt, a tight-packed little woman, with bulging calves and the same brown skin tone as Trish, our Bajan child carer, but with none of her gentleness.

She nodded back, with just a little deference, not because of who my husband was, I knew, but in spite of it, since there was a fair chance that a year down the road I'd be sitting on the other side of the First Minister's desk.

'Bollocks,' I barked.

Clive pushed backwards in 'our' chair. 'Aileen,' he exclaimed, his tone a little pained.

'Toni's no more dropped in for a chat than I have,' I continued. 'I know full well why she's here; she's reporting back to you on yesterday's ACPOS meeting, the one you set up to rubber-stamp the police unification process. I even know what she's told you, that my husband squeaked a negative vote through, courtesy of his best pal being in the chair, but not to worry, that she'll see him off next time.' I looked at her, sideways. 'Am I correct, Chief Constable?'

She smiled, a condescending little smirk that enraged me, but she didn't reply. I wanted to tell her that she'd made two mistakes in as many days, first underestimating Bob, second, pissing me off, but I decided that could keep, that I'd choose the moment when she found that out for herself, the little mass of political correctness.

She's so much modern cop that she even has her own Twitter account. A few evenings before Bob had ranted about her, and it, after dinner. 'She posts everything on it, Andy told me,' he'd bleated. 'Her diary for the coming week; she's even listed our bloody ACPOS meeting on Thursday. What next? Her bowel movements?'

I couldn't quite share his outrage. The Labour Party press office publishes my engagements too, every day.

'Let's take that as read,' I said to Clive. 'Now go ahead, First Minister. Since you're not going to offer me tea, coffee or Irn Bru, you'd better ask me the question you invited me here to answer.'

Unlike Field's superficial smile, his was open and genuine. In truth, Clive Graham is one of those colleagues that I regard as a friend, all politics set aside. Sometimes I regret that we aren't in the same party, but no way am I going to join his, and he left mine twenty-five years ago. 'Okay, Aileen,' he chuckled. 'Did you talk to him?'

'Yes,' I replied. 'At least that's how it started. But I am not going into detail, not even with you, Clive, and certainly not with a third party who doesn't seem to have any regard for my husband, or any idea of what makes him tick.'

'And you do, Ms de Marco?' Field murmured.

Second time around I didn't even bother to look at her. 'Oh yes, dear. Be sure I do.' I focused on the First Minister. 'Well?' I challenged.

He nodded. 'Do we have a problem with him?' he asked.

'Oh, yes,' I replied. 'We certainly do. And if the chief constable here thinks she can sweep him aside in ACPOS, she really doesn't have a bloody clue who she's dealing with.' I held his gaze. 'I'd like her to leave now,' I said.

He shifted in his chair, awkwardly, as if his nuts needed rearranging, but Field removed his problem. She stood. 'As it happens,' she drawled, 'I must go anyway. I'll leave you to your plotting. I find politics so intriguing,' she added. 'All that stuff behind the Speaker's Chair, when we all know how it's going to finish, even you, Ms de Marco. Your husband is a dinosaur, and their time is long past.'

I couldn't hold back any longer. 'And what are you?' I snapped. 'The fucking meteor that wiped them out? Alongside him, you're a pebble.'

I watched her, every step of the way to the door. 'God, Aileen,' Clive Graham gasped as it closed, 'you don't mind who you cross, do you? That woman is powerful. If she tries to influence her force and their families against you . . . '

'What's she going to do? Book me for parking every time I step out of my car?'

'She has ten thousand people under her command,' he pointed out. 'If she spread the word that you were to be opposed at the next election . . . '

'I'd find out about it the day it happened.' I glared at him. 'Clive, I am up to here with being underestimated. Don't you bloody start or . . . '

'Or what?' he chuckled. 'You'll wind up the Lib Dems and the Tories to back you in a no-confidence vote? You know that neither of us want that.' He frowned. 'So, things did not go well, I gather, when you had your discussion with Bob?'

'It wasn't as calm as that,' I told him.

'Do you want to back off from public support for the bill?' he asked.

'Hell no! The day I vote according to the whim or instruction of Bob Skinner, you'll know I'm finished in politics.'

'Fine, but if you want to take a step back when the bill is published, I'll understand. I appreciate that you're in a very difficult situation, domestically.'

'I'm not the one who's making it difficult,' I snapped, 'so I'll cope.'

'What's he saying? Can I ask that? Not to leave this room, of course.'

I looked him in the eye. 'Can I trust you on that?'

He nodded. 'Yes, because I know you'll kill me if I break my word.'

'True; keep that thought in your mind because it's apposite. Bob is saying, 'Over your dead body,' almost as directly as that. He's said that he will oppose an all-force merger publicly, and that if he loses and it happens it'll be a resignation issue for him.'

'You've pointed out to him that the police are meant to keep out of politics?'

'Of course I have,' I sighed. 'You can tell him yourself if you want. He'll assume that we're having this conversation, so if you call him in here and warn him off, it won't make it any worse between us.'

'Would it work, do you think?'

'Hah!' I laughed. 'No chance. You make your speech, and issue as formal a warning as you like; he'll point out to you that 'politician' and 'policeman' both have the same root and mean essentially the same thing, interpreted in different ways. That's one of his dinner table favourites when he's among my colleagues. Some of them call him Bob the Greek.'

'And would it matter,' he wondered, 'if I told him he was wrong, that while the two English words are similar, 'police' flows from the ancient Greek 'polissoos', meaning city guard, while the derivation of 'politics' is the word 'politika', and that comes from Aristotle?'

'I'd like to be there when you tell him,' I said, 'if only to mop you up. You might want to change the waistcoat for a tartan with a bit more red in it.'

He winced. 'Do think Toni Field can swing ACPOS behind her?'

'Bob does,' I conceded. 'I'm not so sure. When he goes to the next meeting, or even gets on the phone before it happens, and tells them that the main parties are ganging up to force their will on the police service, he may well pull some waverers behind him. And now that I've seen how presumptuously fucking arrogant the woman is . . . '

'Damn,' the First Minister muttered. 'I'd hoped to avoid this. I like Bob; I don't want a confrontation.'

'Then don't have one,' I advised. 'Ignore him.'

'I don't know if I can do that,' he replied. 'If

he really cranks up his public opposition, I may have to do something about it. I hate to think of suspension, but . . . '

My mouth fell open. 'Are you crazy?' I gasped. 'You suspend him, and you will have one of the smartest young solicitors in the country briefing the best QC in the country, to take you to court. You'll have made this into an election issue, when that's exactly what we want to avoid. If that happens my party might well reconsider its support for the bill.'

'How would you feel about that? Are you one hundred per cent behind it?'

'Yes, I am,' I admitted, 'and not just on cost grounds. But I don't want to have to tell Bob that. Christ, we're shaky enough.'

'I'm sorry,' Clive said, and I could see that he was.

'Let it lie,' I urged him again. 'Bob won't keep quiet about the bill, but he won't lead protest marches either. He'll use what media contacts he has, the likes of June Crampsey in the *Saltire*, but he has no power base in our world. Live with it; we have the numbers, and we will win.'

'But how will you come out of it? Your marriage? What if he does resign, and blames you?'

I shrugged. 'There's another side to that coin. Suppose he does kick up a big enough media storm to swing my lot against the bill, with me on record as supporting? I'd have to quit if that happened. Either way, one of us is going to wind up blaming the other. Will we survive that as a couple? To be honest, Clive, I don't know.'

84

'My sympathies, Aileen,' he said. 'I'm truly sorry I got you into this.'

'You didn't,' I retorted. 'He did, by being the most intractable son-of-a-bitch on the face of the earth.'

He reached into the drawer to his right, the one where I'd kept my personal stuff, and took something out. 'In the spirit of amity,' he murmured as he pushed an envelope across to me. 'There's an event in the Royal Concert Hall in Glasgow tomorrow evening, a concert in aid of a range of charities including police, and one that supports battlefield casualties and the families of the dead. I'm the guest of honour: they've sent me four tickets. I had thought to take my private secretary and his wife, but his boss has vetoed it on some spurious ground of official impropriety. If you'd like to come, I'd be very pleased; and if you could talk your husband into escorting you, it might cool things down a little.'

I picked up the tickets. 'Thanks, Clive, I'll try to persuade him. If he won't I'll come anyway. My stepdaughter might join me, if it's her scene. Who's performing anyway?'

'A classical pianist that I've never heard of; I'm more of a jazz man, myself. His name's Theo Fabrizzi. Quite a star, apparently.'

'Theo Fabrizzi?' I repeated. 'I didn't know Italy had any pianists. I thought they specialised in tenors.'

'He isn't Italian, although most people assume it. They sent me his bio. Yes, his great-grandfather was an Italian prime minister, back in the very old days. He was a socialist, so it got very uncomfortable when Mussolini came to power. He left the country in a hurry and settled his family in Beirut. That's where Fabrizzi lives.'

'So he's actually Lebanese?'

'By nationality, yes.' I stood to leave. 'Would you like to be collected?' he asked. 'I can arrange for a government car.'

I smiled. 'No thank you, Clive. We're still political opponents, remember. I expect to have access to those in my own right before too long. Until then, I'll make my own way.'

*Mutual interest is one thing*, I thought as I left him, *but fraternising with the enemy is quite another*. But then I wondered, after the set-to of the previous evening, should I regard my husband as the enemy?

If that was the way he wanted it, yes.

# Andrew Martin,
# Director, SCDEA

Mario McGuire and I go back a long way, fifteen years at least, to when he was a plod and I was still a raw detective constable. I've made chief officer status, and he's only one rung short, so you could say that our careers have developed along parallel lines. You could say that, but I've always believed secretly that Mario has more ability than me, but less ambition.

I played rugby in my youth, at a very high level, but I set it aside when the job demanded, for that was my priority. As far as I know Mario never played any organised sport in his life, and certainly not rugby; probably just as well, because I'd have hated to have scrummed down against him. But if he had, and had been given the choice between an international future or early entry to CID and a fast track to the top, he'd probably have grinned that piratical grin and gone on to win a boxful of caps for Scotland . . . or Ireland, or Italy, as he'd have been qualified for all three.

He and I do have one thing in common; it's a link on which nobody ever comments, but I'm only too well aware of it, and I know he is.

Both of us made the same mistake: we each married cops. Mario and Maggie Rose got together on an investigation years ago, when they took the concept of undercover policing very literally indeed; they drifted into a union that seemed happy at first, until the smiles left their faces and the whole thing fell apart. Maggie had a brief breakdown, and Neil McIlhenney dropped a hint about a suicide attempt, but I didn't pry.

Mario moved on, giving the force a wide berth second time around in his choice of partner, and I hear that Paula's pregnant: great. Maggie remarried also, only she stuck her head in the lion's jaws for a second time. But that's too painful even to think about; it would only depress me.

Karen and me? That's a long story. At first, she and I . . . honestly, it was lust, pure and simple. Then I had a bad day at the office, a very bad day; my counsellor told me I could expect to experience post-traumatic stress and I told him he could expect to experience my boot up his arse, because I had always been mentally tight and able to walk away from a bad experience then move on to the next good one.

But he was right. I did have problems in the aftermath; nightmares, cold sweats, all the stuff that was only supposed to happen to other people. When they hit me, Karen soothed the fever when I needed it and I decided that what she gave me was what I wanted for the rest of my life.

And yes, I decided that I was well and truly over Alex Skinner.

I'm a Catholic, something else that McGuire and I have in common. But he's pretty much lapsed, whereas I'm devout . . . when it suits me. That's why I went off the end when Alex had a termination without telling me. No, let's be totally honest, Andy. While that was the reason I gave to everyone, myself included, I know now that the real truth was that I resented the fact that she'd made what was in effect a career choice that didn't fit with the way I'd imagined our future.

I've known Alex since she was a teenager, a kid not as precocious as she looked, following her then single dad around like a puppy, and eyeing up every woman he ever dated, even Alison Higgins, whom he did a lot more than date, as a potential interloper.

When she grew up, she did so fast. The kid just disappeared and someone completely different took her place. When she and I got together, as she was moving into her twenties, I hadn't kept up with her development as a woman, not at all.

Confession: I was pretty dumb where the female psyche was concerned. I had spent too much of my time sowing wild oats to notice that society had moved on from the one I'd grown up in. My mother was a traditional housewife, and I thought of my new young fiancée along those lines. Bottom line, I saw my career as more important than hers.

Alex? Homemaker? Mistake.

When he realised what had happened to us, her father actually apologised to me. I remember it well. 'Your trouble, Andy,' he said, 'is that you're an old-fashioned Scots proddy cunningly

89

disguised as a Tim. There's a lot of John Knox in you, not far from the surface. Okay, you might not see women as weak, sick and impotent like he did, and in the workplace you accept them without question as your equal, but at home, whether you know it or not, you're still the sort of guy who wants the little woman there, tea on the table, kids fed and bathed, when you get home at night. I should have realised it earlier and warned you off, for my daughter will never be like that. I'm sorry, mate, for both of you.'

At the time I told him that he was talking bollocks, but he was right, as I proved with Karen, for that's exactly what I made her into. I took a strong vibrant woman, encouraged her to leave a job that she probably did as well as I do, and in the process I diminished her being.

Where once we had been two pieces of flint, in the end she and I couldn't manage a spark.

Alex and I, though, we always did that. When our paths crossed again, after a few years, we found that our flame had never gone out, for all that we had stamped on it, hard.

Yet I insist, that wasn't why Karen and I finished. 'It isn't unfaithful Andy I can't live with any more,' she told me in the end. 'It's the boring middle-aged fart you've become at home and the person you've made of me.'

We could hardly post that on the bulletin board, so when I moved out, everyone and his uncle assumed they knew why.

So, Alex and Andy, where are we now? Not where we were, and that is for certain. She will never give me dominion over her and I will never want it, never again. Yes, we have a relationship, but no, there's no commitment on either side. The only rule is the one that she made, after her first surprise visit to my place, that neither of us will ever arrive unannounced on the other's doorstep. What she does when I'm not there, I have no idea; and my job as Director of the Serious Crime and Drugs Enforcement Agency involves quite a lot of travel.

It was by sheer chance that I was around when Bob Skinner called me to ask if I could do him a professional favour. 'No worries if you can't handle it personally, but if you can't, I'd appreciate it if you could send me someone senior to sit alongside Mario.'

But I was clear, and to be honest, I saw it as a chance of a long weekend in Edinburgh, since the interview he wanted me to do would inevitably last too long for me to get to my base in Paisley for any sort of meaningful work.

My SCDEA badge didn't work when I arrived at the police headquarters building in Fettes Avenue, not even with 'Director' on it in bold print. The door security officer didn't know me from Morecambe and Wise . . . his lack of humour was written all over his face . . . and he made me wait until I could be fetched by someone from CID.

Mario came down himself. He was ready to take a piece off Cerberus, but I hauled him away before he could do too much damage. 'That's the trouble with these civilian staff,' he growled, 'no nous, no initiative. Ah, it's not their fault, I suppose. The politicians want to see as many uniforms on the street as possible so we con them by hiring civvy security officers. We have to vet them to make sure they're legit, and that takes time, then once they're in the job, they don't have any flexibility about them. Last month, one of them made Aileen wait down here until Gerry Crossley came to collect her. You can imagine what happened when Bob found out.'

'Oh yes,' I laughed. 'Has the fall-out cleared or is the place still radioactive?'

He walked me up to the head of CID's office. It hadn't changed a bit since it was mine, save for the photo of Paula (and bump) on the desk and a couple of very classy landscapes on the walls.

I took a guess. 'Your mother's work?'

He nodded. 'That's what she retired to Italy to do. She gives them away, you know.'

'Literally?'

'Well, no,' he conceded, 'she's still a Viareggio. No, she sells them through a gallery in her village, when they're easily good enough for her to get them into an outlet in Firenze and make three times the money.'

'How does she feel about being a granny?' I asked.

'Ecstatic. She's talking about moving back to Scotland. I'm doing my best to talk her out of it, but I've never been any effing good at that.' He frowned, suddenly. 'Hey, by the way, I'm sorry about you and Karen. Haven't seen you since it happened, but . . . You know, sorry.'

'Yeah, thanks; appreciated. Now, brief me. Bob

only gave me the bare bones yesterday. What am I here to do?'

'He said that you don't know Jock Varley . . . Inspector John Varley?'

'No, I don't in any personal sense of the word. I know who he is, obviously, but we have never actually met face to face, not that I can recall.'

'And you would,' he snorted, 'given your legendary memory. You're right; he's spent virtually all his career in uniform, while you've been in CID. The situation is that he has an in-law called Freddy Welsh, whose name came up in an operation that the Torphichen Place team had under way. There was a meeting between him and our target, and Varley stopped it with a phone call.'

I asked the obvious. 'How did he know about it?'

'His niece told him. DC Alice Cowan.'

I did know her. 'Special Branch Alice?'

'Not any more, she got booted off SB about a year ago for tipping off Uncle Jock about something else he was involved in. Obviously you didn't know that.'

Actually, I did. 'Oh shit, yes, he was that guy.' It came back to me. I'd been in a similar situation then, an outside force officer brought in from Tayside as an objective eye, but not too objective.

'You got it. Varley was, very briefly, a suspect in a murder investigation, but he was exonerated.' Indeed: I had come very close to meeting him at that time. 'He was in Livingston then, and

93

he was moved to Gayfield afterwards, diplomatically.'

'How seriously are we taking this?' I asked.

Mario stared at me; he was offended. 'Very. We don't want you to help us rubber-stamp a cover-up here. Nothing is off the table in terms of action as far as we're concerned. If you say at the end of the day that we should hand the whole investigation to another force, or to your agency, we will do that.'

That was what I'd wanted to hear. 'That's good. You want me for just the one interview, then?'

'That's all it was going to be,' he said, 'but I've had a rethink overnight. I saw Alice myself yesterday; she said she'd co-operate and I suspended her, pending a full hearing. But I want us both to interview her as well, again so that you're happy with the way I'm proceeding.'

'Fine, but there's another officer in the chain, as I understand it. What about him?'

Mario frowned. 'He's being dealt with separately; I've taken a statement from him and I'm satisfied that he's guilty of no more than careless talk. But I don't want to handle the discipline. He'll be on Maggie's carpet later on.'

'But shouldn't I interview him too,' I wondered aloud, 'as part of this process?'

'That wouldn't be appropriate, Andy. It's DC Montell, and he has . . . ' He hesitated, and I knew why.

I nodded, and said it for him. 'He has a history with Alex. You're right; that disqualifies me. But let's be clear; you're satisfied that he hasn't done

94

anything that could possibly be seen as criminal.'

'Absolutely.'

'Okay, that's enough for me,' I said. 'Is he suspended too?'

'Hell no! That would have emptied the Leith CID office; Sammy Pye would have done his nut.' He paused, his face twisting into a grimace. 'Would you believe, I called him 'Stevie' the other day? At a meeting Maggie was at, too.'

I shrugged. 'Come on, they worked together. It's an easy mistake to make. Plus it would show her he's remembered.'

'That's what Maggie said; it didn't stop me looking for a hole to hide in, though.' He stood. 'You ready to go?'

'Sure. Downstairs?'

He shook his head. 'No. I've had Varley held overnight, down at Leith. We'll go there.'

Bob had said no half measures when he'd asked for my help, but that took me by surprise. 'You serious? He's a cop and you've held him in custody?'

'I've got grounds,' he insisted. 'If he wasn't a cop, what would I have done, or what would you?'

He was right; I don't take prisoners either.

Mario drove us down to Leith, since I'd walked the ten minutes from my place to Fettes. There are no attractive police offices in Edinburgh, damn few anywhere for that matter, but at least the building on the corner of Constitution Street and Queen Charlotte Street has the benefit of being old. It has an impressive pillared entrance and if the stone was cleaned up it wouldn't look bad, not the best piece of architecture in the city, but the most distinguished nick, and certainly more attractive than Torphichen Place; to my eyes that's always managed to combine age and ugliness.

We paid a courtesy call on Detective Inspector Sammy Pye as soon as we arrived. He hadn't expected me, but he seemed pleased to see me nonetheless. He and I, and Alice Cowan for that matter, go way back, to our days in uniform in East Lothian, when I was on sabbatical from CID. He met us at the top of the stairs and led us straight into his office. Through the glass I could see the back and shoulders of Detective Constable Griffin Montell, hunched over his desk with the phone to his ear.

Yes, he did have a history with Alex (they lived next door to each other for a while) but she'd told me that it had never been serious with either of them, and that the physical side of it had ended for good when she'd discovered that he had an ex-wife and two kids in South Africa that he'd neglected to mention. However, he did once get her out of a very nasty situation, which had earned him so many bonus points with her dad . . . and with me for that matter, though I barely knew him . . . that it would take him a long time to run through them.

'How is Griff?' Mario asked Pye, as the DI handed him a mug of coffee.

'He's a mess; he's angry, he's feeling guilty and he's resentful, all at the same time. He's angry that Alice let him down, yet he blames himself for putting her in a position where she felt she had to warn her uncle; all that aside, I get the impression he's thinking that she's being too harshly treated.'

'And how do you feel about that?'

Sammy frowned at me. 'Feel about Alice? I don't want her back here under any circumstances, not even out front in a uniform. I'm sorry if that seems hard, but . . . '

'No,' I said quickly. 'That was the right answer . . . not that my question was a trap. How do you feel about Montell?'

'I'm sorry for him. I talk to my wife, don't you?' Words spoken can't be recalled, as many a TV pundit has found out after thinking that his mike wasn't live. 'Ouch,' he hissed.

'That's okay, Sam. I did,' I acknowledged, 'in the certain knowledge that what I said wouldn't be all over the supermarket checkout queue next morning.' I turned to Mario. 'Where is Alice?'

He checked his watch. 'She should be downstairs. She was told to report here at ten o'clock sharp.' He drained his mug, laid it on the desk and smoothed down the lapels of his immaculate jacket. 'Let's go.'

I followed him out and down to the foyer. 'Is DC Cowan here yet?' he asked the desk sergeant.

'Yes, sir,' she replied. 'She's waiting in interview room two, as DI Pye requested.' I sensed a vibe coming off her. Inevitably, the suspension must have become public knowledge in the office, and the absence of detail would have led to speculation. Sides would be taken, until the full story was known, and probably afterwards. I guessed that the sergeant was leaning towards another female officer.

If Mario picked it up too, he didn't react, not even when she added, 'She has a Fed rep with her.'

He led the way out of reception and through to the interview rooms. He knew the place better than I did, so I tagged along like his nee'bur, as they say sometimes in Strathclyde.

Alice was standing when we walked into the room, in earnest conversation with her Police Federation representative. God, but she had changed since the last time we'd met. She'd been a fairly conservative dresser in those days, and even in CID she'd managed to make her civilian clothes look like a uniform. Her hair had been dark and simply styled, hanging down to her shoulders. She'd also been fairly well upholstered, not fat, I wouldn't put it that way, but solidly built, if that's not politically incorrect . . . although it shouldn't be, since I'd say the same about a guy.

The Alice who turned to look at me was clad in what I'm told are called distressed denim jeans and a white, knitted, sleeveless top that emphasised her tanned skin, and the slimness of her arms and shoulders. Her hair was bleached blonde, cut short, probably done at home from the look of it, and gathered into spiky clumps, that I guessed were held in place by gel.

The rep stuck his chin out aggressively as he stepped up alongside her. I'd seen his sort before; confrontational by instinct. He was well into his forties, and his face was familiar to me.

Mario put a name to it. 'Sergeant Gahagan,' he said. 'I'm surprised to see you here.'

That helped me place him; a capable officer frustrated because his career had stalled at sergeant, and who became active in the Federation as a way of gaining a little more influence, a little more authority. There are a few like him in every professional body.

The Scottish Police Federation isn't a union as such; indeed by definition it isn't. It was created by statute in 1919 by the same act that banned the police from membership of trade unions, to give them an acceptable . . . to the establishment of the day . . . means of voicing concerns about their welfare. It looks after all ranks below superintendent and it's run by serving officers, elected to full-time posts. There's a branch structure as well and within that each force chooses a full-time local representative. Gahagan is Edinburgh's; why they picked him, given the bag of chips on his shoulder, heaven only knows.

'Don't know why you should be,' he snapped. He thought his position entitled him to leave out the 'sir'. 'Detective Constable Cowan is entitled to Federation support, and I'm entitled to sit in on this interview, which I fully intend to do, otherwise it won't take place.'

Inwardly, I moaned. The idiot was waving a red flag in the face of the bull that is Mario McGuire. He might have thought he was armed with the sword of justice, but it was going to be as much use to him as a strand of wet linguine, cooked just past *al dente*. I decided to save him.

'That would be the case,' I told him, 'if this

99

was purely a disciplinary matter. But it isn't. You know who I am, Sergeant?'

'Yes, Mr Martin,' he replied.

'And that I'm now a senior officer in an outside agency?'

'Yes.'

'Yes what . . . Sergeant?' I murmured.

His body language altered, subtly; his posture became just a little defensive. 'Yes, sir,' he grunted. He resembled a man crossing a lively stream on stepping stones, not sure if he was going to reach the next one or take a dip.

'The fact that I'm here, and that I've been asked by the chief constable to be here, should indicate to you that this isn't an ordinary disciplinary hearing. It's part of a wider inquiry into a crime that may have been committed and DC Cowan is a potential witness. I can understand why she asked you to be here . . . ' I paused as a possibility ran itself past me. 'You did ask Sergeant Gahagan to attend, Alice?'

'Actually, sir,' she replied, 'I didn't; he volunteered. I think it was Griff who called him.'

I'll swear I heard a hungry growl from McGuire, beside me. 'Do you want him to remain?' I went on. 'Even though he's got no locus here, I'd be prepared to allow it, provided that he says nothing without invitation, and agrees not to reveal anything he may hear.'

'No, sir,' she declared firmly. 'Since I'm going to be talking about my uncle, I'd rather he wasn't here. That's what I was saying to him when you came in. Besides . . . ' She peered into the bag that was slung over her shoulder, then withdrew a white envelope and handed it to Mario. I looked in her eyes; they were clear and calm.

'What's this?' he asked as he took it. I glanced at it and noticed that the letter 'R' was printed on it.

'It's my resignation. I reckon I should beat the system to the punch, if you'll accept it, that is. I've got some pension accrued, and I'd like to keep it.'

'I understand,' he murmured. 'I'm sorry, Alice. I'll take this, but whether it's accepted or not . . . that'll be the chief constable's decision.'

'Hold on a minute,' Gahagan protested. 'There's no need for that, Constable Cowan.'

She turned on him. 'Of course there is,' she snapped. 'I know it and you know it, or you would if you were halfway to being a decent cop. Now please go away.'

Gahagan picked up his briefcase from the table. 'I won't forget this,' he muttered, glaring at McGuire.

'Neither will I,' the big guy promised. 'You won't always be a full-time Fed rep, Sergeant, so be very careful who you try to threaten from now on.'

Silence followed him to the door, but it didn't end with his departure. Cowan stood, backlit by the sun streaming through the small window behind her, with her eyes on me at first, then switching to Mario, then back to me. She wasn't quite sure who was taking the lead, and at that moment, neither were we.

McGuire ended the impasse by walking round

behind her and adjusting the venetian blind to give us complete privacy. 'Sit down, please,' he said, drawing a chair out from the table and offering it to her.

She made herself comfortable, and he and I settled down opposite her. There was a dual deck recorder on Mario's right, with two blank CDs still in their boxes. He unwrapped each one and loaded the machine. 'Ready?'

'No.'

'What's the problem? Would you like water, a coffee? A lawyer, even?'

She smiled, as if he'd said something funny. 'None of the above, thanks.' She delved into her bag once more and produced a second envelope, marked 'S'. 'That's my written statement,' she announced, pushing it across the desk and leaning forward, shoulders hunched.

'It's all I'm prepared to say on the record, so I thought I'd save us all some time by getting it down in advance. It says that DC Montell told me on Wednesday evening, at his flat, that he had to go out for a while. He said that he was sitting in on an operation as a substitute for DS McGurk, who had an important personal appointment. I asked him what it involved, casually, with no specific interest. He said that he and Sauce Haddock were staking out a meeting in a pub between a man called Kenny Bass, and another called Freddy Welsh. Both names were known to me. Bass had been mentioned in connection with another inquiry, about six months ago, but he wasn't involved, so I never had cause to meet him. But I had met Welsh, socially, several times over the years, most recently at a party in my Uncle Jock's house a year or so back. He's a relation of my Aunt Ella, Jock's wife.'

'And you phoned your uncle,' I said. I needn't have interrupted her, but I wanted to remind her that she was in an interview situation whether she thought so or not, and to exercise a degree of control.

'Yes, sir, I did.'

Mario stepped in. 'Why?'

'My written statement explains that. I had no idea that Inspector Varley would act on what I told him. I passed it on as a piece of family gossip, no more. Obviously, I'm now sorry I did it. The statement includes an apology to the team involved in the Bass operation and also to the chief constable for bringing the force into disrepute. I know that won't save my job, but I feel it should be there.'

'You're right on both counts, DC Cowan,' I told her. 'Now, what do you want to say to us off the record?'

Still hunched forward, forearms on the desk, she looked up at me, eyes hooded. 'What makes you think I do?'

'I know you, Alice. And so does Mr McGuire. You're not the sort who gossips.'

'I did once.'

'Yes,' Mario snapped, 'and Neil McIlhenney and I booted you off Special Branch as a result. You're not stupid, so please don't imagine that I am. I don't buy the notion of you making the same mistake again, on the basis that it was

103

family gossip. It was more than that last time, so come on. We'll do this off the record for now, if you like, but we do it. Otherwise I hand you back your letter of resignation and you go down the full formal dismissal route, plus I rip up your statement, we caution you formally and I switch the recorder on.'

She sighed and sat back in her chair, running her fingers through her spiky hair. 'Okay,' she whispered. 'Off the record.'

'That's better. So, why did you call Jock?'

'I wanted to tell him about Freddy Welsh. The truth is, I didn't want him to have any nasty surprises if Griff and Sauce wound up lifting his wife's cousin. I expected him to warn Auntie Ella, not bloody Welsh.'

'How close were he and Welsh?'

'I've no idea. He was always at family dos, not just the formal ones, but the kind where all the blokes wind up in the kitchen, and all the women are in the front room. As I remember, he and Uncle Jock seemed to get on fine there, but other than that I do not know.'

'How about you, Alice?' I asked. I didn't really know why, but something in her body language told me I should. 'Did you ever talk to Welsh at these parties?'

She paused, considering . . . considering something, but I couldn't tell what. 'Yes, a few times,' she conceded, eventually. 'I danced with him at a wedding once.' An eyebrow twitched, and I thought that I caught a slight flush under the tan.

'And?' She looked back at me, without

104

expression. 'Come on,' I said, 'don't get coy on us. It won't help.'

'Nothing really, he just got a bit smoochy, that was all. It was quite late on, and we'd all had a couple of drinks by that time.'

'Just a bit smoochy,' I repeated. 'Sorry, Alice, but I've got to ask this. How smoochy are we talking about here, and did you smooch back?'

The flush deepened. 'Is it relevant?' she murmured.

I thought Mario was about to explode, so I kicked him, quickly, under the table, not too hard but enough to get his attention. The volcano rumbled, but didn't erupt.

'I won't know until you tell me,' I replied. 'Look, Alice, we can stop this at any time, but as DCS McGuire said, if we do, we go on the record, it's interview under caution, and we'll advise you to be legally represented. If you would like us to bring in a female officer, that can be arranged. We'll take a break for that.'

I stopped, to give her a few moments to consider her options. Mario had cooled down; he even offered to fetch tea or coffee. I'd have been for that, but Cowan shook her head.

'No thanks,' she said. 'Yes, I did smooch back, as you put it. Probably harder than he did. When the dance was finished, we went outside and I had sex with him in the back of his car, in the hotel car park.' She stared at the tabletop. 'I'd been without a man for a while, plus I'd had a few drinks, as I said earlier; other than that, no excuses.'

'No excuses necessary,' McGuire murmured.

He nodded sideways, towards me. 'If there was a vacancy for guardian of public morality, neither of the two of us would be in with a chance of the job. But what you've just told us makes things very difficult.'

'Why?' she protested. 'Sir, it was a one-off; I patted him on the bum when we were finished and sent him back inside to his wife. She and Auntie Ella had been gossiping in the bar, so she never had a clue. That was it. We didn't exchange phone numbers and neither of us ever mentioned it again when our paths crossed in the future.'

Mario sighed. 'Alice, the number of times you did it, that's irrelevant. The very fact of you having sex with Welsh, even just the once, that's what matters. If this investigation does lead to criminal charges being laid against Jock Varley, you'll be a key witness, and wide open to any suggestion that you had a reason to warn Welsh yourself that he was walking into something.'

'Uncle Jock wouldn't say that,' she protested.

'If Uncle Jock winds up in the dock, he's going to be looking at time inside,' I pointed out. 'You have to assume that if his counsel comes up with that as a line of defence, he'll go along with it. Look,' I added, 'I have to put this to you, straight out. Is that what happened? Did you in fact call Jock and ask him to warn Welsh off because of your previous relationship?'

'Absolutely not!'

'Did you call him in the hope that he might do that?'

'No!' she shouted.

106

'Okay. I'll accept that your anger is genuine, Alice, and that you didn't. But will the jury believe you if the accusation's put?'

'That'll be up to them, won't it?' Her eyes were belligerent.

'Yes, but before it gets to them,' McGuire interjected, 'the Crown Office has to believe you. Alice, I'm sorry, but I repeat, the fact that you screwed Freddy Welsh, even if it was six years ago, does put a whole different slant on this. For a start, it's a hand grenade chucked right into the middle of this informal, unrecorded, discussion we've been having. You've told us, we know, and whatever the basis, we can't ignore it. We will have to include it in the report we make to the fiscal, and he may then have to take a view on whether any conspiracy might have been between Inspector Varley and Welsh alone, or whether you were part of it.'

'Fuck,' she whispered.

'I know,' he said, 'you're wishing you'd kept your mouth shut just now.'

Her laugh took us by surprise. 'Actually I'm wishing I'd kept my legs closed six years ago. But I hear what you say; it could look bad for me. All I can tell you, again, is that it's not true. What else can I do?'

He pushed the envelope marked 'S' back across the table. 'Take that away,' he told her, 'and revise it, adding in everything that you've told us here, and anything else that you haven't. If Welsh sent you flowers afterwards as a 'Thank you' gesture, you must declare that. List every contact you've had with him since your encounter. Once you've done that, bring it back and we will treat it as if it was in the first envelope you gave us, as if you volunteered everything in it . . . as, eventually, you did.' He turned to me. 'You all right with that, Andy?'

'Yes,' I replied, 'as long as you understand that after it goes to the Crown Office it's out of our hands. We can only recommend; any decision on prosecution is theirs.'

'I understand.' She picked up the envelope, then looked me in the eye. 'Should I take legal advice?'

'That's up to you,' I replied. 'If it's any help, I would in your shoes. If you want to run your statement past a solicitor before you submit it formally, that's fine by us. But be wary of anyone who tells you to say nothing at all. In reality, you've already said it; while this has all been unrecorded, it's not privileged, and if necessary we'll be obliged to disclose its contents. Apart from that though, the fiscal takes a dim view of people who stare at the wall and decline to answer any questions.'

'Okay. Thanks.' She stood. 'Where do I hand it in, when I'm ready?'

'My office,' Mario told her.

'I don't have to come back here?'

'No.'

'That's good. I don't want to bump into Griff.'

'Are you and he . . . '

She took a quick bite of her lower lip. 'He is.'

I walked her back to reception, to the front door. Not that she didn't know the way out, but I felt that if she was seen with me, looking

108

reasonably relaxed, it would be better than if we'd left her to walk out on her own, head down, every eye in the place following her. 'So you're in the doghouse?' I asked as we reached the door.

'No, it's worse than that. Seafield cat and dog home, unclaimed, on death row.'

It was my turn to chuckle. 'Been there,' I confessed, 'but I survived.'

'How? I could use a tip.'

'Look as pathetic as you can manage,' I advised her. 'Eventually someone'll take pity on you. It worked for me.'

'Mmm. In that case you might know where I can pick up a length of sackcloth. The ashes of my career are still warm, so I don't need any of them.'

I hadn't expected to, but I felt sorry for her. She'd been no more foolish than many, but a lot less lucky than most. 'Listen, Alice,' I said, quietly. 'Once this is all sorted, and some time's passed, give me a call if you want to.' I gave her a card. 'My office number. I won't make any promises, but you never know. Resignation is probably the right move just now; much cleaner than the alternative, and no public stigma attached.'

'Thanks, Mr Martin,' she murmured. 'I'll keep that in mind.'

As she walked away, I called after her. She turned. 'What?'

'One thing; if you decide to use that card you'll need to lose the hair gel.'

Mario was still in the interview room when I returned. So were two tall Starbuck containers, and a couple of croissants. I stared at him. 'Where the hell did those come from?'

'Paula dropped them in for us. I told her we'd be here about now.'

'Some girl, Paula. How's she doing?'

'Magic. She's just magic. She's had all the scans going and every one's a photo opportunity. The wee fella looks so comfy in there he might not want to come out.'

'A couple of months without a full night's sleep and you'll want him to crawl back inside,' I told him. 'Will you be looking to move house?'

He looked at me as if I'd asked him if he wanted a ticket for the next Hearts game, and answered me as if I had. 'Why the hell would we want to do that?'

'You live in a duplex, man,' I pointed out. 'However many floors up.'

'We have lifts, Andy, and two parking places in the underground garage.'

'But lifts break down.'

'They don't, actually. They're serviced more often than a police car, and they're driven a hell of a lot more kindly.'

'But the height, the balcony . . . '

'The windows are secure, you couldn't fall out if you tried, and his name's going to be Eamon, not Spiderman. Your kids come to visit you from time to time, yes?'

'Yes.'

'Do you ever worry about them falling in the Water of Leith?'

'Well, no . . . ' I admitted.

'Exactly. Look, if Paula says we'll move we'll

move, sure, but as of this moment, she doesn't want to. Do you see us in a nice big house with a garden?' He shook his head. 'Fuck no.' He killed half his croissant in a single bite.

'That was a turn-up with Alice, was it not?' I ventured.

'Sure was. Getting pissed at a wedding and shagging a married bloke in the car park? I did not have her down for that at all.'

'Me neither,' I agreed. 'But I wonder if Uncle Jock did. Ready for him?'

He raised his coffee. 'Let's kill these first. I need the caffeine rush. I always have a couple of espresso shots in my Starbuck's; does much more for me than any of that ersatz cream they stick on them. Yours is the same.'

I took a mouthful of mine, and imagined that I could feel my heart rate increase by about twenty beats. 'This is as bad as Bob's stuff,' I gasped.

When we were finished Mario dumped the empties in a bin in the corner, then left the room to have Varley brought along from his overnight accommodation. By the time he arrived, brought in by an escort, we were both seated behind the desk, but on the same side. I had binned the unused CDs and two fresh ones, still wrapped, lay beside the recorder.

I'd wondered if I might recognise the inspector after all, but I didn't. There are over three thousand people in the Edinburgh force, more than the population of many a small township, and it is possible to be a serving officer for years and still bump into strangers, even though they may have been around for longer

111

than you. He recognised me, though; I could tell by the way his eyes narrowed.

Although he'd been held in custody overnight he looked smart. He was wearing his uniform, having been arrested, discreetly, at his office, and he'd been allowed to shave, under supervision, I assumed. Unlikely or not, the last thing Mario would have wanted was a suicide attempt in the custody suite. His grey-black hair was neatly and recently cut and his moustache was as sharp as the edge of a well-trimmed lawn.

'We've got to stop meeting like this, Jock,' my companion said. 'You under arrest, me on this side of the table.'

His mouth tightened. 'Not funny, sir.'

'I wasn't laughing.' He picked up the CDs, opened them as theatrically as before to demonstrate that they were virgin, loaded the machine, and switched it on. He began with the date and time, then, 'I am Detective Chief Superintendent Mario McGuire accompanied by Mr Andrew Martin, director of the SCDEA, based in Paisley, present at the request of the chief constable. Please state your name for the recorder.'

'Inspector John Varley, aged forty-four, a uniformed officer stationed at Gayfield Square.' He was calm and controlled; no histrionics, no show of indignation over his detention.

'Again for the record, Inspector Varley, although you haven't been charged you have been offered the chance to have a lawyer present at this interview, and you have declined. Is that correct?'

112

'It is, sir.'

'You may reconsider that if you wish.'

I knew why Mario was being so particular. For years Scots law allowed the police to question suspects for up to six hours without having access to legal advice. Then, out of the blue, that situation was overturned by a Supreme Court decision, controversial in itself since that London court wasn't given oversight of Scottish criminal appeals when it was set up. Chaos ensued and since then cops everywhere in Scotland have erred on the side of caution. As a ranking officer, Varley would have been only too aware of the new ground rules, so my crafty pal was making certain that he couldn't use it to create any loopholes he could slip through later.

But the inspector didn't seem to have that in mind. 'No, sir,' he declared, 'I'm okay to proceed as we are at this stage. I spoke to a lawyer on the phone this morning and he's given me general advice on my rights.'

'Are you happy to have a voice recording only,' I asked, 'or would you like video also? Again, that can be arranged.'

'No thank you, sir. I don't want to find myself appearing on *Reporting Scotland*.' He allowed himself a small smile, at the reference to another controversy that had followed the release to the media of a filmed interview with a suspect who was later acquitted.

'All right, let's get down to it,' Mario said. 'Were you on duty on Wednesday evening at Gayfield Square?'

'Yes, sir, I was. There was a pre-season football

match at Easter Road; the division was heavily involved, but I wasn't at the ground, I was in charge of the office.'

'Did you received a phone call that evening?'

'Yes, sir, I did.'

I could see that Varley was doing things by the book, volunteering nothing, making us work for every detail of every answer. I wasn't having that. 'Yes,' I repeated, cutting in. 'It was from your niece, DC Cowan. She told you that she'd just picked up some gossip from her boyfriend about . . .'

'No, sir,' he said, sharply. 'She didn't say that at all.'

'Oh?' I exclaimed. 'Then what did she say?'

'She asked me to meet her.'

I tried to hide my surprise, but didn't quite succeed. Mario didn't even bother trying to conceal his. 'She did what?' he barked.

'She asked me to meet her; that's what I said.'

'So, when you were caught on the station CCTV ten minutes later, you were actually going to meet DC Cowan. That's your story, is it?' Varley nodded. 'For the record!' McGuire bellowed.

'Yes, sir, it is.' The inspector paused, and smiled. 'Would you like to suspend the interview, sir?' he asked. 'I don't mind.'

The big guy was incandescent; he was anticipating the gambit that was going to be played, and so was I. 'People who try to take me for a ride, Jock,' he growled, savagely, 'they don't usually like the destination when we get there.'

That sounded too much like a threat for my

114

liking and the recorder was live. Time to intervene, I reckoned. 'Chief Superintendent,' I said, 'perhaps I should carry on the interview.'

He drew a huge breath, then exhaled, very slowly. 'Perhaps you should, Director,' he murmured, never taking his eyes off Varley.

'Where did you meet, Inspector?' I asked.

'At the end of the street; the top of Leith Walk.'

'When DC Cowan called you, where was she?'

'I've no idea, sir. But from the background noise, I'm sure she was on her mobile, not a land line.'

'I see. So you put on your coat, and left the office?'

'Yes.'

'Why did you do that?'

'Why, sir?' he chuckled. 'To go and meet Alice, of course.'

He was trying to wind me up, as he had Mario. 'Sorry, Inspector. Why did you put on your overcoat? Do you know what I was doing on Wednesday evening, around the time you left the station? I was sat out on my balcony, looking down at the Water of Leith, with a beer in my hand. I was wearing shorts and a T-shirt, and I was killing midges by the dozen. It was a warm, muggy evening, and you're telling us that you put your uniform coat on to go out and meet a family member? Enlighten us, please. Why would you do something so strange?'

He shrugged, and smirked at me. 'I didn't want to be seen in uniform.'

'Meeting your niece, and her a cop as well?'

'Yes, sir. It might seem strange but that's what I did; you know it, you've probably seen the CCTV.'

'Sure, it's the 'Why' I'm still struggling with. Let's go back to DC Cowan's call. Did she say why she wanted to meet you?'

'No.'

'Did you ask her why?'

'No.'

'Why not?'

'Why should I have?'

'Because you were on duty,' I suggested. 'In charge of the station. Come on, man; your niece calls and you walk off the job just like that?'

He spread his hands. 'Point taken, sir. I shouldn't have. I'm sorry.'

'Not accepted,' I snapped. He was beginning to rile me too. 'However, that's probably a matter for a different inquiry. So, you put on your overcoat and stepped out into a warm steamy evening, to meet Alice. Who got there first?'

For the first time, Varley hesitated for a second before replying. 'I think I did,' he offered.

'You think?' I repeated. 'Come on, man; this was less than forty-eight hours ago.' I leaned forward, hustling him.

'Okay, okay, I was first, definitely.'

'How did she arrive? Was she on foot? Did she get off a bus?'

'Taxi. She got out of a taxi.'

'How was she dressed?' I fired the question at him.

'In civvies.'

'Don't be evasive, Mr Varley. What was she wearing?'

'Jeans and a blouse,' he retorted.

'So, she hadn't got dressed up to meet you. Did she seem in a rush?'

'Yes, I suppose she did.'

'Make-up, was she wearing make-up?'

He shrugged. 'You can't always be sure with Alice.'

'Come on, Inspector, you must know. We've just seen her. She's got this big bleb on her nose just here.' I touched mine, on the right side. 'Was it covered up or not?'

'No,' he answered. 'No it wasn't.'

Beside me, McGuire didn't move a muscle. 'Good,' I said. 'We're making progress. So there you are on the street, the pair of you, she with a bleb on her nose, you sweating like a pig in your uniform coat. That's the scene, is it?'

He nodded. 'That's the scene.'

'Who began the discussion?'

He frowned. 'I did, as I recall. I said, 'What's the panic, Alice?' or something like that.'

'And she said?'

'Her reply was 'Freddy's in trouble'. Naturally I asked her 'Freddy who?' and she replied that she meant Freddy Welsh, Ella's cousin.'

'And your good friend.'

He stared at me. 'I wouldn't say that, Mr Martin. He's more a friend of Alice.'

I let my eyebrows rise. 'Is he? Why do you say that? He's a cousin of your wife and your relationship with Alice is on your side of the family, not by marriage. So why should he be more friendly with her than with you?'

Varley winced, as if it was paining him to go on. 'This is where I get into really deep water,' he murmured. 'Alice and Freddy, they've . . . ' He let his voice tail off.

'They've a what? Spell it out, man.'

'A relationship, sir.'

'Do you mean a sexual relationship?'

'Exactly.'

'How long has it been going on?'

'For six years that I know of.'

I leaned closer, pressing him. 'How do you know about it?'

'I saw them, at a wedding,' he replied. 'They'd been dancing, and I saw them go outside. I followed them. They got into the back of Freddy's car and he gave her one.'

I frowned. 'That's pretty specific; you're sure they had sex?'

'Her legs were practically round his neck, and his arse was going like a fiddler's elbow; I was close enough to see. What would you call it?'

I looked at him, letting my face register disgust. 'You spied on them?' I gasped, contemptuously.

'She's my niece,' he blustered. 'I was worried about her.'

'Wow!' I exclaimed. 'Six years ago, Alice was well into her twenties, Inspector. Her sex life was entirely her own business. Did you get a kick out of it? Did you masturbate?'

He stiffened. 'Fuck off!' he yelled.

'So what did you do?' Mario asked him, rejoining the interview. 'Did you give them marks out of ten, or did you express your concern to Alice later?'

'No. I did speak to Freddy, though. I told him he was out of order.'

'How did he take that?'

'He said much the same as Mr Martin, that she was a big girl. I never mentioned it again.'

I waited for a little before I picked up the questioning again. 'Let's go back to your street corner meeting and to Alice telling you that Freddy Welsh was in trouble. Elaborate.'

'She said that her boyfriend, Montell, had mentioned his name in connection with a job he'd been pulled into, close observation in a pub up in Slateford. And then,' another pause, 'and then she asked me if I'd call him and warn him.'

'Which you did.'

'No!' We'd arrived at the point to which Mario and I had known we were heading. We'd even warned Alice about it, but neither of us had really believed in the possibility. 'No, I did not,' he declared, solemnly. 'I refused point blank. I reminded her that she was a police officer and told her to behave responsibly. Then I left and went back to the station. I was pretty angry with her, as you can imagine.'

'No, Jock,' McGuire said, shaking his head. 'I can't imagine that at all. What I can imagine is you thanking her, when she phoned you to tip you off that a relation of your wife was in the spotlight. Then I can picture you digging out the phone book to find the Lafayette's number, and going out to phone it from the call box up the road.'

119

'No, sir,' he replied, quietly, looking at the table.

'Your prints are on the handset, man,' he pointed out.

'I've used it,' Varley conceded. 'I admit that. I don't like calling in bets from the office, so when I have a flutter I use the phone box to ring my bookie.'

'The bar person,' he fired back, 'who took the call in Lafayette's, told DC Haddock that it was a male voice.'

'Oh yes?' the inspector challenged. 'You know Alice, DCS McGuire, so you must realise that she has a deep voice. I've heard her sing; contralto, she is. If you heard her for the first time, on a phone line in a crowded pub, could you be sure it was a female calling?'

Mario hesitated, for only a second, but it was enough. 'See? You wouldn't,' he exclaimed.

'I suppose you realise,' I murmured, 'that DC Cowan's, that Alice's, story is the complete opposite of yours.'

He nodded, his mouth tight. 'I suppose I do, but this is my story, and I'm sticking to it.'

'Why didn't you want a lawyer here?' I challenged him. 'Was it because you didn't want to trot out that pack of lies in his presence?'

'I don't need a brief. I've given you my account of what happened, and if it's at variance with Alice's, then I'm sorry for her, but it's her problem.'

McGuire smiled, and looked him in the eye. 'No, Jock,' he said 'it's still yours. You don't know your niece as well as you think, if you imagine she'd go anywhere with a big bleb on her face. She'd sooner saw her fucking head off. There never was such a spot. If you'd come clean and told the truth, it might have gone better for you. As it is, I'm going to charge you with attempting to pervert the course of justice.'

Varley's eyes hardened. 'The Crown Office will laugh at you,' he hissed. 'You haven't a chance of making it stick.'

'Nevertheless, I'm going to try. Stand up.' He rose to his feet. 'John Varley . . .'

When it was done, we released him on police bail, with orders to remain at home until the following Monday morning, when he was to report to the Sheriff Court for an initial hearing. Before he left we gave him one of the interview disks, signed by both of us.

When he had gone, we returned to the interview room. 'Bastard,' Mario growled, as he closed the door. 'Can you imagine that? Trying to stitch his own niece up. What a ruthless . . .'

'Maybe, but he's right, it is his story versus hers,' I pointed out.

'Aye, but he fell for the bleb trick, didn't he? Well done, by the way; you rushed him into that.'

'Sure, he fell for it,' I conceded, 'but a good defence counsel will blow that away in a trial. It's not enough to send a man to jail, least of all a cop with twenty-five years' more or less exemplary service. And you can bet that Alice, in the witness box, will be taken all the way back to that car park, with her legs in the air, screwing a married man. She'll be shredded. No, big fella, all you've got is breathing space, and maybe not much of that, unless you can come up with something more to show the fiscal, something that ties Varley and Welsh together.'

'In that case,' he said, gloomily, 'we're in the hands of Mackenzie and the Strathclyde guy, Payne. That's their job. A recovered alcoholic and the boss's sister-in-law's husband.' He sighed. 'I hope they're up to it, otherwise, you're right; Jock bloody Varley might just walk.'

# Detective Inspector
# Becky Stallings

'What the devil am I doing here?'

That's what I ask myself sometimes, when I think of the world I left. Of course, Edinburgh has its attractions. It's a much gentler city than London, and the pace of life is so much easier. From the job point of view there's less serious crime, the body count is lower, and I never feel that I'm taking my life in my hands when I go to work of a morning.

But it's about one-fifteenth the size of the capital (you can shove the nationalist nonsense: I'm British, we have one capital city and that's London), and the force I left to move north is eighteen times larger than the one I joined, with promotion prospects commensurately better for a smart cop, and even better for a smart female cop — both of which boxes I tick — in this politically correct century. Plus, I liked being called 'guv'nor', not plain 'boss' which is all I get here, and that's on a good day.

So what the devil am I doing here? Well, it's Ray, innit? This flash Detective Sergeant Wilding pitches up in London in hot pursuit of some bad guys, I'm assigned to him and his mate, DI Steele, and the next thing I know he and I are staring at my bedroom ceiling and I'm in love with the guy. It might have stayed unrequited from then on if I hadn't found myself loaned to his big boss for the duration of the investigation and impressed him enough to be offered a permanent transfer, but that's how it played out.

The love thing hasn't worn off, no, that's gone from strength to strength, and there's still enough about Edinburgh's social life to interest me, but from time to time I miss the thrill and the pace of the job that I left. Not the mindless street violence side, oh no, that's just sordid, but the pursuit of the unusual, of villains with a bit of class and imagination about them. Because, to be honest, your average Edinburgh criminal mastermind wouldn't go halfway to meeting the Mensa IQ requirement. (That said, the only Mensa member I've ever known wound up shooting himself, so maybe a great big brain can be a curse as well as a blessing.)

Ray can read my occasional frustration, and bless him, the love's even offered to put in for a transfer to London himself if I want to go back. We could probably have worked it too, on the coat-tails of Neil McIlhenney's move down south, but Ray's only just made DI and as a new boy down there he'd probably have been given the jobs that nobody wants, like cleaning up the mess that youth gangs leave, and investigating drive-by shootings. So we're staying put, he and I, although we have discussed the possibility of me applying for a spot with the Serious Crimes Agency.

All that said, the job isn't always boring; the oddest things can happen, and they don't come any odder than a call-out to a grave site in the grounds of a crematorium. Funny, I take most things in my stride, but that one threw me right off kilter, especially when I saw the body, as it had been left. It gave me the creepiest feeling.

Every death is sad, and every homicide is positively tragic, but there was something about that one that I found unnerving. It even brought a couple of tears to my eyes, although I hid them from the rest of the team. And then the chief constable turned up, and said what I'd been thinking, that the burial was a thing of honour and respect, not violence and hate.

I couldn't work out what had happened to the dead man, though. Like the rest of us, I had to wait for the pathologist to tell us. That pathologist; she's a cool one. I had no idea about her back story with the chief until Jack McGurk filled me in, and I gather that Sauce hadn't either. Not that I'd have dropped any clangers. She isn't the sort of woman that you can dig in the ribs and whisper, 'Hey, see the chief? I fancy him a bit.'

Not that I do; I've always been good at reading men who are dangerous. I don't mean potential wife-beaters or anything like that. No, I'm talking about men who radiate sexual attraction, without being aware of it. In my experience guys like that are emotional train crashes waiting to happen, and I've always avoided getting on board with any of them.

That's my take on Bob Skinner, and the fact that he's on his third marriage, not counting what I'm told was a serious thing with a woman DI about fifteen years ago, is proof enough for me that I'm right. As for Dr Sarah Grace, she's his female equivalent; aloof and a bit of an ice maiden when she's at work, but she's as sexy as hell, and I'll bet she's hardly ever been without a man somewhere around.

I was wondering, idly, how Sauce was getting on with her when he walked into the CID suite. Detective Constable Harold Haddock makes me laugh, but always with him, never at him, for all that he can look a bit like Tintin with muscles.

There are those who do make that mistake, usually time-serving officers who can't see behind his gawky appearance and think he's gullible. I've noticed them size him up, and I've heard them take the piss. He never reacts, never gets riled, never rises to the bait, but I'm quite sure that he's filing everything away, and that those comedians might live to regret their mistakes.

Jack McGurk, his sergeant, was Sauce's mentor when he came into CID, but those days are over; the long fellow has nothing left to teach him. Now they're equals in rank, since Sauce's move down to Leith to replace my Ray in the DS slot there. But that was still in the wind on the day he attended the autopsy of Mortonhall Man, as we were calling him then.

He was frowning as he came through the door, as if his mind was still in the mortuary. 'Tough day at the office?' I asked.

He stared at me, surprised. 'Sorry?'

'The autopsy,' I said. 'Gruesome, was it? Don't worry about it, they always turn my stomach too.'

He smiled. 'My Uncle Telfer, that's my mother's brother, was the manager of an abattoir before he retired,' he replied. 'He took me to work with him one day, when I was fourteen. I didn't say so to Dr Grace, in case the comparison offended her, but a post-mortem's nothing earth-shaking compared to that.'

'Jesus, Sauce,' Jack exclaimed, 'are you saying that animals mean more to you than people?'

'Of course not, ya daft . . . ' He shook his head. 'The big difference is that in an autopsy, you don't see the thing that's going to be carved up walking in through the doorway. Try watching what happens to it and see how you react.'

I shuddered. 'Are you trying to put me off black pudding for life?'

He laughed. 'Boss, if you saw that being made . . . '

'Enough,' I declared. The boys weren't to know it, but I'd been sick that morning . . . and I was nearly four weeks late. 'Come on; tell us what we want to hear. What are we dealing with?'

'Nothing, boss; this is officially not a suspicious death. The man died from natural causes, namely a spontaneously ruptured artery in the brain. There were no contributory factors, no signs of trauma and he was in perfect health otherwise. A man in the second half of his twenties in an athlete's body with just one fatal weakness, Dr Grace said.'

'Did she tell you what his name was?' McGurk grunted.

'Sorry, no. She's a remarkable woman, but

she's not that good. Tracing him is still down to us.'

'Did she tell you anything at all about him, other than that he's male?'

'His blood type was O positive,' Sauce replied, 'the most common there is. His last meal looked as if it had fish in it and some other stuff, washed down with mineral water, and he ate it no more than a couple of hours before he died. Analysis will tell us exactly what he had. His prints are being emailed to my address, for checking with NCIS, and the lab's going to give us his DNA profile, to be run through the national database. That's as much as we have to work on, but don't get too excited about that.'

'Why not?' I asked, catching up with him. My mind had paused to reflect on 'remarkable woman'.

'Because Dr Grace suspects he isn't British.'

'Remarkable indeed,' I muttered, dryly. 'How does she work that out?'

If he caught my sarcasm, his face didn't betray it. 'His teeth are too good. She told me that she's never done an examination in this country, or in America, where the subject's been dentally perfect. This man was; she reckons he had a sugar-free diet because there's no sign of decay, and that he never drank tea or coffee because there's no staining.'

'So,' McGurk boomed, stretching his absurdly long frame in his chair, 'why the hell are we dealing with it? In case you've both forgotten, CID stands for Criminal Investigation Department. The chief constable himself said he doesn't

128

believe that a crime's been committed, and now we know that for sure. It's a sudden death. Okay, someone chose to park him in a grave, temporarily. It's not a homicide, and it wasn't concealed. So? One for our colleagues in the furry tunics, surely.'

I picked up the phone on his desk and handed it to him. 'Give the chief a call,' I challenged. 'Tell him that.'

He wasn't up for that, so I went into the office and phoned Bob Skinner myself. Gerry Crossley, his civilian doorkeeper, told me that he had someone with him, but asked me to hold on. A couple of minutes later he came on line. I started to brief him on Sauce's report from the post-mortem, but he knew already.

I asked McGurk's question, but less bluntly. 'Where do we go with this, sir?'

'Good question, Becky. As far as you can; that's all I can ask.'

That wasn't quite the answer that I wanted. I'd been hoping that Jack was right and that the weird problem would be dumped on a uniformed colleague's desk. My fingers had been crossed for that. I'm like any other punter; I'm only interested in backing winners, and I didn't see much chance of a result with Mortonhall Man.

# Deputy Chief Constable
# Margaret Rose Steele

I've stared into the pit, and a couple of times, I've fallen in, only to be caught by strong hands and pulled back to safety. My life has been saved twice, once figuratively by Mario McGuire, my first husband, then literally, by a surgeon called Aldred Fine, who operated on me when I contracted ovarian cancer, removed the tumour, and saw me through the follow-up therapy.

Now I am, officially, in remission; I'm not sure when I'll be pronounced cured, but I must behave as if I am. *One day at a time, sweet Jesus.* Didn't Kris Kristofferson write that song? If he did I wonder if he has any idea of how it feels to live that way. I tell everyone that I don't dwell on it, but don't kid yourself. I've never been more aware of my body. Every small twinge magnifies itself in my mind and when I go for what are still my six-monthly scans, I am nervous, right up until the moment when Aldred comes in smiling and says, 'Everything's normal.'

If it wasn't for Stephanie, I don't know if I'd have made it. Indeed if it wasn't for my daughter I don't believe I'd have tried too hard, after Stevie was killed on duty. But now I have her, and I must keep well for her sake; regression isn't an option.

I never thought I'd have a child. To be honest

with you, when Mario and I were going through the motions of trying to conceive I was privately relieved when my period came along, month after month. There was the possibility of adoption for a while, but when that fell through, it didn't bother me either. That was just as well, for by that time our marriage was broken beyond repair.

He and I split up and I concentrated on my job; that I could do, very well, much better than marriage. Then out of the blue, Stevie happened, and I fell pregnant, and the world was wonderful, for a few precious weeks.

I should have known better.

I did something bad in my life, something I saw and still see as justifiable, but I crossed a line. Mario, God bless him, cleaned up after me and nobody ever found out about it, but afterwards I carried this foreboding around with me that one day, Nemesis would tap me on the shoulder and say, 'Excuse me, Margaret, there's something we have to discuss.'

But she didn't stop at me, that vengeful old Greek cow; as well as giving me cancer, she fingered Stevie as well. His tragedy happened and that bottomless pit opened up under my feet again, until . . . she relented and I was saved.

It used to be that there wasn't an hour went past without me thinking about it, remembering the shock, and then the horror, when they told me Stevie was dead. It was the darkest, darkest time. Having Stephanie, recovering from my surgery, and then going back to work all combined to bring me into the light once more, not least since I was secure in the knowledge that Bet, my sister, is happy as Larry (whoever he was) combining the roles of Steph's carer and freelance designer. Being promoted into the deputy chief vacancy helped a little too; now I find that several hours can go by without me finding myself staring at the wall, remembering.

That's what I was doing when the intercom buzzed and my secretary told me that DC Montell had arrived for his scheduled appointment.

Bob had given me his file, and, he said, carte blanche to proceed as I thought appropriate. But he'd also reminded me why he couldn't deal with the matter himself, knowing full well, I believe, that I'd feel constrained. The man Skinner is many things. He's bold, he's brave, he's brilliant. He'd have made a great soldier, but a lousy general, for he can only lead from the front; those are some of his strengths, but make no mistake, he has his weaknesses.

The one that's quoted most often is his eye for the ladies, and I can see why, but I'll defend him on that front. He has never made a pass at me in all the years I've known him or offered me a single improper word, glance or suggestion. But I doubt if he ever has with any woman; from what I've seen he's much more prey than predator. The truth is that Bob's a sucker for a pretty face, as long as a powerful personality goes with it. I doubt if he's ever shagged a bimbo in his life.

You couldn't pin that label on Sarah, no way; oh no, she is smart. He was the head of CID and she was the new pathologist, when she sized him

132

up, saw he was ripe, and flashed the lashes at him. A few of his colleagues saw what was happening, but nobody had the stones to tell him.

When the marriage first hit the skids, and another scheming woman sank her claws in, briefly, that might have finished him, in every respect. It didn't, and he moved on, until eventually it was him and Aileen, and he seemed more content than I'd ever known him. Even then, I had the feeling that he was hiding in that marriage. From what, I don't know; maybe from himself.

His other flaws? He can be cruel, he can be lethal, he can, on occasion, be petty. He makes instant judgements about people and they are usually irreversible, be they right or wrong. That exposes him to accusations of favouritism, of gathering an elite of cronies around him, and when he was less senior it laid him open to the sniping of his enemies, most notable among them a man called Greg Jay, a former CID colleague who found out in the hardest way that it is one thing to dislike Bob Skinner, but that crossing him is a luxury nobody can afford.

His inner circle? I'm one, so is Mario, Neil McIlhenney was a third, before he left for London, and Brian Mackie, my predecessor, the fourth until he went to Tayside. The closest of all, though, is Andy Martin. Bob promoted all of us, but Andy has flown highest, to a level at which there simply wasn't room for both of them in our force.

There are, or have been others; Stevie, of

course, and now DC Haddock. You look at young Sauce and you might well think that he's Bob's diametric opposite. In some ways he is; he's gawky, and he has a tendency to say too much at the wrong time. But he's also perceptive, and he has an analytical brain. It wasn't the first thing that brought him to my attention . . . no, his daft nickname did that . . . but once I could see past the air-scoop ears, I realised that a serious mind lies between them.

Recently, the boy Haddock showed his patron's propensity for landing risky women, but he's come out on the right side of it. From what I've been hearing lately, that relationship survives; the surprising thing is that far from frowning on it, Bob seems to be taking an almost fatherly interest in its health.

And Griff Montell? Where does he stand in the serried ranks of Skinner's army? That's what I wondered as I peered at his file, at the summary of a career that began in South Africa, then migrated to Edinburgh. And what did Bob want me to do with him?

'Your call,' he'd said, 'entirely your call.'

Sure, and what have I just said about Skinner being devious? What had Montell done? Why was he about to enter my office for a disciplinary interview that could lead to proceedings that would fire him from the force? He'd screwed up an undercover operation by telling his girlfriend all about it.

Yes, she was a cop, and yes, he'd assumed she was trustworthy, but the whole thing had blown up in his face, and very publicly at that. A serving officer had just been charged with attempting to pervert the course of justice, and the indications were that he'd defend the charge.

Worse, from what Mario had added when he'd called me to break the news, there might even be a defence of impeachment, putting Montell's girl on the rack. Either way he'd be a witness, and wasn't that the real problem? Cowan was going for sure, but if he was still a serving officer, would he have any career left himself after taking a hammering from the defence in the witness box? Would I be doing him a kindness by recommending dismissal? Was that what Bob wanted me to do?

*What, Maggie?* I asked myself. Was I to assume that he wanted me to fire the guy who, as our whole professional circle knew, used to sleep with his daughter, at least while Andy Martin was otherwise engaged?

'Hardly,' I said aloud. For any appeal to an employment tribunal would go public, and if Montell chose he might allege that he'd been fired for personal, and not professional reasons. It wouldn't hold, but it would be messy. No, there was another solution somewhere. It was in Bob's mind already, and he expected me to catch on without being told.

'Thanks, pal,' I murmured as I pressed the button that would summon my visitor.

# Detective Constable
# Griffin Montell

I took a deep breath and reached for the door handle. I'm not a nervous guy as a rule, but I could feel a fluttering inside. It reminded me of an oral exam I once faced as a student. My degree hung on it, and I knew that I would walk out of that room as a success or as a failure.

Earlier, I'd had a call from Sauce Haddock, apologising for dropping me in it. I admit that the day before I'd been thinking about ripping his head off with my bare hands, but when I'd cooled down, I knew that if our roles had been reversed, I'd have handled the situation in exactly the same way he did. I told him as much. He thanked me and wished me luck with my interview, from which I guessed that it must have been public knowledge.

'You'll come out okay, Griff,' he said. 'I did.'

I was grateful for his support, but I lacked his confidence. I was going in to see the deputy chief as a serving detective constable, one who'd expected, just forty-eight hours earlier, to be promoted to fill a vacancy for detective sergeant. Whatever Sauce thought, there was a chance I would come out with my card marked for dismissal. If that happened, it would have huge consequences.

Having 'Sacked from the police force' on your

CV is not the best reference on the job market. I wasn't even sure I'd be able to stay in Britain. I'm a Commonwealth citizen with a Welsh grandmother, but I haven't lived here for five years, so I don't have permanent resident status. Being chucked out of the country was my biggest fear: I'd left South Africa for a whole raft of reasons, but chief among them was my need to make enough money to support my kids from my failed marriage. If I was forced to go back there, we'd all be in trouble.

I knew the woman who was holding my life in her hands, but not all that well. She has a rock-solid CID background, but she'd been moving back into uniform and heading for the command suite when I secured my international transfer and arrived in Edinburgh. I knew her husband much better, Stevie Steele, God rest him. He was my DI in Leith, before Sammy Pye. We'd got on, and I carried the small lingering hope that his widow might bear that in mind.

I knew why I was seeing her and not the chief; that didn't need to be spelled out. My sister Spring and I moved to Scotland at the same time and bought a flat together in Stockbridge, right on the Water of Leith and right next door to Alex Skinner, his daughter. She and I became friends, and both of us being young, free, single and liberated, there were evenings when the five-yard journey home from her place seemed too long for me to contemplate. We were discreet about it, but inevitably there was a degree of office gossip, at Alex's end, not mine: I don't believe there's anyone in the force stupid enough to accuse me of trying to sleep my way to the top, not to my face.

Our closeness was over by the time Alex moved house; she never spelled it out but I learned later that she'd taken the hump with me because I didn't tell her that I'd been married. Since neither she nor I was looking in that direction, I didn't think it was relevant, but I made a mental note not to be so secretive in the future.

*Mistake, Griffin,* I thought as I turned the door handle and stepped into the deputy chief constable's office.

She didn't stand up to greet me, and she wasn't smiling either. She was too busy frowning at an open folder on her desk, at some documents whose crest I recognised, even upside down. It was my career file, going right back to the beginning in South Africa. She finished the page she was on, and then looked up.

'Good afternoon, DC Montell,' she said. I tried to read her eyes as she looked at me, but they weren't telling me anything. She was in uniform, but she wasn't wearing her jacket, a small informality that might have been a good sign . . . or might have meant, on the other hand, that she didn't want to get blood on it. For a second I wondered if I should have worn mine, then was happy that I hadn't, in case she'd taken it as an indication that I'd settle for being booted out of CID, as a better option than the sack.

She pointed to the corner of the big wood-panelled room, towards a low L-shaped leather seating arrangement, set on two sides of a coffee table. She rose to her feet. 'When the chief had this room,' she explained, 'he held most of his meetings over there. I like to do the same.'

I looked at her as she led the way. DCC Steele is at the low end of medium height for a modern woman, five feet six tops, and her standout feature is probably her reddish hair, which she wears fairly short and has done, they say, since she went back into uniform. She has a figure that my sister, who works in Harvey Nichols ladies, would find easy to clothe. If she'd a mind to, Spring could make her look voluptuous, but that's no way to think of a deputy chief constable, especially when she holds your career in her neatly manicured right hand. Neat: if there's a single word to describe her, that's it.

She steered me towards the seat facing the window. 'Would you like coffee?' she asked.

I hadn't expected that. 'No thank you, ma'am,' I replied. 'I've had my quota for today, I reckon.'

'Then I'll follow your example,' she said, favouring me with her first small smile. 'The chief's an addict, and it's bloody near compulsory in his office. Some of the stuff he brews can make you hyperventilate.'

She sat, and I followed, perching on the edge of the squab, not wanting to appear at ease, which I wasn't in any case. She looked at me, then smiled again. 'Relax, man,' she exclaimed. 'Whatever happens here, it's not going to be fatal. I'm probably more nervous than you are. I've never been in this situation before.'

I took her at her word and settled myself into the well-worn leather; the tension was still there, but I did my best to hide it.

Then she was serious again. 'Do you think you have any leverage in this room?' she asked. 'Your sister Spring is in a gay relationship with one of our senior officers. You have a past friendship with Alex Skinner and those of us who know her well, know also that she isn't famous for celibacy. D'you reckon any of that's going to get you off the hook?'

I shook my head. 'No, ma'am. Nor would I want it to. If you're working up to ask me to resign quietly because of it, I will, for my sister's sake, and for her partner's. As for Alex, she's a big girl, she can look after herself and she wouldn't expect me to do anything so noble on her behalf.'

The DCC laughed again. 'Christ, you do know her well.' She paused. 'Do you know what carte blanche is?'

Was she patronising me? 'French has reached Cape Town,' I replied. 'It means . . . open season?' I suggested.

'That's as good a translation as any,' she agreed. 'Well, that's been declared on you, for that's what Mr Skinner says I've got.'

That brought me up short; privately I'd been hoping that the boss would weigh in discreetly on my side. I helped Alex out of a scrape a while back, and I knew that I had his personal gratitude; but not professional, it seemed.

'What have you got to say to me?' she asked.

'Sorry,' I said, immediately.

'That's a start, but to whom?'

I didn't have to think hard. 'To the force, to

140

the chief, and to the guys who were involved in the Bass investigation. I screwed it up for them.'

'What's your relationship with Alice Cowan, away from the office?'

I'd been asking myself that one for more than twenty-four hours. 'We're close . . . or we were until yesterday,' I added.

'Would you say that you were a couple?'

'Informally. We've never discussed the long term but we've been in a relationship for a few months now.'

'Which you did not disclose to your line managers.' That wasn't a question.

'No, we didn't,' I conceded. 'We didn't think we were at the stage where we had to. It has no bearing on our . . . ' I didn't complete the sentence as I realised how wrong that was.

'Indeed.' The DCC frowned. 'Did you know how Alice came to be posted to Leith?' She paused. 'Just in case you're thinking about protecting her, I'd better tell you that she's resigned from the force.'

That was news to me; I hadn't spoken to her since the previous morning, after my DI had called me into his office and ripped me to shreds. Sammy Pye's a nice, friendly guy, which means that being taken apart by him hurts even more. Alice hadn't appeared for work; she'd been ordered to stay at home. As soon as Sammy had thrown me out I called her on my mobile, from the toilet, yelled at her, thanked her for what she'd done to my promotion prospects and told her that was the last way she'd ever be fucking me. I felt bad about it a few hours later, but I reckoned that the bridge was burned right down to the water level. I probably would have protected her, or tried to, but her quitting had made that pointless.

And so I answered, 'Officially, no, because as you know, the reason was never made public within the force, but she told me.'

'Did you know where she'd been before?'

'Yes, Special Branch.'

'You know where I'm going with this, Griff, don't you?'

*She used my Christian name*, I thought. *A good sign.*

'Of course. You're going to ask me why it didn't occur to me that she might be a security risk. I can't answer that properly; all I can say is that I trusted her.'

'And she let you down.'

The interview was taking a turn I hadn't expected. I'd assumed that it would have taken her about two minutes to bust me down to village cop in Breich, or to have me sign my goodbye letter. Instead she appeared to be offering me a way out; shop Alice and let them rubber-stamp the official inquiry.

'No, ma'am,' I contradicted her, regardless of it. 'I wouldn't put it that way. I let her down by being indiscreet, and putting her in a position that's led to her blowing her career.'

She smiled again. 'That's noble of you. But there's still a question left, the key one as far as I'm concerned. Did you know of her family connection with this man Welsh?'

'Absolutely not. I knew that Inspector Varley

142

was her uncle, but that's all. I've never met any of her family, and I didn't know of the Freddy Welsh connection until DI Pye told me. I'd never even heard the man's name until I was pulled into the Lafayette's thing.'

'So you didn't know that she had a personal connection with him?'

*What the hell did she mean by that?* My face must have answered her question and asked one of my own.

'I've got to be blunt here,' she said, gently. 'Alice was interviewed this morning at Leith, by DCS McGuire and another senior officer. She admitted to them that she had a brief sexual encounter . . . a quickie, if you like . . . with Welsh at a family celebration about six years ago. Did you know about that?'

And if I had, then I was done for; out on my ear, and that would be at best.

I took a long breath, blew it out and looked her in the eye. 'No,' I replied. 'She told me . . . ' I began, then stopped, considering how best to put it. When I saw how, I continued.

'At the beginning of our sexual relationship, I told Alice all about me, about my marriage, about my family, and about the extent of my relationship with Alex Skinner. I've come to believe that it's best to be frank about these things.' I didn't tell her how. 'Alice told me that she didn't have a past anything like that. She said that she'd had very few relationships, that she wasn't promiscuous, and that the worst thing she'd ever done, and I quote, 'was banging a married guy at an in-law's wedding a few years

143

ago, after too many tequila sunrises, and feeling guilty as hell next morning'. She added that she'd hardly been able to speak to the man since. It sounds as if that was Freddy Welsh, but she didn't put a name to him, not then and not since. In fact we've never discussed it again.'

'Sure?'

'Certain.' I held her gaze. 'Look, ma'am, Alice is not routinely untrustworthy. Yes, she told me she'd been booted out of SB for tipping off her uncle about something, but when she did she was cracking a joke at my expense. Usually she's tight-lipped about the time she spent in the Branch. You have to be . . .'

# Detective Chief Inspector
# Lowell Payne

I came close to saying, 'No thanks,' when my boss told me that Bob Skinner needed a senior officer from another force to work on a sensitive investigation, and that he'd asked for me, specifically. I've nothing against Bob, but when the chief super went on to say that I'd be working with Bandit Mackenzie, the prospect of a few days in the capital became less attractive.

He used to be one of ours, and I remembered him as an arrogant bastard; he made DI after I did, but he made no secret of the fact that he expected to leave all of us in his wake. When he left to run the drugs squad in Edinburgh, very few people contributed to his going-away present, but we'd all have been happy to chip in for his train fare.

The gaffer read my mind. 'He's changed,' he rushed to tell me. 'Apparently he's cleaned his act up. He had some sort of a breakdown, possibly alcohol-related. When he recovered he was a different man. He's a superintendent now, in uniform, and he's the exec officer in the command suite through there. It seems that nobody calls him 'Bandit' any more.'

'Mmm,' I grunted. 'Have you ever seen a stripy leopard?'

He laughed at that one. 'Come on, Lowell,

forgive and forget. Look, Bob Skinner would not have entrusted this investigation to him if he had any doubts about him. From what the ACC told me, it's a very delicate situation. You should take it as a compliment that you're wanted on it. Do it, get a result and . . . no promises mind, but it might give you an edge when the next superintendent slot comes up.'

I took that with a pinch of salt. I'd been passed over for promotion three times already, and I was pretty sure that them upstairs had decided I'd reached my ceiling. Not that I was complaining; I'd never expected to make it beyond inspector, but my career surged in my mid-thirties. It started with a move to CID about fifteen years ago, as a DS. I was promoted fairly quickly after that and for the last five years I've been a DCI. I'm a year short of fifty and have thirty years' service, so I'll be in the happy position of being able to retire on full pension while I'm still young enough to enjoy myself, and with a lump sum that will help Myra, my twelve-year-old, through university if that's where she wants to go.

One more promotion would be nice, but that wasn't the carrot that made me say, 'Okay, sir, I'll take it on.' No, when it came to it, it was the prospect of working close to Bob Skinner. It's not that I'd ever held that ambition, rather that I was curious to find out what sort of a boss he really is, without it being permanent.

I first met Bob at the funeral of his father-in-law, Thornton Graham. Thornie would have been my father-in-law too, but my wife Jean and I weren't married when he died. I'd heard of Skinner even then, and not just from her. He'd been running the drugs squad in Edinburgh for a few years, he'd had a number of high-profile results, and the grapevine talk had him as a certainty for the top job in Strathclyde one day, since he'd been a Motherwell boy. A few senior officers were said to be afraid of that happening, for he was reputed to be a very hard man with no sense of humour and no time for below-average performance.

Some of that talk must have come from his enemies, for when he and I did meet, he didn't scare me a bit. Yes, he'd just made detective super at that time, while I was still a sergeant, and yes, since he's only a couple of years older than me, that did put our careers in perspective straight away. But he didn't treat me as other ranks. He was polite, pleasant and generally friendly, although I did have the impression that behind it all he was quietly assessing my suitability for Jean, his late wife's sister.

His daughter Alexis was there too, early teens, a year or two older than my lass is now. I recall that one or two of the senior relations frowned on the way she was dressed, but Jean would have none of it, telling them that Thornie would have wanted her that way. She told me, afterwards, when the funeral sandwiches were finished and everyone had buggered off to get on with their lives, that one of them had also muttered that the kid took after her dead mother, and that it hadn't been meant as a compliment.

'They thought our Myra was flighty,' she said, 'to put it politely.' Then she laughed. 'She was too, and Bob was putty in her hands.' Another crack in that legendary armour. 'He's been a lost soul since my sister died; maybe the one he had with him today will make him happy.'

She did, as it happened, but only for a while: Alison, her name was. When they split, Jean's take was that it hadn't worked because she'd been as career-driven as him.

Since that first meeting, I haven't seen a lot of him, but Alexis has always kept in touch with her aunt and with the younger Myra; she takes a special interest in her cousin, because she was named after her mum. His path and mine did cross, professionally, though, just after the funeral. He had an investigation in progress and a line of inquiry led him to Hamilton, where I was stationed, in the sergeant's uniform that I thought I'd be wearing for another twenty years. I checked something out for him, informally, but I never did find out if it led anywhere. It wasn't long afterwards that I hung up the tunic and moved into CID. I did wonder at the time whether he had anything to do with it, but when I asked him, at my wedding reception, he laughed, and said, 'Do you think your bosses would listen to a single word of mine, Lowell?'

'When do I start?' I asked the chief super.

'Tomorrow afternoon; ask for the chief constable when you get there. Stay till you're done, in a hotel if you have to. They'll be paying your expenses.'

'Jesus. It's that urgent?'

He told me to report to the Edinburgh headquarters building, two o'clock sharp. I'd been there once before, for a liaison meeting, but that had taken place in what looked like a gymnasium, near the entrance, so I knew very little about the layout of the building. I showed my ID, two minutes early, to an unsmiling civilian on the reception desk. He peered at it until a light went on in his eyes, then he nodded, with an attentiveness that would have shamed Uriah Heep. 'Yes, Mr Payne. The chief constable's asked me to send you up to his room. Go up those stairs behind me, then along the corridor that you'll find straight ahead of you. You'll see his office on the left. I'll call and let his assistant know you're coming.'

The directions were spot-on. When I reached the chief's outer office, the door was open and a man stood framed by it. He was in his thirties, medium height, well groomed and in civvies. 'DCI Payne,' he greeted me. 'I'm Gerry Crossley, Mr Skinner's personal assistant; he's asked me to show you right in.'

The Man Himself was standing in front of his desk when I entered. He stepped towards me, hand extended. 'Lowell, I'm glad you can do this,' he greeted me as we shook. 'How are Jean and the wee one?'

'Jean's fine, thanks, and the wee one's not so wee any more. She's twelve.'

'Twelve?' he gasped. 'Bloody hell! It all goes by so fast. But why should I be surprised? My own kids are shooting up. Mark's starting high school, James Andrew's becoming a bruiser, and

149

Seonaid's too damn smart for her own good.' There was a gentleness in his eyes as he spoke of them. Then he switched to official mode; in that instant they turned hard as steel, and I admit that I was shaken as I found myself looking at a man I'd never met.

He led me to a small meeting table in the corner of the room; as I sat he poured two mugs of coffee from an ancient, battered, filter machine on a stand against the wall. 'Milk?' he asked.

'Yes, please, but no sugar.'

He nodded. 'Alf Stein, my old boss, gave me this contraption when he retired and I succeeded him as head of CID. He also taught me how to get the most out of it. When I leave, it'll stay here.'

He handed me a mug. I took a mouthful and wondered how Stein had survived to retirement.

Bob spotted my reaction. 'Alf smoked a pipe,' he volunteered. 'His room was always as stuffy as hell, but nobody ever got drowsy at his meetings, not when we were drinking that stuff.' He sat, facing me.

'David Mackenzie's going to join us shortly,' he continued, 'but I want a quiet word with you first. I need to emphasise that he's not the character you knew. I'm well aware of what he was like. He tried to come the smart-arse with me once, and I had to put him right. But I still rated him highly enough to poach him and bring him to Fettes.' He leaned forward, frowning. 'David had a rough time, in a rough situation, a few years ago. He came out of it full of self-doubt, and for someone as he was that's not good. He hit the bottle, and it hit him back. For a while I thought we were going to lose him from the job, but I refused to allow that. Now he's one of my real trusties, and a better officer than he was before he crashed. Just don't call him 'Bandit', not even in fun.'

'Noted,' I said.

'Good; now, the job I've brought you here to do. I've got a cop who's gone bad. I need to know how bad. Best case, you may come to say simply that he's let himself down. Worst case, you might find that he's disgraced my force. If that's how it turns out, I will fucking crucify him, upside down.'

'What's your instinct?' I asked him, bluntly.

'Worst case,' he grunted. 'This man has had a respectable, but low-profile career, so circum-spect that a man who left this force with the rank of chief superintendent was able to come back this morning as an independent interviewer because he'd never met him. When you're that good at not being noticed, what the fuck else are you good at?'

I took another swig of the coffee. It must have made me reckless, for I asked him, 'What about you? Presumably you knew him.'

'Yes,' he confirmed. There might have been a warning in his tone, but I pressed on.

'In that case, has he ever crossed you?'

He stared at me, and I knew how the legend had risen up around him. 'Are you asking whether I have a personal grudge against this man?'

151

I nodded, because if I'd spoken it might have come out as a croak.

Then he smiled, if only briefly, and I found that I could breathe. 'Fair question,' he conceded. 'So it deserves a truthful answer. I hadn't until half an hour ago, when I heard a recording of his interview this morning, and I heard him trying to pin the blame for his own action . . . fuck, no,' he barked, 'his own crime . . . on a junior officer, his own sister's daughter no less. That girl's resignation is in my in-tray, and I am bloody angry about that, because I did not want to lose her, but now I have to, because the way it's turned out, if I accept it, and let her leave chastened but unblemished, I will be saying publicly that I believe her account over his. On the other hand, if I reject it, and let her go to an independent disciplinary hearing, as I'd have to, people might infer the opposite, that I don't . . . and she would be sacked anyway. So yes, as of now, I do have a personal grudge against Inspector John Varley, and I am looking out the longest and bluntest nails I have in my toolbox.'

There was a knock on the door, but he ignored it. 'That's why I'm going to set you and David up in an office outside this building, and why I don't want either of you to come anywhere near me until you're in a position to tell me just how dirty this fucking bastard is.'

# Maggie Steele

'Usually she's tight-lipped about the time she spent in the Branch. You have to be, because that's the way it is.'

It was an epiphany moment. As soon as the words left his mouth, I knew what Bob Skinner wanted me to do.

I picked up Montell's file from the coffee table. His whole police life was in it, and I'd liked what I'd been reading when he'd come into my office. I looked at it, and then at him. I'd done my best to put him at his ease, because I don't believe in treating people with anything but respect, whatever the circumstances, but I could see that he was still a little on edge.

No way was I going to recommend dismissal; that had never been an option in my mind. It would have set an impossible standard for the rest of the force, and it would have been unjust. Technically, Montell had broken the rules, but I've never met a cop who hasn't done what he had, and I don't see one when I look in the mirror. He and Cowan were a couple, as Mario and I, then Stevie and I, had been. I didn't talk shop with either of them over every dinner table, but I shared things with them and they did with me, as Griff had with Alice. We had done so casually; Montell actually had a reason for telling her what was going on, because it had disrupted their plans for the evening.

She'd let him down and she was going to have to pay the price. It was end of story, all done with for her, but not for her uncle, and not for her boyfriend. If Varley went to trial he'd be a key witness, not just in respect of what he had told her, but also where and when. Mario had told me about the inspector's version of events, and I knew that we would have to knock that story down, by demonstrating if possible that Alice couldn't have got from wherever she was, to the place of the alleged meeting in the time available. When Griff went into the witness box to explain that, mud would be thrown at him, it would be reported, and among his fellow officers it would stick, fairly or not.

'You had an impressive record in South Africa,' I commented, as I laid the file back on the table. 'Specialist experience of violent crimes, sex crimes, political protection, and good performance reports in every one; sergeant by age twenty-four and scheduled for promotion to inspector, when you upped and quit.'

'Was I?' he remarked, sounding genuinely surprised. 'I didn't know that.'

'If you had, would it have made a difference to your decision?'

He shook his head. He wore his hair quite long, but not shoulder length. It might have been dark, but the sun had given it straw-coloured highlights, the kind that cost women a hundred quid a pop to maintain. Good-looking with it; I understood why Alex Skinner had been happy to wear him on her arm for a while.

'No, not a bit,' he replied. 'My wife's lawyer

154

and her good friend the judge stitched me up so tight that I couldn't afford to be a cop in South Africa any longer.'

'Will you ever go back?'

He looked me in the eye. 'That may depend on you, ma'am.'

'Would you consider a transfer to another force?' I ventured. 'With nothing on your record,' I added.

'Is that what you're going to propose to the chief?'

'It might be in your best interests. What do you think?'

'With respect, I think no. I like it here, and I'm ... I was ... building a career here. One move on your record is okay for a junior officer, but two? No, I'd rather stay here. If I have to take some flak from colleagues over this thing, if I have to be sanctioned, I'll ride those out.'

He'd said exactly what I'd hoped he would. 'Okay,' I said. 'The final decision on sanctions will be up to the chief, but I'm not going to recommend any. As for the flak, I can do something about that. It is likely that you will have to give embarrassing evidence in a future trial, but there is a way to keep your name off the public record.'

He looked at me, curiosity stirred.

'In certain circumstances, a judge may direct that police witnesses' names may not be reported. For example, if that officer is in Special Branch.' He edged just a little more upright in his chair. 'As it happens,' I continued, 'the chief is looking at some personnel changes there, and

155

there is a vacancy for someone at your rank. DC Singh will be moving to Gayfield, to join DI Wilding, and your overall record makes you an outstanding candidate to replace him . . . as long as you understand that there is an extra need for discretion there.'

He nodded. 'Oh yes, ma'am, I do.'

'Okay, that's what I'm going to recommend to the chief, and I do not believe for one moment that he'll reject my advice.'

He smiled. 'Ma'am, I came in here not knowing if I had a future, and I go out with a new job. I don't know what to say.'

I grinned back; I couldn't help myself. 'I reckon 'Thank you' would just about cut it, don't you?'

# Superintendent
# David Mackenzie

I wasn't sure I'd recognise the guy, but I did as soon as I stepped into the chief's office and saw him sitting at the meeting table. He'd put on a bit of weight since I'd last seen him in Pitt Street, a few weeks before my move to Edinburgh, and he was losing the unwinnable battle against male pattern baldness, but otherwise he hadn't changed much. Same dark suit and tie, same white shirt, the unofficial uniform of Strathclyde CID, the sort of garb that I'd kicked against when I was one of them.

They said I was flash, and they were right. They didn't like me, and I can understand why. To be honest, looking back, I didn't really like me either. I knew how pushy I was, but the nasty streak in me was in full control at the time, so I forgive my peers for the way they felt about me. Mind you, I'd still like to find the comedian who shat in the pocket of my Aquascutum overcoat on the day I left.

I put the notion that it might have been Lowell Payne firmly to one side as we shook hands. His grip was firm and his eyes a little wide, signs of a man just subjected to the chief constable's ordeal by coffee. From their body language I thought I sensed something between the two of them, but I didn't have time to dwell on it.

'David,' the boss said, once the reintroduction was done. 'Welcome. Would you like a coffee?'

'No thank you, Chief,' I replied. The kind that he brews is so powerful, it's akin to the stuff that I have to steer clear of these days. He knows that, though, and when it's offered it's only out of politeness.

He handed me an envelope, brown. 'That's the latest,' he told me. 'It's a transcript of Varley's interview by Mario and Andy; you won't like what you read. That said, do not let it colour your view. There are three things you need to keep in mind in the job you guys have to do: objectivity, objectivity and objectivity. This may be an isolated incident in Varley's career; presumption of innocence applies. But if he's guilty of more, then I want to be able to prove it, and more.' He paused. 'This is the way it's going to work. I don't expect either of you to be investigators; your job is to look for possible lines of inquiry. If you find any you will need leg men, and you will have them, but given the nature of the situation and the fact that it's possible it may lead to links between a police officer and organised crime, they have to be specialised. Therefore, anything you do trigger will be handled by Special Branch.'

That came out of the blue. I'd assumed that we were looking for backhanders changing hands, nothing deeper than that. It raised a question in my mind and I put it out there. 'Chief, have you had specific information about this?'

'Yes, I have, but that's all I'm going to tell you.

158

Even at my level I have informants who need to be protected. So,' he continued 'the Branch: I've just made a change there. The officer who was in charge is being moved back to divisional CID duties. Her replacement is Detective Inspector George Regan, and he'll be your first line of contact should the need arise.'

He looked at me. 'I don't think you've worked with him, David, but you probably know his back story.' I did; I nodded.

'Okay, I suggest that you get along there and introduce yourselves before you leave the building. I've briefed him on the Varley situation, so he's expecting you. Good guy, George. You'll appreciate that SB operates in its own way, and please remember that. Brief him on anything you turn up then leave him to get on with it. And don't take the hump when you find that he shares everything with me; that's his job.'

He rose to his feet, signalling that the briefing was over. Our marching orders were clear; if it's there get a result, and one that is, given the circumstances, unquestionable.

'The rest of the material, and there are boxes of it, will be waiting for you at St Leonards,' he said. 'I want you to work out of there. Sometimes I think I should do that myself; less of a post-modern shit heap than this place. Or maybe I should work from home; maybe that would be best for everyone.'

*What the hell was that about?* I thought, as we left.

# Detective Sergeant
# Jack McGurk

'How are we with missing persons?' the boss called, from the doorway of the glass box that she called an office.

'They're all still missing, Becky,' I told her. 'I had four possibilities from the national trawl that I did this morning, but they've all dropped off. Four families contacted and asked if their loved one was circumcised and had perfect teeth, and all four were negatives. It took time, though; the wife of John Ancram, of Middlesbrough, didn't know what circumcision meant, far less what it looked like, but she did say that his teeth were very good. When the local cops went to his dentist, they discovered that she'd neglected to mention that he kept them in a jar. They told me that they don't want to find John now, for his own sake. The partner of Michael Winterton, of Bourton, was so surprised when he was told he might have been found that the officers who visited him got suspicious. As soon as they started to question the guy, he broke down and now they're digging up the back garden. As for the other two . . . '

'Complete pricks?' Sauce chipped in.

'You got it.'

'Ha bloody ha,' the DI grumbled. 'Do you two schoolboys have anything positive to tell me?'

160

She was getting testy, and young Haddock had the sense not to wind her up any further. 'I'm working on the pathologist's suggestion that he might not be British,' he volunteered. 'I'm looking at immigration, talking to the Border Agency. They're suggesting that we focus on failed asylum seekers; so far they've sent me photographs of males in the age group we're after, all of them currently missing from detention centres. None of them was a match, but they haven't finished. Now they're trawling through people waiting to be sent back who aren't in detention, to see if any of them aren't where they should be.'

'What's the thinking behind that?' I asked him.

Sauce looked at me as if I was thick. 'Let's say a family goes underground,' he replied, 'and one of them dies.'

'Possible,' I conceded, then put a hand to my ear.

He looked at me, puzzled. 'What are you listening out for?'

'The cackle of wild geese,' I told him. 'A well-nourished young man with perfect dentition and an athletic build: I don't like to stereotype people, mate, and I know we look after visitors to our country very well, but does that sound like an asylum seeker of any description to you?'

'He doesn't sound like a runaway steel erector from Middlesbrough either,' Sauce retorted, but I knew that I'd made my point.

So did Becky. 'I know, guys,' she said. 'It's a human needle in a haystack, but you know what

161

they say, once you eliminate all other possibilities, what you're left with is . . . '

Sauce and I looked at each other and grinned. 'Fuck all!' we cried, in unison.

Our DI is a patient woman, with a sense of humour, but she's not at all keen on being leaned on by the head of CID. 'Look,' she began, until the phone rang and let us off the hook.

# Sarah Grace

The lab results had just come back when the call came in, not through the hospital switchboard but on my cellphone. The screen told me that it was Bob's number in Gullane, but I didn't expect it to be him. The witch? Surely not her either.

I hit the green key. 'Mum,' James Andrew began, 'can I have a mobile?'

I had to grin at his tone, that of a boy who knew he was pushing his luck, but who hoped nonetheless. 'Have you asked your father?' I said.

'Yes. He says not yet.'

'Then don't play us off against each other, Jazz. Does Mark have one yet? He's older than you and I don't recall seeing him with one.'

'No, he hasn't,' he admitted, grudgingly. He paused, then added, 'But if he does get one, then I want one too.'

'I'll discuss it with your dad, okay? What's brought this on anyway?' I asked.

'I had to come back to the house to call you,' he replied. 'I was on my way to the beach; if I had a mobile I wouldn't have had to come home.'

'Then the sooner you tell me what it's about,' I pointed out, 'the sooner you can get back on down there.'

'It's the computer. I was on it last, and I forgot to switch it off. Mark says it shouldn't be left on or somebody could hack into it. Can you do it?'

Sharp kid, that Mark. The boys have their own computer at my house and another at Bob's. At some point in time they might have a laptop each, but it can stay as it is for now, as it allows parental supervision. That's one of the things that my former husband and I still agree on.

'Yes, I will,' I promised. 'Now get on back outside.'

'Thanks, Mum.'

I frowned a little, as I heard him hang up. Eight years old, and yet he sounded just like his dad on the phone, give or take a few octaves; the same accent, the same intonation, and even a hint of the same authority in his voice. I took a strong hit of nostalgia.

There were some things I liked about my ex. Hell, face it, woman, there still are, and that voice of his is one of them, that and his presence; charisma is an over-used word but Bob has it, no question, and so, when you see him among his peer group, has James Andrew.

When Bob made his 'we've fallen out of love', speech, I went along with it, even though it wasn't entirely true on my part. If I had told him so, it might have sounded like I was pleading with him, and that is one thing I have never done: this gal has way too much pride for that. Besides he was right about the nub of it, our relationship was a mess and was finally broken beyond repair: probably.

I've always been good at loving Bob. I was crap at being married to him, that was all. Yes, I gave him a hard time when I came back to

Edinburgh to my new job, but that doesn't mean that I'm incapable of wishing him well, or that I never worry about him any more.

As an example, I was concerned about the way he had been at the grave site the night before: there had been something not quite right about it. I hadn't expected him to turn up, but he must have known that there was a fair chance I'd be the attending pathologist, so I couldn't put it down to shock at my presence, or even mild surprise.

Embarrassment? Hardly, for two of the people there didn't know me from Eve, and he and I are an open book as far as Mario and Jack McGurk are concerned.

Professional difficulties? Not a chance. Bob has supreme confidence in his ability to do his job. I've seen him in the most stressful conditions that the most gifted crime fiction writer could imagine, and I've never known him to be rattled.

Trouble at home? No, that couldn't be. Bob was never one for silent huffing and if there had been a barney between him and Aileen, surely I'd have picked up a whiff of it from Mark, a sensitive kid who'd have been upset by it. But hold on, the kids were with me, so . . .

'No, couldn't be,' I murmured. 'It's paradise in Gullane these days, Sarah, remember.' But something had unsettled him: I was sure of that.

I set the thought aside and looked at the lab results from my morning autopsy. I scanned though all the tests and analyses, looking for anything that might have been a contributory factor to the fatal collapse, but there was nothing.

I'd left the stomach contents till last. It's the only part of a postmortem examination that makes me feel at all squeamish. I do not read the entrails if I can avoid it; instead I leave it to the lab to analyse the deceased's last meal. I glanced at it, saw 'chicken' and almost set it aside; then I had a second look and reached for the phone.

I dug out the card that I'd made DC Haddock give me and dialled the direct number of the Torphichen Place CID suite. It was he who answered.

'Sauce,' I began, 'this is Sarah Grace. Have you identified your man yet?'

'No, Doctor,' he admitted, 'not yet; we're exploring possibilities but we haven't had a result. Are you going to tell me you've found that bar code after all? If you have, I hate to think where it was.'

I laughed: I was getting to like the kid. There was a self-confidence about him, but it stopped well short of the arrogance I've seen in quite a few cops. 'No,' I told him, 'I can't put a name to him, but I might let you focus your search a little more tightly.'

'How?'

'Circumcision,' I said. 'How much do you know about it?'

'I know I don't fancy it, not at my age,' he replied, cheerfully. 'Aside from that, it means you're Jewish, doesn't it?'

'That's the stereotypical UK gentile image,' I conceded, 'but actually, those boys don't hold

166

the copyright by any means. Nobody lines them up and counts them but I've seen figures that suggest that about half of the American male population is circumcised. In the Jewish faith, the practice is regarded as a command from God, but it's also widespread in Islamic peoples. Among the rest it's seen as precautionary, or even therapeutic; there's evidence that it lessens your chances of contracting sexually transmitted diseases. The World Health Organisation estimates that worldwide around one in three men are circumcised and that two-thirds of those are Muslim.'

'I stand corrected,' Haddock chuckled. 'So, are you saying that worldwide we can eliminate two out of every three men from our investigation?'

'I'm saying more than that. All I was doing was putting it in context, saying that you cannot look at a man who's had the procedure and say he's Jewish, which is why I didn't do that. But look at a man who's been trimmed, and whose last meal, consumed a couple of hours before he died, was matzoh ball soup followed by geffilte fish, then that, Detective Constable, is the way to bet.'

# Detective Inspector
# George Regan

It was a Thursday morning, and I was on duty in Dalkeith when the call came. I was asked to report to the chief constable's office, twelve noon sharp, with no reason given, not even when I asked the man Crossley point blank what the hell it was about.

I ran through all sorts of possibilities in my mind. I wasn't in any trouble that I knew of, I didn't know anyone who was and I'm not the sort of man you'd ask to organise the force Christmas dinner dance, so I ruled all of them out. That left redundancy at the top of the list.

The country's gone crazy over public spending cuts these days. Apart from the sacred cow that is our Notional Health Service, nobody seems to be exempt, not even the police force. Who would they pick first for the push? I asked myself. How about an emotionally damaged officer with twenty years in the job, but young enough to find a new career outside it? Oh, he'd be well up the pecking order.

Yes, I do consider myself emotionally damaged. I still haven't got over my young son's death. But I can function normally, as I like to think I've proved; my promotion to detective inspector a couple of years ago wasn't out of sympathy. I earned it by performance, and by

168

passing exams. Nevertheless, when I stepped into Crossley's small room that morning, en route to the chief's, I was fairly sure that I was going to be offered a package and shown the door.

I had half expected the Human Resources manager to be waiting with the boss, but he was alone. However in the current climate it was possible that HR was being phased out too, so her absence didn't raise my hopes.

When we sat down at his meeting table and Mr Skinner got down to it, I was even more convinced about the outcome.

'George,' he said, 'you're a good officer, one hundred per cent reliable, you have no skeletons in your closet and I rate you very highly. I want to say that up front. Now, I want to ask you how you'd feel about stepping out of the front line; right out of it'

That was it then; he was making the blow as soft as he could, but it was coming. I know a guy who left the force five years ago and became security manager for the Co-op. *He must be due for retirement*, I remember thinking, all in that couple of seconds. *Maybe there would be a slot for me there.*

'If it's in the public interest,' I began.

He laughed. 'It's in the very private interest, DI Regan. I want you to consider taking charge of Special Branch.'

I wish he'd had CCTV in his room, for I'd love to see a video. My expression must have told him everything I'd been thinking. He read it right and laughed even louder. 'You thought I was giving you the push, didn't you? Jesus Christ, George, when the force starts laying off guys like you, the dark side will have won well and truly.'

I think I stopped breathing for a couple of seconds, because I found myself taking in air in a big gulp. 'Special Branch,' I repeated.

He nodded. 'Yes. I'm not saying it'll be a springboard but it's a key position within the force, even more so in the modern era. Back in the old Cold War days it was relatively simple; there was one potential threat and even that was more imaginary than real, they say now. Even into the sixties, our predecessors checked on who went to Communist Party meetings and that was all, more or less. Then Ireland happened and since then it's all been much more complicated. Tell me what you know about the Branch, George.'

I'd never been asked that question before, nor even put it to myself, but I did my best to answer. 'It's a unit within each police force,' I began, 'that deals with national security, terrorism, etc. Its main job is gathering intelligence on potential threats, but it can investigate too. It can also get involved with serious organised crime as well as subversion. Every force has a Special Branch, but they're independent of each other.'

The chief smiled. 'Dictionary definition,' he said. 'It also keeps contact with the security services, but it isn't under their command. Some forces don't use the name any more: in the Met it's become part of SO15, the counter-terrorism command, and Strathclyde call it something different too. We still use the old name, but I don't give a bugger what we call it, as long as the unit works effectively and doesn't let anyone slip through the net that it should be catching. One other thing; it isn't part of CID, although its officers use detective ranks. Its head reports directly to me, and my deputy. That doesn't mean every day, but I like to be up to speed with everything that's going on, so you will be seeing a lot of me,' he paused, 'assuming that you want the job. You may decline without any offence being taken on my part, as long as the fact of the offer remains within this room. What do you say?'

There wasn't a chance of my turning it down. I was getting stale in CID; I knew it and it was only a matter of time before my line managers did as well. I needed a new challenge, so badly that I'd even been contemplating asking for a move to uniform. However, I didn't want to give the impression of being too keen, so I let it appear for a few seconds that I was engaged in sombre thought.

When I decided I'd pondered enough, I looked back at him and said, gravely, 'I'd like to do it, sir. I'm honoured even to be considered for the post.'

'It's gone beyond consideration,' he retorted. 'It's yours. I've talked it through with DCI Leggat, and he's onside with the idea.'

Fred Leggat was my immediate boss. I'd had to tell him about my meeting at HQ and the sod hadn't given me a clue that he'd known what it was about. 'When do I start, sir?' I asked.

He shrugged. 'You're here. You might as well start now.'

'But . . . ' He'd stunned me again. 'What about vetting?'

'That's all been done; you're cleared. You'll be replacing DI Dorothy Shannon. It's time for her to move back to CID. I'm doing a straight swap; she's going to your job in Dalkeith. The pair of you can spend the rest of the week doing a handover to each other.' He looked at me. 'How's Jen?'

The sudden switch of topic threw me off balance. In the middle of giving me a career-changing move he was asking me about my wife?

'She's okay, sir,' I replied. 'She's a full-time housewife these days.' I was going to leave it at that, but I realised that his question had come from genuine concern, not casual curiosity.

'By which I really mean,' I continued, 'that she doesn't go out any more unless she really has to. She's never got over losing the wee fella, and I don't believe that she ever will. She's withdrawn from all her circle of friends. I'm told that's not unusual in these circumstances, but she hasn't made any new ones. Our house is like a builder's show home, and the garden's like a Chelsea Flower Show exhibit, because she has nothing else in her life. When I say she doesn't go out, I am not kidding. She does all the shopping, food, everything, on the internet. If you ever run short of double A batteries, just call by our place. Jen buys them by the box.'

172

He frowned. 'Has anyone suggested medication?'

'For what, sir? There's nothing medically wrong with her. She's just sad, for a terrible reason, and the pill that will make her happy again hasn't been invented. I've tried, believe me, in all the ways you'd expect. Nothing worked. I booked a surprise break in Paris a year ago. She wouldn't go. I'd packed our case, there was a taxi at the door, and she refused point blank to get in it. We don't sleep together now: it's not that she'd refuse, but I know that I'd be imposing myself on her, just using her body, and I'd rather pay a hooker than do that.' I gasped at the enormity of what I'd just said. 'Not that I have, sir,' I spluttered, 'or ever would.'

'I know that,' he said, sympathetically. 'Your vetting was very thorough . . . but I know you better than that anyway. But if you ever feel the need . . . '

'Don't worry,' I exclaimed. 'If I ever do I'll resign from SB rather than compromise myself, or the job.'

'Hell, George,' he chuckled, 'I wasn't going to say that. I was going to ask you to be open with me if you do get involved with a third party. If I know about it, then, unless you really are paying ladies of the night, you're not in any professional difficulty.'

He paused again. 'Do you want to bring anyone with you?' he asked.

*Will the surprises never end?* I wondered. 'To SB?' I responded. 'Can I?'

He nodded. 'It's possible. I may have made

mistakes in the past by moving people into the Branch one at a time, so, if there's anyone you've worked with that you feel might be an asset . . . '

I didn't have to think about it. 'Lisa McDermid,' I said, instantly, 'my sergeant. She's a top operator.' *And she might not get on too well with Dottie Shannon if she stays in East Lothian*, I added, but only in my thoughts. However I did say, 'By the way, sir, she's single, but she and I, we're not . . . '

The chief grinned. 'I know that too,' he chuckled. 'Fred Leggat's not going to be too chuffed at losing both of you, but Dorothy's a good operator, so yes, you can have McDermid. You'll have someone else in your team too, since DC Singh's due for rotation as well, but at this moment I'm not entirely sure who it'll be.'

At that moment I didn't give a bugger. I used to work with big Tarvil and I was sorry he'd be going, but the boss could have dropped old Charlie Johnston on me as his replacement and I wouldn't have cared. I'd been re-energised. I'd gone into that room afraid, because I'd thought I was facing the end of a stagnant career, and I'd come out with a new one, and with my self-confidence restored.

Fred Leggat tells a story from the past, about seeing Bob Skinner dealing with a couple of lazy officers who thought they could get away with anything. 'Scary, George. Fucking scary.' If that's so, being praised by the man is at the other end of the scale. He hadn't even said all that much to me, yet I found myself . . . inspired isn't too strong a word.

It wasn't the prospect of redundancy that had frightened me. No, it was the thought of what might have followed if I hadn't been able to find another job, of being stuck in that refrigerator of a house with no escape other than to the golf course during the day and to the Longniddry Inn in the evening. I've forbidden Jen from making our newish home a temple to wee George's memory ... that will never fade ... and so she's gone to the other extreme, making it everything that it wasn't when he was around, neat, ordered, everything in its place, so unnaturally tidy that it reminds me of him even more and now, even though he never lived in that house, my heart breaks all over again every time I walk thought the fucking door. I've thought about leaving her, but I couldn't be that cruel. I confess that I did harbour thoughts about Lisa McDermid for a while. I never said anything out of place, but she cottoned on anyway, and very gently, very kindly, told me to forget it. She suggested that Jen and I find a shared hobby, and for a couple of months, I tried, but it was no use. Wrapped in her green housecoat, my wife is dying of grief, a terrible affliction; it may take another thirty, forty years to run its course, and while it does I've pledged to be as kind to her as I can, and to love her, as I always have, while spending only such time as I must in her company, lest I fall victim too.

My career move, to a job with irregular hours in an office further away from home, offered me another avenue of escape, and I was buoyed up by the prospect as I walked from the chief's

175

office to the small suite that houses Special Branch.

Some might imagine there's a keypad on the door, or a secret knock, but I just walked in. The first person I saw was Tarvil Singh, dwarfing his desk, as always. He was my DC when I'd worked in Edinburgh, before he'd been moved out of mainstream CID. He's a Sikh, but he doesn't wear a turban when he's working, because he says it makes him too conspicuous. Given the size of him, that always makes me laugh. He wasn't surprised to see me; that told me who'd done my vetting.

DI Shannon was expecting me too. I hadn't seen her for a while, not since her uniform days in Leith. Before that, there was a time when I'd seen quite a lot of her, including the pink bits, and the scars from a bad car accident she'd been in as a kid. Back then, when I was another man, she and I had what is called, euphemistically, a 'fling', until a very good friend made me sec sense. She's the one blot on my marital record, and it was so short-lived that it hadn't occurred to me to wonder whether it had showed up on my vetting. When I worked out that if Tarvil had done it, she'd probably signed off on it, I knew the answer.

She hasn't changed much since then; her hair tone might be a little more subtle, but that's it. One thing I did notice fairly quickly; I didn't see as much of her gold tooth as I remembered. That was because she wasn't smiling as she began to brief me on the contents of the two trays on her desk.

'Are you sorry to be going, Dottie?' I asked her. 'The county patch is okay, I promise you.'

'That obvious, eh?' she muttered. 'Yes, George, you're right; I'm a bit pissed off. Most people leave this job on promotion, but not me, oh no. And there I was thinking that the glass ceilings had been shattered for good.' She sighed. 'I suppose I've only got myself to blame. I had a run-in with the new deputy chief's sainted husband not long before he died. I guess he must have told her, and my card was marked from then on.'

As I looked at her, I recalled how I'd got myself involved with her. In the workplace, Dottie is not one of those sparkly women, and I'd decided that my mission in life was going to be to make her laugh. When I succeeded, after a couple of post-shift drinks, I found that there was another side to her.

'Hey,' I said, quietly, 'will you fucking lighten up on yourself, woman.'

Her eyes narrowed. 'You can talk, George. You were the one who got all uptight on me, remember? And it stuck, so it seems; look at you now, Mr Serious. What makes you think you can tell me to . . . ' And then she remembered. 'Oh, George. Shit, listen to me; you of all people can do that. I'm sorry, love, I forgot.'

She forgot? She fucking forgot? Lucky her.

'You poor man,' she exclaimed, but I stopped her in her tracks with an upraised hand.

'Please don't, Dot. This is where I work and I don't bring that here. I said you should lighten up because you were sounding more than a wee bit paranoid there. Maggie Steele is evidence that the ceiling's smashed, and as for her blocking your promotion, that's plain daft. Our moves had sod all to do with her; they're down to the big man, and he's not holding you back as I see it. You're going to work with Fred Leggat. He's about three coughs and a spit off retirement and when he goes that opens up a DCI slot. Who's going to get that?'

'Becky Stallings, probably,' she said, gloomily.

I laughed. 'Becky? She thinks Edinburgh's the countryside. No way will she get a rural job.'

She looked at me over her reading glasses, doubtfully. 'You sure about that?'

'Certain of it, so brighten up.'

'Okay, if you say so.' She paused. 'How's life anyway, if I'm allowed to ask?'

'I'd rather you didn't; you probably read my vetting report anyway.' Her eyes flickered and I knew she had. 'How's yours?'

'Private life?' I nodded. 'Crap, since you ask. My man got bumped by his bank and left town for a job in Hong Kong, without as much as a goodbye dinner. Four years down the pan. Some pair, aren't we?'

'At least we're not security risks. Come on, brief me on the job and I'll buy you a drink when we're done.'

By the end of the afternoon she had brought me up to speed on the dark and mysterious ways of the Branch, which turned out to be more routine than anything else. There were no major crises, and the threat level was officially 'substantial', mid-point in the five grades. 'It's hardly ever below that these days,' she said. She also gave me a list of contacts in SB offices in other forces, and in the security services. These were locked in a wall safe; she showed me how to change the combination, then turned her back as I did so.

She turned down the drink afterwards; I was quietly pleased about that, as I'd regretted the offer as soon as I'd made it. Instead we arranged to meet the next morning at Dalkeith, to go through the same process in the other direction.

I broke the news to Lisa McDermid, in a bizarre cross-purposes discussion . . . when I asked her to come into my room, she got the wrong idea . . . as soon as I got back to Dalkeith, and so she was gone when I got there next morning, to brief Shannon. Fred Leggat wasn't, though. He was in his office and his face was tripping him, as I'd half expected. He was cruising and hadn't planned on breaking in a new support team in his last few months in office, but I managed to persuade him that Dottie would hit the ground running.

I got back to Fettes by mid-morning, to find Lisa and Tarvil in conversation in the outer office, and a summons from the chief waiting for me on my new desk.

'Did Shannon brief you on the Varley situation?' he asked, as soon as I was through his door.

'Yes, sir, she did.'

'Did it come as a surprise?'

Skinner is good at bouncing the unexpected at his colleagues. I suppose the time it takes them to respond tells them how sure they are of their answers. 'Not as much as it might have,' I replied, quickly. I'd asked myself the same question the afternoon before. 'I was in the same office as Jock about eight years ago. I don't know why, but I didn't take to him. He struck me as a guy who always wanted to know more than he'd let on.'

'Yeah,' he murmured. 'Have you ever heard of Freddy Welsh?'

'I know nothing about him,' I confessed, 'other than he's a general builder and contractor, in quite a big way.'

'Yes,' he nodded, 'and now we need to know more. Dottie and Tarvil had a look at him yesterday, but only to check out his background and contacts. I'd like you to go a bit deeper. Maybe I'm wrong, but I can't see a well-set-up guy like Welsh being personally involved in something as small time as fag smuggling. That said, he wasn't going to meet Kenny Bass for a tip on the three-thirty at Lingfield. So what was it about? Put McDermid on to it; she isn't known around town. See if she picks up any hints.'

'Yes, sir. What about Bass?' I asked. 'Is he saying anything?'

His eyebrows rose. 'Take a guess?'

'How about, 'Who's Freddy Welsh?' Is that close?'

'Right on the money, George, right on the money.'

# 'Sauce' Haddock

Most of the time, when someone begins a sentence with 'I have to say . . . ' what it really means is, 'I'm going to say . . . whether you like it or not.'

I probably shouldn't say that I was beginning to get very fond of the chief constable's ex-wife, but I will . . . regardless. I don't mean that I fancied her. If I did I would definitely keep that to myself. No, I liked her, pure and simple. I could tell that Jack had reservations about her but I found her bold and provocative, things I like in a person, and I could detect no side to her, none of the aloof superiority that cops, and particularly young ones like me, often encounter in our dealings with those my mum calls 'members of the professions'. She was friendly and had treated me as an equal in every encounter we'd had.

'What are those?' I asked her after she'd finished describing Mortonhall Man's last meal.

'Classic kosher dishes,' she replied. 'Jewish food, as approved by ritual and the local rabbi. One of the few things I miss about New York City are the delis.'

'Are there any of those in Edinburgh?'

'There's the Viareggio chain,' she pointed out, 'but they're Italian. There are no kosher ones that I know of, but they're not places I've ever looked for over here.'

181

'His last meal,' I continued. 'Would it have been homemade?'

'Possibly,' she conceded. 'If you can trace kosher-approved suppliers in the area, you might get a lead to him.'

'How about kosher restaurants? Are there many in Edinburgh?'

'From memory,' she murmured, 'I think there's only one . . . and it's entirely vegetarian, so you wouldn't get chicken broth there, or stuffed fish either.'

'What about the matzoh balls?'

'Nor them; there's egg in the recipe. Hey,' she laughed, 'did you hear about the blonde who thought the matzoh was an endangered species?'

I was still grinning when I put the phone down.

'Who's made your day?' the boss called to me.

'Dr Grace, the pathologist.'

'What were you talking about?'

'Circumcision.'

Even Jack reacted to that. 'You what?' he exclaimed. 'With the chief's ex?'

'I'm not kidding,' I told him. 'She gave me a lecture on the subject: not how it's done, but who has it. Are you circumcised?' I asked him.

'Mind your own fucking business. What are you asking me that for?'

'Call it a statistical survey. More people are than you'd imagine.'

'Ray is,' Becky volunteered.

McGurk actually started to turn pink. 'Can we leave DI Wilding's tackle out of this, please,' he moaned. 'If you must know, yes I am.'

'And you're not Jewish.'

'Of course not. You don't have to . . . '

'I know,' I said, cutting him off in mid-sentence. 'That's what Sarah explained.' I paused, for a little effect. 'That's before she said firmly that our man was.'

'Come again?' the DI murmured, dryly. 'Did the rabbi who did it put his initials on his work?'

'Hardly,' I replied, slightly narked by her sarcasm. I shook my head and repeated what Sarah had told me . . . leaving out only the line about the blonde and the matzohs.

Her reaction was the same as if I'd shaken her awake. She blinked, once, twice then focused on me. If Becky Stallings has a fault as a team leader, it's her occasional tendency to slip into cruise mode, rather than driving full on at the task in hand. When she snaps out of it, though, she's a formidable operator. Half an hour earlier she'd begun to echo Jack, chuntering on about her team having been stuck with a job that uniform should be doing, putting a name to the dead man from the evening before, when we should have been tasked with putting the screws on Kenny Bass. That disappeared in an instant as she started to gnaw on the bone I'd given her.

'She's a hundred per cent certain about that?' she exclaimed.

'As near as damn it. 'That's the way to bet,' is what she said.'

'How much do you know about the Edinburgh Jewish community? How big is it?'

'I've got no idea,' I admitted.

'Then find out.'

Half an hour later, after some intensive research, followed by a few phone calls, I was up to speed. 'There are around eight hundred Jewish families in the Edinburgh area,' I reported to the DI. 'They worship in two active congregations but there's only one full-time rabbi in Edinburgh, Rabbi Hyman. I've just spoken to him. He doesn't know of anyone who's missing, and he's certain that if there had been a death among his flock, he'd have been called in. But he's willing to look at the body, to see if he knows him.'

'When?' she asked.

'Right now. It's Friday; their Sabbath starts in a few hours. He's preparing for this evening's service, but he's agreed to meet me at the mortuary in half an hour.'

'No great hopes, though?'

'No,' I admitted. 'I described our man. He said that it only fitted three or four people, no more than that. Those are all active in the community and he said that if any of them died it would be big news. He was shocked when I told him how we found the body, but he did say that the white shroud was 'appropriate'; his word.'

'Okay,' Becky said. 'You'd better get down to the Cowgate, now.'

'Yes, boss, I will, but there's more. I did a search on kosher food as well. Like the pathologist said, there's only that one vegetarian place in Edinburgh, and the food itself wouldn't be easy to source. There's one supermarket that stocks a range of kosher products, but it's not extensive. However, I did find a kosher restaurant in Glasgow; it's called Solomon's, and it isn't veggie. I phoned it, and spoke to the guy who owns it; it's named after him, by the way. Chicken broth with matzohs and geffilte fish are both regulars on the menu. The timescale we're looking at, according to the autopsy findings, has Mortonhall Man eating his last meal on Wednesday evening. Mr Solomon says he was open then, and busy, but when I described the man, he said yes, it was possible he might have been a customer.'

'Did you tell him that we're trying to find a dead man?'

'No. I didn't need to do that. All I said was that we were trying to trace a man who might have eaten there. Then I said that I'd pulled his menu off the internet, and I asked him how the broth and the fish were, casual like. I said they were my favourites. He said they're his best sellers, and that I should call in.'

'Do you have an address?'

'Sure.' I checked my notebook and read it out.

'Then what are you waiting for? Get the most presentable face shot that we have of the body and take him up on his invitation.'

I raised a slightly impertinent eyebrow. 'Is that before or after I go to the morgue?'

'Sod that,' she grunted. 'I'll meet the rabbi. It'll be a waste of time anyway. I'm beginning to get an idea of what's happened here.'

# Lowell Payne

It's as well that Bob had told us that the Special Branch guy was new. It went a long way to explain the caution with which he greeted us when his monstrous Indian sidekick showed us into his office. 'George Regan,' he said, almost apologetically, as he extended his hand to me. His grip was firm, that of a golfer. He was immaculately dressed, in a blue suit with some silk in it. *What gives with these Edinburgh guys?* I wondered, looking at him in Austin Reed's finest and Mackenzie in a uniform with creases so sharp you could have shaved Parma ham with them.

David and he seemed to be sizing each other up. I wondered whether their obvious appraisal of each other had something to do with the fact that they both seemed to enjoy Bob Skinner's confidence, and that they saw themselves as rivals as a result. If that was so, I'd be watching my back if I was Regan. The Copper Formerly Known As Bandit might have cleaned up his act, but whatever his bosses think of him I suspect that it was because he had no other option, and that an ambitious, calculating bastard still lurks close to the surface.

He was under wraps, though, as we took seats at Regan's desk. 'Quite a task we've been given, George,' he said. 'The chief's briefed

186

you on what we're doing, I take it, and how you relate to us.'

The DI nodded. 'Yes, he has.' He paused. 'But I'm not completely reactive in this. He's given me a separate task.'

He went on to explain what it was. 'Look,' he continued, 'I know you're reviewing the Varley career files, to check for any possible improprieties, across the board. We know, for example that he's got a track record with women, and he was even, briefly, a murder suspect because of it.' That was news to me; I suspected it was to Mackenzie as well, although he did his best not to show it.

'In practice though, all we have on him at the moment is his warning to Freddy Welsh. We have nothing at all on Mr Welsh, so that gives him priority status in my book, and in the chief's. He's told me to fill in the blanks. So, what I suggest is that you gentlemen concentrate on Varley's dealings with Welsh, while my colleague and I do the same thing, but in reverse; we go for Freddy and tie him to Varley. Hopefully we'll meet in the middle and get the complete picture.'

CoFKAB nodded. 'Fair enough,' he agreed. 'What about this man Kenny Bass? He seems to be pig in the middle between them.'

'Not necessarily,' Regan pointed out. 'There's no evidence of any connection between Varley and Bass. However, we don't need to get involved in that, not for the moment anyway. Bass will be re-interviewed separately; hopefully it'll be more productive this time.'

'Who's doing that?' I asked him.

'The head of CID; DCS McGuire.'

'Ouch,' Mackenzie chuckled. The SB man smiled too; an insider joke, I guessed. It passed me by because I was too busy wondering what the hell I'd become involved in. Bob Skinner seemed to be playing us all like the conductor of a small orchestra. Yet he was the chief constable. Jesus! Things were a lot different in Strathclyde where you rarely saw anyone more than two ranks above you, and didn't want to either because it usually meant you were in the shit.

This was very true, by all accounts, of our new gaffer, Chief Constable Antonia Field. She hadn't been in Pitt Street long before she became known as 'the queen of mean', for the way she scoured the place, identifying weak links and showing them the door. Quite a few senior faces were no longer around, and there were even rumours that Max Allan, our old school ACC, was for the chop. The one thing that worried me about the Edinburgh assignment was that it was bound to bring me into her field of vision.

*Better make sure you get a good report, then,* I decided. 'Then let's get to it, gentlemen,' I said. 'Since this isn't a nine to five job, the sooner we get it done, the sooner we can all get back to the wives and kids.'

The look that Mackenzie shot me didn't have a trace of smooth David; it was pure Bandit. *What the fuck was that about?* I wondered.

188

# Aileen de Marco

'Bob, can we talk?'

Unlike my husband, I have no previous experience of being married. So I didn't really know what to do when you've had a real up-and-downer, the kind that leaves a chill in the air even after the combatants have quietened down, and when the concept of not letting the sun set on an argument has gone for a burton. But one thing was for sure; I didn't reckon it was up to me to make the first move. Bob was the one who'd blown up, who'd refused to listen to a single word I'd said, or to consider the logic of what the government was proposing and what I felt it was my duty to back.

I waited all day for him to phone; waited in vain. When I got back to my office from Clive's, I hoped there would be a message from him, but there wasn't. With nothing else to do that my stubborn gene would permit, like ringing him myself, I called my stepdaughter. I don't like disturbing Alex at work, because her time is valuable and she has to account for every minute of it, but I felt that I had to do it; she's her father's vicar on earth.

'Have you heard from your dad today?' I asked her, once I'd persuaded her secretary that it was important, and been put through.

'No,' she replied. 'Was he supposed to call me?'

'No, no.' I felt stupid; I had no idea what I was going to say next.

She helped me. 'What's up, Aileen?'

'Oh, I thought he might have, to sound off.'

'Let me guess,' she said. 'You've had an argument.'

I sighed. 'Have we ever. I've never seen him like that.' I explained what had happened, and why. 'Alex, I really need your help.'

'I see,' she murmured, when I'd finished. 'Let me see if I've got this straight. You and the First Minister are ganging up to threaten my father's career.'

I'm not easily rattled, but the sudden, unexpected chill in her voice shook me up. 'No,' I protested, 'that's not how it is. We're going to advance it, if anything. He'll be the only serious candidate to head the unified police service.'

'In which he doesn't believe. I know he doesn't; he's told me, and he's passionate about it. You must have known that.'

'Maybe,' I conceded, 'but his opinion's irrelevant at the end of the day. It isn't his decision. It's a matter of public policy.'

'What's that got to do with it? If this creature is introduced in the face of his protest and counter-arguments, he's supposed to live with it? That's your position, is it?'

'Yes. He'll have to live with it,' I insisted.

'But he doesn't have to be a part of it,' she snapped. 'My old man has principles. Do you expect him to betray them?'

'I have principles too.'

She laughed scornfully. 'No, you don't, you're

190

a politician. Your principles change with the tide, they're based on expediency, yet you expect my father to put his own aside and yield to them.' She paused. 'Why did you marry him, Aileen?' she asked me.

'Because I love him,' I said, quietly.

'So you say,' she retorted, 'but you know what? I don't actually believe that. I think you married him mainly because you saw it as a formidable alliance, one with a man who's a constant, a far bigger figure than any of your crew, but one you thought you had wrapped around your pinkie. Now you find that you don't and you're furious.'

She was right there; I was, with the whole bloody Skinner family, and especially with her, at that moment. Before I could tell her as much, she went on.

'Well,' she declared, 'don't look to me for help to persuade him to see it your way. As it happens, I don't agree with what you and your pal are up to, but even if I did, I'd never lean on him like that. I'll say to you what I said to Sarah when she came back: don't hurt my dad. But with her I didn't really need to: she wouldn't, because it would hurt the kids,' she paused for a second, 'and also, by the way, because she still loves him, although she might not even know it.' That was a possibility I hadn't considered, not for a second.

'I do need to spell it out to you, though,' she said. 'Don't! Hurt! Him!' She spat the words out. 'You do that and you'll have made a lifetime supply of enemies, with me at the head of the queue. I was content, you know, Aileen, not because I like you all that much, which I don't, but because I saw my father settled and happy with you. Now you've gone and screwed that up.' The line went dead, as she hung up.

I hadn't realised until that moment how like Bob his daughter is, and the sudden recognition left me shaking, literally. When she'd let go at me, she'd sounded almost exactly like him, but not quite, for there had been even more venom in her. That crack about Sarah; Jesus, that was brutal. I know the woman can't stand me, but no, it hadn't occurred to me that she had any feelings left for Bob. Yet it didn't occur to me either that Alex might have made that up; there had been a certainty in her voice.

Had she been right about me also? Had I seen my husband as a good strategic match? Well, yes, I had. However, that's not to say that I don't love him; I wanted him from the moment I saw him, and I didn't let his rocky marriage stand in my way. Then again, neither did he. 'Scotland's couple of the year', a Sunday newspaper had christened us. It was beginning to sound like football's 'Manager of the Month' accolade, or its near relative, the chairman's vote of confidence.

Normally, I am a clear and decisive thinker. As I sat there, I realised that I didn't know what to do, and that scared me. So I picked up the phone again, and did what I'd been determined not to: I called my husband, on his mobile.

'Can we talk?' he repeated. 'Sure we can. Will either of us listen? For my part I will, I promise. Will either of us budge an inch? What do you think?' I had no answer to that but silence. 'Come on,' he continued, after a while, 'admit it. That story of yours about being persuaded by the cost argument: that was bullshit, wasn't it? You believe in a unified force for its own sake.'

'Yes,' I whispered. 'I'm sorry, but I do.'

'Aileen,' he said, heavily. I had a sense of alienation; he never calls me by my given name. Once I asked him why; he replied that he didn't need to, that he talked to me in a different way than to anyone else. 'Don't apologise, please,' he said, 'that's demeaning. It's what you believe, and I'll respect you for it. I'm sorry I roared at you last night; that was demeaning too. I was angry that you're prepared to shaft my career, and I let it get the better of me.'

'It's not a matter of shafting your career . . . '

'It is from where I'm standing,' he declared. 'Tell me something. Have you and Toni Field had your heads together over this?'

'What?' I hadn't intended to snap at him, but he'd set me off again. 'Do you think I'd plot against you with that bloody woman?'

'No,' he replied, calmly. 'Of course I don't, not as such. But the two of you are in the same camp.'

'For entirely different reasons.' Change of subject called for, urgently. 'Bob, Clive Graham's given me a couple of tickets for a charity gig in Glasgow tomorrow evening. It's a classical pianist called Theo Fabrizzi. Let's go to it, eh?'

'Will Clive be there?'

'He's the guest of honour.'

'And Toni Field?'

'I have no idea.'

'Doesn't matter, I'm best avoiding Mr Graham for a while. Sorry, love, but he can stick his tickets up his arse, and the piano with it.'

'Oh please,' I sighed.

'No, really, it's better I don't go. I couldn't trust myself to stay quiet if my dear colleague was there and tried to stir it.'

*God forbid*, I thought. 'Okay,' I conceded, 'I understand. I'll have to go, though, now I've accepted the tickets.'

'Fine,' he replied with an equanimity that might have annoyed me at another time. 'You do that. Why don't you take Sarah with the spare ticket? You can spend the evening picking me apart.'

'I don't think she'd come, somehow,' I murmured, dryly.

'I wasn't being serious,' he said sharply. 'How about Alex?'

'I don't think she would either.'

My tone must have given me away. 'Oh my God,' he exclaimed. 'Please tell me you didn't ask my daughter to try and talk me round.'

'I didn't get that far. Bob,' I moaned. 'I thought she liked me.'

'She does, as far as I know. She's never criticised you to me, not ever. But if you asked her to side with you against me . . . ' He didn't have to finish. 'I'll talk to her,' he said, 'and try to repair the damage.'

'Maybe you have to talk to me as well to do that,' I pointed out.

'I meant the damage between you and my kid,'

he replied, quietly. 'Between you and me, I'm not so sure. Something broke last night; we both know that. Now,' he continued, abruptly, 'about that spare ticket. Given the guy's name, why don't you ask Paula Viareggio if she'd like to go. She's mightily pregnant, but she still has a couple of weeks to go and she's bored as hell with it all. She might jump at the chance, and you'd be doing Mario a favour too; he has his hands full right now. We all have.'

# Paula Viareggio McGuire

'You will never guess, Mario,' I said, 'who I've just had on the phone?'

'You are almost certainly right, love,' he replied, 'so save us both some time and tell me.'

'The once and future First Minister, that's all.'

'Aileen? What did she want?'

'Does the name Theo Fabrizzi mean anything to you?' I asked him.

'Not a light,' he admitted. 'Should it?'

'If he was Italian, maybe, but he's not, he's Lebanese, so we're both off the hook. He's a classical pianist, and he's the attraction at a charity event in Glasgow tomorrow night. Aileen's got a spare ticket and she's asked me to chum her. Front row seats; the First Minister himself is the guest of honour.'

'That's very nice,' he murmured, 'but why isn't Bob going with her?'

'She said he doesn't fancy it.'

'Mmm.' Nobody is better than Mario at making a mumble sound sceptical.

'That's what she said. I don't care why he isn't; I am going to have very few more opportunities to get glammed up, so I'm going . . . if it's all right with you. Be warned; it's advisable to answer 'yes' to that.'

'Yes,' he chuckled.

'I'll cook tonight, to make up for it.'

'No you won't. I will, or I'll bring something

196

in. You're not coming in from a day at your office to stand around in the kitchen.' He can be a doll sometimes: most of the time; with me, all the time. 'Anyway, you're well in credit for the Starbucks and the croissants. Andy says thanks, by the way. They came in handy, saw us through a difficult interview. The gentleman in question . . . well, he's no bloody gentleman.'

'You poor love,' I murmured. That might sound soppy, but I know Mario's secret side. He's more sensitive than he would ever let on, and when someone he's trusted . . . and that means every cop in the force . . . lets him down, it makes him very sad, as well as very angry.

'Bah!' he grunted, for he won't admit it to anyone, not even me. 'Listen,' he continued, 'in the wake of that I might be a wee bit later than usual this evening. I've got a call to make.'

'Where? Out of town? Can you tell me?'

'Not very far. Saughton Prison, in fact. The chief wants Andy and me to have a serious conversation with the man who set this whole sorry Varley business in motion.'

# Alexis Skinner

I must have raised my voice during my discussion with my dear stepmother. I may be a partner in the august firm that is Curle Anthony and Jarvis, but I'm still well down the pecking order and the office that I rate didn't have too much spent on its sound-proofing. I had barely hung up before the door opened and my secretary's frown came into view.

'Is everything all right?' she murmured. Clio Lomax and I are still new to each other: her predecessor Pippa finally pushed her flippancy far enough for it to earn her a rollicking from the chairman of the firm. When she came crying to me and I told her that it wasn't before time, her lip became so petted that she called me a 'fucking establishment lackey' and walked out, never to return. Now she's working in her father's investment management business; God help the clients.

Clio was available as a result of one of our departments having been downsized during the recession, and she moved straight into the vacancy. Her inquiry wasn't entirely solicitous. It was her way of suggesting that I turn down the volume.

'Sorry,' I said. 'You weren't meant to hear that. Just a small family disagreement. You don't want to know about the serious ones. You know who my stepmother is?'

She nodded. 'I take it you won't be voting for her next year.' I grinned, and she left.

I tore into the project I'd been assessing before Aileen's call; her interruption had taken fifteen minutes out of my midday break, but since I hadn't been scheduled to meet anyone, it wasn't a big deal. The day was warm and sunny, so I cleared out of the office, walked down the steps that lead from Castle Terrace to Princes Street Gardens, and bought a sandwich lunch at the Fountain Cafe. I was eating it, on a bench, when my mobile sounded.

I looked at the screen, and felt instantly brighter. 'Hiya,' I said. 'How's the sex slave business?'

'Getting worse by the day for the traffickers,' Andy replied, cheerfully, 'I'm glad to say. So is drug-dealing, and the Agency's internet team just busted a rock singer for having some very bad stuff on his computer.'

'Once upon a time, sex and drugs and rock and roll were reckoned to be very good indeed,' I laughed, 'until Director Martin became head of the serious crime-fighters. How's the weather in Paisley? It's lovely here in the Gardens.'

'No idea,' he replied. 'I'm enjoying the sunshine on Leith. It's an outside officer job that your father asked me to do; it'll take up the rest of the day.'

'Are you around this weekend?'

'I am tomorrow, unless this goes pear-shaped. Sunday I'm going up to Perth to take the kids out. You?'

'I'm clear. Fancy meeting up tonight, and

taking it from there?'

'Deal. I'll call you when I'm done.'

That's the way it is with Andy and me now. We have no ambitions for our relationship, but we enjoy it. I know what a lot of people think of me . . . yes, they think it of me, rather than him . . . but I did not set out to bring it about, and I'm sorry that his marriage didn't work. I've had hate mail, the old-fashioned kind, addressed to me at the firm and always anonymous. There's been shit posted about me on Facebook too . . . Faecesbook, as I've come to call it. I assume it's all come from people who are, or consider themselves, friends of Karen, Andy's wife. He hasn't had any of that stuff, but you'd have to be seriously mental to send poison pen messages to a cop. If anything was too heavy, I'd ask him to deal with it, but I would never, ever mention it to my father.

It's strange, that people can come back into your life when you believe that you've consigned them entirely to your past. When Andy and I split and he married Karen, I didn't see him for a few years, even though he's my old man's closest pal, and I never expected to have anything to do with him, ever again. Same with Sarah and Dad; when they divorced and she went back to the US, I assumed that it was for good. Her latest comeback was as unlikely as *Rocky Seven* but it's happened. Sarah says it was a career move. Yes, and next year I will be the fairy on top of the Christmas tree on the Mound.

I shouldn't have said what I did to Aileen

about her, in the midst of the only major row we ever had. I knew that Sarah detested her, but I was just as sure that Aileen had no thoughts about her at all, that she saw her as being as distant a figure in my dad's past as my mother is. And there she's wrong on two counts.

Sarah is in the present and she's alive; so is my mother, in my father's heart. Sarah found that out and stopped trying to compete. Aileen? She didn't even know she was in a contest. She lived in a world that she'd created in which her husband is settled and content, domestically, and in the job about which he was always ambivalent, but which she manoeuvred him into accepting.

Great, until she tried to push him that one step too far and it all went up in smoke. She came to me in the hope that I could put out the fire, and I threw petrol on it by telling her that her predecessor still loved her husband. I'd told her she'd screwed things up, but what had I done myself?

I was by the bin, recycling my sandwich wrapper, when my phone rang again. 'Yes, Dad,' I said.

'You had a call from Aileen?'

'Yeah,' I admitted. 'I'm sorry. I lost it.'

'You and me both,' he sighed, 'last night. We should be ashamed of ourselves, shouldn't we?'

'That depends. Were we right on the principle?'

'Of being against police unification? I believe so, absolutely. Trouble is, Aileen believes the opposite.'

'And she wants you to subordinate your view

201

to hers, and me too, by implication?' I put the question to him as if I was leading him, in court. 'That's what she expects, yes?'

'Yes, that's how it seems. But it works both ways; I recognise that. It's an impasse.'

'Will it happen, Pops?' I asked. 'The unified force.'

'It's shaping up that way,' he admitted. 'You only need to look at the numbers. If the Nationalists and Aileen's crew both back it, then it'll walk through the parliament. She and Clive Graham probably think I'll keep quiet if ACPOS support it, but I won't. Any journo who asks me a straight question will get a straight answer, and I'll bloody well make sure that I am asked. It won't make any difference, though, for all the friends I have in the media, and in the parliament itself, because when it comes to it, there won't be a free vote.'

'Will you really quit over it?'

'That's my intention, although Aileen imagined that I could be bought off with the top job. No chance of that,' he said emphatically.

'What would make me reconsider? If you asked me not to, I might not.'

'If I asked you to betray your principles?' I exclaimed. 'Why would I ever do that?'

'Look, kid, if I go balls out over this I could make myself pretty unpopular with some people with a lot of power. There could be backwash, you know.'

The waves would have to be high, I reckoned, to reach a fifth-floor office in the biggest commercial law firm in Scotland. But they could be as high as the castle that I could see through my window and they wouldn't make any difference to me.

'Remember that song,' I said, 'the one you used to sing to me when I was wee, in the years after Mum died, whenever I got sad and started to cry because really she wasn't coming back?'

I could see him smile, as if we were on Skype. 'Yeah. The one by Paul Williams: wee guy, glasses, dodgy hair; 'You and me against the world'. I've still got it, you know, that record. It was your mum's favourite.'

'Then dig it out and play it, because it was never more true.'

Nobody really understands about my dad and me; there's a bond that ties us together, one that will never break, although she who formed it has been dead for twenty-five years.

# 'Sauce' Haddock

Satnav guided me all the way into the heart of an old-established residential area called Newton Mearns, to the south of Glasgow. What it didn't tell me was that I'd been there before, not on police business, but for an away tie in a national foursomes competition against a pair from Whitecraigs Golf Club. I have very warm memories of that place; my partner and I handed the opposition a dog licence, in other words we beat them seven and six.

Solomon's restaurant was situated only a few streets away from the clubhouse where we'd eaten after the match. That was a friendlier snack than it might have been, given what we'd just done to the locals. I've been to golf clubs where I haven't even been offered a drink in those circumstances.

Solomon himself, a cheery, dark-haired wee guy . . . think of Ben Elton with a refined Glasgow accent . . . just short of forty, first name Jeffrey, 'but call me Solly; everyone else does', kept up the local standard of hospitality. He took me into his small office, and gave me sparkling mineral water, then produced a plate of buns that he called rugelach. I tried one, then another, then another. 'Cream cheese cookies,' he explained. 'Kosher, of course. Go on, have another.'

I did; I hadn't realised how hungry I was.

'So,' he said, once we had cleared the plate, 'this guy you asked me about. What's the story?'

'I have a photograph,' I told him, 'but I have to warn you, it's not the nicest.'

'I have a strong stomach, Mr Haddock.' He grinned. 'Unsullied by pork, that's why. You know the story about the rabbi and the priest?'

I did, but I let him tell it anyway, and I laughed when he was done. Then I took the mugshot from my pocket, slipped it from the evidence bag that held it and showed it to him.

It wiped the smile off his face, but it didn't take the colour from his cheeks. He shrugged. 'So he's dead. I've seen worse: I did some kibbutz time when I was a kid, and we had trouble once. Rocket attack. What happened to him?' He paused, and his eyes widened slightly. 'You're not going to tell me it was food poisoning, are you?'

'No,' I replied, smiling vaguely for a second or two, as I tried to work out whether his concern was real or just part of his shtick. 'He had a brain haemorrhage, no warning. Pretty much instant cheerio. If it's any consolation, he seems to have enjoyed his last meal. He ate plenty of it and he didn't have time to digest it. That's how we linked him to you.'

'So what can I tell you about him?'

'His name would be nice. Was he a regular?'

Solly shook his head. 'Never seen him before. I have lots of regulars, and I know them all, but equally, because this is the only kosher restaurant in a long day's march, I have a lot of occasional trade.'

'How about his bill?' I asked. 'Can you identify that? I might be able to trace him through his credit card slip.'

'I can find his bill, no problem,' he told me, 'but there ain't no transaction slip, because he paid in cash. That's why I remember him so clearly. You have any idea how few cash customers pass through here, or through any retail business these days? I love those guys. When someone offers me real money rather than plastic I knock the bill down to the nearest fiver, out of pure sentiment.' He winked at me. 'And when I do, the tip is always bigger. Works every time, and it did with him. I've still got the notes, by the way.'

'You have?'

My tone must have rung a warning bell. 'All above board,' he insisted. 'It all gets declared, honest. It's just that I have so little currency that I don't bank it very often; I tend to keep it as a float.'

'Solly,' I told him, 'when I showed you my warrant card, it didn't have HMRC on it. I don't care about that. Anyway, I don't imagine there's any way you can tell which are the notes he gave you.'

'Hell yes,' he laughed. 'I know exactly which ones they were. The only two Bank of England fifties I've taken in here since I opened.' Just as I was thinking that his prices must be sky-high if it took two fifties to cover chicken broth with matzohs and stuffed fish, he added, 'He didn't give me them, though. It was one of his mates.'

'He wasn't alone?'

'No. Party of three.'

That was news indeed. 'Can you describe the other guys?' I asked, trying to sound casual. Solly struck me as a man with an imagination and I didn't want to get him so excited that it ran riot. 'Age bracket, for example?'

'Same ballpark as your mate, I'd say. Medium height, all of them. One of them was fair-haired, sort of ginger, with a crew cut, a real flattop; reminded me of that American wrestler guy, Brock Lesnar, only smaller.' I'd no idea who that was, but I made a mental note to Google him and find a likeness. 'Otherwise,' Solly continued 'they were ordinary-looking guys. Nondescript,' he declared. 'I could do a photofit if you like,' he added.

'I'll bear that in mind,' I said; a nondescript photofit, indeed. I reckoned that Brock Lesnar was as lucky as I was going to get, but I was wrong.

'One thing, though,' Solly chirped on. 'The other two guys weren't Jewish. They hadn't a clue about the menu. Your dead guy had to explain what everything was, and in the end they let him order for them.'

A bit more, but it didn't really take me beyond 'nondescript'.

'And they weren't British.'

That was more like it. 'Explain,' I murmured.

'They spoke English, to me and the staff, but with accents. The dead guy, the Jew; his was closest to normal, but it still wasn't. The other two, I dunno; Australian? New Zealand?'

'To you and the staff, you said. What about

among themselves?'

He shook his head, firmly, sending a white shower of dandruff on to the empty plate. 'No, they spoke something else then. But don't ask me what it was. I don't have a bloody clue, other than that it wasn't Hebrew. I'm not fluent, but I'd have picked up some of it if it had been that.'

'Okay, thanks,' I said. 'That's something to go on. I wish you had a credit card slip, though.'

'Sorry.'

But . . . wait a minute, Sauce. 'You said one of the other guys paid the bill?'

More dandruff flew. 'Yes, the other dark-haired one, not the wrestler lookalike; seventy-two quid and twenty pence, I knocked it down to seventy. He peeled two fifties off a roll and told me to give him back twenty and we'd be square.'

'And you've still got them?'

'Like I said.'

I picked up the evidence bag that had held the photo. 'Solly,' I began.

He rolled his eyes. 'Ah, I know what you're going to ask.'

'I'll give you a receipt.'

He laughed. 'Now, I really will have no choice but to declare it to the tax man.'

He took a cash box from his desk and unlocked it, then pushed it across to me. I tipped the contents out, a few hundred quid, and saw the two fifties straight away, reddish things with the Queen's head on the front and some bloke in a wig on the back. I wondered how much fifty pounds had bought in his day as I picked them up, each one by a corner, and slipped them into

208

the protective case. They looked fresh, and hardly used; bound to yield decent prints and, with luck, not too many of them.

I wrote Solly the promised receipt, signed it and clipped one of my cards to it for added authenticity.

'Will you let me know what happens?' he asked. 'Whether you get a result or not?'

'I don't even know what the game is, sir,' I admitted, 'let alone how to work out the score.'

He offered me a sampler of the chicken broth, but I declined. Undeterred, he pressed a bag of rugelach on me, for the road, he said. I thanked him and headed for my car.

I didn't rely on the satnav for the return journey, for that would have taken me through the centre of Glasgow at gridlock time. Instead I took a simpler route through East Kilbride. I had just cleared the place when my phone sounded. I hit the Bluetooth button on the steering wheel and said, 'Sauce.' That's my standard greeting; on the rare occasion I have a wrong number it confuses the shit out of the caller.

I expected to have Becky Stallings in my ear, wondering why I hadn't given her a progress report . . . as I'd neglected to do. Instead I heard someone I hadn't expected, not at all.

'Chief Constable here. Are you on the road?'

'Yes, sir. I've been to Glasgow, in connection with Mortonhall Man.'

'Oh yes? Any progress?'

'Of sorts, sir. I don't have a name for him, but I've got a couple of new lines of inquiry.'

'What are they?'

I paused as I was overtaken by a clown in a Mercedes, braking as he pulled in too soon, to be overtaken himself by an even bigger idiot in a Golf GTI. 'Fingerprints and a wrestler,' I said, when I could.

He laughed. 'Where the hell are you, son? It sounds like Brands Hatch. I couldn't make out a word you said there. Tell me all about it when you get back.'

'Sir?'

'I want you to come straight to Fettes, to my office. I need to speak to you.'

If the great man wants you to know why, he tells you. When he doesn't, don't ask. 'Yes, sir.'

'Oh, and Sauce,' he added. 'Switch your phone off, now. Just in case DI Stallings or Jack try to call you. I don't want them in on this, and I wouldn't want you to have to lie to them.'

The buzz of an empty line filled my humble, non-racing, Astra. 'Me neither,' I murmured.

# Mario McGuire

Some people actually volunteer to visit prisons. I can never get my head round that, because they are the most depressing places I know. Even today, when our society is forced by human rights conventions and such to care about the conditions in which it locks people up, even without pisspots during the night, they are grim places, devoid of all but the darkest humour, and with an air of pent-up aggression that's so pervasive it's almost palpable.

I've helped to send a right few people there in my career. While all those results were satisfying professionally, I've taken no personal pleasure from any of them, save one, perhaps, a police officer who'd betrayed us all, and who'd earned our righteous anger. That guy killed himself inside, possibly before someone else could do the job for him, and as I turned into the access road that leads up to HMP Saughton, I found myself wondering what would be waiting for Jock Varley when he found himself banged up, as I was determined he would.

'That sign always gets my attention,' Andy Martin said as we drove past a pole by the roadside.

'How come?' I asked. I'd never noticed it.

'It says 'Beware possible traffic queue'. It's

211

hard to imagine folk queuing to get into a jail. Out, yes. In, no.'

'You're in a cheerful mood,' I remarked.

'Am I?' He sounded genuinely surprised. 'Yes I suppose I am. I've got my weekend sorted out.'

'Are you going to see the kids?'

'Sunday, yes.'

'How's Karen?' I've known Andy's soon to be ex-wife for as long as he has.

'She's fine. We've sold the house up in Perth, and she's bought a place in Lasswade; she moves in September. Once Robert's old enough for nursery school she's going to apply to rejoin the force.'

'She won't have any problem getting back in, not with her experience.'

'I know that, Mario,' he said. 'But everything will have to be done by the book.'

And I knew whose book it would be. Karen's re-employment was a racing certainty.

There was no traffic queue at the newly built entrance to the prison complex, and there was plenty of space in the car park. The video camera picked us up as we walked to the door next to the vehicle entrance. I told the entry system who we were and why we were there, and it was opened for us.

Kenny Bass was waiting for us in an interview room in the remand unit, to which we were led by one of the gate officers. He'd been told that we were coming and had called in a brief, a smart-suited mid-twenties kid from Criminal Lawyers R Us or some similar operation. His name was Laurence . . . his surname escapes me; I don't think I'm ever going to need to remember it . . . and he was keen, but he had the wrong idea.

'Let me set the ground rules for this meeting, gentlemen,' he began. 'My client . . . '

'That won't be necessary,' Andy murmured, just as I was about to tell the lad to shut the fuck up. 'This is an informal interview with your client, and it doesn't relate directly to the offence with which he's charged. So you don't need to worry about him incriminating himself, or about protecting his human rights.'

'Nevertheless . . . ' the young solicitor exclaimed, then stopped short, as Andy nailed him with those green eyes of his. They're made unnaturally bright by the tinted contact lenses he wears, the only sign of an affectation in the man. He can make them seem as if they might turn red in an instant, without pausing at amber, and I guess that's what he'd done with Laurence.

'There'll be nothing recorded,' he promised. 'Unless your client wishes it, of course.' He beamed at Kenny. 'Do you, Mr Bass?'

The prisoner shook his head. 'It'd be a waste of a tape,' he muttered. 'I've got fuck all to say to yis. I'll take my chances in the Sheriff Court.'

'Oh yes?' I laughed, softly. 'It may not stay at that level, Kenny. You should know the Edinburgh sheriffs by now. Plead guilty if you like, and I'm sure your lawyer here will put in a very eloquent plea in mitigation for you, but the guy on the bench will have your whole criminal history in front of him. Worse, you might get that new lady sheriff, Levy. Have you heard about her? A pal of mine in the fiscal's office told me they call her Miss Whiplash in the court. She's allowed to put you away for five years, but on her current form, she might decide that's not enough. In that case she'll send you to the High Court for sentence.'

He frowned and tried a shrug that didn't quite come off.

'But as my colleague said,' I went on, his attention secured, 'we're not here to talk about that. Are we, Mr Martin?'

Bass glanced across at him. 'I didnae know you were back,' he muttered. Many members of the alternative society in Edinburgh have come to know Andy Martin personally, and nearly all of them, apart from the very young talent, will have heard of him. They've never quite known what to make of him, not since the early days when he was very obviously Bob Skinner's pupil.

Some believe that he only ever played Good Cop to the chief's Mr Nasty, but there was always much more to him than that. I could read the ambition in him on the day I met him. He knew from the start that it wouldn't be realised by standing in someone else's shadow, so he made his own space early on, and made himself memorable. That's what the green contacts are about, and that leather jacket he wore for ever, and still has, I believe. He's the second most visible cop in the country, and it's no accident. As for those assumptions, big Bob has never gone in for that sort of stereotyped role play. Most of the time, the people he interviewed were only too keen to tell him what he wanted to know.

'I'm not,' Andy replied. 'This is a special guest appearance, Kenny, just for you. We want to ask you about a man called John Varley.'

'So ask.'

'Do you know him?'

'The name's familiar. Is he no' a comedian?'

'No relation. This would be Inspector Varley.'

'One of your lot? He'll no' be funny at all, then.' He started to smile, but then flinched. I guessed that Andy had given him another warning look. 'I think I met him a few years ago,' he volunteered. 'He might have been a sergeant then; aye that's right, he was. I had a massage parlour then and he came in to check on the licence.'

That was news to me. 'Why did he do that?' I asked him. 'Those places all have public entertainment licences; you can inspect them in the council offices.'

'You tell me; that was his excuse for coming in. He wanted to look over the premises.'

'And you let him?'

He sniffed. 'Aye sure, Mr McGuire. Like I was going to tell a uniform sergeant to fuck off.'

'Okay, so he looked over the premises. Then what?'

'Then he left.'

I laughed; couldn't help myself. It was so spontaneous that it startled Laurence the lawyer who sat bolt upright in his chair. 'Bollocks, Kenny,' I chuckled. 'A cop comes into your massage place, has a quick look round then goes

215

away. That's all, and yet a few years later you remember the incident then him. Something else happened, didn't it?'

He shook his head. 'No, nothing,' he murmured. 'Nothing happened, nothing else.'

I leaned forward, not laughing any longer. 'Don't bullshit us, now. Did he try to extort money from you?'

'No.' He was staring hard at the tabletop. If Laurence hadn't been there I'd have made bloody sure he was looking at me as he lied to me, but I couldn't.

'Then what, Kenny?'

'Nothing.' His voice was so quiet that if we'd been recording I'd have asked him to repeat it.

Andy leaned forward. 'Listen, this is not going to get you done,' he said. 'I don't give a fuck about . . . ' Bass flinched again and he hit on it. 'A fuck,' he repeated. 'Varley leaned on you for a freebie from one of the girls, didn't he?'

Finally Bass raised his eyes from the furniture and met ours. 'I'm saying nothing, okay.'

'Why not?' Andy asked. 'Is it because Varley's related to Freddy Welsh?'

Those eyes went blank, as if two shutters had dropped. 'Who's Freddy Welsh?'

'Freddy Welsh is the guy you met for a drink in Lafayette's pub last Wednesday night,' I reminded him.

'Gentlemen,' Laurence intervened, tentatively.

'Shut up!' Andy snapped. He did.

'I was on my own.'

'You were sitting with Freddy Welsh,' I countered. 'We've got you on video.'

'Sure,' he blustered, a little animation restored, 'a guy came and sat at my table, but I didnae know him.'

'That's not what the video shows.'

'Fuck your video; that's what I'm saying.'

'He took a phone call then he left,' I continued, 'without looking at you.'

'Exactly,' Bass exclaimed, as if we had made his point for him.

'Then you left too. Right away, straight after him.'

'I finished my drink. I was leaving anyway.'

'No, Kenny, that's mince, and we both know it. You were there to meet Freddy. Look, we don't want to ask you about these fags you're being done for. We want you to tell us about Freddy himself, and why a supposedly straight-up reputable businessman should be involved in a pretty run-of-the-mill tobacco smuggling deal.'

'Who's Freddy Welsh? Who's Freddy Welsh? Who's Freddy Welsh?'

Andy stopped any further repetitions, with a warning, pointed finger. 'He's a guy who's got you scared shitless, Kenny. You might be relatively small time as criminals go, but you're experienced and you know the ropes. The fact that Welsh can do that to you makes him a person of interest to us.'

'Fine,' Bass hissed. 'Then go and ask your pal Varley about him, if they're related like you say they are, because you're getting fuck all out of me.'

# David Mackenzie

Since I became executive officer to the command ranks in Bob Skinner's regime, I've met most of the senior people in the other Scottish forces. Graham Morton was an exception. As chief constable of the Tayside force, he'd been notoriously insular, always reluctant to set foot outside Dundee. They said that Edinburgh and Glasgow were as far distant to him as New York or LA. And so, when he retired, and bought a house in sunny Cramond, one of the posher parts of the capital, it made front-page news in the *Courier*, and even rated a mention in the *Police Review*.

When I mentioned it to the boss, all he did was smile and murmur, 'Watch this space.' Morton had been a civilian for two days when the announcement was made of his appointment as director of security for First Caledonian Bank, a small Scottish outfit that does mostly retail business, which is why it managed not to get itself massively over-exposed to toxic debt. As a result it emerged from the global catastrophe smelling distinctly of roses, and its key staff were able to trouser their modest contractual bonuses without anyone batting an eyelid.

First Caley is popular with cops, and it values us as customers, so it wasn't a surprise when Payne and I were told that Inspector John Varley did his banking there. Straight away, I put in a call to Morton; I didn't give his secretary any details, only that I needed to consult him on a confidential professional matter. He took my call at once.

'Thanks for speaking to me, sir,' I began.

'It's my job, Superintendent Mackenzie. Give me a name and come to my office.'

I was taken well aback. I'd expected all sorts of ritual dancing. 'Sir?' I said, cautiously.

'I know who you are, and what you do. You're one of Bob Skinner's close people but you're not CID. You've got a bent cop, am I guessing right?'

'Yes you are, sir; spot on.'

'But you're not discipline and complaints either, so this one is extra sensitive.'

'True again,' I conceded. 'We need to look at bank records, to trace payments from a particular person who may be involved in organised crime.'

'Is that person one of our customers?'

'To be honest, I don't know yet.'

'I can find out for you. Give me his name as well.'

'Will do, sir. When can we see you?'

'Now,' he exclaimed, with a laugh in his voice. 'It's Friday afternoon. Do you imagine I'm going to keep a police investigation waiting over the weekend?'

'You're not going to ask for a court order?' I'd been expecting that he would; the Data Protection Act allows exceptions for police inquiries, but I knew from my CID days that most people like to cover their backs.

'No,' he replied firmly. 'In this bank, decisions

on the release of personal information are in the hands of a designated person, and that happens to be me. Give me those names now and get yourself along here; I assume you know where we are. By the time you get here I'll have accessed all the records.'

I did what he asked. 'Come on,' I said to Lowell Payne as soon as I'd hung up. 'We're dealing with someone who knows what 'urgent' means.'

The headquarters of First Caledonian Bank are located in a modest building in the big business park on the west of the city. Unlike the monster of which I'm still a customer, it doesn't trumpet its existence, or build bridges across a main road into the city, or run stupid television advertising for no obvious reason. I'd never been there before and I was so impressed by its simplicity that I made a mental note to talk to Cheryl about moving our family banking.

Graham Morton's office had a whiff of newness about it. He'd only been in post for a few weeks and I guessed that the place had been refurbished for his arrival. His desk was shiny, without a coffee ring in sight, and the carpet was thick and springy.

He was beaming as I introduced myself and my Glasgow sidekick. Morton struck me as a man who'd been re-energised by his new role. The word was that latterly in his career, Andy Martin, as his deputy, had been carrying him on his shoulders, and that his retirement notice had gone in on the same day that Andy was appointed to the Serious Crimes and Drug

Enforcement Agency. I made my second mental note within fifteen minutes. *Don't exceed your 'best before' date, David.*

The table in his room was strewn with papers. 'Everything's on computer these days,' he told us. 'I thought it would be easier if I printed these out.'

'How about Welsh, Mr Morton?' Lowell Payne asked.

'Not one of ours, I'm afraid.'

'Pity,' he grunted. 'That would have made it even easier for us.'

The former chief smiled. 'Too easy is bad for the soul,' he murmured as he offered us seats at the table. 'So,' he continued, 'tell me about Mr Varley. How bent do you think he is?'

I was happy to let Payne answer that. He was the seagull, you know, the guy who flies in, shits all over you and then flies away again, so he could deal with it with no issues of loyalty to the force, if not the man.

'We don't know,' he said, bluntly. He ran through the events that had led us to Morton's office. 'It may be there's no more to it than Varley digging a cousin out of an embarrassing situation,' he admitted, 'but it's the words Welsh used . . . 'weighed in' . . . that led the chief constable to set up our investigation. That and the fact that Varley's lied to his interviewers about even making the call. We're in no doubt that it was him, but he's accused Cowan.'

'Are you examining her bank transactions?' That was a bloody good question, and one that I could not leave to the visitor.

'No,' I answered. 'The investigators are satisfied that Varley did call Lafayette's.'

I was on slightly wobbly ground, and we both knew it. To an extent, Mario and Andy were taking Cowan's integrity on trust. If he'd still been in uniform, Morton might have pressed me further, but he didn't. Instead he just nodded, then waved a hand in the direction of the printouts on the table.

'There you are, gentlemen,' he declared. 'Current account statements for John and Ella Varley for the last three years. They have two; one seems to be reserved for household costs; mortgage, car loan, insurance, utility bills, council tax, dental plan all come off that, plus there's a credit card that's settled on it every month. It's one of our Mastercard products so I've been able to access that too. I can tell you that it's used for food and petrol, mostly. The household account is funded by monthly transfers from the other one. Both their salaries go into that . . . she's a civil servant, if you didn't know. Their personal spending is modest, and they manage to save regularly, making irregular transfers into a high-interest deposit account that we offer our customers.' He paused. 'As I said, I've called up three years. I can and will go back as far as you like, but I can tell you that in what's there, I don't see a trace of payments from any Mr Welsh, or anyone resembling him. All their income comes from employment.'

I didn't know whether to feel relieved or frustrated. I didn't want another cop to be crooked, but on the other hand I'd been given a task and I hoped that it was going to be wrapped up very quickly, to my satisfaction and, more important, to the chief's. From what Morton was saying, that wasn't going to happen.

There was something else: I had a gut feeling about Varley, and so had Lowell Payne, for we had compared our impressions on the drive to the First Caley office. We were sure he was wrong. If we found nothing there, as it seemed we hadn't, we were going to dig until there were no more holes left for us to make.

I looked at the Strathclyde seagull on my right and could tell that his thoughts mirrored mine. Then I looked back at Graham Morton, and I realised that he was smiling.

'That was the bad news,' he murmured, 'now the rest. In addition to this absolutely routine account portfolio, the Varleys are clients of another of the bank's departments. We don't shout about it, but we have an international division. It's based in the Isle of Man and it's home to an offshore account in the name of E. Varley.'

'E. Varley,' I repeated. 'As in Ella Varley? The inspector's wife?'

He nodded. 'The account details show the same address. It's been active for eight years and the current balance is one hundred and thirty-seven thousand pounds. It was set up with a deposit of fifteen grand, and similar amounts have been paid in there every year since.'

'Who by?' Payne asked, eagerly if ungrammatically.

'A corporate entity by the name of Holyhead

Enterprises SL. That's short for Societat Limitada.'

'Spanish?'

'Actually the language is Catalan; the company's registered in Andorra and the transfers are made from a bank there.'

It's not only great minds that think alike. So do those of opportunistic, cunning investigators presented with the possibility of foreign travel. I looked at Lowell, but he said it first.

'What's the handiest airport for Andorra?'

# Detective Sergeant
# Lisa McDermid

When George asked me his question, last thing on a Thursday afternoon, I seized the wrong end of the stick and grasped it hard. He'd asked me to come into his room at Dalkeith, and that was unusual. He's not the sort of man who keeps secrets within the office. Anything operational is always discussed openly; anything private is usually a telling off, quietly, because he isn't the sort of man who's given to raising his voice to junior colleagues.

No, I'd better qualify that: he isn't now. I have no idea what he was like before his son was murdered. Maybe he was your stereotypical twentieth-century macho male cop before that, like our celebrated chief constable, a man I avoid at all costs, because there's something ferociously arrogant about him that I just cannot stand. (By the way, I'd avoided him successfully for most of my career, since I've always been 'other ranks' material and unlikely to drift into his orbit, or even show up in the distance on his radar.)

Actually, I could have understood it if my boss had become a Skinner clone, if George junior's pathetic death had turned him into a shouting, quick-tempered, rage-filled bully, ready to take out his loss on anyone who crossed him, colleague or client.

But that's not him. He's a quiet respectful man, who seems to take pride only in his work and in his immaculate appearance. I cannot imagine George Regan ever slobbing around in a vest and jeans with a Sunday morning hangover, or ever being a month past his due date for a haircut. This may be fantasy on my part, but to me, it's as if he dresses to impress someone who isn't here any more.

So when quiet DI George invited me into his room after he came back from some away trip or other, with no hint of what he wanted to talk to me about, my mind sifted through the possibilities. There were only two that I could see, and I dismissed the first one out of hand. We're an excellent team, he and I, and we have a good record of success. There has been nothing of late that I've screwed up, nothing that I've done without his knowledge and approval; so I crossed off 'bollocking' on my short list.

That left personal. George rarely speaks of his home life, and I never ask, but I know that it isn't happy. There was one time, a few months ago, when I thought that he was working up to unburdening himself to me, and possibly angling to take it further than that. I headed him off, politely, and as gently as I could. My guess had been spot on, but he took it well, and I came to believe that it had strengthened our relationship rather than weakening it.

Still, as he closed the door behind him, that was all I could think of, and I decided to deal with it in the same way, full on.

'Things bad with Jen?' I asked.

His eyes widened, very slightly; then he sighed. 'It's the same old story, Lisa; same old story. She'll never get over it.'

'I'm sorry,' I said, 'sorry for you both. George, I wish there was something I could do to make your life better, but honestly, that wouldn't. If it's still preying on your mind, then please understand that it's not that I don't find you attractive, I just know that sleeping with me wouldn't make you any happier.' His mouth seemed to quiver, very slightly. 'Hey, don't get me wrong,' I added. 'I'm not saying I'm lousy in bed, and I'm sure you're great. It's how we'd be the morning after, not the night before.'

He grinned. I hadn't seen him smile as broadly as that in all the time I'd known him. 'I can only speak for myself, Lisa,' he chuckled, 'but I'm sure I'd feel fucking magic, for an hour or two at least. I'm just as sure it wouldn't bother Jen at all, not even if we filmed it and I showed her a video. But can we discuss that later,' he paused, 'because there's something work-related that I've got to ask you first. I'm being moved to a new job, and I've been given clearance to take you with me . . . if you want to come, that is.'

It takes a lot to make me blush but I did then; I even felt my chest go pink beneath my shirt. 'George, boss,' I spluttered. 'I'm sorry, I thought . . . '

'I know, and to be honest I'm flattered. I like you, lass, and I'd be lying if I said that the thought doesn't cross my mind any more,' he grinned again, 'but you're right in what you say, so I don't come to work every morning consumed by lust. Now . . . '

'Yes,' I said, grateful for the chance to move on. 'Your new job, what is it?'

'Special Branch.'

'Jesus,' I gasped. I had not expected that, not in a month of those Sunday morning hangovers. 'SB? And I can come with you?'

'Yup. Fancy it?'

I was ready to bite his hand off but I made myself consider some practicalities. 'Where's it based?' I asked him.

'HQ. Fettes building.'

That sounded good; I'd always wanted to work there, but never thought it would happen. But it did mean . . .

'What's the chain of command? Do you report to DCS McGuire?'

He shook his head, and his expression returned to the norm; serious. 'No. Direct to the chief constable.'

'I see,' I murmured.

He caught on. 'Look, Lisa, I know he scares you, but . . . '

'He doesn't scare me,' I retorted. 'I just don't like the man, that's all.'

'Well I promise, he's got nothing against you,' he replied, 'because he approved your transfer without question. Look, we don't have to like our colleagues. I could list a few that I can't stand. But we do have to respect the system that put them where they are and work within it . . . especially when they're the chief bloody constable. Anyway, you'll be reporting to me, not to him; I'll be your buffer.'

There's something reassuring about George; when he said that, I felt all right. 'When do we start?' I asked.

'Clear your desk,' he replied. 'Report there first thing in the morning.'

He wasn't kidding either; I said my goodbyes, with no mention of our destination and turned up at Fettes next morning as instructed. George's predecessor had gone . . . I didn't learn until a few days later that they'd done a straight swap . . . and I found myself at a desk facing an enormous Sikh DC called Tarvil Singh. He was being moved out too, but not until the following Monday, so he gave me a briefing on the practical work of the Branch and on what was hot and what was not.

Naturally, there was also the obligatory welcome by the chief constable, barely fifteen minutes after I'd arrived. To my surprise, he came to me. I must admit that he was very pleasant, very polite and very proper, no question of that, but I had a mental picture of arriving at an old-fashioned boarding school and being greeted by the smiling headmaster, knowing that the next time you saw him would be in his study and he'd be standing there with cane in hand, ready to leave stripes on your arse.

In this life there are some people to whom we will never take, and for me Bob Skinner is one of those. He reminds me of the Robert Duvall character, Colonel Kilgore, in that old seventies movie *Apocalypse Now*: I guess I must hate the smell of testosterone in the morning.

Once he was gone, I spent a couple of instructive hours with Tarvil . . . I really did take to him . . . before George, the boss once more, as if our strange cross-purposes discussion had never happened, called me into his new office and gave me my first real SB task.

He handed me a folder. 'That tells you all there is to know at the moment about a man called Freddy Welsh,' he said. 'I want you to find out everything else. There isn't very much there, just his business details, home address and that's all. What it certainly doesn't tell you is that Welsh is related by marriage to Inspector John Varley, who's just been charged with perverting the course of justice. Varley's niece is DC Alice Cowan, who used to work in this place.'

'I know that,' I told him. 'Alice is a friend of mine, from her days in East Lothian. She called me last night to tell me she was in the shit. Her boyfriend told her something and she passed it on to her uncle. He went and did something crazy and tipped off a guy involved. She's scared she'll lose her job.'

George frowned. 'It's gone beyond that. She resigned this morning. What did you say to her?'

'Apart from telling her that I think her uncle's an arsehole? I told her she should do what's best for her in the circumstances.'

'Do you feel compromised?'

I wasn't sure that I understood his question so I made him spell it out.

'Will your friendship with Alice make you less than objective in investigating Welsh?' he asked.

I was almost offended by that. 'No, why

should it?' I retorted. Then the penny dropped and I saw the wider picture. 'It was Welsh who was tipped off?'

'That's right.'

I shrugged. 'I'll be objective,' I promised, 'don't you worry. I'll also be well motivated.'

'Good. Now here's what I want you to do. First, run a check on Companies House for every company of which Freddy Welsh is a director. Find out who the other directors are; you never know, maybe Varley's name will be among them.'

'What's his business?' I asked. 'What does he do?'

He tapped the folder. 'That much is in there,' he said, 'from what Tarvil tells me. I haven't had time to read it. He's a builder, incorporated under the name Anglesey Construction PLC. I want you to access his company records, preferably without him knowing about it.'

'All of them? That might not be easy.'

'I know. It may be we'll have to go in with a full search warrant for his home and office premises, but our brief is to try and avoid that. His company will have auditors; they will have signed off on his annual accounts. Find out who they are and then go see them, armed with a court order to access information.'

'Won't it be difficult to get one?'

George winked at me. 'This is Special Branch, Sergeant; we deal with national security and organised crime. A sheriff will give you an order just for the asking.'

I was sceptical about that, but I shouldn't have

been. Just over two hours later, I was in the offices of an accountancy firm called Garland Pyke, facing a rather uncomfortable but sharp-suited thirty-something auditor across a designer desk that was so large that if I'd been a client I'd have demanded to know how much it cost before I signed a cheque to cover a fee note. I'd gone on my own; I could have taken Tarvil with me, but he's so large that I was worried he might have frightened the guy.

'I feel a little awkward about this,' Mr Magnus Garland admitted. 'Mr Welsh is a long-standing client, and his business is of great value to our firm. It could be very awkward for us if he found out about this.'

'In what way?' I challenged. 'You're not afraid of him, are you?'

He flinched, slightly. 'I wouldn't say that, Detective Sergeant, but he's certainly not a man I'd go out of my way to cross.'

'Don't worry about that,' I assured him. 'What we do is as confidential as it gets. This is one of those meetings that never took place. Now, can we get down to business? I've established that Mr Welsh is the controlling shareholder in a company called Anglesey Construction and that you're his auditors.'

'That's correct,' Garland acknowledged.

'That's his only business?'

'To the best of my knowledge.'

'And it's profitable?'

He nodded. 'Very. It's ridden out the recession well. The pre-tax profits have dropped, naturally enough, but the last full year figure was still in excess of two and a quarter million.'

'Where are the records kept?' I asked: a big question.

'The books for the current trading year are in Mr Welsh's office, as you'd expect; but everything that's been audited is stored here.'

That was exactly what I wanted to hear. 'How far back does it go?'

'By law a company must retain its records for seven years,' he explained, 'but Mr Welsh insists that everything about his company should be demonstrably above board, so everything's here, going all the way back to the formation of the company, what, fourteen years ago.'

'Have you been his accountant all that time?' He didn't look old enough.

'No,' Garland replied. 'Initially, my father handled his business, but he's . . . no longer in practice.'

'I can still speak to him, though?'

'He isn't in practice anywhere,' Garland said, laconically. 'I'm afraid he's dead. He passed away three years ago. I had to work hard to persuade Mr Welsh to let me keep his business. Sometimes I feel as if I'm still on probation with him, so you'll forgive me for being nervous about this.'

'I understand that,' I told him. 'Look, I might as well ask you straight out, when you sign off on the Anglesey accounts as true and accurate, are you always satisfied that they are?'

'Absolutely,' he insisted, a wee bit huffily. 'We're stringent in our interpretation of what's allowable and what isn't. HMRC can inspect a company at any time, and nobody wants to fall foul of those people. Mr Welsh's standing instruction is that when there is doubt over whether a particular piece of expenditure is allowable against tax, the benefit of it always goes to the Revenue. In other words, we don't take any chances. As a result, on the two occasions that the accounts have been inspected, they've passed with flying colours.'

'Was there any specific reason for those inspections?'

'No. They were purely routine, I'm sure of that.'

I pressed him a little. 'If there had been a motive for those checks, would you have known?'

He pursed his lips. 'Not necessarily,' he conceded, 'but I'm sure there wasn't.' He leaned forward, his elbows resting on the enormous desk. 'Look, I'm not naïve, Ms McDermid. I can work out why you're here. You suspect that Anglesey Construction PLC might have been used for the purposes of money-laundering.'

I didn't; I'd gone in there with an open mind, but I let him run with what he'd begun.

'Well,' he went on, 'I can disabuse you of any such notion. We've been scrupulous in examining the source of every payment made into and out of the company and you can take it that the firm's bankers have also. Even if we wanted to turn a blind eye to something, we couldn't; regulation and supervision are too tight these days. As for Mr Welsh's personal dealings, we supervise those too; one of my partners handles his tax return, and I can assure you that it's a true account of all his income.'

'What happens to the company profits?'

'Some are retained, some go into the pension funds of Mr and Mrs Welsh . . . I assume you know she's his co-director . . . and the rest they draw as dividend. It's paid into a personal bank account from which they pay any higher rate tax that might be due, calculated by this firm, as I've said, and agreed with HMRC. Clean as a whistle, I tell you, clean as a whistle.'

To my ear, he was a wee bit too insistent; he had the sound of a man who hadn't questioned his client in as much detail as he might have, and was hoping that the wool hadn't been pulled over his eyes.

'That's all very instructive, Mr Garland,' I told him. 'But it's not the main reason why I'm here. We've got a particular interest in any payments that might have been made to a Mr John Varley at any time.'

'Who's he?'

'You don't need to know that.'

'Is he a supplier? I've supervised the audit for a few years now, so I'm familiar with most of them. That name doesn't ring any bells. Give me a clue. Come on, I'm being frank with you.'

'No,' I said, 'I can't do that, not at this stage.'

He leaned back in his leather swivel chair, the kind that I'd love but can't afford. 'Have it your way, then,' he drawled. 'I might have been able to make it easier for you. As it is, you're going to have to go through the purchase ledgers and thirteen years of receipts. You can take it that my staff will have cross-checked one against the other, so that will save you a bit of time, but you

235

won't be able to finish them before we close, so I suggest you come back on Monday and do it then.'

I pushed the court order that I'd shown him earlier back across the desk, or rather, halfway across, because that was as far as I could reach. 'Read that,' I told him, 'and you'll see I'm authorised to remove all the records I need. I can do that, or you can leave someone here with me to lock up after I'm done. Your choice.'

'Oh really!' he moaned. 'I can't ask any of my people to do that.'

'Okay, I'll take them with me.'

'No, no.' He held up a hand, palm out, as if to resist. 'No,' he sighed, 'I'll wait with you. Not that it's going to do you any good,' he added. 'You won't find any payments to anyone called Varley in there.'

He was right, God damn him. I didn't.

# Bob Skinner

I was checking my watch, and wondering where young Haddock was, when Gerry stuck his head round the door to tell me that front desk security had called to warn him that a young guy had walked straight past them and was headed for my floor. He had barely finished before Sauce came into view behind him.

'You have to wait to be escorted up here,' I said, as he joined me.

'I'm sorry, sir,' he stammered. 'But it sounded urgent, so . . . '

'That's okay,' I laughed. 'I'm only repeating what my wife was told when she came here earlier on this week.'

'I did show him my warrant card,' the lad volunteered. 'Twice.'

'Once more than should have been necessary. I must do something about that outfit,' I muttered. 'Between you and me, lad, I don't like paramilitaries, and too many of these private security firms behave as if they are. Do you want a coffee?'

'Yes please, sir,' he replied.

I noticed that he was carrying a brown paper bag. 'What's in there?' I asked.

'Kosher cookies, sir. They're called rugelach. Solly pressed them on me; I couldn't refuse. Would you like some?'

'What's this? An apple for the teacher?' I

handed him a mug. 'Aye, why not? Let's have a taste.'

They weren't half bad; a lot of cream cheese about them, but okay. I let Sauce ingest some of the coffee. It had been on the warming stand for a while, so it must have been well stewed, but the boy took it without flinching.

'What was that you said when you were driving?' I asked him. 'What you got from your interview? It sounded like 'wrestler' to me. What was it really?'

'That's what I did say, sir. Solly, that's Mr Solomon, the restaurateur that I went to see, confirmed that Mortonhall Man did eat there, very shortly before he died, with two other guys. Solly said that one of them looked like a smaller version of Brock Lesnar. He's a . . . '

'I know who he is,' I said. 'My younger son is into that sort of stuff.' I wonder how many dads there are like me, people who would never dream of admitting that they watch TV wrestling themselves, and blame their knowledge on their kids. 'I doubt if we could circulate his picture, though.'

'No, sir,' he conceded, 'but there's a good chance I've got a set of the third man's prints.' He slipped an evidence bag from his jacket pocket and held it up. It contained two large banknotes. 'He paid with these.'

'Good work, Sauce,' I told him. 'Banknotes though,' I wondered, 'how many prints will they have on them?'

'Hopefully, not too many, sir. These are brand new. Solly's agreed to give us his fingerprints, for

238

elimination; I'll have to arrange that. I thought that if we circulated all that are left . . . '

I nodded. 'Yes, you're right, son. You will never know, unless you ask the question. Feed them all into NCIS and see what pops out. If your friend Solly doesn't have a record you can circulate his too, and no harm done, so forget about printing him.'

I could see something else in his eyes, the hesitancy of a young man who doesn't want to seem to be too pushy. 'Go on,' I said to him. 'Jack isn't here to take the piss. What else have you got?'

'Maybe nothing, sir, but if Solly's right we might need to go beyond the NCIS if we want to trace these men. He doesn't think they were British. He told me that they were speaking a foreign language among themselves, one he didn't recognise.'

'Could they have been Israelis?'

'No, sir, he said he'd have known their language and also the other two guys didn't have a clue about Jewish food.'

That did set my antennae twitching. But I wasn't about to tell young Haddock as much. One thing at a time with him, and that wasn't why I'd asked him to come to see me.

'Let's not fly too high,' I told him. 'You get those banknotes processed straight away up at the lab, priority job on my orders, and run what you get through NCIS. You should send me copies of all the prints through the force intranet, but on the quiet, to keep me in the loop without Becky thinking I'm looking over her

239

shoulder. Meantime,' I added, 'I've got some real undercover work for you.'

I thought I detected a tremor of excitement run through him, but maybe it was just the coffee. 'The tip that you brought me,' I continued, and knew right then that his reaction had nothing to do with caffeine, 'the one about Kenny Bass and his import venture, the one that opened this whole pit of mischief that Jock Varley's fallen into. You told me that your source insisted that you brought it to me and me alone, and that there wasn't to be a hint to anyone else in the force of where it had come from.'

I stared at him until he nodded.

'If that had been anyone but you, Sauce,' I murmured, 'I'd have melted you into fucking ingots. But I didn't; I went along with the whole presumptuous thing. As a result, only you and I know about this, as requested; nobody else, not the deputy chief, not the head of CID, just the two of us. I agreed because we both know who your source is, although you never named him: it's your girlfriend's grandfather.'

He opened his mouth, but I closed it for him. 'Shut up,' I said. 'You don't have to break any promises. I don't need you to say his name. I'm fine with the way it is. I bought into it because I reckoned that it was Grandpa McCullough's way of sending me a signal that he wasn't thinking at all of using your relationship with Cheeky to suborn you. But when one of the top figures in organised crime that this country has seen since Perry Holmes died co-operates with the police in any way, at any level, I have to treat it very warily.'

I took another kosher cookie from the bag and made him wait while I munched my way through it. When I was good and ready, I went on. 'I'm sure that when Grandpa told me, through you, that he'd heard on the grapevine that a wee crook from my patch called Kenny Bass was trying to make himself a big crook in the illegal tobacco business, he reckoned that I'd take it as some sort of peace offering. But with the intervention of Freddy Welsh it's become more than that. Welsh is a completely unknown quantity, a surprise player. Whatever his role is, he's caused chaos within this force. Therefore, I need to know . . . and that means that we,' I said, heavily, 'need to know, Sauce . . . whether Grandpa's playing some game or other. You're the conduit, or part of it, and so, even though it's way above your pay grade, it's down to you to find out. This is what I want you to do.'

# Lisa McDermid

It was well past eight by the time I got back to my flat in Haddington, and my evening was well and truly busted. I'd had a supper and possible shag date with a guy I'd been seeing for a couple of months, and I certainly wasn't up for the second without the first, so I'd called him earlier to cancel. I would have been happier if he'd sounded more disappointed.

I'd picked up a takeaway tandoori on the way home, and chose a nice Semillon blanc from the fridge to go with it, but when I looked at it on the plate I decided that I didn't really fancy it at all, so I binned it and settled for the wine and a bag of crisps.

Then I thought about George. He'd told me to check in with him in the morning, but I was restless, so I picked up the phone and dialled his number. The dead voice answered. I've never met Jen, but I've spoken to her a few times. She's always polite, and never asks me why I'm calling, but her tone still gets to me. That's because there isn't one, no intonation at all; she sounds as if she's medicated, but apparently that's not the case. I can't imagine what their home life must be like but I hope to God nothing like that ever happens to me. I have quite a few childbearing years ahead of me, and I can appreciate the horror of having one then losing it.

He took the call on an extension; I knew this

because there was television noise in the background when he picked up. 'Hi, Lise,' he murmured. 'You done?'

'Yes,' I told him. 'I got as far as I can go; the well's dry, trail's cold, whatever.' I looked at my glass; it was still half full, so I was nowhere near the limit. 'Fancy a drink?' I asked, taking myself completely by surprise. 'Business meeting,' I added.

'Nice idea,' he replied, 'but I've had a couple already, and I don't think you and me should meet in the Longniddry Inn. People who know me might wonder. So maybe we'd better not. Another time, yes?'

'Sure,' I said, wondering how likely that was.

'No links to Varley in Welsh's records then?' His voice changed, became more businesslike; I wondered if Jen had come into the room.

'Not a light. The auditor said the accounts were meticulous and he wasn't kidding.'

'Nothing at all out of the ordinary?'

'Nothing that I could see; trust me, boss, I spent long enough looking. The bookkeeping's flawless and every tax return is accepted. There are even a couple of over-payments, where the taxman's issued refunds without even being asked.'

'God, the man's a philanthropist,' he chuckled. 'Over-paying tax indeed.'

'What about Alice?' I asked him, changing the subject. 'Has she been interviewed?'

'Absolutely. High level too; by Mario McGuire and Andy Martin. The chief's accepted her resignation, by the way.'

'Ah, that's a bugger,' I sighed, but in truth it wasn't a huge surprise to me. I'd sensed things were heading that way. 'What about Griff Montell? He'll be okay, I suppose.' Don't let anyone tell you the police force isn't still male dominated.

I heard another soft laugh at the other end of the line. 'There'll be a note on his record, and he'll be taken out of the limelight for a while.'

'What the hell does that mean?'

'You're going to love this,' George chuckled. 'He's replacing Tarvil. The chief told me, just as I was leaving tonight.'

'Jesus.' I'd never worked with the guy, but I'd met him, through Alice. I wasn't sure about him; he struck me as another testosterone-fuelled type, like Skinner, maybe even higher octane, being twenty years younger and a bloody Springbok into the bargain. 'When does he start?'

'As soon as he can be replaced in Leith; might even be Monday.'

'Mmm,' I muttered, not trying to hide my cynicism, letting him make what he would of that. 'Listen,' I went on, 'the bigwigs' interview with Alice: what did it cover?'

'Not much; she gave them a written statement along with her resignation. Why?'

'I'm wondering if I should talk to her, that's all, about Varley and Welsh.'

'On or off the record?'

It was my turn to laugh. 'I thought everything we did was off the record, boss.'

'True,' he conceded. 'Okay, do it, but there's

244

one thing you might not know. There's history between Alice and Freddy Welsh.'

'As in sexual history?' I asked

'Just so. She owned up to it at interview. Years ago and a one-off, she says, but it's best if you're aware of it when you speak to her. Have a good evening.'

'Thanks, you too.' As if, poor sod; his good evening would only involve another couple of drinks. 'I'll let you know how I get on.'

I finished mine, refilled my glass and dialled Alice's mobile number. 'Yes?' she answered on the third ring, cautiously.

'It's me,' I said, 'Lisa. Didn't your phone tell you?'

'No, it came up as 'Private number' that's all.'

'I see. Maybe something to do with my new job,' I surmised.

'Your . . . ' She stopped. Having worked there herself, she knew the form. 'Probably, if I read you right. When did that happen?'

'This has been my first day in the office.'

'Lucky you. No more of those for me. You'll have heard, I take it.'

'Only just. I'm sorry, Alice.'

'Me too,' she sighed, 'but I fucked up big time, so I'm blaming nobody.'

'Not even the Springbok?'

She hesitated. 'No,' she murmured, eventually, then added, 'It would be nice if the sod would stop blanking me, though.'

'If he does that, he's not worth the grief. He's come through it all right. Same old story,' I snapped, 'the boys always stick together.'

'Hey, you'd be best to keep your feminist tendencies under wraps where you are now,' she warned. 'Shannon's one of the boys herself; God knows, she's test-driven enough of them in her time. Including your ex-gaffer, from what I hear.'

'George?' I exclaimed. 'You're kidding.'

'Nope. It wasn't recent, though, long before . . . '

'Well, there's a surprise. And here's one for you; he's still my gaffer. I've just finished speaking to him, in fact. I asked his permission to call you.'

'All change, eh,' she chuckled softly. 'But you don't need his okay, surely. Am I really as non grata as that?'

'Not at all,' I told her. 'It's what I want to ask you that I thought I should clear. I'm looking into possible historic links between your uncle and the guy he called in the pub the other night.'

'A call,' Alice boomed, angrily, 'that the son-of-a-bitch tried to claim I made, incidentally.'

'Don't worry,' I assured her, 'nobody's buying that.'

'I should think not.' She paused. 'Lisa, I suppose you know about the other guy and me.'

'I've been told,' I admitted.

'And were you told what my shit of an uncle said when he was interviewed? That he'd spied on us when it happened.'

'No, that's news to me.'

'That's what he said, apparently; in fairly graphic terms too. Mr Martin called me to warn me that he'd been bailed. He said I'm to report any approach he makes to me, and he also filled me in on what he'd claimed, about me making the call, and why. Hell, Lisa, my dear uncle will be bloody lucky if I don't approach him, armed to the teeth!'

'Alice,' I said, 'I have to ask you this. You're clear that there's been nothing between you and this man since?'

'Absolutely. I was drunk, he could barely get it up, plus he had BO, so it was an experience I regretted as soon as I'd sobered up. You know the kind, I'm sure.'

I could have lied and told her that I didn't; instead, I let it pass. 'Is there anything you can tell me about his relationship with your uncle, anything I don't know?'

'Other than just family?'

'Yes.'

'I wish I could. I wish I could give you a nice big juicy secret that would lead to the sods being banged up for five years, but there isn't. There is no relationship between the two of them that I know of, other than him being my aunt's cousin. Nothing professional, apart from the conservatory of course, and that was Jock and Aunt Ella giving him business.'

'Say that again,' I asked. 'What conservatory?'

'The one they had built on their house in Livingston. It's a full-scale extension really, but that's what Aunt Ella calls it. Bloody huge thing it is, not your bog standard double-glazing job. His company built it for them.'

'It did? When?'

'Can't say for sure; five, six, seven years ago.'

'Alice,' I said, 'I've just been all over the

records of Anglesey Construction, from its very beginning. There's no mention of any job with your uncle's name on it. I will double-check with his auditor, but I'm bloody sure of it.'

# Bob Skinner

I wasn't planning on rushing back to Gullane that night, for reasons that were both personal and domestic. I knew the kids would be back home, so I called them and had a chat with each of them. They'd had a good week with their mother, and didn't sound as if they were missing America one bit, although Mark took me by surprise by asking if he could have a mobile phone. He's a responsible kid and he's never given me a moment's trouble since he came into our family, so I said that he could, subject to Sarah's agreement, yet when I hung up the phone I was left with an inexplicable notion that, somehow, I'd been stitched up.

I was pondering this when my personal mobile sounded: as you'd expect, I have two, police and private. I checked the screen and saw that it was Aileen calling. I thought about letting it go to voicemail, but I couldn't let myself be that petty, so I picked up.

'Hi,' I said, quietly, ready to signal a truce.

'How are you?' she asked; something in her voice told me that she wasn't.

'Busy,' I replied.

'Me too. Listen, Bob, I've been thinking. I have some constituency stuff to take care of in Glasgow tomorrow. Rather than have you glowering at me across the table before you disappear off to the pub for your Friday swill, I'll go through there tonight and stay in the flat. Okay?'

Enough of being conciliatory. 'Would it matter a toss if I said it wasn't?' I snapped. 'You suit yourself, dear: as usual.' I hit the red button to end the conversation.

I sat there for a couple of minutes, wondering how something could go so wrong so quickly. I could have made it right with one phone call. All it would have taken was for me to hit the return button and say, 'Aileen, you're right and I'm wrong. Your crowd are the policy makers and I'm the public servant. I'll keep my mouth shut from now on and let you get on with your job.'

Why not? Why didn't I do that? After all, and you can trust me on this, I knew that I had no chance of winning the war I'd declared. I have power, sure, but not Clive Graham's kind, not Aileen's kind. Yes, I could have faced the facts, accepted the inevitable and tried to live with it.

And lived with myself at the same time? Not a chance, because I believed then, as I believe now, that what they were planning to do was not in the best interests of the people that I was appointed to serve. Not a chance, because a man can't preach about values and principles to his children when he's abandoned his own.

'Bugger!' I growled, then turned to my computer, opened a new document and started to type, to draft the letter of resignation that I would submit on the day that the unification legislation was passed.

I was still considering whether to begin 'It is with great regret . . . ' when my personal mobile

250

trilled again, on my desk beside the keyboard. I assumed it was the bell for round two. I'd have stayed in my corner had I not glanced at the readout. Wrong wife.

'Hello, Sarah,' I answered.

'You sound beat,' she said.

'Do I? I'm sorry. Tough twenty-four hours, and I'm still in the office. I shouldn't let it get under my skin.'

'Trouble in Harmony Row? Or am I not allowed to ask?'

'You are very definitely not,' I warned her. 'What's up anyway?'

'Nothing specific. I was worried about you, that's all.'

'Why, for heaven's sake?' I exclaimed.

'I dunno. Last night at the crime scene, you didn't seem yourself.'

'How do you know what my self is any more?'

'Hey,' she protested, 'how many years were we married?'

'More than enough,' I chuckled.

She sniggered too. 'Probably, but in the time we were you don't think I got to know you? I can tell when you're not focused and last night you weren't. You're okay, aren't you, physically? Your pacemaker hasn't been playing up, has it?'

'What pacemaker? I barely remember that it's there. I have my annual check-up and each year they tell me that the battery's going to last a little longer than they expected.'

'That's a good sign,' she said. 'It means your heartbeat needs very little regulation.'

'You wouldn't say that if you'd heard it . . . ' I

stopped, but by then I'd said too much.

'I see. I won't pry, honest. Actually there was a work reason for me calling you. I wondered if you had any feedback from the autopsy on our client from last night.'

'Yes,' I replied. 'I'm completely up to speed. I don't just know what he had for dinner, I know where he had it. I know also that he was with two other men, and I'm assuming that when he died they were the ones who buried him and called us.'

'Hey,' Sarah exclaimed, 'young Sauce is on the ball, isn't he?'

'More than you know,' I told her. 'Things happen to Sauce. He's a magnet for them.'

'You should be careful. You sound paternal when you talk about him; if you let other people in the force hear that tone they'll get to resent him pretty quickly.'

She had a point. That woman always could read me like a Kindle. 'I'm aware of it,' I said. 'But the people he works with rate him just as highly as I do. He's about to be promoted, on his DI's recommendation, but he doesn't know yet.'

'Thank God you'll be retired,' she murmured, 'by the time our kids are old enough to join the force.'

'As they will over my ancient body!' I retorted. 'Speaking of our kids, Mark's just asked me if he can have a mobile. I didn't think he was interested in one, but it's okay with me if you're onside.'

I heard a gasp. 'The cunning little . . . ' she exclaimed. 'Mark isn't interested, not really; he's

252

been played by his brother. Jazz nagged me about that very thing this afternoon. I told him no way was he having one before Mark, and that I would talk to you about it.'

I had to laugh at that one. 'What a player! Hey, maybe I should encourage him to be a cop after all. If he's as manipulative as that now . . . I may have to head him off from being a politician.'

Fortunately, Sarah didn't latch on to that one. Instead, after a few seconds' silence, she asked, 'Are you really still at work?'

'Yup, 'fraid so. I'm waiting for a couple of things, then I have to make a call. No rush, though. Aileen's going to Glasgow and Trish is looking after the kids.'

'In that case,' she hesitated, then . . . I could almost hear the splash as she took the plunge, 'would you like to eat with me?'

'Are you kidding?' I exclaimed.

'No, I'm not. We have matters of common interest, three of them. Surely it's not unreasonable for us to meet to talk about their future.'

'When you put it that way, no it isn't.' I stretched in my chair, feeling, all of a sudden, as tired as Sarah had claimed I sounded. 'Ah, what the hell! Where? Nowhere too crowded.'

'Everywhere's crowded on a Friday night, Bob. Come to my place. I'll burn you a steak . . . '

I smiled, and finished the quote for her. ' . . . and smother it in onions.'

She'd taken that line from an old Paul Newman movie she'd seen as a kid, and made it

253

real many times when we were together. Sarah can burn a steak to perfection, and as for the onions . . .

'Okay, I'm sold,' I said. 'I'll bring a bottle of something decent, but you'll have to drink it.'

'Not me, hon. I don't partake these days.'

'Eh?' How many surprises in one day? Sarah loved fine wine.

'It's too easy for a single woman to sit at home and sink a bottle a night,' she explained. 'I've looked at too many diseased livers to want anyone looking at mine one day and wincing. But I do like Vichy Catalan, that mineral we used to drink in Spain, if you can find any of that.'

'Okay, I'll try to be with you by eight,' I promised. 'But don't cook anything till I call to tell you I'm on the way.'

'As if I would!'

She hung up and I turned back to my computer. I aborted my draft letter to be resumed at a later date, then opened my intranet mail box. Young Sauce had moved fast. The images and the report he had attached told me that the banknotes had been dusted and had yielded only eight prints in total, but four of them were common to each note. There was a thumb in the corner, index finger in the centre, same side, where someone might leave them when peeling them from a roll, and two others, fainter, one on the front of the fifties and the other on the back. Sauce guessed that these might have been Solomon's as he took the money from his customer.

The lad had been smart enough to have the

notes scanned, and sent four images, with the serial numbers showing clearly. 'Good boy,' I murmured, then reached for the phone, not a mobile, but a secure line on my desk.

It's good to have friends, but it's great when they have influence. I've known Amanda Dennis professionally for years, and whenever I'm in London I try to meet her socially as well. She's one of those people who keep a low profile. Indeed there was a time not so long ago when she didn't even exist, officially. Her business is national security, and on occasion it overlaps with mine. She's the deputy director of MI5, although there was a period when she ran the whole damn show, on an acting basis.

'Bob,' she said, 'this is a surprise. Does it mean you're coming to the capital?'

'Hey,' I laughed. 'I'm in the capital.'

'Oh, you bloody Scots. You know what I mean.'

'Yes, but I don't have a trip south in my diary at the moment. There's something I want to run past you, to see if you can help. I've got an odd situation in Edinburgh and it's getting odder by the minute.'

I ran through the story from the beginning, from the anonymous call and the discovery of the body, though to Haddock's trip to Glasgow and what he had found there.

'You can't help it, can you?' she murmured, when I was finished. 'You're a chief constable, supposed to be a pen-pusher, yet here you are on a Friday evening, up to your elbows in an investigation when you should be in your club with your cronies. Does the phrase 'get a life' mean anything to you?'

'You can talk, woman,' I grunted. 'Do you actually have a home, or do you have a room in that building?'

'I have a very nice flat,' she replied, but I'd known that all along.

'Sure, in Dolphin Square. You could throw a tennis ball from your office window and it would hit it without a bounce.'

She sighed. 'Maybe, but you know how it is. The bastards who are trying to get us don't work office hours; for example, there's live intelligence about a plot to assassinate a leading British political figure. Whitehall's on a virtual lockdown because of it. Even without that, the threat level's constantly high these days. From both sides,' she added, 'theirs and our own. Ever since we became a more open book, as it were, we've been under more political scrutiny. You know what those chaps are like; Commons committees are stacked with ambitious people looking for a cause that's going to generate headlines for them, and bashing the security service has become very popular.'

'Tell me about it,' I murmured.

'Oh, do you have problems too?'

'Do I ever.' I paused. 'Amanda, between you and me, what do you know of Toni Field?'

'Enough to know that I never want to work for her,' she said, firmly.

'You're career Five, chum, going nowhere else; there's no chance of that.'

'To the first, yes, I agree. To the second, don't

be so confident. That woman's ambitions know no boundaries. She cultivates the powerful everywhere she goes. Doesn't matter who or what they are. She's the poster girl in the Met at the moment . . . the Mayor of London thinks she's wonderful . . . plus she has contacts deep into the Home Office and Justice Ministry, at political and civil servant level. She sees herself running this place one day; the way she operates makes me certain of that. The present Home Secretary hates her, thank God, but nobody stays in that office for long. When I heard she'd got the Strathclyde job, I knew there would be trouble between you two, I just knew it.'

She was so insistent that I had to chuckle. 'Fact is,' I said, 'I have bigger problems than her, but to hell with it, I've had enough of them for today. Amanda, I've got some fingerprints, and an image of the dead man. We're running them through conventional databases, naturally, but I wondered if you'd be prepared to do some wider checks for me, within your community. The fact that these guys seem to be foreign . . . '

'I agree. They could just be a trio of tourists, but . . . To dispose of a body like that? Worth a check.'

'And it might be worth checking with your Glasgow office, too,' I suggested, 'to see if there have been any undercurrents there. The three men ate in Glasgow; the guy died very soon afterwards, and yet his friends buried his body in Edinburgh and then pointed us at it. Why would they do that? They must have known we'd be chasing our tails in the aftermath, so was that deliberate? Create a mystery in Edinburgh, focus attention there. Smokescreen?'

'Yes,' she agreed. 'I'm not aware of anything specific in Scotland but I'll ask. Send me the image and the prints and I'll have people work on them, straight away.'

# Lowell Payne

I hadn't really fancied a trip to Andorra. I went there on a skiing holiday with Jean in the first year of our marriage, before our daughter was born: I didn't like it. The country looks as if God landscaped the Pyrenees with an axe when he was making the world. It's a drab, claustrophobic canyon of a place. Our travel agent fed us a line about how cheap the shops were. Crap! When we got there we found that for most things they were cheaper than Harrods, but nowhere else. An ex-pat resident told me there were bargains to be had in diving equipment . . . in a ski resort: work that one out . . . and in firearms, but we were in the market for neither.

As it turned out, one phone call was all Mackenzie and I needed to make progress with our investigation. A quick online check told us that while there's an honorary consul in the mountain state, he operates under the supervision of the British consulate in Barcelona. I called there, and was put through to the Andorran expert, a lady called Betty Ireland.

'How can I help the police?' she asked, sounding as if she was genuinely pleased to have a chance to do so.

'I want to find out all there is to know about a company called Holyhead SA,' I told her. 'It's come up in an investigation. Can you give me some pointers?'

'A criminal investigation?'

'Potentially,' I conceded. 'We're interested in some payments that have been made and Holyhead's the source.'

'I can make enquiries. Do you know anything about it at all?'

'We believe it may be owned by a man called Welsh.'

'Is he a resident of Andorra?'

'No, he's Scottish. Lives in Edinburgh. Does that make a difference?'

'Not necessarily, but you may find that the gentleman isn't the owner of record. In the past that would have had to be a citizen, but the law is changing, to encourage foreign investment and to encourage the setting up of holding companies there.' She paused, then switched into full lecture mode. 'Andorra isn't your classic offshore tax haven, you understand. It doesn't have the sort of regime that attracts financial institutions, nor is it the sort of place where you'd set up an offshore trust.'

'So what's the attraction?'

'Income tax: there isn't any. The taxation is all indirect.'

'I see.' *Wouldn't be enough for me*, I thought. *They'd have to pay me to live there.* 'Can you give me any pointers,' I asked, 'on how to investigate this company?'

'How urgent is it?'

I grinned. 'We're the police, Ms Ireland. Everything's urgent.'

'In that case I'll speak to my contacts and get back to you as soon as I can. I'm sure you won't mind giving me your main switchboard number, so that I know you really are the police.'

'Sounds reasonable to me,' I said. 'Time frame?'

'With luck, tomorrow morning; I'm assuming that you're on weekend duty.'

'We are on this one. Thanks.'

# 'Sauce' Haddock

Cheeky and I don't live together, you understand. We each have our own place, and don't plan on moving in together until we're sure that the time is right . . . and yes, I'll admit it, when I feel one hundred per cent sure of her. At the moment we tend to get together at weekends rather than during the working week. We're pretty conservative in what we do, given that we're both still only twenty-something: we'll go out for a meal at least once, do a movie at one of the multiplexes. If the weather's nice we might go for a drive on a Saturday or Sunday, usually as far away from Edinburgh as we can get, and if we're feeling flush, stay over in a hotel.

We'd been talking about going to Loch Lomond on the Saturday in question, and maybe beyond, up towards Oban. There are all sorts of wee bed and breakfast places up that way, and we thought we might try one of them. The chief had buggered that plan up, well and truly.

He'd put me in something of an awkward position as well. As I've said, I've built Chinese walls into our relationship, to keep Cheeky and my work well apart. Her having given me her grandpa's tip was one thing; it didn't break any of my self-drafted rules. But me, involving her in my work, that did.

But what was I going to do when the boss asked me? Refuse? Tell him politely to go and fuck himself? Bob Skinner? Are you kidding? I might be self-confident, but I'm not suicidal. No, I'd said, 'Yes, sir, how many bags would you like me to fill, sir?' and a few hours later I was sitting in Petit Paris in the Grassmarket . . . we'd decided to stay at my flat that night . . . feeling decidedly shifty, and I am certain looking it as well.

Some nights, I'll look at Cheeky and I'll say to myself, 'You know, Sauce, you're crazy.' My favourite band is Del Amitri, and of all their songs, my all-time number one is called 'Be my downfall'. Every time I hear it I think it could have been written about me, and often I find myself singing it in my head, sounding remarkably like Justin Currie in the process.

She could have been my downfall, and no mistake. Her grandfather is from the Dark Side, so dark that when the local villains in Dundee mention Darth Vader, they ain't talking about the black sheep of the Skywalker family, or Sammy Pye's secret father as a CID in-joke has it. She and I got together for all the wrong reasons, lust on my part, the fact that I'm a cop on hers. She kept her background from me and when she walked out the door one time, she might have been carrying the corpse of my career on her shield.

But she came back, remorseful, and when she did, I found that I couldn't slam that door in her face. I've told her that if she ever lies to me again, that'll be it, we'll be finished. I was so firm about that, I almost believed it myself. The truth is that she has a hold over me. I love her. She says she feels the same about me, and I do believe that. We don't discuss the future, we don't think about it. We have what we have and that's cool.

She's the spawn of one of those families from hell, product of a relationship between the jailbait teenager that became her mum and a guy who really should have known better and is probably now part of the foundations of a choice property on Tayside. Her grandfather has been in the dock, in a situation where the wrong outcome would have seen him in jail for most of the rest of his life. He isn't, because when it came down to it his resources were greater than those of the hapless cops who tried to put him away, and indeed because his assets included a couple of their colleagues.

Grandpa McCullough is retired from all that now. He's a legitimate businessman whose interests are property and leisure. That's what he says, and I tend to accept it as fact, because since Andy Martin became head of the Serious Crimes Agency, every time Grandpa takes a shit, that organisation is likely to know about it.

However, straight or not, I have nothing to do with him. That is a given between Cheeky and me. I will never go home to Dundee with her and I will never meet him . . . unless on some inconceivable occasion in the future I go to arrest him. That's the one thing that the chief made me promise when I told him that if I was forced to choose between her and the job, she would win.

And that's why, when Cheeky came to me one

night and told me that her grandfather had given her a message that he wanted me to pass on privately to Mr Skinner, I was more than a little doubtful.

'What the hell's this about, love?' I asked her. 'What's he up to? What's in it for him?'

'I wanted to know those same three things myself,' she told me. 'He says that it's something he heard from a guy in his health club, somebody who doesn't know he's out of the life and thought he'd be interested. He says that it's a gesture of goodwill . . . his words . . . but that he doesn't want anyone to know the source. He doesn't even want you to mention his name to Mr Skinner, but to let him figure it out for himself.'

'Jesus, Cheeky,' I protested. 'I can't do that. If I get a tip I'm supposed to take it to Jack McGurk, or DI Stallings. The head of CID would fry my balls and eat them if I went over their heads, and his.'

'I told him that too. He said that you're only a sprog detective and that if you went through the usual channels they'd insist that you told them where the tip came from. He says that he can't be seen to be an informant, and he only trusts Skinner to keep the secret.'

'I don't know,' I muttered, doubtfully. 'What do you think?'

'I think nothing. I'm an unwilling messenger girl, Sauce, that's all. Of course you could always forget it. There would be no comeback.'

But I couldn't forget it, could I, because I'm a cop, and I'd been given information about a possible crime. I could have gone by the book, indeed I almost did. It wasn't Grandpa's reputation that stopped me, it was Cheeky; I was taking enough flak about her from Jack as it was and I didn't want him knowing about her involvement.

So I plucked up the courage, I called Gerry Crossley, and I asked to see the chief. He asked me why, but all I said was that it was for Mr Skinner's ears only, and very confidential. I had visions of being back in uniform next morning, but that didn't happen. The boss said he'd see me when I'd finished my shift.

When I told him my story, he sat stone-faced all the way through it, and for a couple of minutes after. 'Let me get my head round this,' he said, as the sweat began to trickle down the back of my neck. 'Your mystery informant wants me to take all this on trust, and commit police time to an operation that might be a complete fucking smokescreen for something else. That's how it is?'

'Yes, sir,' I replied. 'But I don't believe it is. If it was a con, the information wouldn't have come to me in the way it did.'

He frowned. 'Luckily for you, son, I don't believe that either. I'll pass your tip on to Mr McGuire myself, and I'll tell him to put DI Stallings' team on the investigation. Nobody will ask me to name my source. But I warn you,' he growled, giving me a look that scared me, 'if this goes pear-shaped, your girlfriend will be in big, big trouble, and that will just be for starters.'

And so the operation started, with my fingers

266

tightly crossed that it would all be plain sailing, that we would all have a nice arrest on our records and a shed-load of potentially toxic ciggies would be taken out of circulation. It nearly worked out that way too, until the complication of Freddy bloody Welsh popped up.

'The weather forecast's nice for tomorrow and Sunday,' Cheeky said, breaking a bread stick in half. 'When do you want to start off?'

'Ah well,' I murmured. 'We might have to change that plan. How do you fancy St Andrews instead?'

'St Andrews?' she repeated. 'In July? God no. The place will be crawling with caravaners and golfers. We wouldn't be able to move. No, I want to go west. What brought that on anyway? I thought you did too.'

'I did. I do, but . . . ' I paused. 'Remember that message you gave me the other night?'

'Of course. How could I not? Why? Did something come of it?'

I'd said nothing, as usual, and she hadn't asked, as usual. 'Did it ever,' I told her. 'We followed it up and a large bucket of shite hit a very big fan, in a way that nobody expected.'

I must have been looking even more mournful than usual, for her eyes creased and her smile appeared, the one that turns me into very spreadable butter. 'And you've got to clean it up?' she chuckled.

'Not exactly,' I replied. 'You have.'

The laugh lines vanished in an instant. 'Me?'

'Only if you agree,' I said, quickly and firmly, finding some of the balls that I'd been missing in the chief constable's room. 'If you don't want to do this, you only have to say so, and it will not happen. I'll understand and I won't say another word about it. That's a promise.'

'Then you'd better tell me what it is.'

'I've got a message for you,' I replied. 'From my boss; my Big Boss. He wants you to go back to your grandpa and ask him some questions.'

'Such as?' She seemed anxious, and for some reason that pleased me, made me happy that if there had been a set-up she hadn't been in on it.

'I need to know whether when he gave me that tip about Kenny Bass, he knew of the involvement of a man called Freddy Welsh. I need to know whether he knows Welsh himself, and even if he doesn't, I need him to tell me everything he knows about him. Can you tell him that?'

I chose not to add the chief's parting words: 'Make sure she tells him that if he holds back on this, I'll come up to Dundee myself and knock his fucking door down.'

She nodded. 'Yes, I'll do it,' she said. 'How soon?'

'As soon as possible.'

'So that's why Oban's scrapped?'

I nodded.

'Then maybe we can rescue it. We can drive up there first thing in the morning. I'll drop you somewhere or other while I go and see him. Then I'll come back and we'll head off from there. It can be just as quick as going from Edinburgh.' She looked me in the eye. 'That's the deal.'

I nodded. 'That's okay by me. If he's got anything to tell you that can't wait, I can pass it on to the chief over the phone.'

'From Oban?'

I laughed. 'From Oban, if that's how you want it.'

She smiled at me once again, any worry gone from those sensational eyes. 'We'd better skip the nightclub after dinner,' she said. 'We'll have an early start. We should turn in.'

I grinned back at her. 'See you,' I murmured, 'you'll be my downfall.'

# Andy Martin

'I'm worried about my dad.'

In the fifteen years or so I've known Alex, she's never said anything to me that's surprised me more than that. They've had occasional differences, the pair of them, but she has never displayed anything other than a total belief in him, and an inbuilt certainty that whatever happens he will come through, that whatever obstacles are put in his way he will prevail. She has reason to feel that way, for she's had some dark times herself, one very dark, when she was kidnapped. He was there, with a metaphorically flaming sword in hand, to lay her abductors low and pluck her from danger. If it wasn't for him, she'd be an atheist: she worships him, and him alone.

So, when she said that, it was as if a temple lay in ruins, in some unseen place.

We were sitting on what the builder described as a balcony in my house beside the Water of Leith. I suppose that's a fair description; it's big enough for two people and a very small table, it's angled to provide privacy, and when the weather's okay, it's a very pleasant place to sit, taking in the evening sun and listening to the river flow by, as we were. There's woodland on the other side; another plus point in that it means the neighbours opposite have feathers rather than annoying personal habits.

I could have sold the place when I landed the Tayside deputy chief job and Karen and I moved to Perth, but the market wasn't great at the time and the rental income was way in excess of the mortgage overhead, so I hung on to it, maybe with half an eye on the possibility that I might move back to the Edinburgh force one day as Bob's number two, a role that I'd filled, officially and otherwise, for much of my career.

I put my beer on the table. These days I tend to drink Mexican, complete with wedge of lime or lemon. If I still hung around the rugby club, they'd call me a poser, or something worse, but my laddish days are long behind me.

'Run that past me again,' I said, quietly.

'I mean it, Andy.' She turned her head and looked at me, displaying that deep chasm that appears between her eyebrows when she frowns. 'I'm worried about him, seriously. I'd hoped that finally, all the pieces in his complicated world were in place and that he could look as far down the road as his contract as chief constable extends, and then beyond, to nice happy years getting older and watching another generation of kids grow up. I'd made myself believe that Aileen was the right woman for him. Politicians seem to have a short shelf life these days, so I'd assumed that when hers came to an end she'd be there alongside him. I certainly didn't expect her to put herself on a collision course with him.'

I peered at her through my glasses . . . I don't wear my contacts around the house any more . . . and made my 'What the hell are you talking about?' face.

'You mean he hasn't told you?' she exclaimed, her voice rising. 'I was sure he would have.'

I put a finger to my lips; my neighbours and I don't overlook each other but they're not that far away. 'Told me what?'

'You know this talk of police unification?' she asked, more quietly.

'Of course I do. We discussed it at ACPOS yesterday, and voted against it.'

'It looks as if you were wasting your time. The government's determined to force it through before the next election, to take it out of the political arena, so they say, and my dear stepmother's party is backing them.'

I picked my beer up, and killed it, then went to the kitchen for another couple to give myself some thinking time. The first half of Alex's revelation hadn't surprised me, given the choice of venue for our meeting and given the evangelistic support for the idea that we'd seen from what Bob and I had taken to calling the Toni Field Tendency; but the second part had.

'Labour's going to line up with the Nats on this?' I said as I handed her a fresh Corona.

'Yes, and Aileen wants Dad to back off from public opposition to the bill when it's published. He's told her he'll resign if a single Scottish force is created, but that doesn't seem to make any difference to her.'

'Do you think he would?'

She shot me a 'silly boy' smile. 'Andy,' she murmured.

Yes, rhetorical; of course he would.

'Do you know,' she continued, 'Aileen actually

had the nerve to call me today. The woman was working up to asking me to try to talk him round . . . '

I put my hand over my eyes. 'Oh dear,' I murmured, for I knew what was coming.

'Exactly!' she hissed. 'I didn't let her get that far. I told her what I thought of her. I blew up at her, I'm afraid. Honestly, I never thought that would happen with Aileen and me. Now it has, and I don't know whether there's any way back from it.'

I reached across and tugged her hair, gently. 'Hey,' I said, 'there's always a way back. Look at you and me.'

'One marriage and two kids later?' she muttered. I must have winced, for she bit her lip and exclaimed, 'Oh I'm sorry, love, I didn't mean that.'

'It's true, though.'

'On the face of it, but it's not the same; we're not going back to where we were. Whatever the rest of the world believes, I didn't break up your marriage, not by myself. No, the thing about Aileen, she seems to want unconditional love, yet she applies conditions to her own. I didn't expect that of her. I don't think I can ever respect her again.'

'But isn't Bob the same?' I asked her.

'No.' She didn't take a second to consider the question. 'You're sat beside living proof of that. I've done some silly things in my life, but never once has he wavered in his love for me. And even you; the two of you have had your differences over the years, your fallings out over me, yet he's always seen you as the brother he should have had rather than the one he did.'

'Surely there's a solution, though, for him and Aileen?'

She pressed the cold beer to her forehead for a second or two. 'You mean like parking their differences in the street outside?'

I nodded. 'Something like that.'

'I don't know about Aileen, not for certain, although present evidence says 'no'. But as far as he's concerned . . . ' She hesitated.

'Andy,' she continued, slowly, 'I barely remember my mum, that's how young I was when she died in that accident, but I can tell you this. If she'd told him to swim the ten, fifteen miles, whatever it is, across the Forth from Gullane to Anstruther for fish and chips and bring them back, he'd have done it with boots on. They'd have been a bit soggy, but they'd have been as good as on the table. And for all that she wasn't perfect, Mum would have done the same for him. If they'd faced a fundamental issue like this, they'd have realised that they, together, were far more important than it was and they'd simply have left it for others to sort out.'

'Couldn't he and Aileen do that?' I ventured.

'Put it this way. If she asked Dad to swim to Anstruther, his trunks would never be wet. If he asked her to walk to the Gullane chippie and bring back a couple of suppers, she'd probably phone for home delivery. And that's why I'm worried about him, Andy. I'm afraid that things between the two of them are past fixing, and I

274

don't know that he could stand another broken marriage.'

'And what about Aileen?'

'She'll survive.' There was a bitter tone to her voice that wasn't very pretty.

'Don't be like that, Alex,' I told her. 'Bob's been ghost-hunting for as long as I've known him, even though it's futile. It isn't Aileen's fault that she's not your mum.'

# Bob Skinner

'I'm a lousy dad, and I'm ashamed of it.

'That's not what my daughter would tell you, and I don't imagine that my younger children would either, if you were to put the question to them. But it's what I believe.

'Jesus, what have I just said? How self-revelatory is that? I called Alex, 'my daughter', as if I had only one, yet I have two. Seonaid's approaching the age that her half-sister was when Myra's car hit that tree. When that happened, afterwards I was consumed by the need to care for Alexis. My employer, the police force, understood completely; my bosses went out of their way to ensure that my shifts were synchronised with the hours of my childcarers, even though I was in CID, at the sharp end. They told me that they wanted to keep me, and that they'd do whatever it took to make things work. But it wasn't easy. I was demanding of the people looking after my kid, and a few of them bit the dust. It reached the point when I was considering walking away from the job, but just then we found the perfect woman to take care of Alex. Daisy was an artist, and she lived in the village, so her career dovetailed perfectly with mine, and everything was sorted. I was able to do a proper job as a police officer and be a responsible loving dad at the same time, and Alex and I made it all the way through as a family unit until she flew the nest and went off to university in Glasgow.

'I look back on that now, and I ask myself, 'Skinner, how selfish was that?'

'For I had an option all along: my old man was a successful solicitor in a prosperous town. He was the founder and head of a law practice that could easily have accommodated me while I finished a law degree, and would have given me a job for life afterwards. The firm would have become mine. That route was open to me at every point in my young adult life. I could have taken it whenever I chose, moved back to Motherwell, studied, and then put in a conventional working day that would have let me spend as much time with my kid as other dads did. Mr Skinner junior, man about town, director of the football club, member of Bothwell Castle Golf Club, Rotarian, all that conventional stuff that we need people to do to make the respectable world turn. Would it have harmed me as a person? No. Would it have been better for Alex? Yes.

'But you know that I didn't. No, I stayed put in Gullane and I would not be moved from the cottage that in truth had been Myra's more than it had been mine. I stayed in the force and with Daisy Mears' help I climbed that fucking ladder . . . as relentless and ruthless as folk will tell you I was. In other words, I put my career before the best interests of my lovely wee daughter. I was a hands-on cop; I was famous for never holding back. And no kidding; there were times when if things had gone wrong, Alex might have been an orphan.

'I'm not proud of that, any of it. I'm not proud of the fact that I haven't learned either. Did you hear me just now? It was as if I was ignoring Seonaid's very existence. I have a second family, and I love them, yet it feels as if they're on the periphery of my life, in a great big bubble. I can see them, touch them, be with them, but somehow they're not real . . . apart from James Andrew that is, apart from the Jazz man.

'He's my firstborn son, and in my macho mind that makes him special. Mark, though, he's more like my charge, my ward . . . which he is in a way, I suppose being adopted. And Seonaid, she's lovely, just lovely, but she's like a wee doll, and I just can't relate to her, because I don't know how to, I've forgotten how to, because my second family has become almost entirely subordinate to my job. Just like my third marriage is, and ours was, only now I'm married to a woman who seems to have the same crap priorities as I do.'

'Wow,' she said. 'And all I asked was what was on your mind.'

I gazed at her.

'I haven't learned a fucking thing, have I, Sarah?'

She gazed back at me across the breakfast bar in her brand new kitchen, in her brand new old stone house. Two plates lay between us, each one cleaned of all but a few strands of dark fried onion, and a couple of smears of mustard. Her elbows were on the dark wood surface and her hands were cupped around a crystal tumbler, half filled with clear sparkling water.

'Not a fucking thing,' she agreed. 'But you're not a lousy dad. You've just described most of the men in this country; job first, family second. Overall, in terms of your contribution to parenting, I'd say you were ahead of the game. What about me? I'm a career mom, always have been, always will be; that's my choice. Do I beat myself up over it? The hell I do.'

She took a mouthful from her glass then set it down. 'As for differentiating between your two daughters, I see it, but I can understand it. It doesn't rile me, even though I'm Seonaid's mother. I can put your past behind me, Bob, even if you can't.' She let her point sink in, before continuing.

'Alex is an adult now, and she's been part of your life for the best part of the last thirty years. By the way, you go ask her whether she'd rather have been brought up by a lawyer in Lanarkshire or by a cop in one of the nicest places in Scotland and see what she tells you. Our Seonaid, she's just past being a toddler. If anyone who didn't know you saw you, Alex and her in the street they would assume that she was Alex's kid, your grandchild, not yours, your daughter. But what they would see, and they'd be right about, is that you love her like crazy, and if you haven't learned yet to relate to her in the same way you do to her sister, then that is no big deal to me.'

'And my marriage?' I said. 'That's all perfectly normal and understandable as well, is it?'

279

'Now that,' she replied, 'I cannot say. I'm not part of it. You have to work that one out for yourself.'

I whistled, and took a sip of the red that I'd brought for my own consumption, although I hadn't planned on drinking more than a glass. 'At the moment, that's a hell of a lot easier said than done. I wouldn't know how to begin, that's my problem. Give me a clue.'

'I'm a bad person to ask,' she warned. 'I don't like the lady; I never have, and I never will.'

'Nevertheless, you're honest.'

She smiled, in a way that I hadn't seen for a while. 'Thank you, sir,' she said. 'Okay. Describe your marriage to Myra, in one word.'

'Passionate,' I replied instantly.

'Beyond doubt,' she agreed. 'Now describe ours.'

I had to think about that, but not for too long. 'Volatile,' I replied.

'Agreed. Now describe your marriage to Aileen in one word.'

That took me much longer. Eventually I murmured, 'Sanitised.'

She nodded. 'I think I get your drift. Everything clean and stainless steel, all the forks and knives in their own section of the drawer.'

'That's it.'

'And now it's been pulled out and the cutlery's all over the kitchen floor.'

I chuckled softly. 'You could say that.'

'I just did. But the thing is, do you prefer it that way? Would you rather have it chaotic than neat and ordered?'

'I . . . ' I hesitated.

'You don't need to answer that one, honey,' she told me. 'You can't do neat and ordered. It's not how you are. You might have been repressed for most of your childhood, but once you broke out there was never any going back.'

She picked up the crystal and took another drink; I saw that her hand was trembling slightly. 'From what I know of Aileen, she must,' her forehead wrinkled, as she leaned on the word, 'have everything neat and ordered, including you. Ah, but now she's discovered that she can't bend you to her way . . .

'Fuck me, Bob,' she exclaimed; her change of tone startled me, 'isn't it obvious? The woman's the leader of a political party, she's led the country for Christ's sake! She's a fucking dominatrix, but you, my man, will never be dominated.'

She paused. 'You shouldn't have got me started on this,' she warned. You thought you had this nice new family unit, with wild, unpredictable Sarah three thousand miles away, and the kids loved and looked after by new step-mommy. Well, do you know what? None of our children have ever mentioned the woman to me, not once. The only mother figure they ever talk about is Trish. With the boys, that might just be sensitivity, but not with Seonaid. She prattles on about everything that happens around her in Gullane, and she only ever mentions you, her carer and occasionally, Alex . . . although I reckon she thinks she's her aunt. That's what I resent most about Aileen, Bob, not the fact that

281

she lured you away from me with smooth talk, sympathy and some probably indifferent sex; none of that matters alongside the fact that she's my children's stepmother and she doesn't care about them! She doesn't fucking care!'

She was glaring at me, a tear tracking down each cheek. 'Shit,' she shouted. 'Get me a proper glass and give me some of that fucking wine, will you.'

I fetched another goblet from the kitchen cabinet from which I'd seen her take mine. 'You sure about this?' I asked, holding the bottle poised.

'Oh yes,' she said, 'I'm very sure.' I poured a large measure of the robust red from Oregon that I'd spotted in Waitrose and bought because I like West Coast American wines, preferably from north of California. I made to set it in front of her but she shook her head. 'Not here; living room. There I can turn the lights down . . . for no other reason,' she added, 'than because I look a mess.'

Actually she didn't. Sarah doesn't cry very often but when she lets go, it makes her look angry, and gives her eyes a light that's anything but weak. I followed her through to her living room, carrying my glass and hers, with the bottle jammed under my arm. She'd given up on the Vichy Catalan. We didn't need to turn on any lights, far less turn them down; there was still enough outside to give us all we needed. She flopped down on to a big brown suede couch and motioned me to join her. I handed her the plonk and she killed half of it in a single swallow.

She held the glass at arm's length, peered at it, and nodded approval. Then she picked up the bottle and poured us each some more.

'You and I were having bother long before Aileen came along,' I pointed out, quietly.

'Sure,' she agreed. 'Mutually inflicted, I think you'll agree.'

I couldn't argue otherwise.

'And pretty obvious to all and sundry,' she continued, 'most of all her. You were a sucker for those doe eyes and that gentle but firm demeanour. And so was I for the equivalent, I'll grant you.' She looked at me, sideways. The tears had gone. 'We were pretty fucked up then, weren't we?'

I sank back into the soft upholstery and gazed at the ceiling. 'Sarah, I've been fucked up for years,' I admitted. 'I had all sorts of things inside me, but I kept them all bottled up; you know that.'

'Yeah,' she whispered. 'And I wasn't there for you when it got too much, but she was. So I have nobody to blame but me, have I?'

'Blame,' I repeated her word. 'Blame, blame, blame. Why are we so concerned about blame, all of us? Why don't we allow ourselves our faults, our imperfections? We've all got them.'

I didn't see her smile, but I sensed it in her voice. 'That you should say so. You've spent your life fighting against yours.'

'Oh yes? And what are they?'

'All the things that make you strong,' she replied, cryptically.

I drained my glass and shared the rest of the

bottle between us. 'What am I going to do, Sarah?' I asked, as night fell in her living room.

'About being a lousy dad? Nothing, 'cos you ain't one. About fighting for what you believe in? Same as you always have done. March forward into the shell-fire and go down in a blaze of glory, if that's what it comes to. About your marriage? That's not for me to say, but you must stop feeling fucked up, because you aren't, not any more. The way I see it, your confidence has been undermined, but you could never admit that, not even to yourself. You used to have nice long thick hair, Samson, even if it was grey, but you've been shorn. You can still see what's happening around you though, and those locks will grow in again.'

'That's very biblical,' I murmured. 'Need I ask who you've cast as Delilah?'

'No, you need not. Can I ask you something?'

'And if I said no?'

'Indeed,' she chuckled. 'Bob, you always fought against the idea of being chief constable even when Jimmy Proud tried to talk you into it. You were afraid it would sideline you as a cop. What made you change your mind? Or was it a who?'

'It was a few people, a few things said; but finally,' I conceded, 'it came down to one person.'

'But it hasn't sidelined you, has it? Not like it was supposed to.'

'No.' I stopped her before she got to where she was headed. 'It's a mess, Sarah, isn't it?'

'You're an expert in those, honey. You'll get

284

by.' She turned to look at me and her eyes were bright. 'I'll promise you one thing. Before, when you needed me, I wasn't there for you. Well, I'm here right now.'

I leaned towards her and kissed her, and that's when I knew I was in real trouble.

# Mario McGuire

I'd known my weekend wasn't going to be one of leisure, so I'd been quite happy to give the nod to Paula going to the Glasgow concert with Aileen. She wasn't so close to her due date that I was afraid to let her out of my sight, although I knew that would happen soon.

I rose early and caught up on the morning news headlines on Sky, then shaved and showered. Paula was stirring by the time I was ready, so I fixed her breakfast to order, muesli with cubed beetroot all mixed with pouring yoghurt . . . don't say it, I know . . . and with a Berocca drink on the side. I had coffee and a couple of poached eggs on toast; conservative, that's me.

These days I don't like going into the office on a Saturday. I'm pretty much on call twenty-four seven, so I value my free time even more than I did when I was other ranks. Indeed I'd been grabbing as much as I could, well aware that when Junior arrived I wasn't going to have any.

It had to be done, though. The chief was steamed up about Varley, and wanted the investigation wrapped up as quickly as possible, so I'd told Mackenzie that I wanted a progress report, ten thirty that morning, from him and Bob Skinner's ex-brother-in-law or whatever the hell he is. There was also the consideration that Payne didn't come for free. In the old days, the command at Pitt Street would have lent him to us for as long as we needed him, simple as that, but that type of inter-force courtesy had been swept away by its new broom, so we were hiring him by the day with expenses, invoiced by Strathclyde, plus VAT.

It was just short of ten when I got there; that gave me enough time to shift some paperwork, the kind I like the least, overtime analyses, division by division, and senior CID officers' expenses claims. And it let me do something else. On a whim I took out my mobile and made a call.

'How's tricks?' Neil McIlhenney asked, as he picked it up. I could hear road noise in the background, so I assumed he was on Bluetooth.

'Tricky,' I replied. 'How's London?'

'Exciting. It's like a language school. My people are chasing Russians, Mexicans; God, you name it we're after them. I can understand most of them; it's the cockneys that could be speaking Greek as far as I'm concerned. Lou's had to interpret for me. But I'm loving it, and so are the kids. You know, Mario, I never dreamed for a moment that I'd ever leave Edinburgh. I was nervous as hell when I started here, but not any more.'

'Different atmosphere?'

'And then some,' he laughed. 'The organisation's huge. I'm surrounded by Very Important People. Some of them actually are, the others act the part regardless. I'm a chief super, and I'm only halfway up the ladder. I'll probably be a commander in a year's time, but you aren't really somebody here until you can call yourself Commissioner, even if it's only Deputy Assistant.' He paused. 'The talk down here is that's what they're going to call the new super-chief in Scotland: Commissioner.'

'Is it now?' I murmured. 'So they know more than we do.'

'Oh yes. In New Scotland Yard it's regarded as a given. Naturally, they reckon it's going to be Bob that gets the job.'

'Word to the wise, my friend. Don't be calling to congratulate him; your VIPs may not have noticed that ACPOS voted against it the other day, with him leading the opposition.'

'That doesn't surprise me, but it won't make any difference. Some people here would like the same thing to happen in England. They're watching with interest.'

'Indeed? Well, maybe once your feet are a bit further under the table you'll tell them to mind their own fucking business.'

'Hey,' he said, 'you're tetchy. Is Paula keeping you awake?'

'No, Paulie is wonderful, blooming, radiant, everything you can imagine.'

'And running to the bog a lot?'

'And running to the bog a lot, but she does it very quietly. No, McIlhenney, I am pissed off because it is a lovely summer Saturday morning and I am in the office.'

'Pity; I'm on my way to the Oval with Spence to watch some cricket. Say hello to Uncle Mario, Spence.'

'Hello, Uncle Mario,' Spencer shouted. His

voice was starting to break. I felt old.

'And to you, lad. Don't let him take you to the cheap seats.'

'Crisis?' Neil asked.

'The worst kind. One of our guys has gone rogue.'

'Anybody I know?'

'Jock Varley.'

Few conversations between my soul brother and I are punctuated by silence. That one was, for so long that I thought the connection had gone.

'Indeed,' he murmured, eventually.

'You don't sound astonished.'

'I wish I was. I never trusted the man. There was a whisper years ago about him looking after a couple of pubs on his patch, and about withdrawn police objections to licensing extension applications that might have been paid for.'

'Didn't you report them?'

'I had nothing to report. I only heard the stories second-hand. Besides, they probably started with the unsuccessful applicants, just like football fans always reckon the ref's on the payroll when he gives the opposition a penalty.'

'But you still remember them,' I pointed out.

'Yes, because while these stories do the rounds all the time, it's not very often that a cop's name's mentioned. Varley's was.'

'Mmm,' I mused. 'Give it some more thought, Neil, if you would. If you can add any details, for example when this happened and the pubs involved, that might be useful next time I have a face-to-face with the man.'

'Will do; there's a chance of rain here so I may have time to do it today.'

'Thanks. While you're at it, maybe you'd think about a guy called Freddy Welsh.'

'Now that's a name I've heard. Let me think. Yes, when I was in the Branch, I had a look at him for an outside agency. The one I'm with now, in fact. They didn't tell me why they were interested and I didn't ask.'

I was puzzled. 'Did you report it to the boss?'

'No, he was on holiday at the time, and I found nothing to report, so it never came up when he got back. You won't find a file on him for the same reason. However,' he paused, 'he is bent.' He said it so firmly that I was surprised; Neil's middle name would be circumspection, if only he could spell it. 'I don't know how, and I couldn't get anywhere near proving it at the time, but he is. I turned his business inside out, and he never knew a thing about it. Couldn't find a hair out of place.'

'So why are you sure he's twisted?' I asked.

'Precisely because I couldn't find a hair out of place, man. Have you ever known a business that was absolutely spotless, where none of the staff had as much as slipped a sandwich or a Mars bar on to their petrol receipt?'

'CID?' I suggested. I'd just found twenty cigarettes and a *Playboy* magazine on one of those, in the expenses claim of a detective chief inspector.

'Better get out of the office, bruv,' he replied. 'Clearly, your brain needs more oxygen. Okay, we're here now,' I heard him brake, and then a sigh, no, two of them, 'and bugger it, the rain's starting.'

After he'd gone I checked the London weather forecast on my computer; mainly fine with showers. Not too bad, but what did they know really?

I was looking up Sunday in Edinburgh . . . warm, sunny, five per cent chance of light rain . . . when there was a knock on my door. 'Yes!' I shouted; it opened and David McKenzie, in uniform on a bloody Saturday, stepped into the room, followed by a man who had to be the chief's ex-brother-in-law, and by a woman. It took me a second or two to put a name to her, then it dawned: Lisa McDermid, detective sergeant, newly transferred to Special Branch with George Regan, over the moans of old Fred Leggat. I wasn't expecting her.

'Sit yourselves down,' I said, moving across to my table. I was ready for another coffee, but Mackenzie doesn't, Payne was a guest, albeit a hired one, and if I'd asked McDermid, as junior officer present, to go and fetch four from the canteen, there would probably have been a sexism complaint, for that's the reputation she carries, so instead I looked in my fridge, found a six-pack of Pepsi with four left in it and handed them round.

I looked at David. 'Fire away,' I told him. 'What have you got?'

'Varley,' he replied, with a vehemence that I hadn't seen in him since the old days. 'By the balls.'

Payne held up a cautionary hand. 'Maybe,' he murmured.

'Come on, Lowell,' Mackenzie exclaimed. 'Of course we do.'

'Yes, I know,' the Strathclyde man said. 'On the face of it we have, but on the basis of what we've discovered, what charge could be laid against him?'

'Guys,' I interrupted, 'I'm not here to chair a debate between you. Enlighten me, and I'll tell you what we can do and what we can't.'

'Sorry, sir.' The superintendent's tone was even but his eyes let me know that I must have barked at him just a little, and that if he ever overtakes me in rank he'd remember it.

'The Varleys' domestic accounts are unexceptional,' he began. 'They take us nowhere. However, there's another that we weren't meant to know about. It's in First Caledonian's offshore division, and there's a hundred and thirty-seven grand sitting in it, paid in, over an eight-year period, by a company called Holyhead SA.'

'Spanish?' I asked.

'Andorran. Lowell's been in touch with the British consulate in Barcelona and they've checked for us. The titular is an Andorran lawyer, but the beneficial owner of the company is Freddy Welsh.'

I shrugged. 'Bloody obvious, that; Anglesey Construction, Holyhead SA . . . the Welsh connection, get it? The offshore account: whose name's it in? Jock's?'

'No,' Mackenzie admitted. 'It's in his wife's.'

'Then DCI Payne is right. What are you going to charge Jock with? We might be able to do her for money-laundering, but if the cash in Holyhead's come from Anglesey Construction, tax paid, then we're stuffed on that too.'

'But it hasn't.' I turned to McDermid as she spoke. 'There's no connection between the two,' she continued. 'Welsh's accountant swears he knows nothing about it. I've just spent some time interrogating him. He wasn't pleased either; we had an extended session last night. All the money going in and out of Anglesey Construction is accounted for.'

'So the Holyhead cash comes from another source, or sources,' I muttered, to myself mainly. 'How much is in it?'

'About seven million,' Payne said.

'Jesus,' I gasped.

'It's an investment vehicle and it's done very well over the years; external deposits are about four and a half, over an eight-year period.'

'Eight years,' I repeated. 'Same length of time as Ella Varley's offshore account's been open?' I asked McDermid.

The sergeant nodded. 'Exactly.'

'How do we know all this detail?'

'The Andorran lawyer coughed,' Payne replied. 'He didn't fancy the Spanish police turning up on his doorstep.'

'Right,' I said. 'So where are we? We've got Welsh owning an offshore company holding funds that don't relate to any legitimate taxed income that we know of.'

'Or that the Revenue knows of,' McDermid

293

volunteered. 'DI Regan's checked that.'

'Thanks. That gives us cause to pull Welsh in. Going on from that, Mrs Varley's account gives us reason to lift her. However it still doesn't let us lay a finger on Jock, and based on what he tried to do to Alice, he isn't likely to lay down his life to save his wife's.'

'No,' Lisa ventured. She doesn't smile a lot does DS McDermid, so when she did I had a feeling a nice one was coming. 'But there is the conservatory.'

I grinned back at her. 'Tell me more,' I invited.

'About ten years ago,' she began, 'the Varleys added a big extension on to their house in Livingston. Alice says it's enormous, and must have cost a packet, but that can't be verified. It was built by Freddy Welsh, but there's no record of the job in his firm's records, and there's no record of the Varleys ever having paid a penny for it.'

'Whose name's the house in?'

'Joint.'

'Lisa,' I laughed. 'You win the major prize. Time we paid another call on Inspector Varley.'

# Sarah Grace

I didn't invite him for anything more than dinner, I promise. Enticing him into my bed was not on my agenda.

It was supposed to be a discussion about the kids, until I asked him what was troubling him and it turned into something else. Cards were laid on the table, by both of us. I told him what I thought about the witch and how she'd operated, how I believed she'd sensed his needs and manipulated him. He didn't deny any of it. Looking back, I realised just how easily and smoothly she'd done it, and when I did, I saw, for the first time, that she'd been even cleverer than I'd thought. She'd manipulated me as well.

I'd been persuaded that the gulf between Bob and me was too big and that the most important thing for us to do was whatever would be best for the children. He said the words, but I'm sure she put most of them in his head. I went along with it with nary a murmur. I decided to make myself scarce, to accept a no-fault divorce and go back to the USA, seeing the kids in the holidays, with their father having custody during term time. For the only time in my life, I gave up without a struggle. Yes, it may have worked to my advantage financially, but if I'd believed that the children would have been better off in America, that wouldn't have mattered.

When I told Bob to get me a glass and pour

me some of the wine he'd brought, what I was really saying was, 'To hell with that! Let battle commence.' And when I fight, there are no rules.

Just before that I'd made a crack about indifferent sex, and I reckon it was right on the button. I've never known him hungrier. After I'd kissed him . . . I'm not certain who made the first move, but I suspect it was me . . . the only thing I said to him, for the rest of the night, was 'Phone Trish.' He did; I heard him tell her he'd be very late and that she should lock up. By the time he'd finished, I was waiting for him, in the bedroom where only Seonaid and I had slept since I moved into the house.

I have no idea when I finally nodded off, but I do know it wasn't for long. I have difficulty describing how I felt when I woke and saw him there, his grey-stubbled face half-buried in the pillow, eyes closed, mouth slightly open. It took my mind a second or two to adjust, to reassemble the pieces of the night before, and as it did a feeling washed through me like a great cleansing wave, leaving behind it a sense of . . . What?

Not déjà vu, for this was no vague feeling, it was reality.

Not triumph, for Bob could never be a trophy, another notch on my bedhead.

Not guilt, hell no, for we hadn't done anything that was going to trouble my conscience.

Homecoming. A sense of homecoming; that's the phrase that fits it best, the way you feel at the end of a long journey, when you're back where you belong, in the place you love.

His right arm lay across my hip. It moved, very slightly, then he farted, quietly. That made me smile; it was just like old times. His eyelid lifted slightly and I caught a glimpse of confusion, then it widened and he was awake.

He rolled on to his side, facing me, then pushed himself up on his left elbow. I looked at him properly, in daylight, for the first time. His body hadn't changed much, since the last time I'd seen it. If anything it was leaner, and his muscles were firmer; to most eyes, that would seem good, but not to mine. When Bob's content, he tends to put on a little weight. 'Where is it?' he murmured, drowsily.

'What?' I was still grinning.

'The fuel can.' He yawned. 'Christ, talk about pouring petrol on a fire.'

'Are you going to blame me for that?' I asked.

'No, not for a second.'

'Are you going to blame yourself?'

'Absolutely.'

'For what?'

'I think it's called adultery. There are cultures where it's still a capital crime.'

I reached up and grasped a clump of chest hair; that's still dark, unlike his beard and his scalp. 'And you're very good at it. And you've got form. You've got a rap sheet as long as your arm.'

A corner of his mouth flickered. 'Pot. Kettle. Black.'

'Yeah. So?'

'Are you going to grass me up?'

I shook my head. 'Never. I will never compromise you in any way, not ever again.'

297

'Why not? You've got cause.'

'Because I love you, fool.'

'Honey,' he began.

'That doesn't mean I want you back,' I added, very quickly. 'I'm settled here. I don't want to uproot myself again; hell, I won't. Also, the kids are used to us now, the way we are, and they're happy with it. Change that and we'd only confuse them. No, lover. Whatever happens to your domestic situation, I'm happy with mine. If this is a one-off,' I flashed my eyes at him, 'or rather a three-off, so be it.'

He sighed. 'You're some woman, you know that.'

'Yes, I do know.'

'Maybe too much for me.'

'Don't bullshit me,' I told him, 'or lie to yourself.'

'In that case,' he said, his smile widening as he slid down beside me once more, 'remember that quirk of mine when we went out for a drink?'

I got his drift. 'Oh yes,' I edged closer to him. 'You never finished on an odd number.'

Later, I made him breakfast, while he showered. I know, without asking him, that he checked the cabinets in my bathroom for razors, shaving cream and all the other guy stuff . . . you can take the man out of CID, etc . . . but there's never been any for him to find. If I'd known that our encounter was going to happen I might have bought some, out of pure bitchiness, but on reflection I'm glad that I didn't.

Just watching him eat, up at the kitchen bar, unshaven and still drowsy, gave me the wobbles again. 'What are we going to do, babe?' he asked, after he'd washed the last of his toast down with the orange juice that I'd made him take, instead of coffee. He drinks way too much of that stuff.

'We?' I began. 'I'll tell you what I'm going to do. Once you're gone I'm going to lie in a warm bath and soothe some parts that haven't seen any action for a while. Then I'm going to do some housework and prepare some lectures for next week. That's the short term. After that, I plan to carry on as before. How about you?'

'Honestly?' he said.

'There can be no other way between us from now on.'

He nodded. 'I'll buy into that. In which case ... I haven't a fucking clue. I don't know anything any more. I'm not sure why I married Aileen, I'm not sure why you and I divorced, I'm not even sure why we married in the first place.'

I laughed. 'Bob, you're a serial marrier; you're an auto-matrimonialist. How about that for a new word? You can't help it; it's what you do. That's what ... ' I had been going to say, ' ... made you a soft touch for her,' but that might have ruined the moment.

'Never again,' he declared. 'Seriously though. What should I do? Tell me. I'll make allowances for your natural bias, I promise.'

'Don't let it fester, that's all I can say; we did, and that was wrong. Clearly, you've got a problem. You have to face up to it, both of you. But whatever you do you, big boy, have to be able to look me in the eye afterwards and make me believe it was worthy of you.'

'What if Aileen comes back from Glasgow tonight,' he asked, 'and tells me that I was right and she was wrong and she's withdrawing support from the police bill? Will we have a problem then?'

I frowned at him. 'Will she say that before or after she tells you that she's pregnant by the Holy Spirit?'

He chuckled. 'Sure, I know it's that unlikely . . . but what if?'

'Then she'll have compromised her principles. How will that make you feel? Are you gonna admire her for her courage or think less of her for her weakness?' I put my hand on his cheek and made him look at me.

'Bob, my darling,' I said, 'you're asking me questions that only you can answer. All I can tell you is what I see in you, now, with the benefit of time apart and a little objectivity. I see a man who's put so much into his career that he has nothing left for himself. I see a man who's in a state of complete emotional confusion, because he can't define his existence outside the police force any longer. You said as much last night.'

'I suppose I did,' he conceded. 'And how long do you think it's been going on?'

'Probably since Alex left home; but it's coming to an end.'

'What makes you a psychology expert?' he asked, but lightly, not challenging me.

'I'm a Bob Skinner expert, that's all; number one in my field.'

'You'd rank yourself above Alex, would you?'

'Yes, because she's too close. I'm standing a

little further back than I used to, so I can see you better.'

'If you're right,' he ventured, 'given your diagnosis, without treatment what's the prognosis?'

'You crash and burn as a husband. That's happening already. Then it begins to affect your judgement and you're no longer the cop you were either. You probably still function in the job, but you become what you've never wanted to be, a wholesale delegator, like Jimmy Proud, but without his skill and subtlety. Effectively, you let Maggie and Mario lead the force, and you push paper around your desk till gold watch time. Then you retire and you have no idea who the hell you are, or what. You pick up a few non-executive directorships, but you don't contribute much and feel like a prostitute. At home, Mark's at college, James Andrew's halfway through high school, and Seonaid . . . you still won't really know who she is. Anyway, by then she'll be living with me; maybe they all will and you'll be alone, playing golf obsessively and drinking too much.'

'Only there won't be a force for me to have left,' he pointed out, 'once this bill goes through, not one that I'll want any part of.'

'And that's what scares you most. That's what's brought you to the tipping point, the prospect of losing the only stable part of your existence. She can see that fear, because she isn't so close to you that she's blind to it, and she thought she could play on it to make you back the bill.'

He stared at his plate for a while. 'That's not the only scary part,' he whispered. 'What you said earlier, that future you painted for me. The man you described just now was my father. That's what he'd become by the time he died. Alex has virtually no memory of him.'

He blinked, hard. 'So, Doc, what's the treatment?'

'The facing of some facts,' I replied, 'the main one being that Myra is dead, that she ain't coming back, and that she was a one-off you can't use as a template for a living partner. The second is that you are far bigger than any police force, not the other way around. If circumstances make you quit, it's not the end of your useful life; it may be the beginning. Accept those truths and everything else will work out, for you will be able to see clearly again.'

'So I should back off from opposing the single force?' he ventured. 'Is that what you're saying?'

'Hell no! You truly are opposed to it, and you alone can put the case against; nobody else will. You'd hate yourself for ever if you ducked out of that. You'd feel like her fucking lapdog. And by the way, if Aileen did come over to your side, you'd think she was yours.'

He reached out for the orange juice carton a couple of feet away and poured himself some more. 'Did I really do that to you?' he asked. 'Try to turn you into Myra?'

'Not so much that; you tried to make me live up to her, at least to your vision of her. You may not have realised it, but there wasn't a single day went by without you talking about her. 'There was this time,' you'd begin, or 'You know what Myra would have done, don't you,' as if I possibly could.'

'I'm sorry,' he said, contritely. 'That must really have pissed you off.'

'It didn't until after you were stabbed, and recovered, then you started to reject me, because you had an obsession about her accident not being an accident. I could handle it until then.'

'Every day?'

I nodded. 'Every day.'

'Now that is odd, because I'm sitting here thinking, how often do I mention her to Aileen, and you know what? I don't believe I do, not ever, not at all. What do you make of that, quack psychologist?'

For a moment I thought he was being sarcastic, but he wasn't. 'No,' I countered. 'You tell me.'

'That I can't see her in the same picture as Myra at all. See, if I did talk about her to you as often as that, I wasn't comparing you, babe, honest. It was because I had this vision of her being there with us, and looking on, and approving of us. Sometimes I felt her presence, love, I really felt her presence.' He looked me in the eye. 'What I'm about to say now, you'll think is bullshit, but it's not. That doesn't happen any more. When I'm in the house with Aileen, in the kitchen or in the garden room or wherever, the only other person I ever think about is you.'

I didn't know what to make of that one so I didn't begin to try. Instead I went round to the other side of the bar, to where he sat, gave him a quick hug and told him, 'You have to be going, honey. Back to our kids.' I looked up at the kitchen clock: seven twenty five. 'With a bit of luck, you'll be there before they're up and about.'

'I won't count on it,' he said. 'You know what they're like when the days are long, like now, especially the wee one.'

'True. All the more reason to scoot, then.'

'Yeah.' He slid off his stool, drew me to him and kissed me. 'Thanks,' he whispered.

'For what?'

He smiled. 'Dinner,' he said, 'and everything that came after it; not least the straight talking. It's been a while since I let anyone in.' He paused. 'And maybe last time I did, I gave away too many secrets.'

I frowned as I looked up at him. 'Do you have any I don't know about?' I asked.

'One,' he replied, and a shadow crossed his face. 'For now I'm keeping it, but I promise I will tell you what it is next time we're . . . like this.'

'You're assuming.'

'I know . . . if we're ever, I should have said.'

I squeezed his butt. 'That's all right; you can come back. I've never been a mistress before; I think I like it.'

'Then I really have got some serious thinking to do, but thanks to you, I'm ready for it. Any more heartfelt advice before I go?'

'Yes,' I replied, 'and this is medical. Give up the coffee; it's the last thing that a man in your emotional state needs. Once you get through withdrawal, you'll feel a hell of a lot better for it. Do that for us?'

'Us?'

'Me and the kids. They don't need any sort of a junkie dad, and I prefer you straight too.'

'I'll try. Promise.'

I watched him from the doorway as he slid into his car, then drove away, with a last wave through the open window.

And then I folded; without warning my legs turned to jelly. I eased myself back to the kitchen and up on to the stool that Bob had been using, then poured the last of the orange juice into his glass. *What the hell have I done?* I asked myself.

Then I answered. 'I've enjoyed the best sex I've had since before the two of us split up. I've made no promises and no commitments. And on top of that, I feel better about myself than I have in years.'

*So why can't I smile about it?*

'Because I'm worried about my man. He's on the edge and I don't know what he's going to be like when he comes through it.'

I took the OJ upstairs and had the warm bath I'd promised myself. I put in some crystals, and wallowed for a while, pleased to find that although I was out of practice and had been holding nothing back, I wasn't sore or even tender. When I'd had enough, I dressed, and began the rest of my day, as I'd described it to Bob. I use a cleaning service, but the kids' bedrooms needed attention. I've never expected Trish to be a domestic as well as a carer.

I put a little less concentration than usual into the tidying of bedrooms and the changing of linen, for my mind was still full and running over. I'd described Bob as a man on the edge, but what the hell was I? I'd been lying to myself, I realised. I hadn't come back for the job and the kids, not for those considerations alone. I hadn't planned the night before, and I repeat, I hadn't invited him for more than dinner, but maybe I'd been waiting for my opportunity all along.

Lecture preparation was out of the question. I owe my students my one hundred per cent attention and they weren't getting it that day. A little girlfriend time might be a better alternative, I decided, but it was a short list, reduced to one, really, by the obvious truth that I couldn't call Alex. So I rang Paula Viareggio; she and I have always got on well from the time that Mario and she came out of the closet, when Bob and I helped them along by inviting them to dinner parties as a couple.

'You busy?' I asked her once we'd got past the opening exchanges. 'Or are you just too pregnant to come out and play?'

'I'd love to, Sarah,' she said, 'but I've got a social event tonight and I'd better rest up for it. Would you like to drop in here instead, for coffee and a chat? Mario's out. There's some stuff going on at work that needs his weekend attention.'

'Fine by me. I'll look forward to it. I'll do some essentials shopping, then come to you. Around eleven thirty suit?'

'Perfect.' I thought she'd hang up, but she

didn't. 'What's put the bounce in your boobs?' Paula doesn't do subtle.

'What do you mean?'

'You sound sparkly. Have you got a new man?'

'Me?' I laughed. 'Honestly, no.' It was the truth; nothing new about him.

I got out of my work clothes and made a list of the things I needed for the house and for the kids when Trish brought them back on the following Monday. I was in the act of reaching for my car keys when the phone rang. 'Dammit!' I muttered. Then my heart jumped a little mouthwards. I wasn't on call, so who . . .

I could only imagine one thing: Bob, full of guilt and contrition, and maybe anger, calling to blame me for the mistake he'd made and threatening me with everything short of deportation if I ever breathed a word.

I was half right. 'Hi,' he said, quietly. I heard a seagull in the background and guessed he was in the garden on his mobile. 'I think I'm calling to apologise. I was way out of order last night, moaning to you about my life, and then taking advantage of you.'

'I see,' I murmured. 'There was a point this morning when I told you I still love you, if I remember right. Or didn't you hear that?'

'Yes, I heard. The bugger is, it's mutual.'

'Then don't go apologising. I also said I won't go back to where we were, and I meant that too. As for . . . all that sweaty stuff, you were a man in great need of getting his ashes properly hauled. If you'd gone anywhere else

307

for that, then I would have been seriously pissed off. Now chill out. What are you doing anyway?'

'I'm playing with our daughter, as it happens. That's it, Seonaid,' he called out, 'pass me the ball. You know what, Sarah? She's gorgeous.'

I had a melting moment, but I wasn't about to let him in on it. 'Yes,' I agreed. 'And she knows it too. Enjoy yourselves. I'm going out.'

I hung up and grabbed my keys, but I hadn't reached the door before the phone rang again. I smiled and picked it up. 'Yes,' I chuckled, 'I still love you in the morning.'

'That may be too much information, Sarah,' Joe Hutchison said, solemnly.

'Then forget you ever heard it,' I replied cheerfully.

'I will, although I'm curious about who you thought I might be. I wonder, my dear,' he continued. I knew it was favour time, 'My dear' told me so, 'I know that you're not on duty this weekend, but something's come up.'

My switch to work mode is automatic. 'Crime scene or major accident?'

'Crime scene. Thing is, Sarah, our Roshan is fine for run-of-the-mill stuff, but this isn't something we can ask him to handle alone. It's multiple and it's messy. I'd go myself, but my dear wife has plans and besides . . . '

*You're the prof, and you're not getting any younger,* I thought, but didn't say it. 'Where is it?' I asked.

'Leith, near Ocean Terminal. DI Pye is the

308

officer in charge. I'll let him know you're coming.'

'It's all right, Joe; I have Sammy's mobile number. I'll call him myself. As it happens, I was heading for Leith anyway. I'll tell my chum I'll be a little late.'

# Cameron 'Cheeky' McCullough

I know there are cops who don't approve of Sauce and me, big Jack McGurk for a start; and I can understand why.

My grandfather has been a very bad man in his time; people like Jack, people who don't know him, think he still is, and that he always will be. People who do . . .

No. I can't say that. The truth is that people who do know my grandpa would never talk to me about him, so I don't have anyone else's educated view to go on, other than my mum's and my aunt's, and you wouldn't hang a rat on the word of either of them.

My aunt, Goldie (her real name's Daphne, but she hates it and nobody ever dares call her by it), is as hard as nails and every bit as dense. My mother, Inez? Grandpa says that Cadburys named a chocolate bar after her. You know, the crumbly one. Dear mother is doing time at the moment for a series of robberies. She even got me involved in the last one, by persuading me to drive for her to pick up a load of gear that she said she'd bought cash from a shop, to be collected out of hours. When we were arrested, Grandpa hired a good lawyer who got me out from under, but to this day nobody in the world, apart from Sauce, believes that I took her at her word and didn't know what was going on. I did, though, I really did; I persuaded myself that she was telling the truth, because what mother would be stupid enough to involve her own daughter in a scam that could put her in jail?

I tell you all this to explain the closeness between Grandpa and me. He's always been the major figure in my life, the one who's raised me and influenced me. He's very young to have a 23-year-old granddaughter. That's because my mother got herself knocked up when she was still under sixteen, and didn't tell anyone until it was too late to have an abortion . . . although Grandpa says he wouldn't have allowed it anyway; he really is a moral maze, that man.

I have no idea who my father is. His name doesn't appear on my birth certificate. My mum's always refused to discuss him, and all Grandpa ever said when I asked him was, 'Doesn't matter, kid. You are you.' When I was eleven, I plucked up the courage to ask Auntie Goldie; she's always scared me, for as long as I can remember. She glared at me with those cold eyes and said, 'Eff you.' It took me another two years to tell Grandpa about that conversation. When I did, he explained that she'd meant, 'Father Unknown.'

It's hard being the light of somebody's life. You have a lot to live up to. When that person is said to be one of the major figures in the country's criminal underworld, you have a lot to live down as well.

He always kept me isolated from that side of his life: I use the past tense because he's promised me that it's over. The closest he's ever come to opening up completely was on my eighteenth birthday. He had a party for me at Black Shield Lodge, his country house hotel up in Perthshire; before it got started he took me into his office. He gave me a glass of Buck's Fizz, and then he started to talk, not in his Grandpa voice but in one I'd never heard before.

'Cameron,' he began; he always uses the given name that we share, not my nickname, 'there's a market in everything: houses, horses, whores, herbs, you name it. For every human need, whether it's as fundamental as a roof over their heads, for entertainment, like a bet every now and again, or just for pure self-gratification, there is commerce and there are merchants, suppliers, providers. Government's attitude to those varied enterprises is inconsistent, to the point of being illogical. It approves of some, and it attaches itself to them like a giant leech . . . that bloodsucker going by the name of Her Majesty's Revenue and Customs . . . drawing its funds from them through taxation. Others it deems to be improper, and it passes laws against them then spends millions on enforcement that's usually futile, because the big G assumes that it's smarter than those it classes as criminals, when at the level that really matters the opposite is usually the case. There's no logic in its demarcation. Government approves of alcohol and tobacco, and taxes both to the hilt. It declares other drugs to be unacceptable and drives them underground, where they're subject to no regulation or quality control whatsoever. Government decrees that prostitution is illegal, yet prostitutes are subject to income tax just like the rest of us.' He paused. 'You with me so far?'

I nodded, wondering what was coming.

'Government has the power to do all that stuff, but there's one thing it can't do, and that's change the basic nature of mankind. Whether they're legal or not, human needs will always exist, and people will always satisfy themselves one way or another. If there were no women selling sex, there would be more rapes, there would be more domestic violence. If there were no distilleries, people would make their own hooch, and for sure it would blind and kill them in their thousands. And so on, and so on.'

He looked right into my eyes. 'Now you're an adult,' he said, 'you're going to start hearing things about me, maybe not to your face, but one way or another, you will. So it's best you hear my side of the story. I have businesses that are regarded as legitimate; this hotel where we are right now, it's one of them. These are very successful, and HMRC does very nicely from them thank you. I should be on the Chancellor of the Exchequer's Christmas card list. You'd think they'd be grateful,' he smiled, 'but that cuts me no slack with them. They say that I have other interests, that I operate on both sides of the fence. Okay, let them try and prove it. I'll always deny it to them, and I'll never admit it to anyone else, especially not you, kid, so there's no chance of you being affected by it or infected by it for that matter.

'You're my future, Cameron. My businesses, the CamMac group, the holding company that contains all my interests in housebuilding, commercial property, hotels and pubs, is mine and mine alone. When I die, which I hope will be a long time off since I'm still only mid-fifties, it's going to be yours. Forget Goldie, forget your mum, they'll have no involvement in it; your aunt's an evil woman, and as for Inez, well, I don't want to speak badly of your grandma, God rest her, but my daughter's brains come from her mother's side.'

He took my hand. 'My will's made already and in it, you're my sole heir. You'll become a director of CamMac, when you're twenty-one. When you're done with university, and have a few years' experience in the wider business world, you'll come and help me run it. In the meantime, I have quite a lot of property and I plan to transfer some of it into your name. I'm not saying, mind, that it'll be yours to do with as you wish, but it's a sensible move, as you'll appreciate once you're a qualified accountant.'

'Grandpa,' I murmured, but he put a finger to my lips.

'Shhh, now. Say nothing. It's your birthright, and it'll be always be ring-fenced for you against anything that might happen to me, whatever those people in government, those people with flexible morality, might try to pin on me in the future.'

They did try, a few years later. He was charged with murder, and with drug trafficking. He sent me a message, telling me he'd be home soon, and asking me to ignore any crap about him I might read in the press. He walked on both charges; no evidence was ever laid. I doubt if the prosecution ever had any.

Now, just in case you think I'm an idiot, I know full well that my grandfather is not whiter than white. The Crown may have wasted money trying to lock him up, but it didn't spend it without reason. He has never once flat out admitted it to me, for the reasons he explained in that birthday chat, but I grew up in the city of Dundee, where you would have to be a chromium-plated bammer not to be aware that Cameron McCullough is the most powerful man in town, that there isn't a door that's closed to him, and that some of those you would not want to knock.

There's only once that he's ever given me a glimpse of that other side and that was last year. I'd gone up to visit him one day, as I try to do at least once a month, because he's a lonely man, when he surprised me with a question. 'You've got a circle of friends in Edinburgh by now, Cameron, haven't you?'

'Yes,' I told him, 'of course. Loads.' That might have been an exaggeration; I had a couple of girl chums from my university days, and I'd had a few boyfriends by then too, but none of them had been keepers. Fact: I'd had to leave Dundee to get laid for the first time. No boy there ever tried it on with me.

'Are any of them cops?' he asked, failing to sound casual.

I frowned at him. 'Why?'

'Ah nothing,' he said. 'Forget it.'

'Like hell I will,' I laughed. 'You wouldn't ask me that without a reason, Grandpa. Come on.'

'Ach,' he was still hesitant, 'I've got a bit of a situation. There's a guy I'm involved in business with, indirectly. Not part of the CamMac group,' he added quickly. 'Nothing you've got an interest in. He might have been a bit naughty. If he was involved with the police, it would be useful to know it.'

'What's his name?'

'Zaliukas, but you'd never have heard of him. He owns pubs and clubs. There's one called Indigo. I believe that's quite well known.'

It was known to me as well. I'd been there a couple of times with a guy I'd met through work. He'd promised me it was drug free because a lot of cops drank there. He'd even pointed a couple of them out, a great tall bloke and his mate, nice, younger and with significant ears.

'Yes,' I lied to my grandfather, 'I know cops. I'll see if the name comes up in conversation.'

'Careful now,' he warned. 'It mustn't get back to me.'

I went to Indigo that same night. The same two guys were at the bar, but they were in a threesome; Lofty had a woman with him. I moved in on his tasty mate . . . and that's how I met Sauce.

I told him my name was Davis, not McCullough; it belonged to my mum's even worse half, so I borrowed it. I hadn't planned anything beyond chatting to him, so what came later was completely spontaneous. I certainly hadn't planned on falling for him. If I'd known that was going to happen, I'd have told him everything about myself from the off, but by the

316

time I realised that, it was too late, and I was compromised.

The thing got messy after that, very, very messy, in fact. Grandpa wasn't involved, thank God, but Sauce was, and when he found out that I'd been less than honest with him, I reckoned we were finished. He's a lovely guy though. I cried on his shoulder, literally and for real, and he took me back. He laid down the rules, though. One of them is that he never meets my grandfather. Grandpa can live with that so I can too.

I'll admit to being a bit worried when Grandpa gave me a message for him. I wasn't keen on doing it at the time, but he told me to trust him, that he had his reasons, so I went along with it, then forgot all about it. I'd never heard of the man that he mentioned, and I didn't expect any progress reports from Sauce, so when he asked me to pass on a few supplementary questions in return, I was surprised to say the least.

Having started it, I felt obliged to carry on. Sauce still refused to deal directly with my grandfather so I set it up that we would go away for the weekend and that I'd call in on Dundee en route. That's what we did. Before we left Edinburgh I called Grandpa to make sure he'd be in; once we were there I dropped Sauce on Discovery Quay and headed for his place.

You hear stories about gangsters, especially the Glasgow kind, having houses that look like Disneyland palaces or medieval fortresses. Grandpa's is an ordinary-looking detached villa on a CamMac development, and the only extraordinary things about it are those you aren't aware of: the garden motion sensors that are part of the alarm system, the infra-red beams that cover the house like tripwires when it's activated, and the fact that it would take an anti-tank missile to penetrate the glass.

'Come away in, lass,' he said, as he unlocked the door. He seemed as fit as ever, lean and trim, the result of regular sessions in the Black Shield Lodge health club. He wore a polo short with its crest on the front. 'How are you?'

'I'm fine, Grandpa. Don't I look it?'

'Aye, but I really meant how's your relation-ship?'

'It's great.' I paused and looked at him. 'I wish we could be like normal people, Grandpa, and that I could bring him here, but he says as long as he's a cop, it's more than his career's worth.'

He shrugged. 'We will never be normal people, Cameron. You can be, Sauce can be, but not if I'm part of it. Your boy's right: I'm the pitch that he cannot touch lest he's seen to be defiled. The only thing I can do for the pair of you is be spotless from now on, and that I'm trying my best to be.'

'In which case,' I ventured, cautiously, 'Sauce passed on your message to his boss, in just the way you asked. But it hasn't been plain sailing. He's been sent back with a couple of questions.'

Grandpa's face changed; it seemed to darken. I'll never be scared of him but when he looks like that I can understand why people are. Funny, I've met Sauce's boss, the chief constable, and he makes me feel exactly the same. 'Such as,' he said, quietly.

'First,' I continued, 'when you gave me your message for him about the man called Bass, did you know that somebody else, a man called Freddy Welsh, was involved in the business?'

'Freddy Welsh,' he repeated.

'Yes. Also, do you know this man, and if so, what do you know about him?'

'I see. Anything else?'

'No, that's all. Sauce is waiting for me at the Discovery; we're going away for the weekend from here. If you've got anything to tell him, you can tell me, and I'll pass it on. He'll phone his chief from Oban.'

His frown was deeper than I'd ever seen it before. His expression was ... ominous. I'd expected that the answers would be short and sweet, 'No' and 'No', but it wasn't shaping up that way. 'Well?' I asked.

He looked at me. His face softened and if it had been anyone else I'd have said his eyes went a wee bit misty. 'What the hell have I done to you, love,' he murmured, 'with my fucking ruthless, reckless life? You and your boyfriend go on to Oban. If you're not booked in anywhere, go on up that coast for a wee bit till you come to a country house hotel called Glen Cameron.'

The name was familiar. 'Isn't that ... ' I began.

'Yes, it's one of ours; you're a director of the company that owns it. I'll call the general manager and tell him you're coming. You two have a nice weekend.'

'Thanks, Grandpa,' I said, 'but what will I tell Sauce about Welsh?'

'Nothing,' he replied, firmly. 'No, don't do that. Tell him that he's out the picture and so are you. Tell him that from now on I'll be dealing with a higher authority.'

# Lowell Payne

The man McGuire decreed that he and I would pay the call on the Varleys. He was head of CID so it was his decision.

I couldn't argue with his reasoning. 'It's not one that I can delegate,' he said, 'but there's no need for more than two of us. Lisa, Special Branch or not, you're still on overtime and we have to keep an eye on that budget. DCI Payne, I still want an outside officer on this. So,' he looked at Mackenzie, 'David, thanks for your significant input to the investigation so far. For now, you can go home to Cheryl and the kids and collect some brownie points.'

The ex-Bandit nodded and murmured, 'Thank you, sir,' but I could tell he wasn't happy to have been excluded. He'd wanted to be part of the end game, and share the credit. I thought I'd seen a certain frisson between McGuire and him earlier, and his reaction confirmed it. I'm a natural sceptic, and I'd been doubtful about the 'reformed character' story from the beginning. I'm pretty sure I'm right, but time will tell on that one. One thing I do know for certain; if it does come to a pissing contest between those two characters, Mackenzie will wind up wet and smelly.

We took McGuire's car. It was a Lexus, four-by-four hybrid, brand new, the kind that gets attention, especially when a cop's driving it.

He caught me looking at it and read my mind. 'It's Paula's,' he explained, without being asked. 'Company car. She runs the company, so she can have what she likes, and with a baby on the way she wants something big and safe. Mine's an Alfa Giulietta,' he added, 'much more modest.'

It would have to be Italian, I guessed, since the Irish don't make cars.

The Lexus was impressive, and very comfortable, but it couldn't fly over the Saturday shopping traffic in west Edinburgh or in Livingston, where there's an enormous shopping complex that attracts people from all over central Scotland.

'Have you been to Varley's place before?' I asked as we broke clear of what I'd hoped would be the last traffic queue and headed towards a housing estate.

'No,' he replied, 'but I've programmed the postcode into the satnav.'

As he spoke a male voice, not the usual patiently polite woman, told him to turn right in three hundred yards. 'There's a speech style option,' he said. 'It seems that Paula prefers the bloke; I must ask her about that.'

One turn later, we were in a cul-de-sac, and our navigator told us that we had reached our destination. 'Obviously, mate,' McGuire muttered.

He didn't tell us which was the Varley home, though; we had to find that out for ourselves.

'Number seven, wasn't it?'

I nodded.

We had pulled up outside number three. The

big man rolled forward, counting as we went, until we found ourselves in front of a detached villa, facing back down the short street. It was the last house in town, literally; behind it we could see open fields. 'That's it.'

There was a car in the driveway, a blue Nissan from the last century: not what you'd expect from somebody with going on for a hundred and fifty grand in an offshore bank account.

The chief superintendent didn't give it a second glance as he braked, switched off and climbed out. I followed him up the path to the front door, crunching small white pebbles under my feet. He rang the doorbell and we waited.

And waited, then waited some more. I pressed the button second time around, with the same non-result. 'Shopping, God damn it,' I said.

'Her maybe, but he fucking well shouldn't be,' McGuire growled. 'Varley's effectively under house arrest. We gave him police bail, but the condition was that he didn't go out.'

'Their car's still here,' I pointed out.

'That heap of shit?' he muttered. 'They must have another. Maybe they're in the back garden.' He led the way again. I knew my role; independent witness more than anything else. 'Inspector,' he called out. 'Mrs Varley.' Consider-ate, in the circumstances, I thought; advance warning in case Mrs V was doing a spot of topless sunbathing; the garden looked secluded enough.

She wasn't, though. There was nobody there, nothing, save some washing hanging on a line, a couple of shirts and a few tea towels. Actually the garden was smaller than I'd expected; much of it was taken up by the extension that had been described to McDermid.

Its size hadn't been exaggerated; it must have made the ground floor fifty per cent bigger. The way the land sloped meant that it was large enough to boast a cellar. McGuire crunched his way up to the back door. It had a bell too, but the result was the same when he rang it. While he was doing that I peered through the kitchen window. There were unwashed plates and pans on the draining board by the sink; next to that there was a chopping board with vegetable scraps on the work surface.

'They must have eaten before they went out,' I said.

'Well I hope Jock enjoyed it,' the chief superintendent retorted, 'for his next meal's going to be fucking porridge. Come on,' he said, and turned away from the door.

'What do we do now?' I asked him. 'Go in?'

'We don't have a search warrant,' he replied. 'In other circumstances, I might be tempted to hear sounds of distress from inside and kick the door down, but in this case I don't want Varley to have as much as one wee toe on the side of the angels. No, we wait. I'll give him half an hour. If he's not back by then, we bugger off and I'll arrange for patrol cars to do regular drive-bys. The first one to find him in will have orders to arrest him and take him to Gayfield Square.'

'Gayfield?' I repeated.

'Nowhere else. The guy's fucked me about;

324

he's betrayed my trust in giving him bail, when a civilian would probably have been held in custody. He can reflect on the stupidity of that when I lock him up in his own station for breaching the conditions. He can stay there until Monday, when he goes before the sheriff. He won't be getting bail then either; he'll be on remand in Saughton, alongside his pal Kenny Bass.'

'You don't miss, do you?' I observed.

'Not when I take aim, Lowell, no.'

# Griff Montell

I hadn't been due for weekend duty, but all things considered I wasn't about to complain about it. The DI had seen his team decimated and I was part of the reason, so when he asked me to work on Saturday, I figured that keeping my head down was best in all the circumstances.

I was glad to be getting out of there myself, truth be told. I'd been due to make DS and although no promises had been made, a nod and a wink from Luke Skywalker had made it pretty clear that I'd be Ray Wilding's replacement after his promotion and move. There might have been a little jealousy from Alice, but I could have talked her through that. She'd have been a bridge between me and a new incoming DC, but she was gone, thanks to my misjudgement, followed by her own, then blown up to disaster proportions by her lizard of an uncle, a man the brass were determined to keep out of my sight, not just because I was likely to be a witness against him, but because I might have decided that taking the bastard apart was worth dismissal.

I saw my promotion as blown, possibly for good; if I'd stayed in Leith as a DC, that would have been tough to take. I'd have felt humiliated by a new guy taking my slot . . . almost certainly Sauce Haddock, if I read things right . . . I'd have been lonely, without both my old sidekicks, and maybe worst of all, I'd have been subjected to the usual Springbok grilling by Alice's replacement. I don't know why, but every Jock guy who meets a South African in my age bracket assumes that he knows Kevin Pietersen, the cricketer.

I'd called Alice that morning. I hadn't slept much and it must have been obvious, for the first thing she asked me was whether I was hung over.

'No,' I replied. 'How about you?'

'Oh yes. I got well smashed last night; what did you expect? You don't want me breathing on you right now, I promise.'

'I'm sorry, Alice. About the job and everything.'

'Don't be,' she told me. 'I should have known better than to trust my swine of an uncle. He's let me down before. I don't know why the hell I did that.'

'I can guess,' I told her. 'You heard Welsh's name and you thought you should give the man the chance to distance himself from him if necessary, before things happened.'

'More or less,' she sighed, 'I suppose. How about your job? What's happened? Nobody would tell me.'

'I'm keeping it. I was worried though; I don't mind admitting it. That's why I went crazy on you, then froze you yesterday. I apologise for all of that; it was the last thing you needed.'

'It's okay,' she said, 'I understood. Friends now, though, yes?'

I smiled. Friends. That's what Alice and I were, more than anything else. There are a lot of things I like about her, not least her spikiness, and her ever-readiness to say what she thinks. 'Yes. Friends.'

'Want to come round tonight?' she asked.

'Yes. We'll go for a meal, somewhere.'

'Okay. But you're paying. I'm unemployed, remember.'

I hung up, feeling glad that I'd taken the plunge, and headed for the office. I'd expected to be there on my own, but I'd underestimated Sammy Pye's ambition. The guy's around the same age as me, and he's a DI already, even if he was accelerated when Stevie Steele was killed. He didn't get there by leaving everything to junior officers; if there's a slot to be filled he's there and he's sharp enough to make sure the bosses know it too.

'Morning, Griff,' he greeted me. 'How are you doing?'

'Fine, thanks. Backside kicked, moving on, then it'll be business as usual.'

'For what it's worth,' he volunteered, 'I'm sorry to be losing you. I'd been looking forward to working with you as my DS, given your experience in the rank back home. You'll enjoy your new job, though.'

'I know,' I admitted. 'I had some of that in South Africa too, but like here it's not something you can put on job applications. Pity about the DS, though: I can always use extra money. I fear I'll be DC Montell for ever now.'

'If you are,' he said, 'it'll mean that nobody upstairs takes a blind bit of notice of anything I

328

say. I sent DCS McGuire an intranet memo saying that I hope what's happened won't hold you back any further.'

I stared at him, taken aback. Ambitious yes, but I hope he makes it.

'I tried to save Alice too,' he added, 'but there was no hope. She was too exposed. If Varley had gone to bat for her, then maybe, but he did the opposite. He claimed in interview that she was the one who called Welsh.'

'He did what?' That was news to me; I rose halfway out of my seat.

'Sit down,' the DI told me quietly. 'Nobody's buying it, but it could be his defence in court, given Alice's history with Welsh. Oh shit,' he murmured. 'You did know about that, didn't you? Short-term; a long time back.'

'I've been told,' I said, 'but as far as I'm concerned, I still don't know about it. It's none of my business anyway, no more than me and that giraffe is hers.'

Pye blinked, and then laughed. 'Catch it kneeling by the pond, did you?'

I was still searching for a comeback when the phone rang. I snatched it up, welcoming the distraction of work, if that's what it was. 'CID, DC Montell.'

'Griff,' a seasoned voice boomed in my ear, 'Bert here, front desk. I've just had a call from a panda patrol. There's a burned-out van on that empty site opposite the Royal Yacht. You're needed there.'

'A burned-out van?' I repeated. 'Have it towed.'

'No' wi' what's in it, son. Like I said, you're needed.'

I passed the message on to the DI. He was pleased, as I was. There's nothing worse than sitting in the office on a Saturday, shifting paper and waiting for something to happen, knowing all along that nothing will. 'My car,' he said as we made for the door.

We didn't have far to go, no more than a mile, but there was no way round the bottleneck at the bridge over the Water of Leith. Mostly it's a stream, on its way through the city; it starts to qualify as a river only when it reaches my flat, which is right on it.

As it turned out there was no rush. The van wasn't going anywhere unassisted, and neither were its passengers. I knew it was a bad one when I saw the younger uniform's face; it was that pale, almost green colour that I've seen a few times in my career, but mostly in the southern hemisphere, where there is a history of people making statements with petrol.

The back doors of the van lay open and the windows had blown out with the heat. I didn't need to look inside to know what was there, but I did so anyway. Black and crispy, definitely overdone.

Pye stepped up like a good leader and stood beside me. 'Jesus,' he whispered. 'How many?'

'Two,' I replied.

'How can you tell?' he asked.

'Simple, count the feet.'

'We need SOCOs,' the boss said, 'and the duty pathologist.'

I'd known that, but I didn't point it out. Instead I called the communications centre and relayed the instruction, leaving them to make the contacts. 'Two corpses in a van on the other side of the Ocean Terminal lagoon; incinerated,' I told them. 'We can dispense with the medical examiner.'

'Do you need Fire and Rescue?' the centre woman asked me.

'No,' I replied. 'The fire's gone out and the victims are well beyond rescue. Everybody else ASAP though. Blues and twos.' For the uninitiated, that means lights and sirens.

The DI had stepped back from the wreck. 'You two,' he told the uniforms, 'get yourselves up to the road end and guard it.' He pointed towards the blocks of flats that overlooked the scene. 'We're in full view here, so there's every chance that someone's calling the press even as I speak. Keep them and everyone else at bay.' The two left, glad of it, and he turned to me. 'It's a wonder nobody reported the fire,' he remarked.

'Not really, boss,' I ventured. 'The doors are facing Ocean Terminal and that's empty at night. Besides, they were probably shut after the fire was lit. To do the job properly you'd turn the thing into a makeshift crematorium.'

'We should back off,' he said. The ground on which we stood was rough and unpaved bare earth, ready for housing development when the economy recovers enough to bring new buyers to the market. 'Look.' He pointed all around us. 'Tyre tracks. We don't want to mess them up any

331

more than we have already. Whoever did this didn't run away from the scene; they drove.'

I nodded. 'Yes, after they'd taken the plates off the van. They've even taken the tax disc, in case it didn't burn properly, I'd guess. They don't want us to identify it too quickly.'

'Or the people inside, possibly.'

The van had been white; it still was recognisably so but its sides were buckled and the remaining paint was bubbled. The tyres had burned as well and the vehicle sat on its bare wheels.

We moved away, as far as the DI's car. 'Gangland?' I asked.

'That's what I'd assume. Maybe I should ask the SCDEA whether they've had any intelligence about tribal warfare on our patch and haven't bothered to share it with us. Although,' he added, on reflection, 'I might put it a bit more discreetly than that.'

'Or even better,' I suggested, 'have somebody else put the question. For example, DCS McGuire; I saw that he had the head of the agency with him yesterday.'

'Yes. He was the outside officer in the interviews with Alice and her uncle.'

'I hope he gave him a really hard time,' I growled, bitterly.

'Time wounds all heels,' Pye chuckled. 'And you're right; it's time also to call our boss man. Big Mario will want to know about this one; I'm sure we'll see him pretty soon.' He pointed east towards the new high-rise Leith. 'See that block over there, on the water's edge? That's his place. Let's haul him out of it.'

# Paula Viareggio

I never thought I'd be a mum, but now that it's going to happen I'm getting used to the idea. It's going to be life-changing, that's for sure, and so, while I'm looking forward to it with an intensity that frightens me at times, at the same time I'm grabbing every chance I can to be the old Paula, the one I'll never be again.

That's why I jumped at Aileen de Marco's invitation to accompany her to that charity gig in Glasgow. Note: she and Bob are married but nobody ever calls her Aileen Skinner; that's one thing she and I have in common, our insistence in clinging to our own family surnames. (The term 'maiden name' went out with the pill as far as I'm concerned. How many Western women these days come as maidens to the marriage bed?)

I don't know her very well, so her call surprised me. I knew that I was third choice, at best, but I didn't give a damn. It was a chance to glam up and put on my glad rags, and I wasn't passing it up. I'd never imagined it was something I'd ever be doing with her, mind you. I have nothing against the woman, but she does strike me as something of a contradiction. As a politician, she's articulate, outgoing, and assertive. I've seen her in parliament, live and on telly, and she seems to have the measure of everyone there, including the current First Minister, the man with the embarrassing waistcoat, without ever rubbing their noses in it. When she appeared on *Question Time* on BBC, the chairman described her as 'the acceptable face of Scottish politics'; I'm sure that's an image she's been careful to cultivate. In private she's much more reserved, much more internalised. I confess that I would never have her on the board of my company, because I could never be sure of what she was thinking.

Mario had just left when she rang again. 'Hi, Paula,' she began as soon as I answered. 'It's Aileen. I'm just calling to check that you're all right for tonight. We're front row centre and I'm sure Clive wouldn't want an empty seat near him.'

'I'm fine,' I assured her. 'I'm still short of going into labour.' *Or voting for them*, I thought, but kept that to myself. 'The wee darling's kicking the crap out of me, sometimes literally, but everything's normal, they tell me. It'll be a couple of weeks yet.'

'That's good. Small change of plan,' she continued. 'I'm in Glasgow already, doing constituency stuff, so, rather than make a double journey to pick you up as I'd intended, I've taken the First Minister up on his offer of a government car for you.'

It was on the tip of my tongue to say that I could still fit behind the wheel of my own, when I remembered that my husband had taken it. With him, there's never total certainty over when he'll be back. 'Thank him for me,' I said. 'Do they need the address?'

'No, they've got it. What are you wearing tonight?' she asked. A woman's question.

'The one and only evening dress I have that still fits me.'

'Colour?'

'Red.'

'Ah,' she sighed. 'Me too. I don't really have a choice at public events,' she explained. 'It's expected of me.'

'Aileen,' I offered, 'I'd wear something else if I could, but I reckon it's either that or a nightgown.'

She laughed. 'Don't worry about it. Between us we'll rub our Nationalist First Minister's nose well in it. Hey, do you want to know about the guy we're going to see? Clive told me all about him.'

'I looked him up,' I replied. 'He's third-generation Lebanese and he's a Muslim. He's a bit of a poster boy in his home country and in the Middle East in general. Famous for refusing to play in the Eurovision Song Contest because there was an Israeli entry.'

'I thought he was classical.'

'He is, but any bugger can turn up in Eurovision these days; he was supposed to play a piano break in the Swedish entry.'

'Maybe ABBA will be on in the interval tonight,' Aileen said. 'But I won't count on it. See you later.'

She left me wondering whether I had time to take a taxi up to Harvey Nicks and look for something classy, roomy, and in any colour other than red. I might have done that too, if the phone hadn't rung again.

It was Sarah Grace: my morning for Skinner

spouses. Sarah's much more of a pal than Aileen though. We see each other regularly, and talk about anything but husbands.

'You busy?' she asked me. 'Or are you just too pregnant to come out and play?'

When I thought about it, I realised that I was. Chauffeur or not, the evening might be taxing, so I reckoned I'd better rest up for it. I told her as much, and we agreed that she'd come to me for coffee. As soon as I'd heard her I realised that I was listening to a different Sarah. She sounded excited, a little hyper even, and happy, as if something good had happened in her life. With her, that could mean only one thing. I asked her as much. Her denial didn't convince me and I looked forward to quizzing her some more when she arrived.

Only she didn't. A couple of hours had gone by before she called to say she couldn't make it, but by that time I knew it, and why. If Mario and I were charged for calls received as well as made, the bill would be horrendous. I was looking through my choicest coffee beans from our deli range . . . the best in Scotland . . . trying to pick one for Sarah's visit, when the phone rang again.

'Yes?' I said as I picked it up.

'Ms Viareggio?' The voice was familiar, but I couldn't place it. As I've said, even though it's ex-directory, our number has some of the heaviest traffic in town. There was background noise but oddly I wasn't certain whether it was on the line or coming through the window.

'This is Paula,' I admitted. 'Your turn now.'

'Sorry, it's DI Pye; Leith. Is the boss in?'

Of course I knew him. 'No, Sammy, he's not. He's working, as I take it you are too. He'll be in the office, or if not, on his mobile . . . if it's urgent.'

'If it wasn't, I'd know better than to call him today. If I can't raise him and he comes in soon, could you tell him that I'm at a major incident on the vacant development site off Newhaven Place.'

'How major?'

'A burned-out van and it's not empty.'

'Oh my God,' I exclaimed.

Sammy panicked, just a little. I think he had visions of me being shocked into labour. 'I'm sorry,' he exclaimed. 'I shouldn't have told you that.'

'No reason why you shouldn't,' I told him. 'I'm not squeamish. I reacted that way because I may have seen it.'

That squared him up. 'What do you mean?'

'I'm not sleeping too well just now. I got up for a glass of water, early hours; half past one, maybe two a.m., I can't be certain. We have a window that faces west. I looked out and I could see a fire, in the area you're talking about. I just assumed it was kids, lighting a bonfire and having a few drinks. I went back to bed and thought no more about it, until now.' I paused. 'Not kids, though?'

'No, not kids. Although to tell you the truth, I'm not sure what's inside the thing. We'll need to wait for the pathologist to tell us that. She's on her way here now.'

I put the coffee beans back in the cupboard.

# Bob Skinner

I was in something of a daze all the way back to Gullane. As my granny used to say when I was very young, my head was full of bumblebees. Physically I knew where I was and where I was going; spiritually and morally, I hadn't a clue. When I married Aileen and put my name to the paperwork, I imagined that I was signing up for a stable life as a faithful husband, putting my wife above everything else, as I expected she would put me.

Within a forty-eight-hour period that ideal was dust; my certainties were doubts, my vows broken. So was my marriage.

I've been there before, so I knew it. Sarah had told me some home truths, and I'd confessed some stuff to her that I'd never articulated to anyone before, not even to myself. The things she'd said about my emotional instability, they were undeniable, and she'd painted a Dickensian picture of my Christmases yet to come, that actually was one I'd seen in my darker dreams.

As I drove home to our kids, I thought of what she'd said.

*'Myra is dead, and you can no longer use her as a template for a living partner.'*

True on the first count, and I suspected I was guilty as charged on the second. Shame on you, Bob Skinner.

*'You are far bigger than any police force, not*

*the other way around.'*

Well now, I'd never made that comparison, but force me to the truth and I'll have to admit that for almost thirty years I've seen the force and myself as indivisible. Maybe that's why Aileen thought she could force me to toe her line.

Had she manipulated me into marriage, as Sarah thought but hadn't quite said? Was ours more a political alliance than anything else? I still can't answer that, but what I will recognise and admit to now is that it was one of convenience on my part. I'd been tired, I was beaten up by endless crises and confrontations, I saw life with Aileen as a place to hide and I crept into it for shelter. I'd been strong, but I'd become weak. Was that before or after she'd cut my hair?

And something else Sarah had said, with real anger.

'None of our children have ever mentioned the woman to me, not once.'

I hadn't dwelt on that at the time, but when I considered it, away from Sarah's vehemence, I saw what she meant. I tried to recall a single time I'd seen Aileen hug one of the kids, or kiss them, or even ruffle their hair as parents do, but I couldn't. Not even Seonaid, who is a mistress of cute.

'Love me, love my kids.' It isn't a clause in the contract when a parent remarries, but it's implied.

Yes, Aileen and I had some truths to face, that I recognised. Would one of them be the fact that I spent the night with my ex-wife? Should I tell her that? Hell, no. How cruel would that be?

'Coward,' I whispered, as I turned into our street.

The kitchen clock read ten past eight when I stepped through the door. Trish was there, supervising Seonaid's breakfast. 'Daddeee!!!' the wee one shouted, then she jumped down from her seat and bounced towards me, all eyes and blonde wavy hair. I swept her up in my arms and hugged her.

'How's my doll?' I whispered in her ear.

'I'm not a doll, I'm a girl,' she scolded. 'Like Lex.' When she was starting to talk, that was as close as she could come to her half-sister's name, and it had stuck.

I sat her back on her chair. 'That you are, Seonaid,' I said. 'That you are.' I glanced at Trish. 'Where are the boys?'

She smiled. 'Still asleep; there was a sandcastle contest on the beach yesterday evening. I gave them both a late pass, after I brought Seonaid home. Their team won; Mark designed, James Andrew and two other boys built.' She paused. 'Would you like some breakfast, Bob? I could whip you something up.'

I almost told her that I'd eaten already, but veered away from that. I was sure she'd be wondering where I'd slept, and I didn't want to feed her speculation. Not that she'd have asked. She's been with us for years, through thick and very thin; she's both loyal and discreet.

'Thanks, but I'm not hungry,' I replied. The truth, if not unbridled.

'Coffee then?'

I nodded, then remembered Sarah's medical

advice. 'No thanks.' I stopped myself in the act of reaching for my mug, and went to the fridge instead. I took out a carton of milk and poured myself a glass. I drank some, then smiled at my daughter. 'If it's good enough for Seonaid, it's good enough for me.'

She beamed back then laughed. 'You've got a white moustache, Daddy.'

. . . thus pointing out to an adult that wherever I'd been I hadn't been able to shave.

I licked my top lip. 'Any calls?' I asked Trish.

'No, Bob, none.'

That was a relief; I thought that Aileen might have phoned to say goodnight. Then it passed and, perversely, I was annoyed that she hadn't.

She did ring, though, twenty minutes later, when I was in mid-shave. Trish doesn't answer when I'm home, unless she's asked, so I snatched it up on the fifth ring.

'You're in, then,' she said.

'Of course,' I replied. 'Didn't you expect me to be?'

'I thought you might have gone to Andy's last night, for a grumbling session, council of war, whatever.'

'I don't grumble, my dear,' I told her firmly. 'And there is no war until you and Clive fire the opening shot.'

'Then you're no tactician,' she shot back. 'In your shoes, I'd be getting my retaliation in first. As it is, you're too late. I've put my name to an article for tomorrow's *Sunday Herald* explaining why a unified police force is essential for Scotland. And they've done an interview with

341

Toni Field to back it up.'

'Hey,' I exclaimed. 'She's a serving police officer. I thought you told me we weren't allowed to get into the political debate.'

There was a moment's silence; I'd caught her off guard. 'She's not debating,' she snapped, when she'd worked it out. 'She isn't arguing with us, not like you are. It's an interview and she's answering some questions, that's all.'

'I thought you didn't like the woman.'

'I don't.'

'But she's useful to you so you'll go along with her. She's your fucking poodle and you've let her off the lead for a bit.'

'Wrong breed, Bob. More like a Doberman.'

'Then I won't try and tame her. I'll just shoot her down the first time she shows her teeth.'

'That's your answer to everything, isn't it? Aggression.'

'Only when threatened,' I countered. 'You should know that by now. You can stand me up at the gates of hell and I won't back down. Or maybe you thought you'd smoothed that edge away too. You told me once I should be the sort of chief constable I want to be. Too fucking right; I certainly won't be the one you want.'

I wasn't making it any better, was I?

'Why did you call, Aileen?' I asked.

'Not to start a fight,' she said. 'To tell you that I'm going to stay in Glasgow tonight as well. The chauffeur will take Paula home, but there'll be a reception after the concert that I really should stay for.'

'And you'll want to check the *Sunday Herald*

first edition. Yes, you stay there, that's fine.'

'It's probably best that I do.'

'Agreed. And maybe the night after that as well. And so on.'

'We have to talk, Bob,' she murmured.

'Why? We're lousy at it, unless the discussion's going entirely to your satisfaction. Aileen, I've had enough of crap like this in my life. If I'm not the guy you thought I was, live with it, don't put pressure on me to comply and don't take it personally if I won't. I don't have strings, so don't try to pull them.'

'Why are you always,' she hissed, 'so fucking sure that you're right?'

'Because in my professional life that's generally been the case,' I replied. 'Personally, domestically, the opposite's been true, for the last quarter of a century. You're the latest in a whole series of mistakes, Aileen. I'm sorry if it's hurt you. Now I am off to spend a lovely day with my kids.'

'To hide behind them,' she sneered. 'Your kids!'

'No,' I laughed, seeing things more clearly than I had in years, 'to give them what they need and deserve: my love and attention. If you'd been prepared to do that it might have worked for us, but that's not what you're about, is it? I don't blame you for it; we are what we are.'

I hung up, I finished shaving, and I went downstairs, feeling much more calm than when I'd climbed them. The boys were having breakfast by then, so I took Seonaid out to the garden, with a ball, and we spent some time working on her close control. On impulse, I called Sarah on my mobile. I felt the need to apologise for inflicting myself on her, but she wouldn't let me. As we talked, I looked down at the little girl we'd made together and realised that I'd never felt closer to either of them. Then she told me again that she still loved me and I had to admit that I'd never got that out of my system either.

When we finished I knew that things were going to be difficult for a while, but that they were going to be a hell of a lot better too.

Mark and Jazz came out to join us. We chose teams, two-a-side, youngest against the oldest, and I made sure that Seonaid won. That wasn't difficult; Mark can beat the world at any game on computer, but put him on grass and he's rubbish, bless him. Once the sun had climbed a little higher, I decided that we'd all go to the beach, not the busy one that we can see from the house, but the secluded one. Gay people, men mostly, are known to go there sometimes for the peace and quiet to which they're entitled. There was a time a few decades back when my force used to give them a hard time. That doesn't happen on my watch, and anyone else who considers pestering them finds out very quickly that it's a bad idea.

As I sat on the edge of the dunes and watched the kids play, I began to imagine a day when I wouldn't have to bring my two mobiles with me, or even one of them, when it would be them, me, and nobody else. It might not need imagination in the not too distant future, I realised, if the legislators had their way with the best interests of our nation.

'Retaliation in first,' I whispered, feeling a grin spread across my face. Compulsory or not, mobiles can be useful. I dug my personal one out, scrolled through my phone book till I reached 'S' and dialled the number I'd been after.

'Editor's office,' a voice chirped.

'Mrs Crampsey, please. Tell her it's the chief constable.'

June Crampsey has been managing editor of the *Saltire* newspaper since Xavi Aislado, her predecessor and its co-owner, took himself off to Spain about ten years ago. She and I get on well, and I've always looked after her, for three reasons: Xavi is a mate, her dad is a retired police officer and she's a bloody brilliant journalist.

'Bob,' she said as she came on line. 'What have we done wrong?'

'You've almost missed out on a bloody good story,' I told her. 'Your Glasgow rival is running it tomorrow. It's all about a secret political pact to turn Scotland into a police state.'

'What?' she exclaimed.

'Okay,' I chuckled, 'that might be a slight overstatement, but given the wrong hands on the tiller at Holyrood, the potential is there. This is what it's all about.'

I spent the next twenty minutes briefing her on what was happening, and giving her my view of it. Most of it was directly quotable; the rest of it, the more florid phrases and the direct attacks on the First Minister and Aileen, was for attribution to 'a senior police source'. The world would guess it was me, but June would never confirm it.

We were both slightly breathless when we were done. 'I owe you one, Bob,' June said.

'I might take you up on that,' I replied. 'I might need a job soon.'

'Any time.' I believe she meant it. 'When can I put it on our online edition?' she asked.

'Any time after seven thirty this evening. My wife and the First Minister will be at a concert in Glasgow this evening. I'd like to ruin their half-time cocktails. It wouldn't do either of us any harm if you fed it to the broadcast media at that time also.'

'Will do. I must get in touch with Xavi,' she added. 'He's going to love this.'

As I ended the call, Mark wandered across. He's a perceptive kid; misses nothing, except for any ball he ever takes a swing at. 'What are you doing, Dad?' he asked.

'Crossing the Rubicon,' I told him, as I slipped my phone back into its pouch on the strap of my knapsack.

'What does that mean?'

'Doing something that you can't go back on. The Rubicon's a river in Italy: in ancient Roman times if you crossed it with an army, it was a declaration of war on the state. Julius Caesar did.'

'What happened to him?'

'Nothing. He won.'

He frowned. 'Will you win?' he murmured.

I smiled, reached out and ruffled his hair. 'I have done already, son. I've done what I believe to be right. If I hadn't, that would have been a defeat.'

I rose and we walked towards the receding tide, out to the spot that James Andrew had chosen for his latest sand sculpture. He was working away, in spite of, rather than with, his sister's assistance.

'Can you tell what it is yet?' he asked as we approached.

'You sound just like Rolf Harris,' I told him.

He stared at me. 'Who's Rolf Harris?'

Wrong generation, Bob. 'A very famous man,' I said, lamely.

'Does he build sandcastles?'

'Probably.'

I dug four drinks from my bag and handed them round, then gave each of the kids a banana, Seonaid's favourite food since she's been old enough to stuff one in her mouth. I cast an eye over Jazz's work in progress. 'A car,' I said. 'It's going to be a car.'

He raised an eyebrow. 'What kind?'

'That's beyond me.'

'Like Alex's,' he revealed, proudly. 'With the roof down.'

His older sister had acquired a new convertible coupé, to celebrate her assumption as a partner in her firm. It could only have been her car that he would have chosen.

'How long can we stay, Daddy?' Seonaid asked.

I checked my watch. I'd told Trish we'd be

back at one; that gave us more than two hours. 'At the very least,' I declared, 'until you've had a test drive in your big brother's car. If you come for a paddle with me, maybe the boys will be able to finish it faster.'

She didn't see the logic in that, but she took my hand as we walked towards the water's edge. 'I like it when you're home, Daddy,' she said, looking up at me.

'I like it too. I promise that I'll spend more time at home from now on.'

Tempting fate is always a bad idea; when you do it with your kids it's criminal. My daughter had barely put a toe in the water before my police phone rang. 'Bugger!' I snarled, quietly. I took a few paces backward as I fished it out of its hiding place. I checked the number before I answered, and recognised it as our force communications centre, our hub.

'Yes?' I snapped, unreasonably. 'Chief Constable.'

'Sorry to disturb you, sir,' a woman began. I didn't believe her. 'Sergeant Christie here. I've got a caller on the line who insists on speaking to you, and to you alone. He says it's most urgent and that nobody else can deal with it.'

'Have you told him that wasting police time is an offence and that wasting mine can be positively dangerous?'

'I've done my best to dissuade him, sir,' Christie assured me, 'but I felt I had to call you just in case it was genuine. He doesn't sound nearly old enough, but the caller says he's your grandfather.'

*Jesus*, I thought, *what next*? I took a deep breath to stop myself from roaring abuse at the woman, and as I did, an outside possibility occurred to me.

'Is that exactly what he said?' I asked.

'No, sir, not quite. He said, 'Tell him it's Grandpa.' Those were his exact words.'

'What a surprise,' I murmured. 'Since it's family you'd better put him through. Understand also, we do not record this call. Got that?'

'Loud and clear, sir,' Sergeant Christie assured me.

A moment later, the background noise changed. I waited for another few seconds to ensure that Christie had cleared off, then said, 'Mr McCullough, I presume.'

'Yes,' a voice replied, one I knew from what I'd assumed would be a one-off meeting a few months earlier, 'it's me.'

'I'm not sure I welcome this,' I told him. 'I'm on the beach with my kids at the moment, so it's a wee bit intrusive.'

'Give them my apologies, won't you. Mr Skinner, if you think I'd be phoning you without a bloody good reason, then the sea air's going to your head. I'd an intrusion myself this morning, from my granddaughter, on behalf of her boyfriend.' The man sounded agitated. That was a surprise; Cameron McCullough had struck me as a man who was never ruffled.

'Look,' he continued, 'when I sent you that message via young Haddock, it was no more than a goodwill gesture, a sign that I am out of that life and that young Cameron should be

349

allowed to get on with hers.'

'Mr McCullough,' this was definitely not someone with whom I'd ever be familiar, 'you're out of the life because circumstances made it so. For example, those two brutes who used to do your dirty work are fertilising a cemetery, because they, and you, crossed the wrong man a while back, and there are no obvious replacements available. If you've seen the light, it was a police officer who was shining it on you. People like you don't reform, you do what's expedient. If you expect me to pass your retirement announcement on to Brian Mackie, the new Tayside chief, or to Andy Martin at the Agency, you're wasting your time. I'm very happy for young Sauce and Cheeky, but you are still going to be under police scrutiny for the rest of your life, and if you make one slip, you will be put away.'

'Tell me something I don't know, man,' he exclaimed. 'I'm not fucking naïve.'

'Then why are you calling me?'

'Because this is no longer something I can have our Cameron involved in, or even her lad. It's dangerous for her and it's way above his rank and station. This has to be between you and me.'

'If that's how you want it . . . '

'It is,' he insisted. 'First off, though, are you recording this?'

'No; I've forbidden it, specifically. You have my word on that. But I can't promise that other agencies aren't listening in.'

'I'm secure,' he retorted sharply. 'I swept my

350

place this morning and this is a throwaway phone.'

I laughed. 'This from a man who assures me he's straight.'

'I value my privacy, Mr Skinner, in every aspect of my life.'

'Fair enough. Now go on.'

'Okay. We've established that I tipped you off about Kenny Bass. I did so for the reasons I mentioned a minute ago, but I'll admit that there was one other. The little bastard really annoyed me. He came to me, in my hotel, and he had the fucking temerity to tell me that he'd moved a load of contraband tobacco into Scotland, too much for him to handle in Edinburgh, and to ask me if I wanted to take some of it off his hands. The bloody cheek of it! Me! Smuggled fags, for Christ's sake! In my hotel!' he raged. 'My legitimate place of business! I turned down his generous offer and I told him to get the fuck down the road and never come back. It niggled me for days afterwards, until finally I thought, fuck it, and decided to sort the pipsqueak out, but do it constructively, if you get my drift.'

'I get it,' I told him. 'Hence your goodwill gesture.'

'Yes,' he continued, 'but I had to be careful. I didn't want to end up on some Edinburgh detective's informant list; those things can leak out. So I passed the message the way I did. I didn't expect any thanks for it, mind; I don't envisage being on the Queen's honours list any time soon. I didn't expect to hear any more about it other than a line in the paper saying that

351

Bass had been sent off on holiday. So when our Cameron came to see me this morning, it threw me right off balance.' He paused. 'What the fuck do you mean, Skinner, using my granddaughter in that way?'

'Eh?' I exclaimed, astonished. 'You were the one who used her in the first place . . . Grandpa.'

'The hell I did,' he protested. 'I just gave her a wee message to pass to her boyfriend to pass to you. I didn't intend for her to be a conduit for a police investigation, to be carrying a fucking questionnaire from you.'

'I'm sorry,' I said. 'Truly sorry. I mean that. There was nothing to stop me sending my head of CID up to see you, with Andy Martin for company. I wish I had now. In fact, I still could. Would you prefer that?'

He got the message. 'No, no, no,' he conceded, sharpish. 'You're right; you were showing discretion, I suppose. It's just . . . when she mentioned the name Freddy Welsh to me, it set off all sorts of alarm bells.'

'So you know him?'

'Yes, but I had no idea that a small-timer like Kenny Bass would have been involved with him.'

'So what about Welsh?' I asked. 'What makes him a man to be feared?'

'He isn't. It's the people he does business with that are.' He paused, for a few seconds. 'You really don't know?' he murmured. Then he laughed, quietly. 'You know something, Mr Skinner, you've restored my faith in human nature and my belief in the frailty of man. I thought my record might have been in danger, but it's intact. I've still never met a copper who's as smart as he thinks he is.'

'I'm under no illusions,' I told him. 'People go out of their way to show me how limited I am, so join the list. But bear this in mind; if I'm that fucking stupid I might be reckless enough to name you as the informant in the report that we're about to make to the Crown Office on Kenny Bass. I've got a police officer implicated in this thing, thanks to Mr Welsh, whatever he is, and I'm not pleased. So you be bloody careful whose tail you try to pull. Now, don't piss me about any further. What do you know about Welsh? You tell me or I'll have you lifted within the hour and brought to my office . . . and yes, there will be photographers outside.'

I'll swear I heard him growl, like a cornered bear. 'Okay,' he murmured, at last, 'but only for our Cameron's sake. That's how this thing started after all. I know Freddy Welsh personally through my main company, the CamMac group. As you'll know, I'm a developer, building houses, offices, small factories, but I don't employ a permanent construction workforce. Freddy Welsh is a building contractor, on a reasonable scale. Not huge, but big enough to take on most of the projects I do, or parts of them.'

'Did you launder money though his business . . . when you were in the life, that is?'

'Hell no. Freddy's accountant lives up his arse. Little chance of that. No, like mine, Freddy's company, Anglesey Construction, he calls it, is completely legit. But there's another side to him.

As a young man, Freddy did some military service as a regular; he learned his trade in the army . . . he's an electrician . . . and he learned some other stuff too. He did a tour in Ireland, and in Kuwait, and while he was there, he became the battalion armourer. He carried the nickname with him when he left.'

'What nickname?'

'The Armourer. That's what they call him, and that's what he does. He supplies weapons.'

'To whom?' I asked, grammatical to a fault.

'To anyone who wants to buy them,' he replied, 'for whatever purpose.'

'You mean he's an arms dealer?'

'Yes, but not in the way you understand. Let's say you're a figure in the other world, and you are planning an operation, an armed robbery, a kidnap for ransom, a hit, anything that needs shooters. It's a fact of life, that when a gun is fired on a job, it creates a piece of history. It leaves a trace. Jails around the world and death rows in many a place are full of people who either didn't know that or didn't take it seriously enough. They use a weapon, they pass it on, someone else gets caught with it, it's traced back to the original user, and he's done. Freddy Welsh takes that problem away. His specialty is the supply of weapons that are absolutely clean. Give him a shopping list and he will fill it; he will source what you need. When the job is done, if the customer wants, he will take that weapon back, and he will rebuild it, change its characteristics, whatever, so that effectively it's become a new firearm all over again. Either that or you use it the once and when you're done just throw the thing away.'

'What sort of weapons are we talking about here?'

'You name it,' McCullough replied. 'You want an American Derringer, something you can hide in the palm of your hand yet blow somebody's brains out, he'll get you one. You want a heavy machine gun? It's yours. Gatling gun? Probably. He sources them all from around the world, and he supplies them, cash and carry.'

'From where?'

'Nobody knows. Nobody asks. His product is too good, so nobody ever rocks the boat.'

'Who are his customers?'

'Everybody,' he said, slowly.

'You mean organised crime?'

'I mean, everybody. If the CIA decided that you knew too much, they'd probably get the gun that killed you from Freddy. If it's that serious, he's where you go. That's probably why you've never heard of him.'

'Have you ever used him?'

'Me?' He chuckled. 'Please, Mr Skinner, you'd never catch me anywhere near Freddy Welsh other than on a building site.'

'No,' I murmured, 'I don't suppose I would. Your two deceased associates though, that might have been another matter.'

'Whatever,' he said. 'The book is closed now, okay. You and I, we never meet or speak again, unless of course you and your highly placed wife happen to be guests at one of my hotels some time, and I'm there. If that happens, you can buy me a drink.'

'Don't let your life depend on it,' I told him. I ended the call, put my phone back in its place and sat down on the sand, feeling its dampness seep into my shorts as I watched Seonaid jumping over small retreating waves, and as I pondered.

'Freddy Welsh,' I murmured. 'The Armourer and a second-division smuggler like Kenny Bass. What's wrong with that picture? Unless . . . I wonder what else might have been on Kenny's truck, apart from those fags,' I mused aloud, 'and I wonder how much Jock bloody Varley knew about it. You're weighed in for this,' I whispered, quoting Welsh's words to his wife's cousin. 'For what, Jock?' I asked myself, deciding as I did that nobody but me was going to put that question to Mr Bass, and that 'No comment' would not be an acceptable reply.

On another day, I'd have driven straight to Saughton to confront the toerag, but I decided that pleasure could keep for a few hours, while I enjoyed another. I lured Seonaid out of the water with the promise of another banana, and together we rejoined the boys. The car was almost finished; it wasn't a bad likeness of Alex's coupé, right down to the kidney grille, even if the upholstery was sand. It had wing mirrors. Mark's idea, James Andrew explained; built around twigs they had found at the high-water mark, and an improvised steering wheel made from a piece of driftwood.

They gave their sister the honour of the first

356

drive. I thought the seat might collapse, but the sand was packed tight, and it took her weight. It even supported Jazz when he stepped over the edge and into the passenger seat. I took a few photographs on my family phone and sent the best of them in an MMS to their mother, with a note that said, 'Being a dad, when the phone allows.'

The work one allowed for another hour, by which time we had started the walk back home . . . or rather three of us had, for Seonaid decided that she'd rather ride on my shoulders. When it rang I was able to reach it without having to set her down. The incoming number wasn't available for display; hardly surprising since the caller was the deputy director of MI5.

'Where do I find you?' she asked. 'At work or at play? Don't bother pretending,' she added, grinning, I imagine. 'I have technology in this building that can tell me exactly where you are.'

'Who's that, Daddy?' Seonaid chirruped. I put a finger to my lips to hush her.

'Ah,' Amanda said, 'I see.'

'Yes, but don't worry, I can still listen.'

'Okay. Your call yesterday, and those items you sent; it seems we have a situation on our hands, one that needs handling, urgently. This isn't one that can be passed down the line, Bob, not too far at any rate. Who's been involved in this investigation, since the body was discovered?'

'The legwork's been done by a young detective constable. He was reporting to me about something else, but I asked him what he'd been up to on Mortonhall Man . . . that's what they

357

call him. When he told me, I reckoned it might be one for you. His line manager's in the loop, though. DI Becky Stallings; she's one of my best, ex-Metropolitan; I can call her in on this. Will I do that?'

'No,' she replied, 'not at this stage. I would like to brief you on this, personally. Once you're up to speed, you can advise on what happens after that.'

'Fair enough,' I told her. 'When can I expect you and where do you want to meet? My place or somewhere anonymous, like the airport hotel?'

'Sorry,' she chuckled, 'communication breakdown; I should have said 'we' rather than I. You never get involved with our regional offices but you know we have them. I have a very bright and very promising man in charge of our Glasgow location. He's heading in your general direction as we speak. Now that we've established where you are, would you mind very much if he came to your home? We can trust your wife's discretion, I know.'

'That's more than I can,' I retorted. 'In any case,' I added quickly, 'she's not here; only the kids and their carer. But yes, he can come; I'll tell Trish he's an insurance salesman.'

'He doesn't look much like an insurance salesman, but that will do well enough. How soon can he arrive?'

'We're about twenty minutes away from home, maybe less if Little Madam gets a pony ride all the way. Any time after that.'

'Good. He was heading for your office, but I'll

tell him to divert to your home address. He should be with you within the hour.' She paused. 'By the way, Bob, I'm not sure why, but he's absolutely bricking it over the prospect of meeting you.'

'He should be,' I said. 'He's buggering up my quiet family Saturday. What's his name?'

'Houseman. Clyde Houseman.'

# Mario McGuire

It would not be an exaggeration to say that I was fucking cheesed off over the absence of Jock Varley from the place where he had been told to go and to remain, when we'd turned him loose the day before. It had been touch and go as to whether he was bailed. I'd been against it, in case we were accused afterwards of special treatment, but Andy Martin was in one of his mellower moods, inspired, possibly, by the prospect of a weekend with Alex, and he persuaded me that it would be all right.

I phoned him. I couldn't help it. When he answered, I could hear someone female singing in the background. 'Mario,' he said, as if I didn't know that, 'this is a surprise. You're not going to tell me you need me again, are you?'

'No,' I said quietly. 'In the circs that the last thing I'm going to do. Guess where I am? I'm at Inspector Jock Varley's house. And guess where he is? I mean it, go on, for your guess is as good as mine!'

'What?' he barked, laid-back no longer. 'You are joking.'

'Do I sound like Les Dawson? DCI Payne, our Strathclyde colleague, and I are outside the place now; Varley's vanished and so has his wife.'

'They've probably gone shopping.'

'That's been suggested already,' I said, 'but I've gone off the idea. Jock wouldn't be stupid enough to break his bail conditions for a trip to the Co-op. No, he's done a runner. We've turned up a solid link between Freddy Welsh and him, or to be exact, his wife. Lowell and I are here to put the thumbscrews on him over it. My feeling is that he's anticipated that and the pair of them are off their mark. They can afford to; they've got going on for a hundred and fifty grand in an offshore bank account, and it won't be easy for us to touch it.'

'What are you going to do?' he asked.

'Wait here for a bit, just in case I'm wrong and Ella has made him take her up to the Almondvale Centre to push the supermarket trolley. When I'm satisfied she hasn't, I'll put a general call out for them, stop on sight'

'Will Varley be safe with you if he does turn up?' Andy wasn't kidding; he meant it.

'Probably,' I replied, 'if only because my minder's with me. But you're right. I'm probably better off picking up Freddy Welsh than sitting here. I'll talk to the chief before I do that, though.'

'Best to do so,' he acknowledged. 'He's got his teeth in this one. And he's got other problems. He needs handling with care just now. One thing I can do,' he continued, 'and I will. I'll warn Alice Cowan. I can't imagine him being crazy enough to go after her but . . . '

'That really would be crazy,' I growled. 'Alice would fucking kill him. But you do that, Andy; you might even ask her if she has any idea where he might go, somewhere we don't know about, a caravan maybe.'

'I'll do that. I'll let you know if she has any ideas.'

I ended the call. 'Come on,' I said to Payne, 'we're out of here. We'll head back to the office and then I'll call Jack McGurk . . . he should be on duty at Torphichen Place . . . and tell him to go and lift Welsh.'

There was no way of avoiding that bloody awful traffic around the shopping centre. I took advantage of the crawl to call the Gayfield Square office and ask them to find the number of Jock Varley's car, figuring that it was bound to be noted somewhere in the station, since he was bound to drive to work from where he lived, and must have had a parking space there.

The duty officer wasn't too sure where to look. I told him to call the station commander if he had to, even if it meant hauling him off the golf course, and get back to me, pronto. 'Is it that urgent, sir?' he asked. I could sense Lowell Payne wince as the question boomed from the speaker of the Lexus's Bluetooth system.

'It's a matter of life and death, Sergeant,' I snapped. 'Yours, unless you get the finger out and do what you're bloody told.'

I was beginning to feel a little peckish as we reached the outskirts of Edinburgh. 'Fancy a bite of lunch?' I asked Payne. 'There's a nice Indian in Davidson's Mains.'

'Sound good to me,' he replied. 'I'll pick up the tab and put it on my expenses.' He may have been joking, he may not.

'Which I will probably have to sign,' I pointed out. 'There may be a slight ethical dilemma

362

there, Lowell. My idea, so I'm paying.'

They do very nice pakora in that place and an exceptional lamb bhuna; I was beginning to salivate as we got there. I found a vacant parking slot right outside and pulled into it. I was on the point of switching off, when my phone sounded. 'Bad timing,' I muttered but I took the call, expecting it to be the Gayfield sergeant, or, with a large piece of luck, somebody from the Livingston office to tell me that Varley had turned up at home and had been arrested, as I'd ordered.

But it wasn't. Instead, I heard the crisp, controlled voice of Detective Inspector Sammy Pye, who is so blatantly hell-bent on being a highflyer that some of his more cynical colleagues call him Luke Skywalker, a nickname that secretly I love. I'm sure he'll get there, but it's not my job to make it easy for him; rather the opposite, I have to make him prove his worth.

'There's been an incident, boss,' he reported. 'I'm there now. You might want to see this for yourself.'

'It better not be a shoplifting, Sammy,' I warned him, 'or a flasher in the Commonwealth Pool.'

'No, sir,' he replied smoothly, 'it's a bit more serious than that. It's a double homicide; found on an open area in Leith that you can see from your house.'

'Are you suggesting that I failed to report it?' I growled. I like to rattle Sammy's cage every so often, for reasons aforesaid.

'No, boss,' he replied, 'but Paula did.' Before I

could nail him for that he moved on. 'We have human remains here, burned very efficiently. Dr Grace has just arrived and had a look. She says she won't even go firm on the gender until she's got them back to the mortuary. Are you coming down or will I let her have them as soon as the photographer and video guy are done?'

I glanced at Payne. He didn't look hungry any more, and I confess that I'd lost my appetite for pakora, let alone the lamb bhuna. 'I'll be down, Sammy,' I told him. 'Won't be long.'

I left our parking place for the next lucky punter and headed for Leith. I didn't need specific directions; the area Pye had described is my home patch. But I hadn't a clue what he had meant about Paula. I thought about calling her, but decided against it, not on hands free with a passenger by my side.

When we got to the scene a perimeter had been set up, bounded by tape. A couple of dozen, maybe thirty spectators stood along it, ogling. A few of them held pint glasses, overspill from the pub along the road, no doubt. 'Excellent,' I grumbled. 'For the benefit of those who didn't know that something had gone off here we have to advertise the fact with a fucking Day-Glo border.'

The entrance was guarded by a couple of plods. The younger one stepped in front of my car. 'Sorry, you can't come in here,' he said.

'Oh dear,' Payne whispered and put a hand over his eyes as if he didn't want to witness something awful, but I'd been that young rookie myself once.

I showed him my warrant card. 'I can, Constable,' I told him before he had time to say 'sorry' again. I patted him on the shoulder. 'But I like to see the job being done right.' I nodded towards the watchers. 'One suggestion: you might like to ask those people with the pint tumblers if they know there's a by-law against public drinking.'

'Yes, sir,' he responded, and headed towards them.

'Is there?' my passenger asked, when he was out of earshot.

'To tell you the truth, Lowell,' I admitted, 'I'm not sure if it covers this area, but all I said was to ask them if they know.' As I parked, I looked across, and saw about one-third of the audience heading back towards the pubs in Pier Place.

Luke Skywalker was headed for us, but I waved him off, for I'd forgotten about a call I'd intended to make. I found the Torphichen Place CID number and hit the button; when Becky Stallings answered I was surprised. 'What are you doing there?' I asked. 'You're not on today.'

'No, sir,' she agreed, 'but my newly promoted partner, the shiny new DI Wilding, is being conscientious. He decided that he needed to go into Gayfield to do some more reading up on the open investigations.' I understood that. Ray's new division had rather a lot of unsolved files; that was one of the reasons why he'd been put there. 'So,' she continued, 'faced with a choice between redecorating our bedroom or coming in here to chum McGurk . . . '

'No contest,' I agreed, 'but come on, Becky.

Get the professionals in. You've got two inspectors' salaries coming into the house now; put some of it back into the economy, even if it is the black part. Anyway I'm glad you're there; this is probably a senior officer job. I want you and Jack to find Mr Freddy Welsh, and invite him to join us for a chat.'

'I thought we were holding off on him, boss,' she said, 'till we had something firm on him.'

'We have,' I told her. 'He's got an offshore company that we didn't know about, and weren't meant to, I'm sure, and he's been using it to bung the Varleys regular slabs of cash, also out of the reach of the tax man.'

'Nice one. That will be an interesting chat. Will Inspector Varley be sitting in on it?'

'That's what I'd hoped, but the so-and-so's disappeared. He seems to have jumped bail and done an effing runner. I'm waiting for Gayfield to get me his registration number so I can put out an alert.'

'That'll be a waste of time,' Stallings chuckled. 'I had my old man in my earhole last night about Varley's bloody car. It's still in the station park, in Ray's space, so he can't get his in. He had to put it up in Greenside yesterday. It cost him eighteen quid, so maybe this isn't the time to be telling him to get the decorators in.'

'Oh Christ,' I moaned, 'that's all I need. Becky, run with this, will you? Varley was bailed yesterday lunchtime; he was lifted from Gayfield first thing Thursday morning, and told not to go back there when we let him go, so he couldn't have picked up his car. I should have worked that out. I doubt if he'd have time to get on a flight to anywhere last night, but he would have this morning. Alternatively, he could have caught a train.'

'He or they, boss?'

'Yes, yes, both of them of course; she's gone too. Get people on to checking all the Livingston taxi firms. See if any of them picked up Jock and Ella. If so, where were they taken? That's not exhaustive though; they may have had a lift from a neighbour. Get some uniforms into their street knocking doors, asking of anyone did help them out but also when they were seen last. Then check with the airlines; find out if anyone flew them out, not just from Edinburgh either, Glasgow and Prestwick as well. They could be in Spain by now. They could be any fucking where.'

'What about the train?' she asked.

'Yeah I know,' I conceded, 'that's just as likely, maybe more so. Not all train tickets are booked on the internet. Simple souls like me can still roll up at Waverley, buy a ticket and get on.'

'Not so easy on a Friday,' she pointed out. 'They're packed that afternoon and evening, with English people who work here going home for the weekend.'

'Do what you can, Becky,' I sighed. 'They could be on bloody Eurostar by now. They could be in Paris. They could be in Bruges . . . that's in fucking Belgium,' I added, lifting a line from one of my favourite movies of all time.

'Get it under way, then you and Jack go and lift Welsh. He'll probably scream 'lawyer' at you. Let him have one, without question, but don't talk to him until I get there. The chief's steaming about this; he may even want to sit in on it himself. Go to it; you're a star. Princess Leia, no question.'

'Who?'

'Sammy Pye's sister,' I chuckled 'Never mind; it's my day for movie metaphors, that's all. It's a habit I picked up from Bob Skinner.'

The van was fifty yards away from where I'd parked. Sammy hadn't mentioned it when he'd called but I knew that was where the action was, as there were lots of people in paper suits gathered around it. Payne was among them by that time; the look on his face made me glad that we'd been summoned before we'd eaten and not after. Arthur Dorward met me halfway there, with a suit for me. The Edinburgh force's forensic genius works for a national resource centre now, but he's still the peppery, irreverent wee bastard that we've all come to know and tolerate over the last twenty odd years.

'Wear it please,' he said. 'We're not anywhere near finished yet and I don't want you contaminating my crime scene; especially not you. With your lineage your DNA must be like a kaleidoscope.'

I did as I was told; there's never an option with Arthur. I approached the burned-out vehicle carefully stepping round several wheel tracks that the SOCOs had marked off for impressions to be taken. I doubted that it could do any good, since some of them must have been made by the van itself and its tyres no longer existed to be ruled out, but thorough is thorough, and it is spelled D. O. R. W. A. R. D.

I knew what was inside the van. I'd been at another fire scene a few months before and I was still having flashbacks to that, but I couldn't bottle it. Word would have spread faster than the flames that had consumed what had once been a Vauxhall Movano, according to the half-melted markings on its grille. I put on a face mask then took a look inside; a long look. The trick is to imagine a bonfire, one made with tree trunks rather than logs and twigs, and pretend that's what you're examining. As I did that, in the same moment I realised what Sammy had meant about Paula.

I had a vague recollection of her getting up in the middle of the night and muttering something when she came back to bed about 'kids having a party over there', and about Guy Fawkes night not being in July.

Mario, Mario, the things we come to dwell on; the destinies, the lives, that hinge on a single action, or on the lack of it. If only you'd got up to see for yourself, and raised the bloody alarm, a lot of things might have been different and maybe, just maybe . . . somebody might still be alive.

But you didn't; instead you merely grunted and went back to sleep.

The logs seemed to be hugging. 'What the hell?' I murmured, to the person who had climbed into the wreck after me. 'Could they have been screwing? Caught in the act by a jealous husband with a petrol bomb?'

'That's if they're man and woman,' Sarah said.

369

'I'll tell you that in a couple of hours.'

'Men get up to naughties as well,' I pointed out.

'But not face to face . . . well, not in that position, if my understanding of these things is correct. Besides, if they were having sex, it was necrophilia on somebody's part.' She used a pen to point to a lumpy bit of the log nearer to us. 'This one was dead before the fire was set. There's a massive hole in the back of the head that, in my opinion, can only be an exit wound. And if he or she was, then the assumption must be that so was the other.'

'Maybe jealous husband . . . ' I persisted.

'Or jealous wife,' she interrupted.

'If you insist . . . or jealous wife . . . caught them in the act and shot them, then torched the van. Or shot them somewhere else, put them in the van and brought them here?'

'And drove two vehicles? Arthur's certain there was another here.'

'In which case,' I offered, hopefully, 'maybe jealous husband of one and jealous wife of another.'

She nodded and jumped out of the van. I followed her. 'That I cannot rule out,' she admitted, pulling off her face mask, 'not until I've separated them from their grotesque dance of death, as at least one tabloid is bound to say when this comes to court.'

'Okay,' I told her, 'you'd better do it. You can have 'em.'

'Thank you, sir,' she grinned. She seemed exceptionally full of life; or maybe it was simply the contrast with her surroundings. Whatever, I found myself smiling with her. She was like the old Sarah back again, the one we knew before everything between her and Bob got buggered up.

'Roshan,' she called to another paper suit, 'the boss man says we can have 'em. Let's go to work.'

'What are you going to be able to give me?' I asked.

'Their genders, and cause of death, certainly. Time of death, no, not unless I'm wrong and the fire killed them. Place of death, the same applies. Identification? Given the material, I'll probably have to do DNA comparisons with people reported missing. I'll give you as much as I can as quickly as I can, Mario. That's all I can offer.'

'I'll take it,' I said.

I stood back and watched as the mortuary crew began the task of removing the bodies. I didn't know where Lowell Payne was while it was happening, but I was bloody sure he hadn't gone for a takeaway. Sammy, though, he stood beside me, shoulder to shoulder, putting down yet another marker.

'Where do I go with this one, sir?' he asked, quietly, as if he didn't want anyone to overhear him sounding uncertain.

'Not far,' I suggested. 'We're stymied for identification until Sarah's done her autopsy. But,' I paused, 'does anything strike you about this, Sam?'

He frowned, considering his answer, considering, as it turned out, whether to tell the head of

CID to his Italian-Irish face that he was talking bollocks.

'I heard what you said to Dr Grace,' he ventured, once he'd decided. 'I'm sorry, sir, but I don't see this being a crime of sexual jealousy. It's not just that there were two vehicles involved, so at least two perpetrators. It's the fact that they've gone out of their way to make it difficult to identify the bodies. The number plates are gone: not melted, gone. The passenger cabin, that's clean. Arthur swears that there was nothing in it, no paperwork, no old crisp packets or drinks cans, none of the stuff you'd expect in a working van. Also there were two seats to the fire, not just in the back but in the cabin too. We're not meant to know who these people are, or who this van belonged to: at least we're not meant to find out in a hurry.'

He was earnest and he was right. I had to smile. 'One thing they couldn't have known, though,' I countered. 'We've got our brightest and best on the case. Plus we've got my remarkable record of being a lucky bastard. Fingers crossed for the autopsy, Inspector, and fingers crossed also that these people didn't know where the chassis number is on Movano vans.'

# Aileen de Marco

I didn't have any constituency business in Glasgow that Saturday morning, but I told Bob that I had as an excuse for getting out from under his roof.

Marriage hadn't been on my agenda at the time I met him. I was Deputy Justice Minister in Tommy Murtagh's Holyrood administration, but my immediate boss was on the way out and I was expected to move up, and into the Cabinet. However, nobody ever imagined that I would replace Murtagh himself . . . nobody but me, that is.

I wouldn't join an orchestra with the sole ambition of playing second fiddle; it isn't in my nature, any more than it's in Bob Skinner's. I am sure that's what attracted me to him, that shared trait that we have, attracted me strongly enough for me to ignore any concerns over the fact that he was married. Not that I had many of those. I've always taken the view that when someone plays away, it's because the game at home isn't so hot, and so as far as I'm concerned Dr Sarah Grace's problems were entirely self-inflicted.

Maybe I should have felt uncomfortable about it, and maybe what happened in the end is my punishment for my lack of scruples. Maybe, but the truth is I don't give a bugger. I fancied the man, I sent out signals and he came homing in on them like a guided missile. Even then, I wasn't bothered about marrying him, but by that time I was First Minister of Scotland, so when he asked me I agreed, on the grounds that it would be seemly, but more practically that the tabloids wouldn't be hounding us if we were man and wife.

Bob would tell you now, I'm sure, that I saw it as a political alliance from the start. You know what? He'd be right. From the day I came into politics, my ambition has always been the same: to go as far as I can. That's true of many of my fellow members of Scotland's parliament, but I don't know any who appreciate that there is a life beyond that building if you're young enough to go for it.

I have never stood for Westminster, but that's only because I haven't tried . . . yet. I will, soon. My party will resume power after the next election; of that I'm reasonably confident. I'll become First Minister again, I will serve loyally and faithfully for a couple of years, and then I'll use my influence in London to find myself a safe seat south of the border at the next Westminster election, expecting to move straight on to the front bench.

That's been my scenario for a while, and when I married, it was in the assumption that I'd have the full support of my husband in making it happen. When I say full support, I mean that exactly. Robert Morgan Skinner is many things; some are pleasant, some are not, but he has one quality that sets him apart. He's an achiever, and I figured that with him spearheading my back-room team, there was nowhere I couldn't go.

My game plan was to take him out of the police force, where he was approaching burn-out anyway as I saw it, and make him my chief of staff. Who better for the job of managing my rise to the top than someone who loved me but loathes just about every other politician in existence? I thought I could bring him onside, I honestly did. I thought that his unquenchable ambition would transfer to me, making that easy.

Unfortunately, my grand design had a couple of flaws. One you know already, I'm sure; Bob's infuriating and unbending resistance to the idea of a single, unified Scottish police force, to which I am committed irrevocably, as part of my plan for stuffing Clive Graham's lot at the next election. I'd prepared the way a year or two earlier by asking Bob to do me a paper on the subject, on how it would work. He did that, without setting out any furious counter-argument, so his blowing up at me when I told him it was going to happen was completely unexpected.

I might have hung in there and gone to work on him. If I had done, I might have, could have, won his support or, if not, won his silence at worst. I've decided not to, because now I know that my ship is sunk, holed below the waterline by the other thing I hadn't anticipated.

When Bob and his second wife split, I assumed that she would take her kids with her wherever she went. Even after she decided to go back to the US, and the children stayed with Bob, I was sure that it would be a temporary arrangement and that once she was settled they would join her. I mean that's what mothers do, isn't it?

But no, not that one. She and Bob worked out their friendly, no-fault split with a shared custody arrangement that meant effectively that the kids were with us most of the time. Was I consulted? Was I hell! No, regardless of the fact that I'm a legislator and leader of the country's largest political party, I found that I was expected to be a Goddamn mother figure as well!

Sorry, that is not me. It's not that I hate kids. What it is, I don't understand them, I can't empathise with them, I have no interest in them. Thank God we had a nanny or I'd have blown a fuse a long time ago. As it was I let Trish get on with her job, and she enabled me to get on with mine.

I probably shouldn't have phoned him that Saturday morning. He assumed I was checking up on him, and maybe I was. He likes having a shoulder to cry on, preferably female. I know that because he used mine for a while. We didn't speak for long, but in the time that we did, things went from worse to irrevocable. At the end of it, we both knew our marriage was in pieces, and that all the counselling in the world couldn't put it back together.

To tell you the truth, for all my blazing anger at his intransigence, I was relieved. No more sham, no more Mummy Aileen, no more Sex By Numbers with sighs afterwards. His, not mine. If he couldn't make me come, that was his lookout.

The only pressing problem I had left after our Saturday conversation was that I was saddled with Paula fucking Viareggio as my chum at Clive's bloody concert.

No, that's not fair. Of all the women in that circle, I like Paula most; she's honest, up front, a truth-talker, and not affected by her business success. The rest?

There's Alex, prodigiously talented they say, but endowed with all the same qualities that I've come to dislike so much in her father.

There's that DI I met once, Stallings; ten minutes with her is like watching *EastEnders* for three hours.

There's a hugely repressed lesbian superintendent called Mary Chambers.

There's the widow Steele, with her miracle child, a police goddess with shards of shattered glass ceiling at her feet, yet with something very cold and rather scary at her centre.

And then there's the newly returned Sarah; if you want him back, you can have him . . . honey.

Yes, you can keep all of those ladies, as far as I'm concerned.

It was only Paula's blooming maternity that made me regret having been manoeuvred into inviting her. But I had been, and I had to make the best of it. So I decided to let the government car service be her taxi, freeing me of the chore of driving her myself, since I no longer had plans to go on to Gullane after I'd dropped her off.

I called her to tell her about the arrangement, and also in the vain hope that she might pull out. She was up for it, though, excited, even. How was she to know that when she told me that she was wearing the same colour dress as me, I almost screamed at her, for putting the glacé cherry on the icing on the pile of shit that my week had been?

# Becky Stallings

The devil makes work for idle hands, and it's been said that there's something dark and Satanic about Mario McGuire. But given the alternative of hanging the flock wallpaper that I'd chosen and was already beginning to regret, I was happy to lend him my soul. There was a second reason why I didn't mind. I was on the trail of a bent cop. I'm old school Met, and when I come across one of them, I feel that I'm defending my own reputation, not just my force's. And yes, there was another: I welcomed a distraction from the reality of another chucked breakfast, and an excuse not to go to Boots for a pregnancy testing kit.

The DCS had given McGurk and me a stack of objectives. I did think about calling Sauce in, but Jack told me that he and his girlfriend were going far away for the weekend. Luckily the uniforms were having a quiet weekend, with no football at Tynecastle, so Mary Chambers, the station commander, was able to lend me three of them to back up the one rookie DC that I had at my disposal.

I set them all to work, looking for two needles called Varley in the twin haystacks that were Edinburgh Airport and Waverley Station, checking the taxi companies and one other possibility that Jack had thrown into the mix, car hire companies. I wasn't optimistic, though, that any of them would turn up anything. Life's never that easy.

While that was happening, Jack came up with a home address for Freddy Welsh. It was south of the city, out in West Linton, a nice rural village, he called it, that straddles the road that leads to a place called Biggar and on towards Carlisle. We headed on out there, taking Jack's car because he's too tall to fit comfortably into mine, and also because he knew where the hell we were going. Neither Ray nor I are country types; we don't do greenery.

'How are you and Lisanne getting along?' I asked him as we drove across the Edinburgh bypass.

He shrugged his shoulders. 'Fine,' he replied.

'Wedding bells?'

He glanced at me and chuckled. 'And you?'

'Not at the top of our to-do list,' I admitted. Not yet, but that seemed to be changing by the day.

'Same with us. But unlike you and Ray, we've both been married before. Neither of us is too fond of the institution.'

'What happened to your first marriage?' I asked. 'Or don't you like to talk about it?' He never had, not to me.

'I don't mind. It started to fall apart when I was posted down to Borders Division. Mary didn't want to go but she was talked into giving it a try. Didn't work.' He paused. 'You'll never guess who did the talking.' He was right, I never would have, but he didn't give me a chance to try. 'Karen Martin, Andy Martin's wife. She left the force when she married him and got pregnant. She set up this thing that she called the police partners' support group, that was supposed to help people like us with job-related problems. It did a bit of good, for a while, then Andy got the Tayside job, they moved to Perth and the group folded. Too bad; she could have done with some support herself.'

'Would it have stopped him bonking Alex Skinner?' I murmured.

He laughed. 'Shhh. This car may be bugged; those Agency guys are everywhere now.'

'What's your ex doing now?'

'She went back to her old job; she's teaching art in a school in Aberdeen, married to a car salesman and I get to see Regan once every couple of months if I'm lucky.'

'Regan?'

'My wee girl. Old George thinks she was named after him . . . as if we'd ever have done that . . . but the truth is we called her after the John Thaw character in *The Sweeney*.'

'Thank God for that,' I exclaimed. 'It would have been weird if it had been the other one.'

'What other one?'

'Have you never seen *The Exorcist*? That's what the girl was called, the one possessed by the Devil.' *Or maybe Mario McGuire?* I thought.

Jack gasped. 'You're joking. And no bugger ever told us? Fucking hell!'

'It's all right,' I said. 'Everyone's forgotten about *The Exorcist* by now.'

'You haven't.'

He drove on in silence, frowning. I looked at

his grim profile and reckoned that my gaffe would cost me a right few drinks in the near future. 'Where did you get that mark on your ear?' I asked. I hadn't noticed it before, but a small piece of it was missing.

'I was shot,' he replied, in the same tone he'd have used to tell me he'd nicked it while shaving.

'Shot?' I repeated.

He nodded. 'An armed operation. The subject fired at me before I could incapacitate him. That's how close it was.'

'What happened to him?'

'I was a better shot than he was.'

'Jesus, Jack,' I whispered.

'It wasn't just me. Another officer fired at the same time. We both hit, and the post-mortem called it a draw.'

'Jesus,' I repeated, but I was talking to myself, asking myself what sort of a boss I was. I'd worked with the guy for over a year, yet all the stuff he'd told me was news to me.

'We're here,' he said, interrupting my guilt trip as a sign told us we'd arrived at West Linton. 'According to the map, Welsh's house should be up the first road on the right.'

He made the turn, into what was more of a leafy lane than a road. Just looking at the bloody place was enough to give me hay fever. Nothing had a number; all the gaffs looked too important for that. Jack drove slowly reading the names on the signs at the entrances to each of the big plots.

'What's it called?' I asked.

'Carmarthen. It had to be something Welsh . . . and there it is.'

He turned into a wide driveway. There was a big double gate but it lay open. I'm not great with areas, but Welsh's house must have stood on an acre of land, at least. It didn't look like one he'd built himself; it was too old, too substantial, although there was a conservatory on the right gable that he might have added.

The blacktop road swung round in front of the house. As Jack stopped I saw that we were facing a massive garage, with two wide up and over doors. Both were raised, and two cars were parked beneath them, a red Vauxhall Astra and a silver Laguna estate. Each had a personalised registration, letters FJW in the three-number format that went out of date in the nineteen sixties.

As we stepped out, the front door opened, and a woman appeared. She had a battle face on, but it softened as soon as she realised we were strangers. 'Can I help you?' she said. 'I imagine you're lost. It happens a lot.'

I put her right. 'No, Mrs Welsh, we've come to the right address. We're police officers, CID; we'd like to speak to your husband, please.'

As I spoke a kid appeared in the doorway behind her, a lad, no more than eighteen, but heavyset. He wore jogging pants and a vest, and he was sweating. I guessed that the Welsh family had a home gym. 'What's up, Mum?' he began, shaping up as truculent until he realised how big McGurk is, then thinking better of it.

'They're police,' she told him, 'looking for your father.'

383

'So are we,' the boy said. 'He didn't come home last night.'

'Graham,' his mother snapped. Too much information, kid.

'Is that so, Mrs Welsh?' McGurk asked.

'Yes,' she acknowledged, 'but my husband often stays in town,' she added, 'if he has a business appointment that runs late.'

'So,' I chipped in, 'when do you expect him home? We're not in a rush. We can wait for him.'

'No,' she said, sharply. 'I'd rather you didn't. I have no idea when he'll be back.'

'Did you know he wasn't coming home, Mrs Welsh?' I pressed.

'No,' she admitted, 'but as I said, that isn't unusual.'

'That's bollocks, Mum,' the boy Graham shouted, taking us all by surprise. 'Dad never stays out all night. You know that.' He was scared, no question.

And maybe he had reason to be. First Varley jumps bail and vanishes, then cousin Freddy goes AWOL; the type of coincidence in which I have never believed.

# Bob Skinner

Clyde Houseman. The name had been kicking around in my head since Amanda's call. I knew it was somewhere in my memory banks, but I couldn't access the file that held it.

I fixed the kids their lunch as soon as we got home, then asked Trish if she'd keep an eye on them, as I had an unexpected business meeting. Officially it was her day off, but she had nothing planned, and she's flexible.

Normally, if I know that company's coming I leave the driveway gate open, but I didn't want any of my village pals turning up without warning, so I left it closed. My house has always been secure but when the First Minister, as she was then, moved in, it was stepped up. Now I have motion sensors in every area of the garden and video cameras that are so carefully placed that an expert couldn't find them.

One of them picked up my visitor before he'd even pressed the button on the entryphone. He was tall and dark-haired, wearing razor-creased trousers and a navy blue blazer that was so well cut it was impossible to guess anything about his body shape, although the way he carried himself suggested that he was a fit guy. The clothes, and his grooming, screamed 'military'.

I opened the single gate to the garden path without even asking him to identify himself. I've

385

met enough spooks to know one when I see one, given advance warning. As he approached the house I opened the front door and stepped outside.

'Mr Houseman.' I extended a hand. As he shook it I studied his face. Yes, I had met him before; I was certain of it, but just as ignorant of the where or when. Nothing about him offered a clue. He was clean-shaven; his hair was short and looked freshly trimmed. At first glance I thought he was tanned, but at second, I wasn't so sure. He was paler-skinned than Trish, but probably of mixed race, some Afro-Caribbean genes blended with the white.

'Come in,' I said, stepping aside to let him enter. 'Let's go in here.' I showed him into my small private study, off the hall, where I'd watched him approach on the monitor. Normally I take visitors into the garden room, but this one wasn't run-of-the-mill.

I sat at my desk; he took the chair alongside it. I opened the small beer fridge I keep in there, and offered him a drink. He peered inside and chose an Irn Bru; I chose the same, but I had a hard time resisting the Red Bull that was in there. That would have negated all my self-denial. I hadn't had a coffee all day and I was beginning to experience the withdrawal symptoms that Sarah had forecast.

All the time I was thinking, trying to nail him down, and all the time he knew it, as he looked back at me, with a faint, nervous smile on his face, incongruous when set against his bearing.

I don't like losing at anything, but sometimes

386

you have to admit your failures. 'Go on,' I said to him. 'Tell me.'

He offered not a word in reply. Instead he slipped two fingers into his breast pocket and produced a white business card. I assumed that it was one of his, but as he passed it to me, face down, I could see that it was old, curled at the corners, and had a couple of stains on it.

I took it from him, turned it over . . . and saw, beneath the police crest, my own name: 'Robert M. Skinner, Detective Chief Inspector'.

'Go back fifteen years,' he murmured, but I was there already.

A call on the mother of a murder victim, a hard-as-nails cow called Bella Watson, in one of those places in Edinburgh that you will never see on a postcard. I'd taken the wrong car with me, my current BMW rather than the battered old Land Rover that was my usual work vehicle in those days. There had been a bunch of kids on the street, eyeing it up, and I'd singled out the biggest, the obvious leader, and explained to him what would happen to him, personally, if there was a mark on it when I got back. When I did, it was pristine. The lad had expected to be bunged for not touching it; I'd explained to him that if certain people in his street saw him taking money from a cop, it could be fatal. I wasn't being a cheapskate; that was his world.

I'd seen something in the youngster as I spoke to him, something in his eyes that said that although he was trapped in his environment, he didn't belong there. Now that I'd found my mental file, I could replay our conversation word for word.

'*What's your name?*'

'*Clyde Houseman.*'

'*Well, Clyde, if it ever occurs to you that it might be a good idea to get out of this hellhole and get a life that gives you a chance to be different, you call me, on one of those numbers, and I'll show you how.*'

And I gave him, with none of his pals seeing it, a business card, the one that he'd just handed back to me.

I felt a huge surge of pleasure, maybe even pride, as I examined it. 'All this time,' I murmured.

'Fifteen years,' he replied. 'At first I kept it as a reminder. Eventually I held on to it in the hope I'd be able to give it back to you one day.'

I laughed. 'Amanda said you were bricking it. That's why?'

'Yes, sir, that's why.' He seemed to have left his accent behind in the slums.

'What happened?' I asked. 'Tell me your story.'

'You scared me that day,' he replied, 'on two levels. One, I was a sixteen-year-old kid, the toughest in our street, no question. I didn't think anyone in the world was harder than me, until I looked you in the eye and realised I was very wrong. Then on top of that there was what you said; it made me look around, and ahead. I lived with my mother and my stepfather in those days. She was a serial shoplifter and he was a serial alcoholic with a gambling habit; hopeless, the pair of them. My father was long gone, doing life

388

in Peterhead Prison for stabbing a taxi driver in a row over the fare. When I met you I was on the fringes of grown-up gang stuff, not dealing, but protecting dealers. I'd never used drugs myself, but sooner or later I would have. You were right, sir; I was living in a hellhole, but it was all I knew so I didn't recognise it as such. When I met you, you opened my eyes. Nobody had ever said anything positive to me before, never.'

'Why didn't you call me?' I asked. 'Why didn't you use the card?'

'I had to get further away,' Clyde replied, 'as far away from Edinburgh as I could, far away from everything I'd known until then.'

'So what did you do?'

'I joined the Royal Marines. I walked into an armed forces careers office and said in effect, 'Please help me, I have a shit life and I want to be different.' They told me I had to prove myself and I did. I blew the preliminary course away; I was a fit strong boy, and a good swimmer, so the physical stuff came easy to me. On top of that I had a stack of O Grades from school, so the intelligence tests were a breeze. To cut a long story down a little I was accepted. I served as a marine for three years, around the world, and I loved it; I made corporal by the time I was twenty, then I was invited to apply for a commission. Two years later, I joined the SBS, the Special Boat Service. That's . . . '

'I know what it is,' I told him. 'Did you see much action?'

He nodded, and his eyes went a little dead. 'Iraq; I did a couple of tours there operating out of Basra, targeting terrorists the Iranians were slipping over the border. When we caught them we sent them back.'

'Intact?'

He looked at me. 'What do you think?' Answer enough.

'After that,' he continued, 'it was Afghanistan; black ops.'

'Not too many boats in Afghanistan,' I observed.

'They put our skills to use where they were most needed, sir.' He glanced at the door; it was closed. 'We were on constant stand-by. If intel picked up reliable information that a Taliban leader was on the move, we'd be mobilised. The Americans would watch them by satellite; if a window opened, we'd go in very fast by chopper, kill the target and get out again before the opposition even realised they were one down.'

'Winning their hearts and minds,' I murmured.

'That was someone else's job,' Clyde said. 'Ours was to blow their heads off.'

I nodded. 'I know. So,' I went on, 'how did you get from being SBS in Afghanistan to being MI5 in Glasgow?'

'My SBS engagement ended just over three years ago. I was Captain Houseman by that time, back in the Marines with a more conventional career ahead of me, but I had the sense that I'd plateaued. My special forces experience wasn't going to help me climb the ladder; there aren't many opportunities at major and above, and my time out of the mainstream had put me at the back of the queue. I had a conversation back in Plymouth with my unit commander. About a week later I was invited to go to London for a meeting in Whitehall. It turned out to be a job interview, with Amanda Dennis. She told me that the security service was responding to the terrorist threat by expanding its operations across the country and was looking for people with . . . a broad range of skills, was how she put it. A few days after that, she offered me a job, and I accepted.'

'What's your area? I asked. I know how the security service works; a few years ago I was asked to help it sort out some in-house problems.

'Counter-terrorism,' he replied. 'I spent my first two years in Thames House, then I was moved up to Scotland, in charge of the Glasgow regional office.'

'How long have you been there?'

'Best part of a year.'

'So how come I haven't heard of you before?'

'Amanda told me not to get involved with the police,' he said, bluntly. 'She feels that the Strathclyde force is too big, and that because of its size the risk of leaks is unacceptable. Its Counter-Terrorism Intelligence Section feeds information to SO15 at Scotland Yard and we work with them. My contact with the locals is at a minimum.'

'So, Clyde,' I asked, 'why are you so keen to

391

talk to me today, other than to give me back that card?'

'The image you sent to Amanda last night, the body that was buried for you to find; we know who he was.'

# Mario McGuire

Once Sarah's people had taken the burnt logs away, Lowell Payne and I were surplus to requirements at the crime scene, four feet that Dorward's crew didn't need on their ground. My appetite hadn't been too badly affected, but I wasn't in an Asian mood any longer; no, my taste buds were talking Italian. Since I was within sight of home, I called Paula, to see if she was okay, and to ask if I could bring a pal with me for whatever we could throw together.

She said yes, on both counts.

I could tell that Payne was impressed by our home, and doing his best not to let it show. I didn't feel like explaining our family circumstances to him so I left him to ponder on how a cop could afford such a pad, even on a chief super's salary of around eighty grand at the top of the scale.

I was going to make the lunch myself, but Paula wouldn't hear of it. She ordered us outside, on to the deck. I gave Payne a beer and watched him with a trace of envy: I knew I'd have to drive again, if only to get him back to his car, and with me, one thing usually leads to another.

My lovely other half joined us about ten minutes later with a couple of sandwiches consisting of warm focaccia bread, spread with olive oil rather than butter and stuffed with sweet red peppers, olives stoned and halved, feta cheese and anchovies. Sure as hell, they put pakora in perspective.

She didn't join us; she'd eaten already. 'You ready for tonight?' I asked her.

'Yup,' she replied. 'Aileen called to finalise the arrangements. Chauffeur-driven car no less. She's staying in Glasgow just now, so it's easier for her.'

I don't know why, but that made me a little curious. She was in Glasgow, the boss had passed on the show; anything to be read in to that? Nah, no chance! Away you go, McGuire, you've been a cop too long.

'I ruined her day, I'm afraid,' Paula continued. 'She asked what I was wearing and I told her, a red dress.'

'So?'

Payne laughed; he got the message.

She nodded in his direction. 'Exactly. So is she. I should have known, her being Labour and everything. However, all is not lost, I remembered that I've got a trouser suit I had let out at the waist just in case. It's black satin and formal enough for tonight. So she can breathe easy again; nobody will wonder which of us is the politician.'

'My darling,' I assured her, 'I don't know anyone who looks less like Maggie Thatcher than you do.'

'Aileen doesn't either,' she protested.

'Facially no, but she has that same air of imperious authority about her. And when she smiles . . . never trust politicians when they beam at you. Isn't that right, Lowell?'

'I never trust them period,' he admitted. 'It's a trait I picked up from my niece.'

'Your niece?' I repeated.

'Yes, Alex. My daughter's her cousin, remember; named Myra after her late mum. Didn't you know that? She visits us every so often to see her Aunt Jean and Junior.'

'I see.' I knew about the relationship, but not that he'd a kid. So Alex didn't trust politicians either; well, well, McGuire. What do you detect from that?

I fetched him another beer, and had just set it on the table when my phone started to sing *Baila Moreno* . . . my phone being a big Zucchero fan. I checked; it was Luke Skywalker. I allowed Sugar another couple of bars then took the call.

'Sam,' I said. 'What's up?'

'We've identified the van, boss,' he replied. There was nothing in his tone that hinted he was about to make my day. 'We found the chassis number; they hide them away, so it was still legible, and I was able to run a trace. It's registered to Anglesey Construction Limited, of Fisher Industrial Park, Straiton.'

I couldn't believe it first time so I made him repeat the name. 'Anglesey Construction Limited. Does that mean something to you, boss?'

'Yes, it does. Problem being I haven't a fucking clue what that might be, or how it might fit. Thanks. Let me think about it.' I hit the end button and turned to Lowell. 'Guess what?' I said to him. 'That van along there belongs to Freddy Welsh's company.'

Remember the domino theory? Maybe you don't but it was the justification the Americans found for the Vietnam War, that if they didn't stop the Communist advance there, all the neighbouring states would collapse like dominoes stood on end, all the way to Thailand and Malaysia.

I don't know why that came into my mind, but it did. I must be psychic, because at that moment, with that vision in my mind, Zucchero started to sing again.

# Sarah Grace

Sometimes I worry about myself. I have the feeling that there must be something wrong with the soul of a woman who can look at the aftermath of the darkest human suffering with happiness in her heart.

That's why I quit pathology when I did. I wasn't past my sell-by date, or even close to it, but I had an underlying feeling that I should be, and that I had become desensitised. In other words, I felt guilty about liking my macabre job too much.

It didn't take me long to get that out of my system, just a few months back in mainstream medicine. I was treated well in practice, my workload wasn't excessive and I didn't make any life-threatening mistakes, but I found nothing inspiring about it and at the end of every day, I got home feeling flat. I'm not saying that I wished my patients were dead, but it came home to me that I preferred them that way.

Joe Hutchinson got it right; I'm an okay doctor, but a gifted pathologist. Maybe that's what I needed to prove to myself all along.

I caught Roshan giving me an odd look as the wagon crew . . . the para-morticians, as little Joe calls them . . . took the entwined corpses from their super-sized body bag and laid them on the examination table, and I realised why. I was smiling. 'Sorry,' I murmured. 'I was somewhere else.'

'Wish I was,' one of the bearers grumbled. 'Wish I was anywhere else.'

'Then go,' I told him, 'but first go get a gurney, please, and set it alongside the table, for when we get these two separated.'

They did as I asked then left. I have a lot of respect for those people; they're not ghouls, they have a job that very few people would tackle, and they do it efficiently, respectfully and without complaint.

'What do you see, Roshan?' I asked when we were alone in the autopsy room. Sammy Pye had sent Griff Montell along as a witness, but he had chosen to stay in the viewing gallery. I didn't blame him. The table was fully lit, giving us a much more detailed view of the remains than we'd had in the van. The extractor fans were going full blast, but they couldn't do much about the smell. I can't describe it adequately; the closest I can get is, imagine marinating a steak in petrol, then putting it in one of big George Foreman's grills and forgetting about it for an hour or two, multiply that by a dozen or so, and you'll be in the vicinity of what it was like.

My assistant walked all round the table, slowly, pausing several times to lean in and look more closely at a detail. 'The body on the right,' he began when he was ready, 'the one that was against the side panel of the van, is smaller than the other and may not have been fully clothed. It is barefoot, whereas the other was wearing shoes.'

'Man and woman?'

'I would say so,' he replied, in his clipped subcontinental accent. He had come to us, just after my arrival, with a BSc in Pathology from the University of Western Australia. Normally we'd have looked for a medical qualification as well, but he'd been quite a find. 'The bodies appeared to have been tied together with some kind of synthetic rope. I believe this was done post mortem, since in addition to the gunshot exit wound which you identified, correctly in my opinion, on the larger body, the smaller, let's call it the female, exhibits three more exit wounds, on the back. One of these has completely shattered the spine, but given their size and position I would say that any one of them would have been fatal.'

'So, for the record,' I said for Montell's benefit, 'we are looking at victims of a double homicide. We're agreed on that, yes?'

'Absolutely. There is no other possibility.'

'Okay, let's try to separate them. Is the rope still intact?'

'I believe that it has melted into the bodies, being synthetic; it is wound round them three times, so yes, it may still be holding them together. I'll take care of that.' He picked up a scalpel, leaned over the mass, and chose a spot to cut the binding. As he did so the remains separated slightly, but not completely as I had hoped they would.

'Hey, Griff,' I called out. 'Would you like to come and give us a hand here?'

'Not on your life, Sarah,' he replied sincerely;

there's a mike in the gallery, and speakers in the autopsy room. I could kid with him; I knew him from his time as Alex's neighbour, and the rest.

Roshan and I decided on the obvious, since it would be easier to move the smaller of the bodies on to the gurney. Luckily they came apart easily when we applied a little pressure. As we rolled the burnt cadaver on to the trolley, it was evident that Roshan's assumptions about its gender had been correct.

'Their killers made a mistake,' I said, for the microphone once again, 'if they were trying to prevent or hamper identification. They should have untied the bodies before setting them alight. Their being pressed together means that the trunk of each is still recognisably human, and that some of the front of their clothing has survived the fire.'

Hers had been a dressing gown, secured at the waist by a sash. It had fallen open at the chest and three entry wounds were apparent, on a group between her breasts.

'This is professional,' I pronounced, speaking once again to the DC.

'What makes you say so?' he asked.

'It's a cluster; three shots close together. I've seen pro hits before. With impulsive, inexpert shootings the wounds are all over the place, and quite often the whole magazine is emptied. Not this one; three taps centre of the chest, quick fire. All done before she'd even hit the ground.'

'What about the other one?'

Roshan had turned the male cadaver so that it was lying on its back. I walked around and examined it, then told him what I saw. 'These are head shots, but the same; a cluster of three, middle of the forehead. No wonder the back of the skull's missing. You'll find that at the murder scene.'

'Wherever the hell that is,' Montell replied, gloomily.

'Let's see if we can help. First step, identify the bodies; bar codes on clothing can help you do that. Roshan, will you take his off, please.'

I stood back and watched as he did what I'd asked. It was easy, since most of each garment had been destroyed; that which was left, simply peeled off, revealing mottled, discoloured, part-roasted flesh. He left the dead man's feet untouched; they'd have come off if he'd tried to remove his shoes, since they were welded to the flesh. When he was finished, he picked up the remnants of what had been the victim's trousers. 'There is something in these, Sarah, in a pocket.'

'Let's see what it is.'

He found a pair of scissors and cut through cloth. A slim wallet, black leather, fell into his hands. He passed it to me. I opened it, and smiled.

'You see, Griff?' I laughed. 'You never know your luck. What we have here is a photographic driving licence, intact.' I took it from its slot in the wallet. 'I can't match the face to the one on the table, not without a very expensive reconstruction, but I don't imagine that he'd be carrying anyone else's.' I read the name on the plastic, aloud.

I glanced up at the viewing gallery. 'Did you

hear . . . ?' I began, then stopped, when I saw that Montell was staring at me as if I'd just told him that the guy on the table, whoever the hell he might have been, had started breathing again.

# Clyde Houseman,
## senior regional field officer, MI5

I didn't know what to expect when I walked into Mr Skinner's house. For all of fifteen years, I'd been carrying a mental picture of the man around in my head, a guy who must have been, when we met, not very far beyond the age I've reached now, a man brimming with self-confidence and with body language that tended to downplay rather than assert how dangerous he was.

By that time, my street gang had rolled a few guys who thought they were tough and found out they weren't, but he was something else. When I tried my hard man act with him, he gave me a look that made my testicles try to retract into my body. What he also did was engage a self-awareness that had never been there before. In that moment, although I didn't realise it or articulate it until some time later, he made me see what I was and what I would become unless I did something radical about my life.

I'd always known I was intelligent, but all my life I'd been conditioned to be embarrassed by the fact. When he gave me that card, he threw that into reverse; he made me embarrassed by what I was.

When I say I didn't know what to expect at our second meeting, I mean two things. First, I didn't know whether he would remember me. He didn't, not until I gave him the card. In a way that pleased me, in that it showed me, if I still needed it, how far I've come, and how much I've changed from that schemie thug. Second, I didn't know what he might have become, whether he was still the guy who'd made that impact or whether he'd been softened and diminished by age.

He didn't look soft, that's for sure. The guy is fifty plus but physically he still looks harder than me. That day he was wearing shorts, a sleeveless linen shirt and thong-style sandals; his skin was brown and shining and his muscles were sharply defined. There was sand in his hair and clinging to his clothing; it made me think of Afghanistan, and of him as a marine from Hell.

And yet he was different; there was an edginess that wasn't part of my vision of the man. Maybe it was there before and I'd been too young to recognise it, but I didn't think so. The thirty-something Skinner had been encased in an aura of absolute certainty. The older version seemed to have lost that; I looked at him and I saw a man with problems that he wasn't sure he could solve.

I'd come expecting to be asked for my life story, and I was happy to lay it out for him. I owed that to him, that and more. The deputy director had told me his security clearance was higher than mine, so I had no problem telling him about my present employment, or about her view of our colleagues in Strathclyde. She had told me I should never be less than frank with him.

He didn't bat an eyelid through any of it, not even when I described my SBS missions in Afghanistan. He asked me very few questions and none of them were personal. He didn't want to know about the family I'd left behind, not that there was much of it left, only my mother. I didn't think of her at all when I was in the Marines, and I listed no next of kin. I'd said no goodbyes when I left. When I joined Five I waited a few months then ran a check on her, with my line manager's tacit approval. She's still in Edinburgh, still drawing benefit, still pulling down convictions for nicking from supermarkets. It seems that she only ever steals food and drink, never clothes. My father never made it out of Peterhead; a friend of the taxi driver he murdered was sent up there and took full revenge by caving his head in with a dumbbell one day in the prison gym. Nobody saw a thing apart from one warder, and it takes two witnesses to convict.

Once my personal history was behind us we got down to business.

'So, Clyde,' he asked, when the time came, 'why are you so keen to talk to me today, other than to give me back that card?'

I tried not to sound too eager, or too pleased with myself. 'The image you sent to Amanda last night,' I replied, 'the body that was buried for you to find, we know who he was.'

He smiled. 'I thought you might,' he murmured. 'What was he? Mossad?'

I nodded. 'Yes, he was a paratrooper first, then Israeli secret service. Not any more, though. He was kicked out.'

'That must be damn near a first for Mossad. What was he caught doing that was bad enough to get him the sack?'

I smiled at his sharpness. 'Using a fake German passport on the assassination of a Hamas official. The German government kicked up such a fuss that he had to be cut loose. His name is Beram Cohen, but he's used a few others.'

'Let me guess,' Skinner said. 'He went freelance.'

'Yes,' I confirmed. 'His name's come up in connection with a couple of operations. It didn't make the press, but last year around two dozen Somali pirates were taken out, in groups of two and three. It put quite a dent in their activities and made those waters a lot safer for a while. The operation was funded by the American State Department and Beram Cohen planned it. That's what he did; he was a facilitator. He used mercenaries, mainly Russians, but a couple of South Africans as well, all of them skilled, all ex-regulars, like him.'

'The sort of people who wouldn't leave a fallen comrade behind?'

'Exactly,' I agreed. 'Like the two men you told the DD about, his companions in the restaurant.'

'The guys he ate with just before he died.'

'Yes. The prints you sent to us meant nothing, but I'm interested in what the restaurant owner said about them speaking in a language he couldn't identify. My guess is that if it had been a European language, Russian for example, he'd have been able to take a guess at that.'

'In Glasgow he might have assumed it was Polish.'

'True. The fact that he hadn't a clue makes me wonder if it those men might have been the South Africans he used on the Somali job.'

'Do you have names for them?' Skinner asked.

'Francois Smit and Gerry Botha,' I told him. 'Smit's a sniper, Botha just a general killer. They're old school. They go back to the apartheid days, but there are no files on them, because they made sure that they were destroyed before the regime changed. We only know about them because the Americans wanted a list of the people Cohen was using on the op, to make sure they were all acceptable, and so that anyone who talked could be silenced.'

'I see,' the chief constable murmured. 'So what we have here is a planner and two hit men. Suddenly, out of the blue, Cohen, the planner, ups and dies from entirely natural causes. Smit and Botha have a problem. They could have stripped the body and chucked it in your namesake river, but their military ethics wouldn't let them do that.'

'Yes,' I chipped in, 'or they could have taken him out on to the Fenwick moors, buried him there and sent us rough co-ordinates, but I guess they didn't know the terrain.'

'So they brought him through to Edinburgh, dug a shallow grave in a city location and told us where to find him. But why Edinburgh?'

407

'So that you'd be searching for them through here,' I suggested, 'while all the time they were back in Glasgow.'

'Maybe,' he said, 'but not necessarily.' His eyes were gleaming. There was something going on behind them. 'But doing what in Glasgow, Clyde? That's the question. You've got . . . or you had . . . the planner, you've got a sniper, and you've got his minder. Who's the target?'

I frowned. 'We don't know for sure,' I confessed, 'but there is one possibility, and that's why the DD has hit the red button. There is a man called Theo Fabrizzi . . . '

'A classical pianist,' Skinner said. 'I know. He's playing in Glasgow tonight at a charity event in the Royal Concert Hall.'

'You know about that?'

'I was invited; turned it down. My wife's going though. Never pass up a photo op, that's her motto.' I couldn't miss the bitterness in his voice, but I didn't have time to dwell on it. 'What's with Fabrizzi?' he asked. 'An Italian musician? Is he Mafia?'

'He isn't Italian. Despite the name, he's Lebanese, and covertly he is a significant financial backer of Hezbollah. He's a sworn enemy of Israel. If they still had a death list, which they say they don't, you'd be liable to find his name on there somewhere.'

'Hold on,' the chief interrupted. 'You told me that Beram Cohen was kicked out of Mossad.'

'I said they cut him loose, that's all. As a freelance, it might actually have been more convenient for the government in Tel Aviv. Fact

408

is, with him involved, it makes Fabrizzi the likely target. With Smit here, the hit could be anywhere. All he needs is a vantage point, and the right weapon. The record distance for a kill shot in Afghanistan is almost two and a half kilometres; Smit's in that class. '

He leaned back in his chair, his hands behind his head, fingers intertwined, and he yawned. 'Sorry, Clyde,' he chuckled. 'Late night, early morning, and I've been warned off stimulants. If the threat is a sniper,' he continued, 'what's the problem? Take the target out of the firing line.'

'This is where it gets difficult, sir,' I said. 'We can't, because he won't let us. I saw him early this morning and suggested that he pulls out of tonight's concert and lets us get him out of the country. He told me no way, that he'd rather be a martyr than back down to an Israeli threat. But there's this too; the Home Secretary's been briefed. She's ordered that these people, regardless of who might have commissioned them, are to be treated as terrorists. They are to be caught, not frightened off, so that, if the Israelis have commissioned this we can hand them their heads on a plate. Her words, according to the DD.'

He leaned forward again, took two more drinks from his small office fridge, and gave me my second Irn Bru of the day. 'You have told Strathclyde, I assume, regardless of what Amanda thinks of their security.'

'No, sir,' I told him.

'But you must!'

'We've been ordered not to, by the Home Secretary herself. This is a secret operation, she says, and that means no police, apart from you, since you brought us Beram Cohen in the first place. Terrorism isn't a devolved function of the Scottish parliament. She's in charge, sir. It's her baby and she gives us our orders.'

'So who's looking after Fabrizzi?' he demanded. 'The guy might be willing to risk his own life but he still has to be protected.'

'We're doing that; the security service.'

'We, being how many?'

'I have a detail of three on it.' Mr Skinner gasped. 'With respect, sir,' I said, 'I'd rather have three of mine than ten of Strathclyde's.'

'That reminds me of the apocryphal story about the guy who left his Bentley in your old street, and reckoned it was safe since he'd left his Rottweiler in the back seat. The flaw in his thinking was that the dog couldn't put out fires. Your guys may be good, but the sniper just needs to have one clear sight of Fabrizzi, and he's up in flames.' He paused. 'All of this puts you in the shit, Clyde, doesn't it?'

We'd come to it. He was right. I'd been tasked not just with stopping an assassination, but with catching the shooters, and I hadn't a clue where to begin. Not one.

Skinner smiled. He pushed himself from his chair and stretched himself to his full six feet and a couple, running his fingers through his hair and sending the sand flying from it.

'In which case,' he laughed, 'the two of us are in it together. But don't you worry, son, because your Uncle Bob has the inkling of an idea.'

No doubt about it, that man moves in mysterious ways.

# Lowell Payne

I'd done my homework on McGuire before I ever met him; I had him marked as a rich kid, maybe a black sheep, a lad who didn't need the money but had joined the police force for a laugh and a fight at the weekend without the risk of being locked up for it, then had found that he was good at it.

It didn't take me long to realise that I'd taken him too lightly. Yes, he does have a tendency to flippancy, and a light touch when dealing with subordinates, but anyone who marks him down as a soft touch is likely to wake up regretting that mistake. Mario is one of nature's nice guys, but I could tell that he also has a formidable temper and no visible tolerance level for fools.

He and Bob's ex seemed to get on very well. I had heard of her, from Alex, and I knew that she was back in town. At first I thought she'd be keeping her distance from the police community, but that would have been pretty much impossible, given her job. From my brief observation of her, I have to say that I like her. She's sexy, beautiful and stacked, but that has nothing to do with it.

I judge people by their eyes; I believe they tell the story of what's behind them and hers appealed to me. I read them as intelligent, kind, and warm, those of someone who at that moment was enjoying life very much. I found myself wondering how she and Bob had split up; she seemed like a good match for him. When I met him first, at Jean's dad's funeral, he was with a DI from his force; that was quite serious for a while, but I never thought it would last, because their eye signals weren't quite right.

I realised from watching her at work that Sarah is also very professional, and that McGuire is too. I didn't step forward to look inside that van, and I stayed well away from what they brought out of it. Maybe that's why Mario's a DCS, bound for ACC rank, and I'll be stuck at chief inspector till I retire.

To be honest, I don't envy him his position; I'm happy where I am. His house, though, that's another matter, a bloody great duplex on top of one of the new high-rises that dominate the Leith waterfront, not far from the Scottish Government building. It goes with the car, Paula's new Lexus.

And Paula? She goes with everything; tall, immaculate hair, archetypically Italian looks, and she has great eyes that go mellow every time she looks at the big guy. She was very pregnant when we met, but she hadn't given in to looking fat and dumpy, as my Jean did when Myra was on the way. She knew how to dress to manage it, probably with the help of a personal shopper at one of those big Edinburgh stores. She had on a maternity day dress that must have made the till ring like a one-armed bandit scoring the jackpot.

She also knows how to make a sandwich. Even now, I salivate when I think of the plate she brought out for us.

I was halfway through mine when Mario's phone rang, or rather played some garish Italian-sounding song. I know that ringtones have to be distinctive these days, but there are limits. He took the call, from DI Pye I gathered, then went bug-eyed as he reacted to what he was being told.

'Guess what?' he said when he was done. 'That van along there belongs to Freddy Welsh's company.'

I was beginning to wonder whether Mr Welsh had been in it when that fucking awful tune sounded again, and I learned that wasn't the case.

'DC Montell,' I heard him say. 'Tell me why you won't let me eat my lunch?'

I watched him again as he listened, saw his face change again, the black eyebrows come together until they were almost, but not quite touching. 'That's reason enough,' he murmured. 'Thanks, Griff.'

He laid the phone on the table and turned to me again. 'Jock Varley's been weighed in, just like Cousin Freddy promised. That was him in the van, and, we can assume, his wife. Just as well we didn't wait for them at their house.'

# Bob Skinner

*The Home Secretary? Who the hell does she think she is?*

That's what I thought when Clyde told me about her 'orders'. I'm a police officer and I'd been given information about a crime, or a potential crime, so I had a duty to investigate it, and to advise my colleagues in Strathclyde of what might be about to go down on their patch. In theory, if push came to shove, I could have the Home bloody Secretary arrested, on the basis of what I knew, for obstructing the police in the execution of their duty.

But that's not the way the real world works, is it?

'Catch them,' she'd said; those were her instructions to the security service, and my protégé's career . . . I'd started to think of him as that already . . . was riding on the outcome. Indeed it was at serious risk, for her 'catch them' was easier said than done, but I could see a line of enquiry, a long shot but one that might pay off.

On the other hand, it might not. If it didn't, although a sniper shot on Fabrizzi somewhere between his hotel and the venue was the likeliest option, we didn't know enough to rule out anything. That meant that a hit within the Royal Concert Hall was a possibility, even if it was the most difficult to pull off, given that there was

415

bound to be a police presence of sorts.

However, among all the doubt there was one certainty; I wasn't having any excitement going down in that hall, not with my wife . . . however I felt about her . . . and Paula Viareggio sitting in front-row seats. That wasn't going to happen, regardless of what any bloody woman in Westminster had to say about it.

'Wait here till I get tidied up,' I told Clyde. 'We're going for a drive.'

I left him in my office while I took a quick shower, shaved and changed into my normal summer weekend gear: slacks, a short-sleeved shirt and a light cotton jacket. That took me fifteen minutes; the call I made to Maggie Steele took five more; three for her to believe I was serious, and another two for her to write down my detailed instructions.

Once I was done I went back downstairs. 'We'll take your car, I think,' I said.

'Where are we going?' young Houseman asked.

'Edinburgh,' I told him. 'We're going to see a man I was planning to talk to anyway. Your visit's made it a little more urgent, that's all.'

'Does he know we're coming?'

'No, not yet. I want to keep it a nice surprise for him. But don't worry, Clyde, he'll be there.'

I gave the directions, back to the A1. All the time I was thinking. 'A man like Cohen,' I began as we were cruising towards Prestonpans, 'on an operation like this one, how would he arm his people?'

'He could bring the weapons in,' Houseman

416

replied. 'But that would be an added risk. If he could source them locally, that's what he'd do. Mind you, sir, they would have to be specialist. These are not the sort of men who blaze away with sawn-offs.'

That's the conclusion I'd come to myself.

'Follow the signs for Glasgow,' I said, when we got to the slip road that leads to the city bypass.

He frowned. 'I thought we were heading for Edinburgh.'

'We are, but it's quicker this way.'

'Come on, sir. Where are we going?'

I laughed. 'We're going to the place where you'd have wound up if I hadn't given you that card.'

Just under half an hour later we pulled into the car park of Her Majesty's Prison, Saughton. 'You may have to pass through a metal detector when we go in there,' I warned my driver. 'Do you understand me?'

He nodded, reached inside his blazer, took an automatic pistol from its holster and locked it in the glove compartment.

I led the way up to the pedestrian entrance. I was ready to show the duty officers my warrant card, but they knew me by sight. I told them that Clyde was with me; that got him in without a pass.

'What can we do for you, Mr Skinner?' the senior man asked.

'My colleague and I need to see the remand prisoner Bass, now.'

He nodded. 'Yes, sir, but won't we have to get him a lawyer?'

'Not this time. Bass has been charged already and he's had the benefit of legal advice. This will be a private conversation, just the three of us. Understood?'

The officer was a veteran; he nodded. His smile suggested that he was a fan of the old-fashioned way of doing things.

He made a phone call, then escorted us to the remand section of the prison. By the time we got there, our host was waiting for us, in a small musty room with opaque glass in its only window. He was cuffed, seated, and a guard stood by the door, watching him.

'You can go,' I told the minder.

The prison officer stood his ground. 'That's against . . . ' he began.

I looked him in the eye. 'Now. No worries, on you go. Wait at the end of the corridor.'

As the door closed behind him, Kenny Bass glowered up at us.

There was only one chair on the other side of the table; I took it, leaving Clyde to lean against the wall. Neither of us spoke. We hadn't discussed our approach but I could tell that he had the nous to follow my lead. I waited, he waited, until Bass's glare faded and was replaced by a look of nervousness.

Inevitably, he broke the silence. 'Who are you guys?' he asked.

'I'm the chief constable,' I replied. 'This gentleman is an associate.'

'What d'you want?'

'We want you to tell us about Freddy Welsh.'

Bass sighed, and leaned back in his chair. 'No'

418

again. Like I said to all the other tossers, I don't know any Freddy Welsh.'

I reached out, grabbed his handcuffs and pulled him towards me, hard. I jerked him right off the chair and his chest slammed into the edge of the table. I leaned forward until our faces were no more than a foot apart.

'In case you didn't hear me,' I murmured, 'let me repeat; I am the chief constable. Ask yourself this: how many other petty cigarette smugglers merit a personal visit from the top cop? The time has come to stop pissing us about, Kenny. You were a trivial little plonker, but now you've acquired significance.' I twisted the cuffs, contorting his arms and drawing him even closer to me. 'You will answer this question, or it's going to get tough for you. Who set up your trip to Spain to pick up those fags? You, or Freddy Welsh?'

I held him, with my eyes unblinking, keeping the pressure on his wrists. He resisted for a few seconds, but no longer. 'Freddy did!' he squealed.

'That's a good start,' I told him, loosening my grip a little. 'What was the deal?'

'He came to me and he told me he had this cargo that needed bringin' over from Spain. He gave me a truck and told me to take it to a place in Valencia; he said there would be serious money in it for me. I did what he said; there were guys waiting for me. They told me to leave the truck wi' them and come back in a couple of hours. I did. They told me I was ready for the road and they gave me papers. They said they

419

were import permissions for what was in the van and that if I was asked, I should show them to the customs guys. That was it; they said I should go, so I did.'

'Were you curious? Did you look in the back?'

'Of course. It was full of fags in cartons; the papers said they were goin' tae a bonded warehouse in Birmingham.'

'Were you stopped at the port?'

A small sneer touched his lips. 'Nah. This country's an open door, mister.'

*Sad but true*, I thought. 'So,' I continued, 'you got home free and clear. What happened then?'

'I met Freddy,' he replied. His tongue was well loosened by that time; he couldn't tell us enough. 'He said well done. He said that I could keep the fags, sell them myself, ken, for whatever I could get for them and that there would be a wee bit of cash in it for me as well. That's why I was in Lafayette's; I was to meet him there and he was going to pay me.'

'So what else was in the truck? He wasn't paying you for nothing. What were you really bringing in for Welsh?'

'A box. That's all I know, honest. A big wooden packing case, about four feet by two, and maybe two deep; I've no idea what was in it. There was a secret compartment in the truck, under the floor. Freddy opened it, we took it out and I helped him carry it into his store. It was heavy.'

I tightened the cuffs a little. 'Where did you take it?' I asked.

'I can't remember. It was dark.'

Another twist, then one more until pain registered in his eyes. 'Kenny,' I murmured, 'people have been trying to lie to me for thirty years and not succeeding. I'm a world expert in spotting bullshit. I tell you again, this is important. If you think I would not break both your wrists, then you're wrong.' As a demonstration I twisted even harder.

He screamed. 'It was a house! It's in Livingston, in a street called the Pines. There's a big extension in the back garden and Freddy's store's under that.' I eased the pressure once more. 'What the fuck are you guys up to?' Bass squealed.

'What do you mean? Why should we be up to anything?'

'I went back there,' he said. 'I was curious. There was too much I didn't know. I wanted to see who owned the place. I knew it wasnae Freddy's. So I parked there and I waited, till the guy who lives there came home. I recognised him. Your guys asked me about him yesterday. He's a polis; his name's Varley. I know him because when I had my massage parlour, he used to come in there. I'd give him freebies with one of the girls; pay-off like, for having a friend on the force. I wasn't the only mug either; that bastard never paid for a thing on his patch.'

I let him go. 'You're an idiot, Bass. You could have told us all this the day you were lifted.'

'Aye sure,' he snorted, clenching and unclenching his fists to set the blood flowing through them again. 'Then one of Varley's pals visits me in my cell and I commit suicide.'

'Varley doesn't have any pals,' I told him.

'Hmm. And I'll believe that. You guys are all the fucking same.'

Clyde pushed himself off the wall and leaned over him. 'If we were, mate,' he said, 'you'd be having a fatal seizure round about now.'

I opened the door and called to Bass's escort; he was at the end of the corridor outside with the man who had brought us across. 'What do I get for this?' the prisoner asked.

'Keep your mouth shut about Varley when you give evidence about Welsh,' I replied, 'and you'll get a suspended sentence for possession of contraband.' I winked at him. 'Opening it might be suicidal.'

We said nothing as we were led back to the prison reception area, nor until we were back in Houseman's car. 'What do we have?' he asked.

'Nothing for sure, only a possibility; no, several possibilities. One of them is that Smit and Botha might not have brought Cohen's body through to Edinburgh. He might have died here, before or after they paid a visit. To test that out, we need to interview Freddy Welsh.'

'But who is he?'

I looked at him as he reholstered his weapon, and pointed to it. 'You know the phrase, 'Gun for hire'. It applies to guys like Cohen, Smit and Botha. Freddy's guns aren't for hire, though, they're for sale. He's a very discreet, very low-profile arms dealer. I'm told that he's operated under our radar for years, and it seems, under yours.'

'How do you know this?'

'Some things, Clyde, I'm keeping secret, even from you, but my information is that if Beram Cohen wanted weapons for his operation, there's every chance he'd have gone to Freddy Welsh.'

He frowned. 'Are you certain?'

'No,' I admitted, 'not one hundred per cent. In theory my source could be spinning me a yarn, but everything fits. The timing, Cohen's corpse showing up in Edinburgh, the pay-off to Kenny that was aborted by Varley's phone call, it all fits. I know what was in that box that the sap Bass brought back in his truck, and Welsh stashed in Jock Varley's house. With a wee bit of luck,' I said, 'it's still there. But I wouldn't bet on it.'

'Where do we find him, this Welsh?'

'In a holding cell in my headquarters, I hope. He was due to be arrested this afternoon. Inspector Varley was on his payroll; we can prove that now, and that gave me enough to have him lifted. We talk to him, and the whole thing's wrapped up.'

'Not quite,' Houseman protested. 'We've still got the threat to Theo Fabrizzi.'

I checked my watch; it showed five forty-five. 'He's okay,' I told him. 'If anything had happened so far your people would have alerted you. He'll be at the concert hall very soon, assuming he makes it, and if he does, that's where they'll be trying to hit him. Only he won't be there; not on stage at any rate. I've taken care of that.'

'How, for Christ's sake?'

'Never you mind. Come on, let's get ourselves to Fettes. Take a left when we get out of here then first right; it's not far.'

I was smiling. I really did think it was going to be that easy. My over-confident grin was still on my face when my phone sounded, and I saw that Mario McGuire was calling; I pressed the 'accept' button; Clyde's Bluetooth system paired automatically and picked it up.

'What's up?' I asked, cheerily.

'Are you at home, chief?' His tone was enough to remind me that complacency is a police officer's worst enemy.

'No. I'm on the road. Are you going to ruin my day?'

'That depends on the mood you're in, and on how you really feel about Jock Varley. We've found him and his wife, shot dead. The bodies were burned beyond recognition, but the pathologist, whom you know, has just ID-ed him.'

'The wife too?' I repeated.

'Afraid so. The van they were found in . . . '

I had a moment of prescience. 'Belonged to Freddy Welsh?'

Mario laughed. 'Have you got a crystal ball in your car, boss? How did you know that?'

'Pure fucking guesswork, honest. Do we have Welsh?'

'No, and that's the bugger of it. He's vanished; he didn't go home last night and his wife's wetting herself about him.'

'Was he in the van too?'

'No, chief, there were only the two bodies.'

'What have you done so far about finding him?' I asked.

'I'm doing it right now,' he replied. 'I've already put a nationwide call out for him, and Lowell Payne's tracing all vehicles registered in his name as I'm speaking. Next, I'm going to send Stallings back out to his house, just in case he does show up there. While she does that, I'm going to check out Varley's place. I'm kicking myself, I should have gone in there this morning when we got no answer to the door. Boss,' he exclaimed, 'what the fuck is up here? Have you any idea?'

'You know me, mate. I never have a clue.' Okay, I was lying about that, but one thing was true: I knew exactly what Mario would do if I told him what I suspected. He'd go straight through to Glasgow like a Chieftain tank and cause all sorts of chaos. The way things were, the last thing I needed to do was to panic him. Besides, I told myself, Fabrizzi was taken care of; the concert hall will be safe because there will be no target, so no danger there.

'Where's Paula?' I asked, idly.

'On her way to Glasgow; the government car's just collected her. Why?'

'Nothing,' I said briskly. 'Mario, change things a bit; you go to Welsh's house, babysit his wife, in case he does come home, but make sure also that she isn't in touch with him. Get armed officers out there as well, just in case. I'm not far from Livingston just now. I'll check the Varley place myself. I know the street name, but what's the number?'

'Seven.'

'I'm on my way there. Keep me informed.'

By that time we were in Stevenson Drive: I told Clyde to do a three sixty at the roundabout then to turn right into Calder Road, heading back to the bypass. There are two ways to get to Livingston from where we were at, the long way and the short way. Unless there are tailbacks on the motorway, and I knew that there wouldn't be on a Saturday, the long way is always quicker, so that's the one I told him to take. As we approached the town I fiddled with the navigation system and worked out how to programme the address into it.

As bad luck might have had it, Varley's house was located beyond the Almondvale shopping centre. It's huge by Scottish standards; I know that because Sarah likes it, and when we were married she dragged me along there on many an occasion, to marshal the kids. The traffic can be intense around it, but fortunately in the early evening it all goes in the other direction, so we had a clear run in. The name of the street was stuck in my head, for there's one in Gullane of the same name and I know the people who live at its number seven. It's a cul-de-sac and so, by coincidence, is the Livingston version.

Clyde turned into it and paused, counting down the numbers. I didn't have to. My body hasn't quite caught up with my age yet, and my long vision is still very good. At the end of the street a single house faced us. There was a car in its driveway, a Mercedes E class, metallic blue. I couldn't make out the numbers, not quite, but the letters of its personalised number were FJW.

I pointed towards it. 'That's number seven,' I said, 'and I think we might just have come up lucky.'

# Maggie Steele

I've learned a lot over the years that I've worked with Bob Skinner, and one of those lessons is never to question him when he's in full flow.

He's a friend as well as a boss, but we've never socialised much, our interests and circumstances away from the office being entirely different. (For example when it comes to golf, I belong to the 'good walk spoiled' brigade.) He's considerate too. Through all my bad times, and through all my worst times, he's been rock solid in my support, and even now, although I hold the second most senior rank in the force, he goes out of his way to ensure that I have as much quality time as possible with my wee Stephanie.

For him to phone me on a Saturday afternoon, it had to be serious.

'Mags,' he began, as soon as I picked up his call, in the kitchen, 'how are you for babysitter cover?' No preliminaries, straight to business; unlike him.

'I think I'm okay,' I replied, 'Bet's here.' I looked at my sister, who was by the sink, and raised an eyebrow. She nodded. 'Yes, I'm clear.'

'Good, I've got a crisis and I need someone with your clout to deal with it.'

'Fire away.'

'Let's hope it doesn't come to that,' he murmured grimly. 'There's a charity concert taking place in Glasgow this evening in the Royal

Concert Hall at the top of Buchanan Street. It starts at seven thirty, with a VIP reception half an hour before. The star turn's a pianist called Theo Fabrizzi. I want you to go there and arrest him.'

'You what?' I chuckled, instantly incredulous.

'I know,' he said, 'it's a bit out of the ordinary, but we've got a problem; no, a whole raft of them. There is a credible threat against this man; he's Lebanese, pro-Hezbollah, anti-Israeli and it is highly like that Tel Aviv wants him dead. We believe there's a hit squad in place ready to take him out. He's been advised of the danger, but the stupid bastard carries a martyr's shroud around with him and he's refusing to back down.'

I knew I was sticking my head in the lion's mouth, but I had to ask. 'Bob, surely the obvious solution is for Strathclyde police to cancel the event.'

'Maggie,' he snapped; then he stopped. 'I'm sorry, I keep forgetting; you're my deputy, you're supposed to question me. The complicating factor is that this is not a police operation. The first objective is to capture or kill the hit team and that's in the hands of MI5. I'm not really speaking to you as a cop here. I'm involved. We've had a specific instruction from the very top not to advise Strathclyde. That said, I'm not letting anyone offer this man as a target, not even the man himself. We have to take him out of play another way.'

'How?'

'As I said, I want you to go to the sheriff and get a warrant for his arrest, then pick up David

Mackenzie, if he's available, if not somebody of equivalent rank, and go through there and arrest him.'

'Eh?' I exclaimed. 'On what charge?'

'Suspicion of the murder of an Israeli national named Beram Cohen,' he said. 'His was the body we found the other night at Mortonhall.'

'But I thought that was death by natural causes?'

'The sheriff won't know that, though. See if you can dig out Sheriff Levy, the one they're calling Miss Whiplash. If she wants to know the grounds for arrest tell her he's a known anti-Zionist and that witness statements place him near where the body was found.'

'Is that true?'

'The first part is,' he chuckled. 'I'll bet you that's enough for Ms Levy.'

'What do we do with him when we've arrested him?'

'Head back to Edinburgh, very slowly. Chances are you won't be halfway there before I call you to say that the witness has recanted his statement.'

'Okay.' I paused. 'Do you know for sure that the attempt will be in the concert hall?'

'No,' he admitted.

'Well what if they try somewhere else?' I asked him.

'Then Fabrizzi will be dead, the career of a certain young MI5 man will be in jeopardy, and I will make it my business to ruin the politician who gave him his orders. Go to it, Mags.'

He was right about Sheriff Levy. I found her at

430

home; all I had to do was mention the words 'anti-Zionist', 'Hezbollah', and 'Lebanese', and her signature was on the warrant.

I'd called Mackenzie before I went to see her. His wife answered and treated me to one of those heavy stage sighs, before calling him. He was all too keen, when I told him that I had a job that required senior officer back-up.

I have to confess that I've never liked that guy much. He's always been a Bob Skinner project. The chief thought he saw a good detective in there behind the flash, when he recruited him from Glasgow to run our drugs squad. I'm sure he also thought that he could knock some of the arrogance out of him, but it took a loss of bottle during an armed operation to do that. Loss of bottle . . . followed by taking to the same in a big way.

There were strong grounds for tipping him over the side, but that would have involved the boss admitting he'd been wrong about him, and that is not something he does with either ease or grace. Instead, Mackenzie was given time to prove that he was off the scoosh, then he was given a uniform and a job in the command corridor, as senior officers' exec. He does it efficiently, I can't deny that, but I always feel that he has something of the Cassius about him, and I don't mean Clay.

I was sure I'd told him 'no uniform' so I was less than pleased when he stepped out of his front door looking like he was going on duty at the Queen's Garden Party. I'd have told him to change, but there wasn't time. Mental note

431

though, Maggie, in future all instructions and requests to him must be repeated, for the avoidance of doubt.

There was little conversation on the way through. I didn't feel like making small talk with him, so I turned down his offer to drive, and then turned up the radio once we were under way.

As soon as we reached our destination, and turned into Killermont Street, it was evident that there was a VIP event on. There was a visible police presence, at the vehicle entrance to the Royal Concert Hall, and a couple of them were armed.

I'd heard from colleagues at inter-force meetings that the new Strathclyde chief had taken no time at all to earn herself a nickname, the 'Gunslinger'. She believed in a show of force, and it had taken the combined efforts of all her assistant chiefs to persuade her that it was a bad idea to have armed officers on view at Old Firm football matches.

Our friends in the west weren't very keen on me parking directly outside the concert hall. Indeed one of them, a big blackshirt PC who'd have done Oswald Mosley proud, was quite abusive until I made him read my warrant card and until Mackenzie stepped out of the passenger seat. I have to admit that the uniform did come in handy, damn him.

I had the Bolshie guy escort us inside, into a foyer that didn't seem to enjoy any natural light. It was ten minutes before seven, comfortably ahead of the official starting time, or even of the

432

pre-show reception, but the organisers were thick on the ground, as were a few others as well. I spotted one of them straight away, just as he clocked me: Max Allan, the senior ACC in the Strathclyde force, the man who wasn't allowed to know that there was a terrorist alert on his patch. Max is a good guy, and not a stickler for formality, but there he was on a Saturday evening wearing every single piece of silver braid to which his rank entitled him and every medal ribbon too.

'Jesus Christ, man,' I said as he approached. I noticed that he managed to ignore Mackenzie completely; some history there, I guessed. 'Have I got this wrong? Is this a royal event?'

'It might as well be, Maggie,' he replied. 'One of our police charities is a beneficiary, as well as the armed forces, and Her Ladyship's representing us.'

'Her Ladyship?' I repeated, then I caught on. 'Oh, you mean . . . '

He nodded. 'The chief constable, our Toni. That means all us underlings have to be in our best uniforms, shoes polished shiny, etc.' He paused. 'That's her way, so I mustn't complain. What brings you here, Maggie?' Finally he nodded to my companion. 'With escort.'

I glanced around the busy foyer. 'Can we go somewhere quiet, Max, please,' I murmured.

He frowned, but he nodded and led us past a broad stairway and round to its side, just as the first of the VIPs arrived. I caught a quick flash of heavy gold chain, the kind that civic dignitaries wear, but I had no time to admire it. Max opened a door and we stepped into a large windowless cupboard. He switched on the light. 'What's up?'

'I'm about to rain on your parade,' I told him. 'Is your guest star here?'

He nodded. 'Just arrived. He's on stage checking the piano.'

'Well, you'd better have someone ask him to join us.' I showed him the warrant.

He read it, at least twice, with incredulity that reached jaw-dropping point. 'You can't be serious,' he gasped.

'Would I make that sort of joke?'

'No, but . . . can't you wait till the show's over?'

'My orders are to pick him up now. Do you want to argue with Bob Skinner?'

'God no, but Field will go fucking ape-shit.'

'Then she'd better not find out till it's done and we're gone. Look,' I continued, 'Fabrizzi's not the only performer, is he?'

'Of course not. We've got the Scottish National Orchestra as well.'

'In that case, they're going to have to improvise. You'll just have to say that Fabrizzi's been taken ill at the last minute.'

'Okay,' he sighed. 'But I'll be taken ill when my chief finds out that I went along with it. She's after me as it is.'

'She never will from me,' I promised.

'I'll hold you to that,' he said. 'Wait here. I'll fetch him myself.'

We did as he asked. He had barely closed the door on his way out before Mackenzie looked at me and murmured, 'Tell me, honestly, ma'am. Don't you feel like an interloper here? This isn't our territory. Has the chief lost his marbles?'

I glared at him. 'You'd better ask him that yourself, Superintendent. Come Monday morning, at his chief officers' meeting, I'll make sure you get the chance.' I waved the warrant in his face. 'Meantime, this gives me authority, and through me, our force. Your view is noted.'

I'd wanted to tell him to shut the fuck up, but that would not have been seemly from an ACC to a superintendent. It might even have led to a complaint to the Superintendents Association, and I did not want to be bothered with any nonsense like that.

Frankly my annoyance with Mackenzie wasn't due entirely to his disloyalty to the guy who'd saved his career; there was also the fact that his point was one that I'd been trying to ignore. We weren't in hot pursuit, and technically we should have advised our colleagues in Pitt Street of our intention before we'd arrived.

Then Max Allan returned with Theo Fabrizzi and my reservations started to melt. First, in his black tie and tail coat, he bore an uncanny resemblance to the Go Compare tenor, minus the silly moustache, and I really do hate those telly ads. Second the man had an air about him, that of someone who believes he's more important than God.

'What is this?' he snapped. 'I very busy man, I'm an artist; I can't be disturbed so.'

'You can, Mr Fabrizzi,' I told him, and showed

him my authority. 'This says so. Can you read English?'

'Of course,' he sneered. 'You take me for a barbarian?'

'Then please read this.'

He did, slowly; clearly he wasn't as fluent as he pretended. When he was finished, he looked at me and he laughed. 'This is preposterous. Is a joke, yes?'

'No joke. Now come with us please, we have to take you back to Edinburgh with us.'

'No!' he shouted.

'Yes,' I said calmly.

'Is conspiracy,' Fabrizzi exclaimed. 'Is the Zionists. What this man's name?' He peered at the paper again. 'Cohen. See? Is the focking Jews. This one is dead, you say? Well, soon they all will be, the focking swine. They hate being called that, you know. Focking swine, focking pigs. We wipe them out, you see.'

I smiled. 'Indeed,' I murmured, then glanced at Max. 'What do you make of that, ACC Allan?'

'I make it inciting racial hatred,' he replied, 'contrary to the Public Order Act of 1986. You may consider yourself under arrest twice, Mr Fabrizzi. But you can have first go at him, ACC Steele.'

'It's an outrage,' the Lebanese pianist hissed. 'You focking Scots, you're Jews as well.'

'Some of us are,' Max told him, 'and proud of it. Now please shut up, sir, or I'll handcuff you myself.'

# Clyde Houseman

There was a gleam in Mr Skinner's eyes, and a narrow, wicked smile on his face as he pointed to the Merc that had been reversed into the driveway of the house that faced back down the dead-end street. As I looked at him, I wondered how a man who clearly loved being in the thick of any action that was going had allowed himself to be constrained in a chief constable's uniform.

'That's number seven,' he said, 'and I think we might just have come up lucky. Drive on down there,' he continued, 'very quietly, and block the exit. Take it easy, though.'

I did as I was told, looking at the house as I approached. It was a villa, with four windows to the front, two up, two down. The curtains were closed on what I took to be a bedroom window on the upper floor, but there was no sign of movement behind any of the others.

There was a second car, some sort of old banger, parked beyond the FJW plate, but the drive was long enough to accommodate a third, so I cruised in there and switched off. 'Quiet now,' the chief murmured, as he opened his door and stepped out, closing it behind him, but not fully, to avoid any risk of noise. I checked my weapon, and then I followed him.

'Back entrance,' he whispered. There was no doubt about who was in command: I knew my role and I trusted him.

The drive was covered in small white pebbles, so we stepped as lightly as we could. We walked silently along the side of the house, past the two cars. The ground at the rear, which sloped down towards fields beyond, was landscaped, with a small neat lawn surrounded by rose beds and a classic herbaceous border, all of it beautifully tended. Someone in the Varley family had been a gardener. I had a fleeting thought of the contrast with the street where I'd grown up, where any flower that poked its head above the surface was liable to wither and die of embarrassment, that's if it wasn't yanked out by a rough and lawless kid like me.

Mr Skinner held out a hand, signalling me to pause. A sound came from somewhere around the corner, a muffled noise of something being dragged. He stepped out beyond the house, into the open, and I followed, my hand inside my blazer, on my gun. There was nothing else to do.

The villa had been extended at the back; it was a proper two-storey construction, not one of those glass box things that the double-glazing guys, and Kenny Bass, call conservatories. Beneath, as Bass had said, there was what appeared to be a cellar, or storeroom. It was windowless, for its door was a little ajar and we could see that it was lit within, on a summer evening. I checked behind me to make sure that no neighbour could overlook and see us, then drew my pistol.

'I go first,' I murmured to the chief, my only show of insubordination.

'You've got the fucking gun,' he replied, his

voice as quiet as mine, 'so fair enough.' He was smiling again.

We crossed quickly to the entrance and I stepped through it. The space was not what I expected, a single room; instead it was divided into two. The side into which I'd stepped was full of gardening equipment, nothing more, but on my left there was a second doorway, in which a large, heavyset man was framed. Even as I saw him he was in the act of throwing something at me, a box; it was aimed straight at my head, and travelling. Instinctively I threw my arm up to protect myself; it caught me on the wrist and sent my weapon flying. And then he was on me, knocking me aside with brute strength as he headed for the exit . . . into the path of Bob Skinner.

The chief hit him, not with his fist, but with the heel of his hand, right in the middle of the forehead, as hard a blow as I've ever seen. It halted Freddy Welsh, big and all as he was, in mid-stride, lifted him off his feet and sent him crashing on to his back, spark out.

'Jesus!' I exclaimed. My first thought was that he'd killed the guy.

'I used to do karate,' he offered, almost apologetically. 'I'm out of practice. A few years back, he'd never have got that close to me.'

I didn't bother to ask him what belt he'd attained; that was obvious.

Stretched out on the cement floor, Welsh proved that he was still alive by making a snorting noise. The chief leaned over him, seized the waistband of his trousers and started to drag him into the other chamber, from which he had come. 'There's a tap over there,' he grunted. 'Fill a bucket, or anything like it you can find. Then close the outer door and come in here.'

I reclaimed my pistol and did as he had said. As it happened there was a bucket just beside the tap.

'Close that door too,' he told me, as I joined him and handed him the bucket. I did. 'This might get a bit noisy,' he added, as if in explanation. I looked around me as he spoke. The room was bigger than the other; it wasn't full, or near it, but there were four crates in the middle of the floor, tea chests, the sort that furniture removers use, and a box with the lid removed.

Welsh was beginning to regain consciousness; Mr Skinner helped him by pouring half of the bucket's contents over his face, slowly.

'Moving the stock, are we, Freddy?' he asked, as the man came to, spluttering and choking.

As he did that I was looking through the chests; they were full of boxes, and most of them bore a manufacturer's name; I recognised them all, Colt, Smith and Wesson, household names, many of them, albeit in the sort of household that watches combat movies, and some more obscure. 'Hey,' I exclaimed, 'he's got a Beowulf in here.'

'Indeed?' he replied. 'What's a Beowulf?'

'A specialist, high-quality rifle; American.'

'Is that what you supplied to Smit and Botha?' the chief asked.

'Fuck off,' Welsh snarled, and started to rise,

but a foot in the centre of his chest slammed him back down.

'No, you stay there. You can answer my questions just as easily from the floor. And those are: number one, did Kenny Bass know what was in the box he brought here hidden among the cache of bootleg fags? My guess is no. Our Kenny might be up for a driving job, but he does not have the bottle for being part of the weapons supply chain in an assassination. Number two, what type of weapon did you supply Cohen? Number three, did he describe his operation to you? Number four, did Varley know anything about the operation you were running from underneath his house, or did he know everything about it? Number five, why the hell did you have to kill him, and your cousin? Number six, who was careless enough to leave Jock's wallet in his pocket, and dumb enough not to realise that even if you can wedge off the engine number, every vehicle can be traced through a unique chassis identifier that's hidden way out of sight?' He paused, smiling down at the man on the ground.

'I'm saying nothing,' Welsh hissed. 'I want a lawyer.'

Mr Skinner shook his head. 'It isn't that sort of situation, Freddy. It's the kind that calls for advanced interrogation techniques, of which officially I do not approve, unless we need information quickly about a potential terrorist assassination, in a venue where my wife and the wife of a friend will be present. Now that I've explained that, let's deal with my questions.'

Welsh stared up at him. He was afraid by then, but there was still resistance in him.

The chief held up the bucket. 'Ever heard of waterboarding?' he asked.

'You're kidding,' our captive grunted.

'Yeah, you're right. We don't have time for that.' He put it down and squatted beside him, leaning close. 'Have you ever seen that Liam Neeson film,' he murmured, 'where he plays a CIA man whose daughter's been kidnapped? There's a bit in it where old Liam . . . if anyone ever makes a movie of my life,' he said conversationally, 'I want that man to play me . . . where he's on the phone to the bad guy and he says something along the lines of, 'I have a particular set of skills; skills I have acquired over a long career.' My young colleague here hasn't had all that long a career, but he has those skills. If you don't talk to me, I'm going to leave the room and let him practise them.'

'I know who you are,' Welsh hissed. 'You're Skinner, the cop. You wouldn't fucking dare.'

The chief stood up again. 'Oh no?' He turned to me. 'The floor is yours.'

I nodded. 'Yes, sir; but you really must leave the room. I'll call you when our friend has something to say.'

'Okay.' He did, and closed the door.

As he left, Welsh tried to rise, but I kicked his legs out from under him. 'Who the hell are you?' he asked.

'That's irrelevant. All you need to know is that I'm the man with the gun. Are you going to talk to us?'

'No fucking chance.'

The truth is, I don't have any advanced interrogation skills. I was planning on making them up as I went along, as once or twice we had to in Iraq. Holding my gun on the man on the floor, I took the Beowulf from the chest with my free hand. 'Lovely weapon,' I said, 'fifty calibre.' I checked the magazine; it held seven rounds and it was loaded; I slipped my pistol into my pocket then hefted the rifle. 'If I shot you in the kneecap with this,' I asked, 'do you think you'd ever walk properly again? Personally I'd doubt that.'

'You can't do that,' he sneered. 'This is Scotland.'

I shook my head. 'No,' I countered. 'This is the cellar of a police officer you've just murdered in the course of an act of terrorism. No rules apply here, and I'm an agent of the state. I can make you disappear. It will be the easiest thing in the world for a third cremated body to be recovered from your van.'

In such situations, there is only one imperative; you must make them believe you. I was getting there with Freddy Welsh, but I could still see scepticism in his eyes. So I shot him.

The bullet creased the back of his right hand, ricocheted off the floor and buried itself in the plastered wall. He screamed, from pain and fright, and crawled backwards, away from me, as I raised the rifle again and aimed at his knee.

'Enough!' he yelled. 'I'll talk to him.' He paused. 'If I do, what's in it for me?'

'I won't kill you. That's all that's in it.' I kicked

one of the tea chests. 'As for your arsenal here, what happens about that depends on the man outside. So my advice to you is, hold nothing back.' I stepped across and opened the door.

Mr Skinner came back into the room. 'I can leave again,' he promised, 'just as easily.' Welsh nodded; he believed. 'So tell me about it.'

'Bass had no idea,' the arms dealer began; he had pulled himself up to a sitting position, leaning against the wall. 'As far as he was concerned, he was only going for the cigarettes.'

'Why did you set it up that way?'

'I didn't. My Spanish suppliers did. It was part of the deal. These people, they'll fence anything. They can source me specific weapons, usually stolen from the police or military, maybe even bought from them, for all I know. But it's knock for knock, and sometimes they want me to take other stuff off their hands. Handy in a way; you were right about Kenny; he'd never have gone just for the guns.'

'Guns plural?'

'Yes.'

'This place,' Mr Skinner said. 'Tell me about it.'

'I built it for Jock, for free. The deal was that I got the use of this room.'

'Did he know what it was for?'

Welsh stared at him. 'Of course he bloody knew. Having built the fucking room, I had to rent it off him as well. The money went into a offshore bank account in Ella's name.'

'Did she know about it?'

444

He shrugged. 'She must have known something went on here. How much Jock told her, I've no idea.'

'That doesn't matter now they're both cinders,' the chief constable said, roughly. 'Go on, tell us about the operation.'

'I was approached about five weeks ago,' Welsh replied, 'by an Israeli bloke called Beram Cohen. I knew him. I'd supplied him before with guaranteed clean handguns. Somebody was paying him to take out radicalised Muslims.'

I laughed. Welsh glared at me. 'What's so fucking funny?' he snapped.

'You are,' I told him. 'You supplied weapons to a guy like him, in his world, and yet until five minutes ago, you didn't realise that makes you part of it yourself, as disposable as he was. If I was ordered to kill you, you'd go into a crematorium oven at night and nobody would be any the wiser.'

'That's what they should have done with Beram,' he muttered.

'Yes, what about that?' the chief asked. 'Tell me.'

'I'd arranged for Beram to meet me in Edinburgh last Wednesday,' he replied, 'at my yard, not here. He was going to pay me for the weapons.'

'What did they buy from you?'

'One of the carbines that Bass brought from Spain,' he explained. 'The other two were handguns from my stock. Anyway, they turned up, the three of them. I wasn't expecting Smit and Botha, but Beram said he'd brought them to

445

drive because he had this bloody awful headache. He had the money in a backpack. He handed it over, and a minute later, he died. Just like that. He stiffened, then he fell over; he kicked a bit, then he was dead. His mates tried to resuscitate him, but it was no use.'

He frowned, as if he was seeing it all over again. 'The three of us, we were all shocked, but those South Africans, they were,' he struggled for words, 'they were just beside themselves. Once we were all back in control, I offered them the money back, but they said no, that they had a commission and that they would go ahead. Beram wasn't involved in the actual hit; he did the planning and took care of the escape.

'I told them they'd need to get rid of the body. I suggested putting it in my truck, driving it out past North Berwick and tipping it into the sea. They went crazy at that; I thought they were going to kill me. They said that he was a fallen comrade and all that guff, and that he had to be treated with respect, not just stuck in a hole and forgotten about.

'I said fair enough but I had nowhere to keep him. We could hardly take him to hospital, and they wouldn't leave him somewhere and call the ambulance service. It was Botha who came up with the idea of doing what they did with him, burying him and then calling your lot. As it happened, I'd bought some bed linen for the house that day. I gave them a sheet to wrap him in; they stripped him and left me his clothes to burn, so they couldn't be used to trace him. They said they didn't want him identified for a couple of days. Smit asked me where they should take him. Given that he was dead, Mortonhall sounded like as good a place as any to me, so I suggested that.'

'So it had nothing to do with setting a false trail for the police,' Mr Skinner asked, 'given that the operation's in Glasgow?'

'Is it?' Welsh asked. 'That's news to me. I never want to know any detail about things like that. Anyway, no, it had nothing to do with that.'

'So they went away,' he continued, 'and last night they came back here, to collect the gun. Is that what happened?'

He nodded. 'Aye. And when I brought them round here, at one in the morning, who was standing upstairs, looking out the window but bloody Jock.' He sighed.

'You see, the arrangement was that every time I brought a client here to collect an order, Jock would always take Ella off somewhere for the night. He didn't last night, though. There he was, as large as life, but not for much longer. He saw both the South Africans, and they saw him. They wanted to know who he was, and I had to tell them. I'd hoped they'd be okay about it, but when I gave them the weapon, the imported one, Botha took it . . . he's an animal, by the way . . . and said he was going to test-fire it.'

Welsh looked away. 'I knew what he was going to do,' he muttered, 'but all I could think about was that he was going to kill me as well. I heard three shots from upstairs, inside the house, then just after, three more. I'd brought my van with me, not the car. I guess you know by now what they made me help them do. When it was finished, they dropped me back at my yard. I stayed there all night, thinking, and most of today. Eventually it dawned on me that you'd be bound to identify Jock eventually, and that I had to clear this place out or I'd be in it up to my nuts. Enter you two,' he took a deep breath, 'and that's the whole story.'

'Not quite,' the chief said. 'What were the weapons?'

'A Heckler and Koch MP3 carbine and two Glock pistols. There were six H and Ks in the box that Kenny Bass brought back from Valencia.' He nodded towards the open box. 'The other five are still there.'

Mr Skinner's eyes widened. 'Cohen ordered them specifically, by name?'

Welsh nodded.

'Is that significant?' I asked.

'Too damn right,' he retorted. 'They're police weapons.' He glared at Welsh. 'Lucky for you that I sent Maggie through there.'

'What are you talking about?' the man on the floor muttered.

'I've sent my deputy to the concert hall with a warrant for the arrest of the target, on a made-up charge that only needs to hold for an hour or so. He'll be halfway to Edinburgh by now.'

'He?' Welsh repeated. 'When Smit picked up the carbine, he said, 'This baby will take her out, no question.' I don't know who you've picked up, but believe me . . . the target's a woman.'

# Bob Skinner

'I don't know who you've picked up, but believe me . . . the target's a woman.'

When he said that, shock, panic, horror, maybe all three swept over me in waves; my heart went ice-cold and for a moment my knees buckled.

Clyde was still holding the Beowulf. I ripped it from his grasp and levelled it at Freddy Welsh's head.

'Are you telling the truth,' I shouted, 'or is that bullshit?'

'It's true, it's true,' Welsh screamed. 'It's a woman, honest; on my life, I swear.'

I jerked the barrel upwards and fired a round into the wall about a foot above his head. Then I turned on Houseman. 'You people got it wrong!' I bellowed. 'You got it fucking wrong.' I was ready to go for him, but he stayed calm.

'Mr Skinner,' he said, 'I promise you, that's the intelligence we have. We know the Israelis have a kill order on Fabrizzi; he's the only possible target.'

A little of his coolness transferred itself to me. 'Not necessarily,' I said. I pointed the gun in Welsh's direction once again. He was cowering away from me, trying to make himself as small as possible. He was terrified; he'd pissed his pants. 'Go into the garden store,' I ordered.

'Find some rope, twine, wire, anything, and

hog-tie this bastard.' I wasn't thinking clearly, my thoughts were jumbled up, my priorities shot to hell. 'Wait,' I snapped. 'Where will your people be now?'

'A couple of them will be on their way home,' Clyde replied. 'The other will be back in the office by now. I told them their job would be over when they delivered Fabrizzi safe and well. The First Minister was going to be at the concert so . . . ' I nodded; standard practice dictated that Strathclyde would have done a security sweep of the hall.

'Bugger!' I hissed. 'That means the Home Secretary can go fuck herself. I'm doing what I should have done from the off, informing Strathclyde. But first . . . '

As the MI5 man went in search of bonds for our prisoner I took out my phone and scrolled through incoming calls till I found the one from Amanda. I pressed redial.

She answered almost instantly. 'Bob, what's happening? Do you have any news for me? The Home Secretary's calling me every ten minutes or so, demanding results. What can I tell her?'

'You can tell her that if this goes wrong, Amanda, then I'm going to kill her. Listen, earlier on you told me about a current threat against a British political figure.'

'Yes.'

'Tell me more.'

'It's serious. It came out of Afghanistan; a source said that the Taliban have commissioned political hits in Britain, the US and Canada, the three major players in the action. They're using

450

specialist contractors, not their own amateurs. You may not have noticed, it didn't get much press over here, but a week ago, there were three arrests in Ottawa. They related to a plot to blow up the Canadian Defence Minister's car. Ever since, we've been on full alert at Westminster.'

'Did it ever occur to anybody,' I asked her, 'that there are two other parliaments on this island, and that there are politicians outside London who might make much softer targets? For example, there's my wife, who was heckled at the last Scottish Labour Party conference for her vociferous support for the Afghan campaign. Didn't that ever dawn on anyone down there?'

'Bob,' Amanda said, as Houseman came back into the room with cut lengths of blue nylon rope, 'please don't shout at me, there's a love.' I hadn't realised that I was. 'What are you telling me?'

'I'm telling you that I've just had reliable information, from the man who sold the team their weapons, that the target is a woman. It isn't fucking Fabrizzi, who is at this moment in my force's custody. But the strong possibility, no, probability, remains that the concert hall is the venue for the hit. This is July; this is Glasgow. The bloody city is closed for the holidays, there's nothing else on, nothing else for professional assassins to be aiming at.'

'And your . . . '

'My wife, my high-profile British politician wife is there right now, in the front row, and sat beside her is the wife of a colleague and very good friend.'

'What can I do?' Amanda asked.

'Three things. You can pass my message on to the Home Secretary, word for word. Then you can tell her that I'm about to call Toni Field and explain exactly why I haven't done so earlier. Once you've done that, I'd appreciate prayer.'

As I ended the call, Clyde was completing a very professional job of tying up Freddy Welsh; he wasn't moving an inch without assistance. I nodded approval, then called Aileen's mobile. It rang four times and went to voicemail.

'This is me,' I said. 'If you get this, and you're in the concert hall, find the most senior police officer there and have him put you and Paula under guard. Instruct him also to disarm any officers there who might be carrying weapons. Then call me.'

I was scared to make the next call. If I'd been in Mario McGuire's shoes I'd have been wanting to knock my head off, for being reckless enough not to warn him as soon as I saw the way the story was heading.

He answered instantly. 'No sign of Welsh,' he volunteered at once.

'No,' I replied. 'There wouldn't be. He's lying at my feet under Jock Varley's extension, trussed up like a chicken.'

Then I told him the rest of it. 'Mario, I'm sorry,' I said at the end. 'I broke my own rule; I listened to a politician. You can beat me up later, I won't resist, but for now, try to get Paula on her phone and, if you can, tell her to take Aileen and lock the pair of them in the toilets till I get there.'

452

'Till we get there, you mean,' he said, grimly. 'But you've got at least twenty minutes' start on me, so go on man, don't waste any more time talking to me. Get on the move and alert Strathclyde from the road.'

We took the keys to both storerooms from Welsh, and left him locked in his own, for collection later, with his arsenal. We ran for the car and burned rubber getting out of the Pines. Clyde set the satnav on fastest route to Glasgow, and thank the Lord we didn't have to retrace our steps: three turns and two minutes and we were on the motorway, travelling like Lewis Hamilton was ahead of us and we had a mind to catch him.

As soon as we were clear I called the Strathclyde communications centre. 'This is Chief Constable Skinner, from Edinburgh,' I told the answering officer. 'I want you to connect me with Chief Constable Field.'

'I'm sorry,' the man exclaimed. 'Who did you say you are?'

'Chief Constable Bob Skinner,' I repeated. 'Now put me through to Toni Field.'

'Oh, I'm sorry, sir,' he droned. 'I'm not allowed to do that. If I put you through without verifying your identity, it'd be more than my job's worth.'

'No, pal,' I roared at him, 'you're not sorry. You don't know the meaning of the word sorry, but you fucking will by the time I'm finished with you. Connect me!'

The bastard hung up on me.

I called back at once; long odds against me

453

drawing the same operator, but I did. 'My name is Chief Constable Robert Morgan Skinner,' I snapped. 'What you will now do is wait one minute then call my force communications centre and ask them to put you through to me on my mobile, as verification. If you are not reconnected to me within two minutes, trust me, you will not have a job on Monday.'

I closed the line, called the comms centre myself, and gave them their orders. Two minutes later I was reconnected to PC Obstinate.

'I'm sorry, sir,' he began.

'No time for that,' I said. 'Toni Field, now: urgently.'

I waited; the only thing I will say for Strathclyde is that they didn't play me the theme from fucking *Z Cars* while I was hanging on the line. If they had, it would have played at least five times as I waited. All I could do was sit there going quietly crazy, no, make that noisily, for at least once every minute I screamed, 'Come on!' into the mike.

I couldn't believe how long he took; we were driving past Glasgow Fort when he came back on the line. 'I'm sorry, sir,' he lied. 'I've tried all the chief constable's numbers. She appears to be incommunicado.'

'Then get me ACC Allan,' I retorted, unimpressed by his vocabulary.

'I've tried him; I can't get in touch with him either.'

Christ! My brain was frazzled; I was fighting to think properly, time flying past while I tried to work out what to do next.

'Okay,' I said at last, when I'd decided. 'Divisional Commander, Glasgow Central. Who's he?'

'That would be Chief Superintendent Reardon.'

'Put me through to him.'

'I believe he's on holiday, sir.'

'Then give me whoever is sitting in his fucking chair,' I screamed.

'Very good, sir,' the communications officer replied stiffly. The waiting hum returned, and stayed with me for another God knew how long. I couldn't look at the car's clock.

'This is Chief Inspector Spencer.' I'd been hanging on so long I was startled when the woman spoke. 'I'm the acting divisional commander. Chief Constable Skinner, is it?'

There was something indulgent about her tone that blew the last couple of shreds of my restraint. 'We've established that,' I yelled at her. 'I have reason to believe that a terrorist operation is under way at the Royal Concert Hall. You need to get an armed response team there now.'

'We have armed officers there,' she protested. 'We always put on a show of force when there are VIPs. Chief constable's standing order.'

'In that case, I'm willing to bet you've got two more people on site than you think. I believe you have a two-man hit team there posing as police officers. Are all your guys accounted for?'

'I assume so.'

'That doesn't cut it . . . '

'Mr Skinner,' Clyde cut in on me. I looked up

455

and realised that we had left the motorway and were heading down Port Dundas Road towards the hall itself.

'We're arriving at the site now,' I told Spencer. 'No debate; get armed back-up here, now.'

We ran two red lights and swung on to the one-way Killermont Street, against the traffic flow, braking and swerving to avoid an oncoming van. Houseman stopped the car and jumped out, unholstering his pistol.

As I followed I could see why he had. Two uniformed police officers lay on the pavement in front of the entrance doors. They'd been armed, but it hadn't done them any good. Two other men stood over them, identically dressed, in blue T-shirts and light cotton trousers; the stockier of the pair, a guy with a low forehead and a crew cut, held a silenced pistol in his right hand. As I looked at them, they registered our approach.

The gunman swung round to face us, but he didn't get his weapon halfway up before Clyde shot him through the head.

By that time his companion was running. I started after him, then something hit me as hard as the other guy's bullet might have if my young ex-schemie pal hadn't nailed him. We'd caught them on the way out, not the way in. They'd done what they came to do.

I stopped chasing after the fleeing hit man. Instead I picked up the H and K carbine that one of the fallen officers had been carrying, sighted it on him as I'd done a hundred times before on cardboard targets on our firing range, and on a couple of live ones in other places, and nailed him, twice, right between the shoulder blades. See how fast you can run now, pal.

Clyde was on one knee, checking the cops for pulses. 'This one's alive,' he said. 'I think the other's gone.'

Then the door to the hall swung open and ACC Max Allan stepped out into the street. His eyes were all screwed up, and I realised that the interior of the concert hall was without windows other than the glass panes of its doors, and that it was in darkness.

He looked at his fallen men, and he looked at me. 'Bob,' he whispered, and I could see he was in shock. 'Bob, she's dead.'

# Paula McGuire

I had to laugh when I got there. As the government car rolled up at the surprisingly anonymous vehicle entrance to the Royal Concert Hall, I saw one of the pair of armed cops on duty outside say something into a radio transmitter. A few moments later, before my transport had even come to rest, the double doors opened and a man emerged. He wore a dark suit and a heavy gold chain round his neck, and I am not talking about the type they sell at H. Samuel.

When my driver opened the door, and I stepped out on to the pavement, the Lord Provost's face registered complete confusion. Glasgow's first citizen glared at the gun-toting blackshirt who'd summoned him.

'I thought you said the First Minister was arriving,' he snapped.

'Sorry I can't oblige,' I told him, wearing my finest arch smile, 'but don't I rate a polite welcome too? I'm accompanying Ms de Marco to the event, and she'll probably be First Minister again by this time next year.'

The civic dignitary recovered his ground, and his composure. 'Of course, madam,' he murmured, schmoozing forward with hand outstretched. 'So nice to see you. In fact our Aileen's arrived already; let me take you to her.'

He escorted me inside. As we approached a

wide flight of stairs, I had a moment of confusion. I thought I'd caught the briefest glimpse of Maggie Steele disappearing from sight round a corner, but I didn't have time to dwell on it as my official greeter led me up and into some sort of anteroom, where the usual pre-concert champagne reception was under way.

Aileen seemed to be its main attraction. She was in the middle of a crowd of people, but she spotted me just as I saw her, and excused herself from them. She stared at me, and I had to laugh again. So had she. Instead of red, she was wearing a dress of shimmering green satin. And there was I, in my black satin trouser suit.

'You too?' she chuckled. 'I decided we'd better not look like twin pillar boxes, so I dug this out. It's from my pre-Bob era and it sends out all the wrong signals to half of Glasgow, but what the hell? I haven't worn it for a while and I want to get back to being the woman I once was.'

Did I detect an underlying message there? Yes, sure, and hadn't I just seen Maggie Steele downstairs when she was for certain back home in Edinburgh fussing over her daughter.

I put both those misconceptions out of my mind. 'I'm sorry, Aileen,' I said. 'After you called, I remembered I had this thing in my wardrobe, and that it still fits, just about. I should have phoned you back to let you know.'

'Don't worry about it,' she assured me. 'We both look fantastic. Let's revel in it. Front row seats, two along from Clive Graham and his partner for the night, whoever she is. Let them all look on our works and despair.'

'Sounds fine to me, Ozymandias,' I agreed, taking an orange juice from a tray that a young blonde waitress offered me. According to her badge her name was Katya, one of the loyal Poles who had stuck with Scotland through the recession, I imagined. Quite a few of them work for me.

A tall, dark-haired, drop-dead good-looking guy came walking towards us. He was wearing a white tux and trousers with a shiny strip down the side; he looked a million dollars and he knew it. I was sure I had seen him somewhere before.

'Joey,' Aileen exclaimed, 'great to see you again.' They embraced and she kissed him on the cheek, for maybe half a second longer than was necessary. 'Paula, this is Joey Morocco, Glaswegian made good, and our MC for the evening; Joey, Paula Viareggio.'

God, and I barely recognised him; showing your age, lady. Joey Morocco is an actor who started his career on a dodgy Scottish soap, then went upmarket very quickly, into network television productions, and most recently into movies. Hollywood has called and there are whispers that he's going to be the next James Bond.

'Hi, Paula,' he said, 'great to meet you.' He sprinkled a little stardust on me, but not as much as he'd given Aileen, I noticed. 'Ladies,' he murmured. 'As well as being host tonight I'm the

460

guy who has to ask everyone to switch off their mobiles. Can you do that . . . if you're carrying, that is?'

'Joey,' I replied, glancing down at my bump, 'if you can't see that I'm carrying, someone needs to have a talk with you. As for my mobile, if I switch it off in this condition my husband will go radio rentals. He might even take it out on you, and you'd hate that. But as long as you're prepared to handle the flak, I'll do that for you.'

'Fantastic,' he beamed, then moved off on a wave of over-statement, after a little squeeze of Aileen's hand.

'Would there be some history between you two by any chance?' I asked her, mischievously.

She smiled as she nodded. 'A brief encounter or two, when he was still on Scottish telly.'

'He still fancies you, I'd say.'

'I know.' She winked at me. 'I could tell by the way he squeezed my bum when he hugged me. The question is, do I still fancy him?'

Before I'd had a chance to take that any further, there were sounds of a small commotion behind us. I looked over my shoulder and saw that the car they'd been expecting outside had turned up at last. The First Minister was among us, with the Lord Provost on one side, and on the other a smallish woman with brown skin, copper hair and the most sexually aggressive body I have ever seen, packed into a tight red evening dress.

'Didn't we do right,' I murmured to Aileen, but she wasn't listening. Instead she was gazing

461

at the new female in our midst with eyes like ice and a wholly insincere smile fixed on her face.

'Clive,' she greeted her biggest political opponent as he came towards us. He wore his usual slightly cautious expression . . . and his usual silly tartan waistcoat, although his evening's choice did match his trews, I'll give him that.

'My dear,' he responded. They shook hands, briefly, semi-formally; no cheek-kissing for them, in case someone snapped it on an illicit iPhone and flogged the image to the tabloids. 'Glad you could come. You couldn't persuade your husband though?'

'Don't go there,' she said, cutting off that line of questioning. 'I brought a friend instead, Paula Viareggio, married name McGuire; this could be her last night of freedom, so we're out to enjoy it.'

'Be sure you do.' As Clive Graham spoke, a tall man moved in behind him; his hair was silver, more or less the same shade as the acres of braid on his uniform.

The First Minister's companion didn't seem to welcome his presence, but she couldn't ignore it. She turned to me. 'Paula this is . . . '

I smiled, not at her but at him. 'I know who it is. Hi, Max,' I greeted him. 'You must be fit, to be carrying all that braid on your shoulders.' Max Allan lives in Lanark, but he and his wife do most of their shopping in Edinburgh. They've been among the Viareggio delicatessen chain's best customers since my grandfather's time. I knew he was a police officer, but I hadn't realised that he was that senior.

He beamed back at me. 'Radiant, Paula,' he exclaimed, 'radiant.' Then he turned serious. 'First Minister,' he murmured, 'can I have a word in private?'

Graham nodded and led the way towards an unoccupied corner, well away from tray waitresses and the savoury tables. His companion went with him.

'He doesn't look as though he's fit for her. Is that really Mrs Graham?' I asked Aileen.

'No,' she replied. 'Mrs Graham's recovering from what the press office described as varicose vein removal, which is true if you regard piles as a type of varicose vein. That wee red dragon is Toni Field, the new chief constable in Strathclyde.'

'In which case,' I murmured, 'Max has just lit her fire.' She followed my gaze. Whatever my customer had told them had made her go absolutely rigid with what looked pretty much like fury to me.

'It can't be bad enough news as far as I'm concerned,' she murmured. 'I can't stand the bloody woman. Unfortunately I'm told that some of my parliamentary colleagues in London think the sun shines out of her fundament.'

'What's she doing with Clive Graham?'

'One of them is using the other to make a point. I'm not entirely sure which; maybe they both are, but I suspect it's her. Clive probably knows he's testing my patience and my loyalty by wearing her on his arm at a do like this, but he doesn't have the courage to put her in her place.'

She was still sizzling when a warning bell rang, and Joey Morocco asked everyone to make their way into the auditorium, apart from the principal guests and charity patrons. We were among the former category, so we hung back, until eventually we were arranged into a line, by a harassed wee man, who seemed to be in charge of everything. He looked like someone who'd just woken on Boxing Day to discover that he'd slept through Christmas.

When we were ready we filed in; patrons first, then the Lord Provost and Mrs Provost, then the First Minister and his 'date', then me and finally Aileen. She'd reversed the order into which the harassed man had put us.

'Do me a favour,' she whispered. 'Don't have me sit next to that bloody woman Field. She's a philistine and I'm sure she'd talk to me all the way through the performance, just to wind me up. She doesn't know you, so that might shut her up.'

As soon as we were settled in our seats, Joey Morocco moved on to stage, to gusts of applause, to stand in front of the assembled Scottish National Orchestra, and beside a piano that seemed to be minus a player. He made a short welcome speech, plugged the benefiting charities, and then went serious on us.

'Now the bad news,' he announced. 'We've

all come here tonight to be enthralled by the great Theo Fabrizzi. Well, I'm afraid I have to tell you,' he paused, then lapsed inexplicably into Glaswegian, 'it's no gonnae happen.'

He waited for the buzz to subside, then he continued. 'Poor Theo has been overtaken by one of those short notice things that can afflict us all, and he regrets enormously that he is not going to be able to play this evening. However,' his tone turned upbeat, 'we still have the nation's finest orchestra to delight us, so the evening will still be memorable. Please just imagine the piano bits, okay?'

He left the stage to applause that was much less rapturous than at his entrance.

I wasn't bothered. The piano has never been my favourite instrument, unless Elton John's sitting at it. I was going to have a good time anyway.

A minute or so later, Joey reappeared on the left of the stage. 'And now, my lords, ladies and gentlepeople,' he announced, 'please welcome your conductor, Sir Leslie Fender.'

A fat man in white tie and tails, with slicked-back hair and an enormously pompous bearing, walked out to centre stage, bowed theatrically, then stepped laboriously up on to his podium. He picked up his baton, raised it, and as if on cue . . . as it probably was . . . the house lights faded.

And that's when it all got very strange. Time seemed to speed up. I was aware of something happening very close to me, of three thudding sounds, of something wet spattering on me . . . then everything went black, as if the darkest night you could ever imagine had fallen in an instant.

Someone screamed. I think it was me.

Books by Quintin Jardine
Published by The House of Ulverscroft:

THE LONER

THE BOB SKINNER SERIES:
SKINNER'S ORDEAL
SKINNER'S MISSION
SKINNER'S GHOSTS
MURMURING THE JUDGES
GALLERY WHISPERS
THURSDAY LEGENDS
AUTOGRAPHS IN THE RAIN
HEAD SHOT
STAY OF EXECUTION
LETHAL INTENT
DEAD AND BURIED
DEATH'S DOOR
AFTERSHOCK
FATAL LAST WORDS
A RUSH OF BLOOD
GRIEVOUS ANGEL

THE OZ BLACKSTONE SERIES:
A COFFIN FOR TWO
WEARING PURPLE
SCREEN SAVERS
POISONED CHERRIES
UNNATURAL JUSTICE
ALARM CALL
FOR THE DEATH OF ME

We do hope that you have enjoyed reading this large print book.

Did you know that all of our titles are available for purchase?

We publish a wide range of high quality large print books including:
**Romances, Mysteries, Classics**
**General Fiction**
**Non Fiction and Westerns**

Special interest titles available in large print are:
**The Little Oxford Dictionary**
**Music Book**
**Song Book**
**Hymn Book**
**Service Book**

Also available from us courtesy of Oxford University Press:
**Young Readers' Dictionary**
**(large print edition)**
**Young Readers' Thesaurus**
**(large print edition)**

For further information or a free brochure, please contact us at:
**Ulverscroft Large Print Books Ltd.,**
**The Green, Bradgate Road, Anstey,**
**Leicester, LE7 7FU, England.**
**Tel: (00 44) 0116 236 4325**
**Fax: (00 44) 0116 234 0205**

*Other titles published by*
*The House of Ulverscroft:*

## AS EASY AS MURDER

### Quintin Jardine

A tranquil, Spanish village by the sea is the perfect place for Primavera Blackstone to raise her ten-year-old, Tom, son of the late lamented Oz, especially when they are joined by his nephew, tyro professional golfer Jonny Sinclair. But when her best friend Shirley introduces her new man, Patterson Cowling, he seems to be a trouble magnet. A casual thief tries to pick his pocket and is found a few days later with his face blown off. Does Patterson Cowling have a past to protect? As the body count rises, and Primavera becomes den mother to an extended golfing family, homicide becomes par for the course, and hazards lie in wait for everyone. Can she save the day, or is the game just too rough?